The Peacock Door

The Peacock Door

❖

Wanda Kay Knight

Copyright © 2017 by Wanda K. Knight.

Library of Congress Control Number:		2017907451
ISBN:	Hardcover	978-1-5434-2182-8
	Softcover	978-1-5434-2183-5
	eBook	978-1-5434-2184-2

All rights reserved. No part of this book may be reproduced or transmitted in any form or by any means, electronic or mechanical, including photocopying, recording, or by any information storage and retrieval system, without permission in writing from the copyright owner.

This is a work of fiction. Names, characters, places and incidents either are the product of the author's imagination or are used fictitiously, and any resemblance to any actual persons, living or dead, events, or locales is entirely coincidental.

Illustrations by Ahmed Shaltout.

Print information available on the last page.

Rev. date: 08/15/2017

To order additional copies of this book, contact:
Xlibris
1-888-795-4274
www.Xlibris.com
Orders@Xlibris.com

To

The six who gave me the eight most incredible, awesome, and lovable treasures imaginable.

Jim, for all the encouragement, love, and support he gave as I typed away in my hobby hole.

Jeannie, Rob, Savannah, Wynn, and the kiddos at Skykomish School for believing.

My siblings and their spouses for being exactly who they are.

EIGHT COUSINS: THREE FAMILIES

Levi, Claire, and Esme

Levi, 13

Claire, 11

Esme, 5

Addison and Brody

Addison, 11

Brody, 10

Eleanor, Tilly, and Ivan

Eleanor, 12

Tilly, 10

Ivan, 9

The Beginning...

It was one of those coastal towns—you know the type—charming in a coastal town sort of way and yet rugged in a coastal town sort of way, with jutting rocks and turbulent waves. And when the sun was shining and the inland waters were sparkling, it seemed crisp and fresh and alive from deep within.

Of course, it had the mandatory white picket fences and the cramped, musty bookstore with the creaky staircase leading to some shadowy place. But then, it also had a cozy little tearoom where the ladies gathered to eat petite sandwiches and dip fruit into three types of sweet melted chocolate while tea is served in tiny flowery cups. A cemetery stood high on a hill right outside of town; and weeping willows sheltered the weathered, crusty graves. Yes, it was one of those kinds of little coastal towns.

And it was on the edge of this town, just where the waters meet with the land, that an older smallish Victorian house with turrets and gables and gingerbread trim sat among uncut grass and ancient rhododendrons. Climbing roses, grasping for their share of sunlight, scrambled upward, falling over the unpainted fence; and purple wisteria twisted across the roof, drooping over the edges of the wraparound porch.

And on a cheerful sort of day in June, a youngish sort of grandma with crinkles around the edges of bright-blue eyes and an unruly mass of tawny curls heavily streaked with silver strands—fidgeted in an oversized red rocking chair. Now and again, after tapping her fingers on the arms of the chair, she would rise and pace back and forth and then plop back down and tap her fingers some more.

And after a little while of rocking and fidgeting, she would get up and wander up and down the lane leading to her house. After sheltering her eyes from the sun and gazing about for a while, she would sigh and wander back to the porch where she would plop back down into the rocking chair and fidget some more as she waited for the arrival of Levi, Eleanor, Claire, Addison, Tilly, Brody, Ivan, and Esmé.

Chapter 1

The Arrival

Gramma jumped up from the red rocking chair as billows of dust and spewing pebbles enveloped the three vehicles jostling up the gravel lane. As the caravan slowed to a halt, doors burst open, and eight kids tumbled out.

"We're here!" Eleanor shouted at the top of her lungs.

"Grammmyy!" Claire yelled, sprinting forward, her husky voice rising above the chaos. Levi and Ivan raced each other for Gramma's hug. Addison held back for just a second, watching the chaos; but when Gramma glanced over with a wink and a smile, she giggled and hurried to join the others.

Tilly and Brody stopped and whispered something to each other before sprinting forward for their hugs. Esmé, the youngest, waited patiently; but once the rest had their squeezes and were clamoring and shouting over one another about ideas and plans for the next three days, she hurried forward, wrapping her little arms around Gramma's waist.

"I'm so glad I'm here," she said, and Gramma tweaked her nose, picking her up and planting a sloppy kiss smack dab on her forehead.

"I'm so glad you are too, sugarplum," Gramma said as she set her back down and patted the top of her head.

Three sets of parents had climbed out of their vehicles, stretched their legs, and observed the scene while pulling suitcases out of the cars and setting them on the grass beside the gravel lane.

"Hey, I got it now," Gramma called, waving a dismissive hand to the parents. Three sets of parents smiled and climbed back into their vehicles. "Good-byes," "love yas," and "see ya soons" flitted through the air as three sets of parents redusted the air as they drove back down the gravel lane.

Chapter 2

The Instructions

Gramma was jittery, bobbling up and down and back and forth until the parents were completely out of sight. As soon as the last set of taillights disappeared around the bend, she plopped down on the front porch step, beckoning for the cousins to come closer. Her face was flushed with excitement.

"I have something very, very special to show you, and I can't wait any longer," she said. The cousins looked at her and then glanced at one another, anticipation bubbling in their bellies. Gramma leaned forward, pointing at the stack of suitcases and backpacks that lay on the ground. "Throw your stuff in the front door and follow me," she said. Abruptly, she stood up, turned, and strode across the grass toward the woods.

The cousins grabbed their suitcases, threw them inside the door, and scrambled to catch up as Gramma tramped away. Almost immediately, Gramma stopped and pivoted to face them. She looked up at the sky, took a deep breath, and tapped her top lip with her forefinger. Finally, she looked directly into the eyes of each cousin.

"I've been waiting for years and years, and I think the time is finally here. I think I can show you, and you won't get lost. It's between here and the water—pretty close and hidden from prying eyes. But there are promises to be made and notions you must accept. Can you do that?" They all nodded. Confused frowns and sidelong glances passed back and forth among them.

"Levi, Eleanor, you two are the oldest," Gramma continued. "You must promise to keep an eye out for the others and make sure nobody gets lost, okay? Do I have your word?"

"Of course!" Eleanor said; but as Gramma turned and hurried off down the path again, Eleanor and Levi glanced at each other, scrunching their noses and shrugging their shoulders. After a few more steps, Gramma spun around again.

"Wait, wait, wait, I almost forgot the most important part," she said, waving her pointer finger. "This path is our secret. Parents are not invited—and I mean that. They would fret and moan and groan and start talking about getting lost and fiction and imagination and—" Gramma bobbed her head back and forth and rolled her eyes. "They just wouldn't get it, okay?" Gramma whirled around again and bustled down the path as eight very perplexed cousins scurried after her.

They hustled down a narrow pebbled path with twisting madrones sheltering it. They ducked under moss-draped tree limbs, hurried past giant toadstools popping out of the ground, and scurried around huge jade rocks stuck in the middle of the path. They pushed swaying branches aside and scrambled through openings in curved trees tunnels.

"Where in the world are we?" Levi asked.

"I know, right?" Eleanor replied. "I thought we had explored every single inch of Gramma's place, but I have never seen any of this."

"Me neither," Levi agreed with a shrug as they hurried along behind Gramma, trying to recognize any familiar landmark, which they did not find.

"Almost there," Gramma called back as she scurried along the path. "Almost there."

And then, all of a sudden, Gramma stopped and pointed up into the top of a mass of trees. And there it was, perched high in an ancient oak and nestled within the branches, an oddly shaped ramshackle treehouse. It was slightly askew, somewhat rickety, and setting a little lopsided with uneven, peculiar angles. It was made of old wooden shingles and tin and such. Branches seemed to grow around the bottom, squeeze the sides and burst out from the top. The entire group stood still, mouths gaping open, peering up.

Levi saw the wooden ladder first and raced toward it. Immediately the others were nipping at his heels as they competed to get to the top. Grunts and ouches and "Hey, stop that!" pierced the air as each one pushed and shoved and as fingers and toes were trampled in the chaos to get to the top first. Gramma watched from the ground, and once they were all at the top, she grabbed hold of the bottom rung of the ladder and began climbing behind them.

Chapter 3

The Peacock Door

The treehouse appeared very different once they were standing on the wooden walkway surrounding it than it had looked while they were on the ground. It was bigger and somehow even odder. A beautiful bluish door stood in the middle of a protruding portico, overwhelming the entire front of the treehouse; the rest seemed to consist only of angles and edges. Levi hurried into the portico, grabbed the copper doorknob, and jerked; but the door did not budge. "Must be locked," he said, so they all hurried back to the ladder to see where Gramma was.

As the tawny head popped up over the edge, Ivan reached down, grabbed Gramma's upstretched hand, and pulled her up onto the platform. Ambling across the wooden walkway, Gramma fished in her apron pocket, pulling out a huge jangling ring crammed full and bursting with all sorts and sizes of skeleton keys. One by one, she sorted through them, mumbling things like "hmmm" and "maybe," until she finally smiled, settling on a tiny blue key with a pearl-encrusted, heart-shaped head. She slipped the key into the lock, tugging on the doorknob, twisting the key back and forth until they all heard the loud click. Exhaling loudly, Gramma smiled, slipped the keys back into her pocket, and turned around. She planted herself squarely in front of the door.

"I have waited a long time to show this to all of you," she said. "And I think the time is finally right, but, whatever you do," she whispered as she slowly turned her head back and forth, gazing directly into the eyes of each cousin, "whatever you do, listen to me! If I show this to you, you have promises to keep. We are going to enter through this door right here, correct?" She patted the door with her hand. They all looked at her suspiciously.

"Yes? And?" Brody asked.

"Look carefully at this door," Gramma continued.

Each one looked at it and then at one another. Claire smirked, shrugging her shoulders. Addison nodded. Eleanor shifted impatiently from one foot to the other. Tilly stood simply gazing at the door, considering each detail. "What color is it?" Gramma questioned.

"It's blue," Ivan said.

"Yes, but what kind of blue?" Gramma asked.

"Kind of a peacock blue?" Addison suggested.

"Yes, good! It is, indeed, peacock blue. Now, what else do you see?"

"It's thick?" Levi suggested.

"It has a rounded top?" Claire suggested, shrugging.

"Both true." Gramma nodded. "What else?"

Tilly stepped forward to touch the door, running her fingers around the raised border. "It has peacock feathers carved in the border," she said.

"Okay, that's good. Now remember, peacock blue, rounded top, peacock feathers carved into the border," Gramma cautioned. "Just in case. Your parents would be so mad at me if any of you got lost. And, quite honestly, I really don't want to lose any of you. It is such a pain to find lost kids. I know I would eventually find you, but what if you got lost and your parents returned for some reason before you got back, and— oh,"—she shuddered—"I don't even wanna think about it." Her head bobbled some more as she rolled her eyes.

"Lost?" Levi grinned, rolling his eyes. "This treehouse seems to have weird angles, and it is big Gramma, but not that big." He chuckled.

Gramma paused, staring straight into Levi's eyes before continuing, "If we go in this door, you've got to promise that you'll use only this door for coming and going. Do I have your word? And remember, a man is only as good as—"

"As good as his word," Levi interrupted, knowing where Gramma was going having heard it way too many times before.

Eleanor's eyes met Levi's. "Gramma," she said rather impatiently, "we've got it."

Gramma cocked her head to the side, this time staring directly into Eleanor's eyes for a few seconds as the cousins stood in awkward silence. Suddenly, the crinkles around Gramma's eyes deepened as she began smiling once more. "Okay then," she said, glancing at each of them as she turned and pushed against the peacock door, "let's do this!"

Chapter 4

The Treehouse

With hinges creaking and the bottom of the door scraping across the floor, the door only opened a few inches before grinding to a stop and sticking in place. "Oh, come on and help me push." Gramma sighed. And so, they joined together, pressing and shoving and pushing until the door burst open so suddenly that they tumbled over one another and fell inside.

But it was during that moment, as they lay in a jumbled mass on the treehouse floor, that the cousins began to understand why Gramma had made such a fuss about the peacock-blue door. For you see, though the peacock-blue door was certainly the exception in beauty and size, and though it was obviously the main entryway into the treehouse, setting as it did in the protruding portico at the front, it most certainly was not the only door.

There were, in fact, eight more doors in the treehouse, and each of those doors was a very different color. There was red and green; there was indigo and purple, gold, bronze, silver, and orange. And each of the doors was in the center of its own wall because the treehouse, you see, was actually an eight-sided octagon with the portico on the front. One by one, the cousins stood up, brushing themselves off and looking around in bewildered silence.

It was as if every section was separate and yet a part of a whole. Each of the eight walls in the room had a colored door, and each door had a tall skinny matching-colored shelf on the wall beside it. And each of those eight shelves beside each of those eight doors in each of the eight walls was overflowing with tiny curios and knick-knacks and precious little whatnots: water globes and kaleidoscopes and golden boxes with tiny bows and music boxes and all kinds of things that sparkled or moved or tinkled or spun in circles.

But the eight walls contained far more than colored doors with their matching shelves. Every nook and every cranny overflowed with clocks or books. Clocks of all sorts and sizes covered entire sections of each wall: cuckoo clocks, windup clocks, clocks with rotating gears, and clocks with crystal balls twirling around the base. There were clocks with little people or little animals or little figurines singing from perches or moving in and out or up and down or through tiny carved tunnels or little villages or tiny snow-laden mountains. And they all ticked and tocked and clinged and clanged.

And books covered entire sections of walls: books filling shelves from ceiling to floor, ragged books with cracked bindings, new shiny books, and leather-bound books, books lying on their sides with other books squeezed on top of and around the fat books, and the skinny books and the ancient books.

Crystal balls suspended from the copper ceiling created floating rainbows bouncing around the walls and over the little curios and across the faces of the clocks and the covers of the books as sunlight filtered through the prisms.

And while the cousins stood there, staring around the room, Ivan happened to glance down. "Look," he whispered, "look at the floor." Levi kneeled down, running his fingers over the tiny mosaic tiles. "It's like the old nautical compasses on old ships or old maps or something. It points in all eight directions."

Brody stood still for a second, glancing around the room. Suddenly his face lit up. "Hey, everyone!" he shouted. "Eight directions, eight doors, eight shelves, and eight of us. That's just perfect! But how do we choose?" he asked.

"Choose what?" Tilly asked.

"Who gets which door and something from the shelf with that door," Brody quickly said. "Gramma always gives us something."

Silence descended like a pebble plopped in water as eight sets of eyes flittered from one shelf to the next as each cousin stopped, suddenly realizing the potential and calculating the possibilities of Brody's suggestion. Curiosity fought with greed as each cousin began quickly scrutinizing the tiny treasures setting on the colored shelves that set beside the colored doors in the octagon shaped treehouse room. And quite suddenly, and without much warning at all, the chaos began.

Chapter 5

The Choice

Claire took a quick glance around the room; her eye caught on a silver hourglass with sparkling white sand pouring through the middle. A small silver vial with a crystal cap and a miniature grandfather clock with swaying gold pendulum set next to the hourglass. An intricately engraved silver mirror hung on the wall behind it.

She dashed for the shelf beside the silver door. For just a second, she watched the iridescent sand pouring through the hourglass; then, picking up the silver vial, she unscrewed the crystal cap and inhaled. *Oh my gosh!* she said to herself. *This is luscious. I must have this no matter what.* She looked around as the others were quickly moving about the room, investigating other shelves. "Hey, everyone!" she shouted. "I picked my shelf. This one is mine."

But as she bent forward to inhale from the vial again, Addison ran for the silver door. "You can't do that!" Addison yelled. "Everybody gets a chance. What if somebody else wants that one? We decide after we all look and choose!"

Addison folded her arms across her chest and planted herself next to Claire. They glared at each other, snarled, and then turned to watch the others. Addison lifted her nose and sniffed. "Where is that amazing smell coming from?" she asked. The edges of Claire's lips turned up into a sly smile, but she didn't say a single word.

Ivan sprinted around the room, scanning everything and knocking over quite a few things before finally stopping in front of the red door. He picked up the embossed treasure chest from the red shelf and gently pried the lid open. Miniature windup pirates with moving arms and legs stood among brilliant jewels and tiny gold coins. "Ooohhh!" He sighed. "This just has to be the best of all!"

Tilly paced about the room, ducking around the others and examining each shelf slowly. Finally, picking up a snow globe from the purple shelf, she turned it upside down and shook it. She watched the flurries of snowflakes fall over a miniature forested village as two tiny ice skaters glided about on an icy pond. She picked up a tiny black bag, loosened the cord holding it together, and poured out a handful of crystals in every imaginable color.

Brody hurried over to the green door, and picking up a gold-trimmed stained-glass kaleidoscope, he closed his left eye and looked through. Reds and purples and greens and blues collided against one another in a mesmerizing spectacle of color. "This is one awesome kaleidoscope!" he said. "I really want this."

Esmé moved slowly back and forth and around, touching precious little curios from each of the different shelves. There were brass rings with jeweled keys and peacock feathers and a stained-glass box with golden coins spilling out and a music box covered with elaborate patterns. When she opened an intricate box on the gold shelf, a ballerina with a rose circlet on her head, ribbon-wrapped legs, and a jewel-encrusted tutu gracefully unfolded from a swan position and spun round and round. "Ooooh!" She sighed, touching the tiny dancer. "I love this."

After pacing between the green door and the red door, Eleanor finally stood still, tapping her fingers against her legs. She especially wanted the painted wooden clock with miniature boys and girls twirling around and through several tiny archways as the clock ticked and tocked from the indigo shelf, but that kaleidoscope from the green shelf was extremely tempting.

Levi hurried quickly around the room. He didn't know which shelf he wanted, but he did know that he didn't want anyone else to beat him to the one he was going to want. He scrutinized each shelf as he strode past each one. But when he came to the bronze shelf, he knew it was his. He reached up and gently took down the ancient leather-bound book with a cracked binding and embossed letters. The bronze lettering simply said What If. Inside, old maps, the kind pirates used to search for buried treasure, filled pages and pages and pages. A small old-fashioned oil lantern hung from the shelf beside it.

Eleanor walked over to take a look at the book, but Levi quickly slipped it behind his back. "Hey," fussed Eleanor, "you can't hide the treasure. What if I want that one?'

"Don't you even try," Levi muttered between clenched teeth. Eleanor started to grab the book from behind his back; but just as she snatched for it, she glanced over, and her eyes met Gramma's. Eleanor instantly decided to take another look at the musical painted clock with the miniature boys and girls twirling through tiny tunnels and archways from the indigo shelf, which was what she really wanted anyway.

For a few seconds, silence settled around the room as each cousin considered the treasures and whatnots they had kinda sorta chosen and then scrutinized the room just to make sure they were picking the best.

During this entire time, Gramma simply stood quietly leaning against the peacock-blue door, watching, listening. The corners of her lips turned up, and her right eyebrow arched up as she watched, analyzing and considering the decisions and choices being made in the little treehouse room.

Chapter 6

The Warning

After the chaos diminished, Gramma suddenly stood up straight. "Dear me, dear me, I forgot to bring lunch. I must have left it sitting on the doorstep. Well, let's go eat and then come back and finish deciding."

A ruckus erupted. "Nooooo! Come on, Gramma, please. We won't break anything. Promise! Please, come on, Gramma!"

Gramma chuckled, looking at them. "Well, I suppose I could leave all of you here and go get the basket—if you promise to be good." She clicked her tongue and drew in a deep breath. "Levi, Eleanor, you two are the oldest—"

"Yes, Gramma," Levi said quickly. The others smiled, nodding innocently. Gramma laughed and turned to go out the peacock door; but as soon as she grabbed the handle, she pivoted back, facing them.

A bizarre expression clouded her face. "Whatever you do," she said, "whatever you do—listen to me!" She pointed her finger at each of them, and after staring directly into each set of eyes, she continued, "There are journeys and treasures beyond those doors," she said. "There are long-forgotten wisps of alchemy and lost keys and crystals and mirrors of illusions, but you must not go out any of those doors." Her voice lowered as she leaned forward. "I gotta tell you, those keys are especially hard to find. You think it's easy, but nooo, it is not! Everything is fine as long as you don't go out any doors except the peacock door, right here. This is the door to use—only this one." She patted the door.

Her voice lowered even more—almost to a whisper. "You see, kiddies, even if you're ready to search for the keys, it's real hard to . . . um . . . well . . . to . . . to feel them . . . to experience them." She rubbed the fingers of each hand together, rotating the thumb around the fingertips. "Yeeessss, to feel them. It's just not the time to feel them. That's the hard part. Do you understand?"

Addison shrugged and moved closer to Gramma. "What's a wisp of alchemy?" she asked, touching Gramma's hand.

"Well, since you asked"—Gramma smiled—"perhaps I can give you an idea." Levi and Eleanor sighed loudly, dropping their heads as Eleanor slipped over and jabbed Addison in the ribs.

"Don't ask any more questions, dummy," she whispered. "Now we have to wait longer till she gets done." Claire and Tilly looked down at the floor, shaking their heads and rolling their eyes. Addison grimaced when she realized what she had done. But it was too late. Gramma's rambling had begun.

"I don't really know how to explain it," Gramma said, not paying attention to the whispers, sighs, and rolling eyes. "Alchemy is kind of like when the medieval people tried to take one thing and make it into something better like turning lead into gold or when they tried to make an elixir so people could live forever. But that's not exactly the point. Hmmm, wait a minute! Perhaps this will give you an idea."

She dug into her apron pocket; keys jangled. She pulled out a large round crystal and held it up so that the sunlight struck the prisms and even more tiny rainbows of colors bounced all around the room. "To find the lost keys, you have to know the difference between shadows and reflections, between real and not real," she said.

"It's kind of like when light reflects rainbows from a prism. You know it's not solid, and your hand can't catch it or hold it, which is, in a way, is kind of like, well, there are all these reflections of things, and they are like the little bits of ideas that you can't really grasp." She scratched her head. "There are facets of truth, parts of the truth, but sometimes as you search for keys, they are in shadows because nobody knows how to grab hold of the reflections. Sometimes black is really white and white is really black, but, you can't tell which is which. Does that make sense?"

Addison stood there staring at Gramma with a very peculiar look on her face, actually trying to decipher the message but not having much success. The others were lost in the ticking and tocking and the doors and the whatnots as they thought about all the treasures buried within the room, and Gramma's rambling faded into the background.

They finally snapped out of their thoughts and looked up as Gramma turned to walk out the peacock door. "Decide what you want, and we'll talk when I get back with lunch, okay?" she said. "And then I promise we will have a very, very fine day."

And with a final glance back, Gramma closed the peacock door, walked across the wooden walkway, and descended on the rickety wooden ladder.

Chapter 7

The Decisions

They all stood still for just a bit listening to Gramma climb down the creaky ladder. Levi motioned to Ivan to look out the door. "Okay, she's gone," Ivan said.

Eleanor moved to the center of the room. "Okay, Gramma put me in charge, so here's—"

"Uhhh, I don't think so," Levi corrected.

"Okay, whatever," Eleanor said, waving the back of her hand dismissively at Levi. "So while Gramma's gone, let's decide. I'm just saying that if Gramma has to make any final decisions or choose between us, we might not be getting what we really want. So we need to choose before she gets back, okay?"

And with that, they all started dissecting the stuff on the shelves one more time.

Now, it is hard to say what really happened next, but you should know that the choosing did not go as anyone had planned. You see, Claire suddenly decided that maybe the music box might be better than the silver hourglass and mirror, but Addison also started having second thoughts when she heard the melody from the snow globe. Suddenly, Eleanor thought the music box might be better than the clock. Brody and Tilly had planned on sharing the spoils of two shelves, but they couldn't decide between the green and the purple shelves. So though it was quite rare for them, they were quite loud and quite cross with each other.

Since Esmé wasn't quite tall enough to see everything on all the shelves, she scooted a three-legged stool over the shelves to examine the curios. But the three-legged stool had one wobbly leg, and so it tipped, and she fell over with it. Her knee and her elbow started bleeding. And since everyone else was busy with their own investigating and choosing, nobody noticed that she was hurt and sad and had drips of blood splatting on the nautical compass on the floor. And so, as she was walking around the room, sniffing and dripping and feeling very sad, her sister, Claire, yelled at her to clean her splatters of blood off the floor, which made her feel even worse.

And in the background, while Levi sat on the floor examining the ancient book with its paths, roads, and symbols, the decisions and the bartering, and the haggling and even the quarreling droned on and on, but Levi didn't even notice. When he looked up and realized that Esmé was crying, Levi finally did try to calm her down, but he would not leave his post in front of the bronze door and give Eleanor a chance at grabbing the ancient map book; so even he grumbled at her, and then she started crying even more.

And so, it must be said, that when Gramma climbed up the ladder about twenty minutes later, singing a song and carrying a very full wicker picnic basket with a very fresh homemade apple pie, she was quite surprised and not at all happy to see folded arms, defiant faces, cross expressions, splotches of blood on the floor, and even a few tears.

"Oh my, oh my," she chided them all as she looked around, set the basket on the floor, and wiped Esmé's tears with her fingertips. "This will not do. It simply will not do. We will eat, and then once our bellies are full, we will sort through all this commotion. I have such excellent plans! It's going to be a very fine day, a very fine day, indeed."

Chapter 8

The Perfect Day

And it is true that they did have a very fine day. Gramma told stories about old times and spiders and snakes and bats and aliens and such, and they ate the best apple pie ever, and the sun was shining, and the day was long and sweet. Addie and Claire made up, and Esmé's knee didn't even hurt much at all after a bit. And all of them hiked to the water, which was very, very blue and very, very sparkly; and they chased scrambling crabs and picked up purple starfish.

Here and there during the day, Levi would slip off by himself and take the ancient map book off the shelf and sit on the floor, leafing through the crisp yellowed tattered pages. He flipped the pages back and forth. Sometimes he stopped and looked into the air, and then he would continue flipping more pages as he puzzled over all those symbols and paths and whatnots.

Now, to tell you the truth, it is very hard to believe that anything at all could go wrong on a day such as that. But it's also true—and you must be told—that something did go very wrong. And the thing of it is, it all started with something very small—actually, it was only a very tiny idea. But unfortunately (and this is also very, very true), sometimes a very tiny idea can turn into something quite strange and can change everything very, very quickly. And that is exactly what happened.

Chapter 9

The Mistake

The little something that changed everything began around the time the sun was beginning to slide behind the distant evergreens. Suddenly, they all realized that they were hungry again (after all, perfect days usually make everyone quite hungry). And so, after warning everyone one more time to stay away from the doors, Gramma tramped off across the field to get some supper.

Claire and Addison decided to go back to the treehouse and read while the others remained at the water. As Claire was sitting on the floor looking at some books and tiny treasures and whatnots, a mischievous smile slowly crept across her lips. After a bit, she glanced over at Addison, who was also sitting on the floor, reading a book from one of the bookshelves.

Scooting closer, Claire laid her hand on Addison's shoulder. "I've got a great idea," she whispered.

Addison raised her eyebrows, tilting her head to the side as a slight frown crossed her forehead. "About what?"

"Just between me and you?" Claire asked, looking directly at Addison and beaming her very best syrupy-sweet smile.

Addison hesitated. "What's going on? I don't like that look. Last time—"

"Geesh, can't you ever just forgive and forget anything?" Claire interrupted crossly, throwing her hands in the air.

"Of course, I forgive and forget, but, Claire, I—" Addison wavered.

Claire looked down at the floor and made her eyes look sad. She slipped her hand over her mouth before a sly smile could betray her intentions. "Now listen," Claire continued with her most innocent expression, "it's just a little idea about the doors."

Addison looked straight at Claire. "What about the doors?"

"Just listen, will ya? Now, I know, I know, I know," she continued, raising her palms up, "I know that Gramma went on and on about how we're not supposed to go out any of the doors except the peacock door. But I've been kinda thinking that—"

"Claairre, don't go there," Addison said, rolling her eyes and shaking her head.

Claire continued quickly, "Listen, Addie, just listen for a second, will ya?" she pleaded. "As I see it, there can only be two things behind those doors. Either Gramma just wants to scare us so we don't go out there or"—she scooted closer and lowered her voice—"and I think this might be the real reason, maybe there is something out there that Gramma doesn't want us to see. Maybe she is hiding something or has a surprise out there."

Addie looked straight at Claire. "Gramma said we could get lost because of some keys and crystals or alchemy or something like that. Maybe there's something out there that could cause problems. Did it ever occur to you that she was telling the truth in some strange sort of way?"

Claire threw her hands into the air and looked up at the ceiling as though trying to receive a message from heaven. "Addie, Addie, Addie! I am three months older than you, so I guess I have to be the one to tell you. It's not real, Addie. It's Gramma telling stories for fun."

"No, she's not!" Addison said, staring straight at Claire. "No, that can't be. Gramma seemed serious about—Gramma wouldn't—" she said, but suddenly a troubled expression flashed across her face, and she began chewing on her thumbnail.

"Well, some of it must be true in some way. She doesn't lie." Addison dropped her gaze to the floor. "Yeah," she said, "maybe you're right. Maybe it's just one of Gramma's games—maybe—but we still shouldn't go out there." Her bottom lip quivered just a little.

Claire jumped in, quickly taking advantage of the situation. "Addie, don't be like that. This is actually a good thing. Think about it. It just means that we can sneak a peek out the door and find out what Gramma is hiding. Maybe that will help us decide which shelf is the best. We'll never know unless we check it out!"

"Yeah, but we still just can't go out there because we would get in trouble if we get caught anyway."

"Addie, I got this! That's why we just open the door a little and take a quick peek. We do this together so that we don't make any mistakes or let the door close behind us or something like that. Think, Addison! Do you really want to go home and not know what's behind the doors when a quick peek could change everything?"

Addison bit the inside of her bottom lip and chewed on her thumbnail again and looked sideways at Claire and then at the door. A little bubble of excitement rolled up from her belly and into her throat, and she giggled. "Well, yeah, it might be interesting."

"Might be interesting? Might be interesting?" Claire raised her palms in the air, shaking her head and rolling her eyes. "This whole treehouse is totally awesome. I bet Gramma's got stuff out there that she is hiding, and if we know about it, we could come up with a plan, and, come on, what can it hurt?" Suddenly, Claire folded her arms into chicken wings and strutted in circles. "Buk, buk, buk, buk," she teased.

"Oh, okay." Addison chuckled.

And so, with a little apprehension and more than a few bubbles floating about in their stomachs, Addison and Claire got up, took a quick peek outside the peacock door just to make sure they were alone, and then slipped over to the silver door. Claire put her hand on the copper doorknob and turned it. The door creaked and squeaked, and Claire pushed it open just enough to peek out. They stuck their heads around the edge of the door, peered outside for a second, pulled their heads back inside, looked at each other, and then stuck their heads outside again.

"Why does Gramma have a huge mirror out there?" Addison finally asked.

"Well, I officially feel cheated," Claire groaned. "All that rambling and going on and on and the only thing out there is a huge stupid mirror propped against the deck railings? Well, if that's all it is, we might as well just go out and take a look. Hey, wait a minute! Since this is Gramma's house, maybe it's one of those trick mirrors that make you look funny or skinny or squishy or something like at the carnivals. We should at least look. Can't hurt."

Addison shrugged. "Might as well," she said. "Especially if the only thing out there is an old mirror." And with that, Claire and Addison started across the threshold. "Wait! Prop the door open just a little," Claire said. "That way, we will be able to hear if anyone is coming up and we get back in before they see us."

"Good thing that you thought of that!" Addison agreed. "Hold the door while I grab something." But just as she bent forward to grab her book and wedge it between the door and the threshold, they heard voices coming up the ladder. Addison stood up to grab Claire and get back inside; but at that same moment, as she turned, a gust of wind rushed across the deck and slammed the door shut.

"Aahhhh, not the best timing," Claire whispered. "Now, we are stuck out here until they leave. Oh well, we'll just have to wait till they're gone. Then we'll slip back in, and they'll never know." But in that very moment, as they realized they were temporarily trapped outside, they both froze. Addison's red summer sweater that she had thrown over her shoulders after swimming had slipped off just as the wind slammed the door shut and the sleeve had caught between the door and the doorjamb.

"Quick," Claire demanded. "Before they get up here. Open the door just a little and grab it. Be quiet. Don't let the door creak. Hurry!" Claire demanded.

Addison reached for the doorknob and froze a second time. "Claire," she muttered, "there's no doorknob, no handle, no anything! We can't get back in. We're stuck. And look!" She waved her hand around. "This balcony doesn't go all the way around. It stops right here, and the balcony is blocked off with this giant mirror. We're going to have to knock to get back in, and we're going to get in trouble. What now?"

Claire shrugged. "Too late now," she said. "We're caught now. But there's always hope," she added, wiggling her eyebrows up and down. "I just might be able to call in a couple of bribes on Levi and get him to keep his mouth shut. Do you have anything on Eleanor?"

Addison shook her head with a sigh. "Oh, Claire."

"Well, if we can't come up with anything, we just might have to face the music. So let's look in the mirror first and then knock. If we're going to get into trouble, we might as well see what we came for," Claire insisted.

And with that, Claire stomped over to the mirror. "Who cares?" She scowled. "It's not like it's the first time we've ever gotten in trouble, and it certainly won't be the last."

Chapter 10

Claire and Addison: Trick Mirrors and Strange Happenings

"This is huge!" Claire exclaimed. "It goes all the way across—like a gate! But why would Gramma have it out here?"

Addison touched the creamy-white wood frame enclosing the mirror. "Look at this frame." She sighed. "It's beautiful. It's huge. Could it be a trick mirror like at carnivals?"

Both girls stood in front of the mirror, staring at it, moving up and down, and swaying from side to side; but there were no squished legs or shrinking bellies, no big foreheads and tiny mouths, and no fat arms—nothing at all. They looked completely normal.

"It's just a regular old dumb mirror, just bigger than usual," Claire complained. She screwed her upper lip into a disdainful pout, crossed her arms, and frowned. "Nothing special at all, and now we have to knock on the door, and we'll get in trouble for no good reason at all unless, of course, I can bribe Levi, but I hate to use up my favors like that. Ya never know when you're going to need 'em for something big. Are you sure you don't have anything on anyone?" she asked.

Addison glanced at Claire, shaking her head. She stood in front of the mirror, straightening her ponytail. "This really is a beautiful mirror," she said, touching the creamy-white carved frame. She noticed a smudge on the glass. She spat on her finger and tried to rub the spot off, but just as she touched the mirror, a little pop and a whirr and a kind of shimmery flick wobbled across the mirror. She screamed and jumped back.

"What was that?" Claire shrieked.

"I don't know, but it was weird!" Addison muttered.

"Oh my gosh! Maybe it's a special mirror after all," Claire whispered. She inched her fingers forward, gingerly touching the glass with her fingertip. Abruptly the mirror popped and whirred and shimmered and flickered.

"Asshhh!" Addison shrieked and jumped back even more. Shimmery waves floated across the glass.

Claire laughed. "I think Gramma has a secret, after all." She gently laid her entire hand on the glass. A little rush of water burst from the top and slid over her fingers, gliding down the front of the mirror.

"Where's the water coming from?" Addison asked, peering around the edges of the frame. "Claire, look behind the mirror! There aren't any steps on the other side. There's a slide or something, but you can't get to it because the mirror is in the way. Why is there a slide instead of steps?"

Claire glanced around the back of the mirror. "You're right. Maybe that's why Gramma doesn't want us out here. Maybe we've discovered her little secret. Told ya so."

"But I still don't see where the water's coming from," Addison said, looking around the edge again. Claire laid her entire hand on the mirror, watching the water emerge from under the white casing.

"Addie, Addie, try this!" Claire insisted. Addison placed both hands onto the glass, giggling as the water flowed over them. The mirror quivered and wiggled even more. Addison laughed, pulling her hands off.

Claire's hands began quivering and wiggling all over the mirror as it vibrated and whirred more and more. Both girls were laughing as Claire tried to keep her hand from bouncing all over the mirror. And without warning and quite suddenly, the mirror kind of groaned and creaked; and before Claire thought to remove her hand, it suddenly slipped right into the glass instead of bouncing on the surface as if the mirror had kind of swallowed her hand all the way to the wrist.

Claire shrieked, jerking her hand back, and it slipped out as quickly as it had slipped in. "Oh my gosh!" she whispered. "Did you see that?" And both girls stood there with huge eyes and open mouths, and then both girls looked at each other again. Then they both crept forward and touched their fingers to the mirror. And the mirror shimmered and wiggled and squiggled and swallowed their fingers.

They tried it over and over. After just a little while, and once they were quite certain that their hands would come back out just as they went in, Claire decided to take it one step further. She pressed her foot against the glass, and it slipped through just like slick soap slipping out of wet hands. She stood there with one foot on one side of the mirror and her other foot on the other side of the mirror. Addison laughed and did the same thing, and they both stood there with one foot on the front side and the other foot on the back side of the mirror.

"Oh my gosh! Addie, I got it. I know how to stay out of trouble. The others don't even have to know what we did. There's a small chance that nobody has noticed your red sweater caught in the door. If they haven't, we just might have time to stay out of trouble," Claire said. "Let's go all the way through the mirror, down the slide, and then run back up into the treehouse through the peacock door. We can slip the sweater out of the threshold, and nobody will ever know anything!"

Addison drew in a sharp breath, clapping her hand over her mouth. "Perfect!" She chuckled. "Let's do it!"

And so, Claire grabbed Addison's hand. "We gotta do this together!" They both faced the mirror and slipped their outside foot through. With their outside foot planted on the back side, they both slid their outside hands and arms through so they were half on one side and a half on the other side of the mirror. They shuffled around so they were facing each other.

"Okay, together now," Addison said with a grimace. And after sucking in several deep breaths, they both laid the sides of their faces against the mirror, grimacing and wincing just a little, because it really is kind of weird to try to go through a mirror even if it is a trick mirror. While gripping each other's hands very tightly, they both closed their eyes, counted to three, and scrunched their faces against the mirror. They pressed the sides of their bellies and their faces against the glass and pushed just a little until they felt a little wiggly kind of something, and there was a jiggle and fizz and a whirr and a pop, and suddenly they were both standing on the other side.

They looked at each other, erupting into laughter at the same time. "Oh, that was so cool!" Claire yelled.

"Wow!" Addison laughed. "I wanna do that again sometime! But for now, let's get down the slide and get back up the ladder, through the peacock door, and hope nobody noticed!"

By this time, Claire was looking over the edge. "Gee, look at this slide. It plunges almost straight down. You can't even see the end of it from here. I think it loops around or something."

"Yikes," Addison agreed. "This is freaky looking. It looks longer than it should be. The ground isn't that far down. How come it looks like it goes on and on?"

"Maybe it has a built-in optical illusion, like the mirror, you know, Gramma and her stuff," Claire said, shrugging. "Oh well, it can't be any worse than that roller coaster. Come on, let's go at the same time. It is wide enough to sit side by side." And at that, they sat down; and after counting to three, they pushed off.

At first, when they swooped down, their stomachs went all tight and bubbly; and they laughed aloud. But then they swooshed, and then they looped into circles and even smaller circles until their eyes felt like they were popping out and they were screaming "Aaahhhhahahhah!" And then suddenly everything was very black and very dark, and they let go of each other's hands as they kept looping and swirling and whirling. Suddenly they shot off the end and went soaring into the light and flying through the air.

Addison landed with a plop and an "Oowww!" and she opened her eyes and blinked and squinted and blinked some more. All she could see was a swirling, spinning world of translucent colors bouncing about as if she had spun her way into the center of a rainbow and all she could feel was a churning tummy that felt quite queasy and gushy. And as she sat there sucking in deep breaths and gasping a little, a kind of scary sensation moved up from her belly and into her throat.

Then, after a few seconds, she heard another "Aahhhhhh!" and she looked up just in time to scramble to the side as a set of sprawling arms and legs flailing about like an overgrown erratic spider came tumbling through the air. Suddenly there was another bump and another plop and several "ouches" and a couple more "ooohs" as Claire landed on the ground and slipped straight toward Addison.

And when Claire sat up, she looked quite green. The entire world was spinning in horrible circles, so she lay back on the ground and whispered, "Wherever we are, I am glad we're here and not on that slide." And then she closed her eyes and waited for the world to stop revolving.

Chapter 11

The Situation

Now, just as Addison and Claire slipped out the silver door, Levi and Eleanor had been walking into the treehouse through the peacock door. "I thought Claire and Addie were up here," Levi mused, looking around. "Where are they?" And just then, he looked over and noticed the sleeve of Addison's red sweater caught in the threshold of the silver door. Levi nudged Eleanor and pointed with his finger.

Eleanor shook her head. "Will you look at that—Addison's sweater!" she said. "Claire and Addison must have snuck out that door. If Gramma finds out, they'll be in so much trouble, but we might be in trouble too because we promised to keep an eye on everyone even though they are almost as old as we are!"

"Claire makes me so mad sometimes," Levi grumbled as he marched to the door, grabbed the knob, and yanked; but the door didn't budge. "This door is stuck. Help me, Eleanor," Levi said. Eleanor grabbed hold, and they both tried to pull at the same time, but nothing happened. Levi pounded on the door, yelling, "Claire, Addison, you better get back in here! We see Addison's sweater. We know you're out there. Get in here before we all get in trouble!"

Just about then, Tilly, Brody, Ivan, and Esmé wandered in through the peacock door, quickly realized what was happening, and joined in the pounding and yelling. But in the midst of all that shouting and pounding, they felt a rumble. They felt the treehouse shake just a little, and then they heard an "aaaah," and then everything went still and silent. Eleanor's hands flew to her mouth. "They fell off the deck!" she screamed.

Levi rushed out the peacock door and practically slid down the ladder. The others ran right behind him. They expected to find Claire and Addison lying on the ground with something broken. But when they got to the bottom, Addison and Claire were nowhere to be found.

They ran all the way around the bottom of the treehouse, trailing behind one another, calling out, "Claaaiiree! Addddisooon!" But there was no sign of Claire or Addison anywhere. So after a bit, the cousins decided to split up and search. They combed through everything: every nook and every cranny, and behind every bush, and even under and around and in all the trees. But they still did not find the girls. After searching high and low, they stopped and looked at one another, and their eyes got very, very large. Well, it was all very confusing and more than just a little scary.

Just about then, Tilly noticed Gramma tramping through the trees with another basket of food for supper. "Come on, there's Gramma!" she yelled as she took off running. They all ran, but Levi got there first because, after all, he had the longest legs.

"Gramma!" He panted, leaning forward, placing his hands on his thighs while trying to catch his breath. "Something terrible has happened."

Gramma smiled, patting his shoulder. "Whatever it is, I'm sure it's quite fixable," Gramma said. "Now, catch your breath and tell me what happened. It's going to be just fine."

By that time, the others were also standing around Gramma, and they all started talking over and around one another and not making any sense at all. Finally, Gramma held up her hand. "Tilly, my little observer," she said, "please tell me what happened."

And at that, Tilly told the story from beginning to end. She told about Addison's sleeve in the threshold, and how the door was stuck. She told about hearing the "aaaahhhh" and how the treehouse had shaken. She told how they had searched in nooks and crannies and trees and bushes. But no matter how much they yelled and looked, Addison and Claire were nowhere to be found.

And when Tilly was finished telling her story, Gramma's face kind of crumpled up, and she put her hands over her mouth. She said, "Oh my, oh my, oh my, the silver door, you say?" And they all nodded. And Gramma kept saying things like "Oh dear" and "Oh my, oh my."

They all stood there, silently observing Gramma. Esmé grabbed Gramma's hand, watching her. Brody paced back and forth; his face was rather red, and he kept opening his mouth to say something, but his voice cracked. He just paced some more. Finally, Brody yelled, "I've got to find my sister! Addison gets scared when it gets dark. Gramma, where can they be?"

Gramma looked at each of them, and then she looked over at the treehouse and heaved a deep breath. She said something about how it would all work out, and she tried to smile, but her eyes didn't crinkle around the edges like usual. She absentmindedly mumbled, "Come on, everyone." And she began walking toward the treehouse without saying another word, and they all trailed silently behind, glancing at one another with curious, worried expressions.

Gramma climbed the ladder and plopped down in the blue rocking chair that sat to the side of the peacock door. "I have to remember." She sighed.

The cousins stood in a semicircle, watching as she rocked back and forth, running her fingers through her hair, and tapping on the arms of the chair until she finally looked up and smiled. The edges of her eyes even crinkled a little around the edges almost like normal. Almost.

"Oh, goodness, children, they are fine, just fine," she said as she noticed the six anxious faces. "I just had to think and get a plan. They'll get back. Since they didn't have a key to come in, I'll have to use my key to go out. What do you think these keys are about? Once that wind slams the door—well, no matter, I have keys, so it's all good." Reaching into her pocket, she drew out the brass key ring, held it up, jiggled the keys, and smiled. For a bit, it almost felt like everything was back to normal. Almost.

They were all feeling just a little bit better until Brody spoke up once more, "But, but, Gramma, it will be dark soon, and Addison will hate that."

"It's gonna be just fine, Brody," Gramma said patting Brody's shoulder. "They will be home before you know it. Dark and light are very different where they are." Levi's and Eleanor's eyes met at that moment.

"Where they are?" asked Levi suddenly, looking quite bewildered and more than a little anxious about his sister Claire.

"Well, yes, where they are, I guess," said Gramma. "Actually, they are quite fine—kinda anyway." She waved the back of her hand at them dismissively. "It's okay. Just eat and play some games and be busy for a bit. I have some stuff to do." She stopped and looked directly at them. "Don't worry," she said, "we will get them back." Levi and Eleanor stood there, feeling quite bewildered and shaking their heads.

Levi motioned for the younger ones to sit down, and Eleanor opened the basket and absentmindedly began passing out the food while observing Gramma who began rushing about the room, opening cupboards and drawers, prying up a couple of floorboards, searching around the room, and studying the curios on the silver shelf. The cousins watched in silence, chewing a tiny bite here and there, not feeling hungry at all, but not quite knowing what else to do. Gramma just kept picking up bits and pieces of things until she had created a pile of stuff on the floor.

Once she seemed content with her stuff, she sorted the big pile into separate little piles. She stopped every so often, tilting her head from one side to the other. After quite a few puzzled looks and after tapping her cheeks several times, she finally slipped a few tiny objects into the little silver bag and smiled.

Finally, she went over to a shelf beside the peacock door and took down an old-fashioned lantern and turned the flame up as high as it would go. She picked up her bag of stuff and the lantern and walked to the silver door and set them on the floor. All the cousins sat slowly chewing their food and watching.

Gramma stood in front of the door, sucking in deep breaths. Suddenly, she turned around and stared at each of the cousins, one at a time. "Levi, Eleanor, Tilly, Brody, Ivan, and Esmé, stay where you are," she cautioned and commanded at the same time. "Don't move until I get back."

Then, after jiggling around in her pocket for the key and sorting through them all, she chose a sparkly silver one, slipped the forked part into the lock of the silver door, and turned it. The lock clicked. The keys jangled as Gramma slipped them back into her apron pocket.

Gramma picked up the lantern and the silver bag of stuff. After taking a deep breath, she opened the door. A huge gust of wind rushed through the door, blowing Gramma backward; but she bent forward, pushing her way out, and slammed the door behind her. Silence hung over the room like a mouse preparing to snatch a piece of cheese off a spring-loaded trap.

Waiting. Waiting. Waiting. Waiting. After a moment or so, another click and Gramma opened the door and stumbled back in with a huge gust of wind pushing her back through the door and practically knocking her over. But this time her face was wreathed in a smile and the crinkles around her eyes were back.

"Oh, it feels so good out there." She gasped. "I almost forgot how good it is." And she sighed a deep, deep sigh and plopped back down in her blue rocking chair.

"Did you find them?" Levi asked, jumping up, knocking his food over.

"Oh no," Gramma said, "They have to find their own way back, but it is all just fine—just fine. They'll be back before you know it."

Chapter 12

Levi, Eleanor, and Esmé: The Search Begins

The floorboards creaked, keeping time with Gramma's relentless rocking back and forth, her fingers continually tapping on the arms of her blue rocking chair, and her humming to some old tune that nobody recognized.

Brody paced around the room, finally stopping and looking around. "Addie and Claire are out there, and we're all just sitting here. Shouldn't we be doing something?"

Gramma glanced at the glass clock with spinning crystals twirling on the base. "Listen, Brody," she said cheerfully, even though a crack in her voice betrayed her, "Claire and Addison will be back really soon unless they get lost, or some shadow tricks them, or they drink too much elixir, or if some path temporarily confuses them. If any of those things happen, they could be slightly delayed. But no matter," she said, glancing at the clock again and smiling, "they'll be back real soon." She leaned forward, gazed directly into his eyes, and smiled her gentlest smile. "All the paths eventually lead home," she said with a wink.

"Now, why don't we all play a game and eat some cookies?" she said, pushing out of her rocking chair and bustling over to the cupboard. "We can get started, and they can join in when they get here." She began opening drawers and shuffling through shelves, pushing and pulling at things, moving things this way and that, and even searching under the cupboard.

Levi slipped over to the peacock door, opened it, and stood staring out across the woods before closing the door again and shaking his head. He watched Gramma rummage through stuff. Ivan slipped over to the silver shelf. He stood with his back to everyone, biting his lower lip and reexamining each of the tiny curios on the shelf over and over and over. Once in a while, he would glance over at Gramma.

Tilly sat with her arm around Esmé, watching Levi, Brody, Ivan, and Eleanor. After a bit, she got up and touched Brody's shoulder. "They will be back soon," she said, trying to reassure him.

Brody stared right at her. "I'm not sure about any of this. I think we should just leave and go look for them. What are we waiting for?"

"Let's give it just a couple more minutes before we panic," Tilly said. "Gramma's lived here a long time, and she keeps looking at the clock. She might know something we don't. But I'll tell you what, if they don't show up in a few minutes, we'll organize a mutiny and take over!" Tilly chuckled, throwing her head up and squaring her shoulders.

Even Brody had to smile. "You might have a point," he said, glancing around at the clocks. "But, really, just a couple of minutes, not more." Ivan had seen them talking quietly together; he had walked over and joined them, listening. He smiled and nodded his approval to the plan.

Esmé sat quietly, watching everything; but after a while, her bottom lip began quivering as she began sucking in deep quick breaths while trying to hold back the tears. "I want my sister, Claire."

Levi sat down next to her. Pulling her close, he kissed the top of her head; and she nestled against him, her shoulders heaving up and down as tears began flowing. "Don't worry, Ezzy, our sister Claire will be back really soon."

Levi looked directly into Eleanor's eyes, and Eleanor stared right back at him. He nodded toward Gramma, who was still humming that strange old melody while pulling out old board games and stacking them on the floor. "Oh, this will be fun," she said, picking the games up and plopping them down in the middle of the room.

"Esmé, sweetie, don't be sad. Claire will be back soon. Here, have a cookie. That'll make you feel better," Gramma added while stooping over the food basket with the red checkered cloth and rummaging through it. Suddenly, she stood up and looked around.

"Oh dear," she said, "now, just where are those chocolate chip cookies? Esmé needs one very badly, and we can't rightly play a game without the cookies! And I crammed 'em full of walnuts and raisins just the way Ivan likes 'em too."

She stood thinking, tapping her cheek with her index finger. Suddenly she brightened. "I've got it!" she said. "They were in the bag, and I bet I dropped the bag on the ground when all of you ran over and gave me that jolt about Claire and Addie. Gave me a little jolt, you did—gave me a little jolt, for sure. Well, I better go and see where I dropped those cookies. But each of you simply must promise me you will stay away from those doors. I don't want any more lost children. It's just too worrisome. Now, promise me!"

They all nodded slowly. And Gramma turned, walking out through the peacock door and climbing down the ladder again. "Stay in there!" she yelled up to them from the ladder.

As soon as she reached the ground, Levi grabbed Eleanor by the arm. "Come on, Ellie. We've got to find 'em. I'll grab the map book just in case there's some area we don't know about." He raised his voice just a little, looking at all the cousins.

"Listen, everyone. Maybe Claire and Addison hurried off into the woods so they wouldn't get caught and got really turned around or something. I don't know how they could get lost. We've all been going back and forth all day. But stranger things have happened, I guess," he added with a shrug. "Me and Ellie are gonna search before it gets too dark—just in case."

"Let's all go!" Brody shouted, looking around at Ivan and Tilly with a smile. They both nodded.

"Wait!" Levi held up his hand. "Just give us a few minutes to check things out. Stay with Esmé and tell Gramma where we went. We'll take a quick look around, and if we don't find the girls right away, we'll rush back, and we'll all go out. I'm sure Gramma will want us all to search if we can't find them. In the meantime, take care of Ezzy and tell Gramma, so she knows and doesn't get too worried. We gotta go, now!"

Bending over, Levi hugged Esmé. "Gramma will be back, and she would be frantic if you aren't here. Stay with Tilly, Brody, Ivan, and Gramma. Be good till I get back."

Eleanor stood looking out the peacock door, watching for Gramma. "Levi, if we are going to go, we have to leave right now! Gramma found the bag of cookies, and she's coming back already!"

Esmé broke into sobs. "Please Levi, take me too. I want Claire."

"We need to go now!" Eleanor almost shouted. "She's almost here!"

"No, Ezzy. We have to hurry. It'll be dark real soon." He patted her head and hurried to the bronze shelf. He picked up the map book. Slipping it under his arm, Levi grabbed the knob on the bronze door. "We'll just go out this door, so Gramma doesn't see us," he said. "A door is a door."

Levi turned, facing the others. "We'll be back soon, and we'll all go together if we can't find them. We can't get lost. I've got the maps. Just tell Gramma we'll make it up to her when we get back."

Levi opened the door, and Eleanor rushed out in front of him. But just as Levi resettled the book under his arm and turned to go out, Esmé ran past him, leaping through the open doorway just as Levi stepped over the threshold. And in the very same second, and just as they were both crossing over, a great gust of wind rushed across the deck, slamming the door shut, shaking and rattling the entire treehouse, and toppling Levi, Eleanor, and Esmé onto the wooden deck.

"What just happened? That was weird!" Levi exclaimed as he stood up, brushing himself off and helping Esmé to her feet.

Eleanor immediately stood up, setting her fists against her hips, glaring at her youngest cousin. She stomped her foot. "Esmé, you go back in there. Right now! Right now!" she yelled. "You'll slow us down. Levi told you to stay here!" Eleanor reached for the doorknob so she could open the door and push Esmé inside, but she stopped short with her hand still suspended in the air.

"Levi," she said, "talk about weird. Look, no doorknob on the outside, just a keyhole! We can't get back in through this door. And look," she added, leaning back to look around the angles of the building, "it looks like there aren't any doorknobs on any of the doors. I bet that's why Gramma told us not to go out these stupid doors. The peacock door is the only one with a doorknob. Mystery solved!"

She drew a deep breath and flicked her hand into the air, glowering at Esmé, "Well, I guess that means we're stuck with you!" Eleanor said, staring straight at Esmé. "You better keep up. No whining! No fussing! We gotta find Claire and Addison." Esmé slipped over and grabbed Levi's hand, leaning against him.

"Eleanor! Stop being mean," Levi snapped. "She'll be just fine!" He laid his hand on Esmé's shoulder, giving her a tiny reassuring squeeze. Esmé looked up, beaming at Levi; then turning her face, she wrinkled her nose and stuck out her tongue at Eleanor.

Eleanor sucked in a deep exasperated breath, shaking her head and rolling her eyes. "Oh, whatever, Esmé," she snarled.

But in that very second, as Eleanor was still shaking her head and rolling her eyes, another blast of wind rushed across the deck, swirling and twirling around them, whipping Eleanor's long hair about in every direction and jolting all three of them one way and then the other way. Levi grabbed Esmé, shielding her as the wind erupted into a violent fury, knocking them off balance and toppling them onto the deck floor again. As Levi tumbled to the deck floor, the map book flew out from under his arm; and the wind picked it up, tossing it into the air. "Ooh no! The book! I dropped the book!" he yelled as the wild wind whipped across the deck again.

Eleanor clapped her hand over her mouth and stared at him. "Oh no!" she shouted over the roar of the wind. "I don't see it anywhere up here," she said, gazing across the deck. "It's probably down there on the ground!"

"Let's get down there!" Levi yelled, grabbing Esmé's hand and pulling her along, even though neither Eleanor nor Esmé could hear anything he said over the howling and the screeching of the wind.

The cousins hunched forward, straining down each step, stumbling and getting pushed against the railing several times until they reached the last step. But strangely enough, in the very second as they stepped onto the ground, the wind slowed to a wispy breeze; and just like that, an eerie calm settled around them.

"What just happened?" Eleanor asked.

Levi shrugged his shoulders and looked around. "Maybe a really bizarre storm is blowing in. All the more reason to find Claire and Addison quickly," he said. "Let's find the map book and get going."

They frantically scanned the ground, quickly searching in and under and around the steps and scouring the entire area. "I don't see it anywhere," Levi muttered after a while.

Finally, Eleanor stopped and shook her head. "Let's go, Levi," she said. "We can look for the book later, but right now, we need to find Claire and Addison before it gets dark."

"Those girls have made such a mess of things!" Levi said, kicking the ground. He took a deep breath and blew it out. "Okay," he said, trying to be calm, "we need to find them. Let's go to the beach area first. I don't know how they could lose their way after all the trips we made back and forth all day, but stranger things have happened. I just wish we had those maps with us just in case there's some weird path that we don't know about. What's Gramma gonna say when that book is gone?"

"When we get back, we'll tell Gramma what happened and search for the book then. I'm sure it'll be fine. You know how Gramma is," Eleanor said with a chuckle. And with that, they turned in the direction of the setting sun and headed toward the turbulent coastal waters.

Chapter 13

Tilly, Brody, and Ivan: Sweet Water

When the bronze door slammed shut behind Levi, Eleanor, and Esmé, the entire treehouse trembled and shook. Tilly, Brody, and Ivan startled and whipped their heads around, gazing first at the door and then at one another. "There must be a huge storm blowing in!" Brody shouted frantically. "Come on, they're gonna need our help. We can't just sit here and do nothing."

"Shhhhhh, quiet," Tilly whispered, holding up her hand for silence. All three leaned forward. Plastic sacks crinkled from below. Gramma had reached the treehouse and was starting up the rickety wooden ladder with her bag of chocolate chip cookies.

"Let's go!" Brody demanded.

He grabbed the copper doorknob on the bronze door and jerked it, but it did not budge. "What in the world?" he yelled, yanking at it again. "What's wrong?"

"What'll we do, what'll we do, what'll we do?" Tilly repeated over and over, bouncing from one foot to the other. Wooden ladder rungs creaked as Gramma climbed up.

Ivan's eyes darted to the closest door. "Try this one!" he shouted as he grabbed the knob on the green door. It flew open. Tilly and Ivan scrambled out simultaneously. As Brody rushed across the threshold behind them, a ferocious blast of wind surged across the landing, slamming the door shut. The treehouse shook and trembled. The cousins whipped around as it slammed, staring first at the door and then at one another.

"That slamming stuff is kinda creepy," Ivan said. "Must be a storm coming or something, but let's get outta here before Gramma figures out what we're doing and tries to stop us."

Brody looked down from the deck, staring across the grassy field and into the wooded area below. "Where'd they go?" he asked. "We were right behind them. How far could they get?"

Tilly stood still, drumming her fingers on the wooden railing, scrutinizing the field and woods. "Hey, guys, something's not right. That field is big. There is no way they've had enough time to get across it. We should be able to see them from up here."

Ivan shrugged his shoulders. "Maybe they ran into those trees," he suggested, pointing to a cluster of evergreens.

Tilly hesitated. "They couldn't get across the field that fast, could they? I just don't know. Maybe we should just go back in and tell Gramma what happened. Something's just not right."

"Come on, Tilly, don't do that," Brody intervened.

Tilly turned around, determined to go back in; but just as she reached for the doorknob, she gasped. "Brody, Ivan, look. No doorknob! And I don't see a doorknob on that door either," she said, leaning back and pointing at the red door. "I bet this is why Gramma told us not to go out these doors! You can't get back in."

"Well," Brody said, shrugging his shoulders, "that simply means that we have to go down the steps and walk around to the front and come in through the peacock door. And," he continued with a mischievous glint in his eye, "since we are all probably going to get in trouble anyway, once Gramma knows what we did, we might as well run over to those trees and help search for Claire and Addison. Then we'll come back and face the music. We're already in trouble anyway now."

"Ooohhh, you're probably right," Tilly conceded.

And so, Tilly, Brody, and Ivan scurried down the back steps and sprinted across the field and into the wooded area.

"Leeeviiii, Ellllleanor, Esméeeee, Claaaaiiire, Aaaddison!" they yelled over and over. When no one answered, they yelled some more. And so, after calling and yelling until their voices began sounding a little like croaking frogs, Tilly pleaded once again. "Let's go back," she begged. "Between the slamming doors and not being able to find anyone, this is just creepy, and I don't like it one bit."

Brody and Ivan finally nodded; but as they were hesitantly turning around to go back to the treehouse, Ivan stopped and pointed to a shimmering pool of water surrounded by trees. "Oh my gosh!" he shouted pointing to a towering oak arching over glistening blue water. "Is that what I think it is? Is that a rope dangling from that high branch? Look, look over there!" he shouted.

"It is!" Brody hollered.

"Wow! Remember climbing on that grapevine and it snapped and we all landed in that creek?" Ivan laughed. "Come on, one good plunge off that rope swing, and then we'll get back to the treehouse and get fussed at. I can't believe Gramma never showed that rope swing to us!"

Tilly giggled. "Yeah," she said, "that's just too sweet."

They ran to the oak tree, and after climbing up onto a massive rock, Ivan grasped the rope, pulling it back as far as it would go. They all three grabbed hold: Brody at the top, Tilly in the middle, and Ivan on the bottom.

"One!" Ivan yelled.

"Don't let the seaweed get you," Brody teased Tilly, knowing how she hated seaweed.

"Two!" Ivan called out.

Tilly's tummy was tight and bubbly as she gripped the rope, squeezing her eyes shut.

"Three!" she yelled, and they went soaring over the water. They swooped up, up, up until the rope was stretched and taut and the deepest part of the water shimmered below them.

Ivan yelled, "Nooowww!" and they let go, flying through the air, legs kicking, arms flailing, bellies flip-flopping as they plunged into the cool luscious water, piercing the surface with their toes and sliding down into the depths of the cool sweet water.

Chapter 14

Gramma's All Alone

Gramma felt the treehouse tremble twice as she climbed up the rickety ladder. She opened the peacock door, looked around, and plopped into her rocking chair. *Oh my, oh my, oh my, oh my,* she said to herself. *They really do not listen very well, now do they?*

She sat in her chair for a few minutes, glancing back and forth between the doors. *Let me think,* she muttered, *let me think. The house shook twice. That means they went out two different doors.*

And, she continued, *I'm gonna guess that Levi and Eleanor decided to go first, and since they were in charge, they told the others to stay for a bit. And then, they probably went out the bronze door since Levi had been looking at the map book. Esmé would have found a way to go with Levi.* Gramma nodded to herself.

Now, Brody, Tilly, and Ivan would have immediately decided to go also. But since the bronze door wouldn't open, they'd have to go through another door. I'm betting on the green door since it's close to the bronze door, and Tilly was wanting that snow globe. Bingo! She chuckled. *I bet that's right.*

And with that, she hurried to the cupboards. Flinging them open, she rummaged through old pens and caps and twisted spoons and crinkled pieces of paper until she found several crystal rocks and a few glass marbles and stuffed them into two velvet drawstring bags. She picked up the miniature compass from the bronze shelf and the snow globe and kaleidoscope from the green shelf and set them on the floor beside the drawstring bags of crystals and marbles.

Finally, she grabbed two lanterns off the peacock shelf and lit them, turning the flames up so high that black smoke poured out the opening in the glass globe. She stood in the center of the room and squinted back and forth at the doors.

I hope I've got this right, she said. *It better be.*

She walked over to the green door and flipped through her keys until she found a large green key with an emerald stone in the center. She slipped it into the keyhole; picked up the lantern, the snow globe, and the drawstring bag of stuff; and turned the key. It clicked. "Yes! Yes!" she shouted, stepping outside. After just a minute or so, she scurried back in with a ferocious blast of wind pushing her through the doorway. She slammed the door and took a deep breath. "Oh, that feels incredible!" She grinned. And she hurried to the bronze door.

Flipping through her key ring again, she found a tiny bronze key with the strange letters engraved on the side. She slipped the key into the lock; picked up the lantern, the miniature compass, and the drawstring bag; clicked the lock; and opened the door. The wind whipped her hair all around her face and back and forth in every direction as she bent into the wind, pushing herself over the threshold, slamming the door behind her.

And after a couple of minutes, the door opened once more; and she stumbled in with the wind, practically toppling her over. But this time, as she stumbled into the treehouse, she was carrying the ancient map book. She slammed the door behind her and stood there for a few seconds, smiling and gently running her fingers over the embossed gold letters.

Oh, that dear boy, she whispered, smiling and slowly shaking her head. *He must have thought he could take the map book with him. Silly child, silly, silly child. It just doesn't work that way.* And with a deep sigh, she walked over and set the book back on the bronze shelf and stood for a minute, just looking around the room.

After a bit, she grabbed a celery stick filled with peanut butter and a chocolate chip cookie from the wicker basket and plopped down in the blue rocking chair beside the peacock door. She glanced over at the large cuckoo clock setting on the mantel. The miniature boy and girl figurines slid around and through the tiny tunnels, singing songs as they rotated around and around in little dancing circles.

I sure hope nobody gets too lost, she muttered, tapping her top lip with her finger and then biting into a celery stick filled with peanut butter. *Their parents just wouldn't understand at all—not at all.*

Chapter 15

Claire and Addison: Ruby-Red Fingernails

Claire sat up looking quite green. Her stomach gurgled, and tiny blips and blops bounced in front of her eyes. Glancing around, she whispered, "Wherever we are, I am glad we are here and not on that slide. That was not good—not good at all." And then, gingerly lying back onto the ground, she closed her eyes, waiting for her stomach to settle and her head to stop spinning.

Addison leaned back on her elbows, gazing up at the sky and down at the ground. A curious frown settled across her face. Reaching down, she plucked a handful of grass; and after scrunching it between her fingers, she lifted it to her nose, inhaling deeply. "Strange," she murmured.

"Hey, Claire," she finally said, "you know what you said about being glad that we're here and not on the slide?"

"Yeah," Claire groaned, turning over and laying her face against the cool earth, nestling her face into the lush velvety grass, letting it tickle her skin. "This smells so sweet," she murmured.

"Well," Addison continued, scratching her head, "I'm not sure where 'here' is."

Claire groaned, pushed herself off the ground, and sat up. Squinting her eyes, she looked around. "We are somewhere near the bottom of the slide." Claire sighed and plopped back down on the grass, slipping her arm over her eyes, shading them from the intense sunlight.

But Addison persisted. "Claire, look at the grass. Have you ever seen grass like this? Look at the sky. Why is it so bright suddenly? It's supposed to be suppertime. This grass is too green, and it's too soft. And the sky should be getting darker."

Claire groaned. "Grass is green. The sky is blue. Addie, you are always—oh, never mind. Just let my head stop spinning, will ya?"

Suddenly, a clicking sound came out of nowhere. Claire sat up quickly, squinting into the distance, shaking her head, trying to focus her fuzzy eyes. Addison glanced from side to side; as she turned, she suddenly noticed a long dark shadow moving across the grass behind them.

Both girls jumped up and whirled around. Claire stumbled sideways.

A tall stunning woman with bobbed blonde hair, a gray pinstriped suit, and very shiny red high heels moved swiftly toward them, clicking across the paved path. As she reached the grass, she hesitated, gently stepping onto it and proceeding to stride straight toward them.

She smiled at them, her ruby-red lips parting to reveal flawless snow-white teeth and dimples on her cheeks. "Did I startle you, darling girls?" she implored as she puckered her lips and batted her long black thick eyelashes. "I didn't mean to startle you."

She scanned the girls. Her cornflower blue eyes sparkled as she continued. "I saw you two sitting over here on the grass, and I said to myself, *Victoria, you simply must go over there and see if those two adorable girls need your help.* So here I am, and I am pleased to make your acquaintance. I am Victoria, and you are?" She extended her hand; the perfectly polished fingernails were the same ruby red as her lips.

Claire reached out and shook her hand but immediately felt her stomach lurch as she touched the hand. "I'm Claire.

Pleased to meet you," she said. "And this is Addison." Addie nodded, smiled, shook Victoria's hand, and then discreetly wiped Victoria's clammy sweat from her hand onto the back of her pants while the other two weren't looking. She noticed Claire had done the same.

Victoria steepled her fingertips against her full lips and tilted her head to the side. The eyes sparkled. The dimples dinted. "Now you girls just tell me what I can do to make your day into a picture-perfect day—one that you would love to enjoy forever."

Claire and Addie looked at each other out of the corner of their eyes. Addison shrugged. Claire spoke up.

"Well, we really would appreciate it if you would—actually we got turned around or something," Claire said. "You see, our Gramma lives right here—somewhere—and we went down the slide from her treehouse just a few minutes ago, and—"

"And the slide was longer than we thought, and we landed here on the grass and—" Addison broke in.

"And we got turned around or something, and we need to get back to the treehouse," Claire finished.

Victoria leaned forward again; her cornflower blue eyes glistened in the sunlight. "Did you two adorable girls say that you went down the slide from your grandmother's tree home?"

"Tree HOUSE," Claire broke in.

"Yes, of course—treehouse—the one with the fascinating doors?"

"That's the one!" Claire yelled a little too loudly, looking at Addison with a "See, I told you so. Everything is fine" glance.

"Why, of course, I know exactly where it is. Such an adooorrable little place." She touched her right hand to her heart and patted her red fingernails against the gray pinstriped blazer. "Your grandmother is so, umm, creative. It is such an adorable little place—charming, quite colorful—and those lanterns, yes, those lanterns. What can I say about all those lanterns?" A small shudder seemed to run straight up her spine and cause her face to grimace just for a second. "Really, what can I say about the place?" She looked straight into Claire's eyes; her red lips seemed to stretch even tighter over her snow-white teeth.

"If you would just point us in the right direction, we will be on our way," Addison suggested.

"Well, of course, of course," Victoria continued, "but first, I have just an itty-bitty favor to ask."

Claire and Addison looked at each other. Addison's eyes got rounder and bigger.

"I would love to have you both come to my house. And it would be so delightful if you would like to join me for just a smidgen of tea. You two have obviously had quite a day. Your hair is a little tousled, and it looks like you have just a little smidgen of dirt on your faces, and I simply must insist that you stop at my house. A little tea and just an itty bit of a cleanup and a look in the mirror might be just the trick. And if you're really good, I'll even give you a taste of my own personal cherry elixir. It is so good. Come in for a little treat before you go on your way."

Addison looked at Claire, making big eyes and a little shake of the head, hoping Claire would just get the idea and say no.

But Claire just shrugged a little shrug and patted her belly to signal that she was hungry. Victoria pretended that she did not see the signals by looking at the trees.

Addison started to get her nerve. "I thank you, but we, uh, no, um, Gramma, and it is late—"

Victoria interrupted, pointing past the cedars to a brick manor house with an immense veranda, diamond-shaped leaded windows, cupolas, gambrels, and even a rounded rock tower with a huge Big Ben–styled clock in the middle. She clapped her hands and beamed, "Well, it's all settled then. Come, come, let's get going, shall we? Time is ticking. Time is ticking, and we all know what happens when time ticks away! We will comb and coif your hair and fill your tummies with sweet treats." She smiled. Her long thick eyelashes batted. Her white teeth flashed.

Victoria nestled her ruby-red fingernails against their shoulders. "Come, come, we'll have those little smudges off your faces in no time—in no time at all—and when you are all fixed up, maybe you'll even decide to stay a while."

With one hand on Claire's shoulder and the other on Addie's, Victoria squeezed just a little, her pointy fingernails jabbing into their shoulders as she guided them across the grass and stepped onto the tiled courtyard. The shiny red very high heels clicked against the slate tiles as Victoria pushed them across the stone portico.

Chapter 16

Levi, Eleanor, and Esmé: Oceans and Waterfalls

"Back to the water!" Esmé called out while skipping ahead on a worn trail through the woods. Levi smiled, letting her take the lead since she already knew the path so well. Even Eleanor grinned as Esmé skipped along, chanting a little ditty that Gramma had been teaching her all day.

> Blue bird, blue bird, what's that song you sing?
> Blue bird, blue bird, keep singing it for me.
> I love to see you flutter. I love to hear you sing.
> Blue bird, blue bird, what's the sign you bring?
>
> Butterflies and lightning bugs, floating in the sky.
> I listen when you flutter. I love it when you fly.
> Show me what you're saying. Make my dreams come true.
> Lightning bugs and dragonflies, I really do love you.

"Don't get too far ahead. It'll be getting dark soon," Levi called out to Esmé. They walked and looked about and called out and walked some more. "Claaairree! Adddissonn! Claaiiree! Addisoonn!" they yelled over and over; and when there was no response, they kept walking and called even more. They continued shouting until their voices sounded quite tired and very uneven. Even after that, they kept walking and calling out some more. And after what seemed like a very long time, even Esmé grew weary. She slowed down and plodded alongside Levi, dragging her feet just a little but keeping up just the same.

Finally, while scratching his head and after flicking his hand in the air, Levi stopped and turned in all four directions. "Where is the water?" he snapped. "This is so stupid! We should have been there long, long ago. It should've only taken a few minutes even if this path is slightly different. How are we so turned around? Maybe this is what happened to Claire and Addison. But I have the solution!" he said as he tapped his head with his finger.

Digging into his pocket, he took out his compass—the one with symbols and strange markings that Gramma had given him years before. "Lucky for us, I brought this," he said with a smug expression. He flicked the compass with his fingers, shaking it and tapping it several times. "Why is the needle spinning in circles?" he complained. "Must be broken or something." He sighed as he stuck it back in his pocket.

And so, they kept walking; and after a while, they stopped and looked in every direction again. "How'd we get lost?" Eleanor grumbled, shaking her head and turning in a slow circle, confused and frustrated. "Wait! Do you hear that?" she shushed them, holding her hand in the air. "Do you hear waves?" She bent forward, staring down the lane and into the trees. "Look! Over there, behind those trees," she said. "Around that bend in the road, listen. I hear something. Maybe the water is around that crook in the road. Maybe that's why we can't see it from here."

Levi scrunched his face, squinting his eyes; and looking toward the sun, he nodded. "I think you're right," he agreed. "Let's give it a try!"

And so, they turned and hurried down the lane toward the curve in the road. As they got closer to the bend, they heard a most excellent sound, the sound they had been waiting for, the sound that instantly fixed everything—the roaring sound of turbulent waters breaking against ocean rocks and washing up onto the shore. "There it is! There it is!" Eleanor screamed. "I was right! I hear the waattterrr!"

"We found it!" yelled Esmé, and again Levi and Eleanor smiled at her as she danced a little jig right there in the path.

"You're right!" Levi shouted with relief.

They broke into a jog that turned into a race, laughing as they sprinted, chasing and dashing to be the first to reach the crook of the road. And after rounding the bend, the roar of the water thundered; and the air became moist with a soft, delicious mist. All three cousins held their faces up, feeling the sweet, cool moisture. Levi chuckled and ran faster, pulling ahead of Eleanor and Esmé, his long legs giving him speed.

Eleanor laughed, shouting she'd get him for that as he surged past her. Esmé giggled. She fell behind but kept running as fast as her little legs would take her. But after running just a little bit more, Levi suddenly staggered to an abrupt stop and stood staring straight up. Eleanor, running hard to catch him, practically knocked him over as she ran into him.

She started to laugh at her own clumsiness, but then she too stopped and gazed straight up into the air. Esmé slowed when she saw the other two standing still in the middle of the lane, and she gingerly moved forward. She drew near, walking softly, hesitantly; and then with an open mouth and huge eyes, she slowly stepped over to Levi and slipped her little hand into his.

For you see, the sounds of roaring waters did not come from ocean waters surging and crashing into misty bursts against the cliffs and bluffs. No, no ocean salt waters at all. The soft and gentle spray on their faces was not from high tides and ocean waters battering the coastal cliffs—no, not this time. This time the mists burst forth from the plunging, pounding waters of a resplendent, pristine waterfall surging over the rock face and cascading down the sides of a magnificent towering mountain. And the three of them simply stood there and stared.

"I think we have a problem," Levi murmured after a while.

"I think you're right," Eleanor agreed.

Chapter 17

Tilly, Brody, and Ivan: Rainbow Swimming

Tilly let go of the rope swing, plunging feet first into the lake, spiraling down into the cold refreshing water. She felt a tickle on her foot, a gentle tug, and a tiny swoosh as something pulled at her leg, jerking her deeper into the water. She opened her eyes, and through the blurry water, she could see that seaweed had somehow tangled around her ankle. She kicked at the seaweed, frantically reaching down and pulling it off.

With deft strokes, she glided back to the surface. When her head popped out, she grinned, shaking her head like a wet dog to get the hair out of her face. Brody and Ivan popped out at the same time, and all three whooped and hollered and began yelling over and around one another, "We gotta do that again!" They laughed, wiping the water from their faces and rubbing their eyes so they could see clearly again. But as they cleared their eyes, they suddenly went totally silent. They looked about in circles, and then they looked at one another. They twisted around, dog paddling and rotating silently in more circles.

"Where's the tree and the rope swing?" Ivan finally asked, breaking into the stillness.

Silence.

"Where's the treehouse?" Tilly whispered.

Silence.

"I-I-I don't get it," Brody stammered. "What happened?"

Silence.

"Everything's gone," Ivan said as his face turned white. "Everything is gone except the water and the sky."

"And that white strip over there," Tilly added as she twisted around. "But everything else is gone."

And yes, it was true. Everything was gone. There were no evergreens lining a bank and no treehouse nestled in a tree. No huge oak tree, no rope swing, no rock. No grass and no sounds. Instead, the entire world was like an artist's palette of vibrant colors and hues.

The entire sky was a kaleidoscope of jeweled tones, weaving, merging, and flowing into one another. Rich peacock blue blended into violet, and violet into rose, and rose into fuchsia, and fuchsia into coral, and coral into jade, and jade into lime. And the water reflected each hue and each tone of the saturated sky. They were encased and drenched in pure color above, around, within, without.

The sky was smooth and silky while the water rippled and flowed; but the drenching, the immersion, and the saturation were complete. It was unbelievably beautiful. It was unbelievably scary.

The only relief from the colors was a thin strip of silvery-white land at the horizon line in the distance. For long astonishing, frightening moments, they stared in silence at the sky, plunging their hands into the water, drawing their hands back out, studying the vibrant colors dripping off their fingertips.

"We can't paddle in this stuff forever," Tilly finally said, her quivering voice betraying the steady expression on her face. "We should swim to that piece of white land over there while we can." Without another word, she turned and began swimming toward the thin strip of silver against the horizon line. Brody and Ivan did the same.

They swam in silence. Fear, determination, wonder, awe, hope, unease, and even terror flitted across their faces; but they kept paddling until they finally reached the silver line and rejoiced to see that it was, indeed, a pure white sandy shore. They pulled themselves onto the glistening white sand and sat in silence, catching their breath. Though the beach extended far and wide, they huddled close to one another, their shoulders touching, their knees drawn up against their chests.

"What if Gramma was telling the truth and we are lost?" Tilly asked.

"Maybe that's why we couldn't find anyone. Maybe all of us are lost," Ivan said as he reached out and picked up some white sand, letting it sift through his fingers.

"What now?" Brody asked after a little while.

"I really don't have a clue," Tilly muttered as she continued to sit and stare.

Chapter 18

Claire and Addison: Mirrors, Clocks, and Elixirs

The floor was shiny dark wood. High stone arches divided the main room from long rows of hallways extending in every direction as if a very rich and very bizarre king from long ago and far away had created some sort of weird castle sanctuary. It was kind of like that, except everything—every single thing—was completely covered either in mirrors or in clocks. No pictures, no shelves, no decorations—only mirrors and clocks from floor to ceiling on every wall and down every hallway.

Mirrors reflecting other mirrors in a perplexing puzzle of cloned images—tall mirrors, round mirrors, short mirrors, square mirrors—and where there were no mirrors, there were clocks: tall clocks, round clocks, short clocks, square clocks. And every clock was set at exactly the same second so that the ticks ticked together and the tocks tocked together. The only relief from the mirrors and the clocks was the stone archways and an immense curved and intricately carved staircase that arose from either side of the room and joined in the middle, creating a balcony above them. A huge hourglass, as tall as the railing, set right in the middle of the balcony. The sand slowly slipped through the center, filling the bottom.

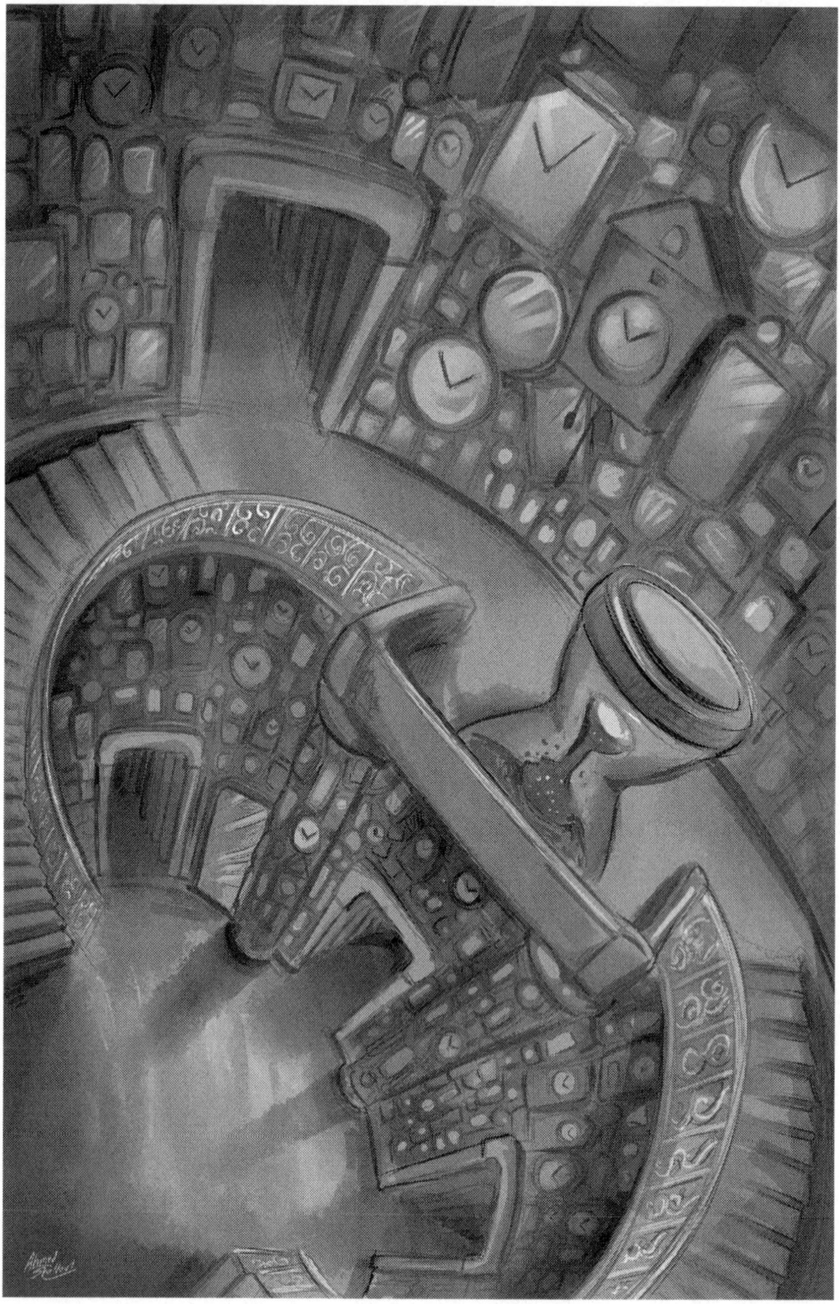

Addison and Claire stood silently, gaping and gazing about and, if truth be told, feeling rather tipsy. They had never been in such a room, and they had never ever seen themselves reflected over and over and over and over from every angle and from every side. And even though both were very lovely girls, it was still rather disconcerting to see so many of themselves repeated so many times and from so many perspectives.

They slid close to each other, shoulders touching. Addison leaned into Claire. "We gotta get out of here," she whispered.

"I know," Claire whispered back. "We'll just say we really have to get home, but," she warned, "be polite, be very polite. From the looks of this place, she might be slightly crazy or weird or—"

But Claire never got to finish her sentence because just then—and very, very suddenly—every single clock on every single wall struck at the very same second so that hundreds of clocks suddenly whizzed and bleeped and cuckooed and chimed in perfect unison. The girls jumped, stared around the room, and with an "aaahh," as they slapped their hands over their ears, their mouths dropped open. They twisted in circles, looking at all those animated clocks and at hundreds of images of themselves.

In that very same moment, Victoria rushed past the girls and ran straight for the largest mirror: the gold one with a frame engraved in fleur-de-lis. She sucked in deep breaths, frantically inspecting herself in the mirror. She studied her hair and her face and her sides and her legs and even spent quite a bit of time looking at her bum—up and down and around and around and in front and in the back. She even looked up at the ceiling mirror and twisted in circles even though she did not need to turn in circles since there were so many of her from all those angles reflecting in all those mirrors.

But just as she appeared to be calming down, she bent forward, looking very closely at the edge of her right eye; she must have seen something very, very bad because she started shrieking in a very strange and unhappy voice, "My elixir, my elixir. I need my elixir."

Tears gushed from her eyes, cascading down her face. Fanning herself with her hands, she kept calling out, "I need my elixir. Quick, quick before the clocks stop. Hurry, hurry—ooooh, hurry!" Twisted lines of black mascara streaked across her cheeks. She wailed even louder, "Huuurrrryyyyy! Oh, the clocks, the clocks."

And at the top of the stairs, a mirror opened, and a short man with a bald head and a brown apron padded out. He stood looking over the railing down at Victoria. After slowly shaking his head, he reached into a huge wide pocket across the front of the apron, pulled out a small silver vial, and tossed it down to Victoria. It landed on the floor and rolled as Victoria dropped to her hands and knees, crawling after the rolling vial. She seized it, and between racking sobs, she popped the cork out of the vial. With quivering hands, she lifted the vial to her cherry-red lips, tilted her head back, sucked in the elixir, swallowed and gulped, and looked around at the clocks, which suddenly stopped whizzing and bleeping and coo-cooing and chiming.

After several deep breaths, her breathing slowed. She licked her lips, set the vial on an end table, and murmured something about that being too close as the little man receded back to wherever he had come from, behind some mirror.

Claire and Addison had watched Victoria with fascinated horror as she rushed to the mirror, screamed for the elixir, crawled on the floor, and gulped from the vial. When the clocks stopped, they stood perfectly still, not sure what to do. As she calmed down, glancing over at them, both girls averted their eyes, not wanting to make eye contact with Victoria in case she was embarrassed. They stood quite still, trying to stare straight forward; but unfortunately, all they could see was whole bunches of themselves staring straight back at them. As you can imagine, it was all really quite uncomfortable and very, very awkward.

Chapter 19

Levi, Eleanor, and Esmé: The Ramshackle Cabin

Eleanor stood with her arm draped across Esmé's shoulder, watching Levi explore a ledge under the waterfall. A soft mist covered them as the plunging waters shattered against the rocks and fogged the air. Levi crept forward, warily planting his feet on the slippery black rocks and then carefully shifting around, so he didn't fall after each step.

He had seen an opening under the waterfall and had decided to explore the crevice, hoping to find clues or any telltale signs about where they were and how they ended up in this place.

Eleanor watched, impatiently tapping her foot and muttering under her breath. "Levi, just stop!" she finally yelled over the roar of the turbulent waters. "Just turn around and let's go back! Come on, you are wasting our time!" At that, she grabbed Esmé's arm and irritably spun around, planning to backtrack in the same direction they had come from. Instead, she froze. "Oh my gosh!" she muttered as spun back around.

"Levi!" she screamed. "Levi, look!"

Levi braced himself against the rock face as he turned to see what Eleanor was yelling about. When he saw it, he slipped, sliding into a sitting position as though he had melted against the rock face. He shook his head, blinking his eyes and rubbing them as he stared across the field in the direction Eleanor was pointing.

The worn-down trail and the bend in the road were simply gone. Instead, through the mist of the waterfall, he saw a ramshackle cabin setting among towering cedars and scrubby, uncut grasses. Wispy smoke rose from a stone chimney. Lit lanterns hung in front of an arched doorway and over windows. A crooked cobbled pathway curved toward the weathered green door of the cabin.

An old bent man stood to the side of the doorway. His head drooped down as he worked. After a while, he looked up, stared at them, and then turned to go inside his house.

Levi cautiously recrossed the slippery stones, and the three of them stood with the misty spray saturating them.

"How did we miss seeing that house?" Levi asked cautiously.

"I don't know," Eleanor said. "Where is the road we just came down?"

"That man looks strange," Esmé whimpered.

Eleanor squinted her eyes, bending her head forward for a better view. "Come on, let's go," she finally said. "Maybe he will be able to tell us where we are and how to get back."

"But he's weird," Esmé whined.

"I don't see that we have any other options right now," Levi said as he looked over to the shack and shrugged his shoulders.

The three of them walked cautiously forward. Esmé held back, clutching Levi's hand. "It's okay, Esmé," Levi encouraged. "We're just asking for directions. Don't worry."

They walked side by side until they reached the cobbled pathway and cautiously stepped up to the splintery faded green door. Levi knocked. They heard muffled groans and grumbling, a chair screeching across a floor, muted, shuffling sounds. And then nothing. Levi stepped forward and knocked again and then again. Finally, the shuffling sounds moved closer—a lock clicking, hinges screeching—and a lumbering old man appeared in the doorway. Muttering under his breath, he emerged from the dark house and stumbled across the threshold.

Chapter 20

Levi, Eleanor, and Esmé: Grizzles and Lola

He hobbled and wobbled when he walked as though sharp tacks protruded from the floor; his shoulders were hunched, and his head bent forward. He was ancient, no doubt about it—he was an ancient, old man. Giant folds and wrinkles covered his face; his white hair fell in large loopy whorls about his head, and they might have redeemed the face if it were not for the huge bulbous nose and the tiny squinty eyes. But the part they noticed the most was the fingers: gnarled, wrinkled fingers with long yellowed talons for fingernails.

He twisted around and snarled at them, his raspy voice interrupted by his own heavy, noisy breathing, "Can't you see that I am busy? I don't like people, and I especially don't like children. I ate the last child that came here." He picked his tooth with a dirty fingernail. "What do you want?"

Esmé hid behind Levi and grabbed his hand. Eleanor scooted over so that her shoulder was touching Levi's.

Levi took a deep breath; his voice trembled, but he managed to force the words out of his throat.

"Bbbeggg your pardon, sir, but—"

"Oohhh," the old man sneered and then snickered, "he's calling me sir. Did you hear that, Lola? He called me sir." His voice grated as though the words were being raked over rocks instead of coming from his throat. "Oh, what has the world come to?? Lola, come here," he grizzled. "Come here. We got a tasty boy out here. You know, a polite one. They are always tastier. Yuumm." And then he threw his head back and snarled, and his mouth snapped, and he clattered his teeth.

Levi pushed Eleanor and Esme behind him, so they formed a triangle.

"Lola," the old man called again, "come here. You have to see this. Polite boys always smell so good—so very good."

Levi stood rigidly; Eleanor stepped up beside him. "Whatever happens," she whispered, "let's just back out of here slowly—very slowly." With imperceptible movements, the three cousins started to move backward, but the old man laid his head over to the side, snarled, and glared down at their shuffling feet. Then he looked straight into Eleanor's eyes with a grimace contorting his lips.

Just then a lovely lady with long black wavy hair framing huge black eyes and delicate nose swept through the doorway in a flowing sapphire gown. She stopped in front of the children and flashed her dimples as her lips curved into a smile. "Oh, what darling children," she beamed as she laid her hand on her heart, "look at the children, Grizzles. They are so cute!"

"Ummmmm," grumbled the old man, "cute indeed and tasty no doubt."

But Lola paid him no mind.

"What do you children want?" she asked as she patted teach of them on the head one at a time.

"Well," stuttered Levi, nervously looking around and down at the floor and then up again, "we, umm, we went out of the . . . treehouse door and lost the map book, and nnnow we are here, aanndd we don't know how to get home. Aanndd if you would just point the way, we will leave you alone," he stammered.

The old man snarled; his upper lip exposed the long yellowed teeth.

"The treehouse, you say?"

All three nodded cautiously.

Lola slapped her hand against her leg and beamed at them. "Well, did you three come through the bronze door with that wonderful map book on that sweet little bronze shelf?" Lola asked with raised eyebrows and sparkles radiating from her black eyes.

They all looked at one another and then slowly nodded to Lola.

The old man snorted and scrunched up his lips. "Well, Lola," he said, "did you hear that? That's why the lanterns turned on. I told you something was happening."

Lola raised her eyebrows and nodded at the old man. "You were right, Grizzles dear. You were right."

"Well, that's no good," grumbled the old man. "Now, I can't eat these. Gotta send 'em back to where they come from. Darn, gotta send 'em back."

Eleanor stepped forward. A glimmer of hope flickered across her face, and she looked straight at Lola. "Ma'am, do you know how we can get home?"

"Why, yes, yes, I do," answered Lola.

"Can you point us in the right direction?"

Lola cocked her head to one side and smiled.

"Why, no," she said, "I can't do that."

The old man threw his head back and laughed and laughed and laughed until the laughter turned into a hideous cough, and even then he kept laughing as he began wheezing and trying to catch his breath.

Chapter 21

Tilly, Brody, and Ivan: What Did Gramma Say?

Tilly, Brody, and Ivan wandered along the glistening beach, each one immersed in their own thoughts. Wavering rainbows of color flickered through the very air they breathed.

Tilly suddenly slapped her forehead with the palm of her hand. "I got it," she said. "There were clues—clues when Gramma was talking! We need to remember everything that happened, anything Gramma said, and see if we can find a pattern in the clues. Without it, we'll just end up wandering around in circles with no idea of where to go or what to look for."

Brody nodded. "Gramma did say we'd get lost if we went out any door except the peacock door, and we did go out a different door, and we are definitely lost," he said, shrugging his shoulders with his palms facing up. "So maybe that's where we should start."

They plopped down on the sand, crossing their legs, sitting in silence, sifting the silky sand through their fingers, and thinking about clues.

"Well," Ivan finally suggested, "when Claire and Addie went missing, Gramma didn't get hysterical or anything. She did say they'd be back."

"That's true. That is true," Tilly replied. "Okay, what else do we have?"

And so, they sat scratching their heads and scrunching their eyes and wrinkling their foreheads and tapping their fingers and staring up into at the sky, trying very hard to think of clues. After quite a while, they finally remembered words like *rainbows* and *crystals* and *long-forgotten wisps* of something that had to do with turning lead into gold or something like that and prisms and lanterns. They were all quite certain that Gramma had taken a lantern out the silver door. And keys—they definitely remembered something about having to find keys. And Tilly was quite sure that the keys had something to do with the shadows and reflections, but the boys didn't remember that part at all.

And so, after sitting and thinking for a very long time, until their heads were feeling quite thick and foggy, they decided that it was too hard to think and that maybe it was time to start walking again.

By that time, they had been sitting for so long that when Ivan stood, his right leg felt very heavy and very strange as if bees were buzzing around on the inside. When he stood up, he almost fell over sideways, which made Brody laugh and Tilly giggle. Ivan limped around, trying to shake his leg, but that made him almost fall over again. "Let's get going," Ivan muttered somewhat crossly as he began stumping down the beach while pausing every now and then to shake his tingly leg, which only made Brody laugh harder and Tilly giggle more and Ivan scowl even more.

Tilly and Brody were following a very grumbly Ivan down the beach when Tilly suddenly stopped and shouted, "Ivan, Brody, how about what was on the shelves? Remember, there was a kaleidoscope on the green shelf. Colors, lots of colors, like here. Look around! Could the kaleidoscope be a clue?"

Both Brody and Ivan looked around. "Oh, that's good, Tilly!" Ivan said.

"I bet you're right!" Brody shouted. "What else was on that green shelf?"

"A little bag of coins!" Tilly yelled. And they all looked around some more.

"And a pair of glasses with different-colored lenses. Those were so cool!" Ivan added.

But then, they just looked at one another and shrugged their shoulders and turned and continued trudging across the sand. Now, if truth be told, they were quite hungry and quite tired and more than a little frightened by that time; but since they had no idea as to where to go or when to stop or even what to do, they just kept walking and hoping.

And so, after walking and walking and walking some more, the landscape did begin to change just a little. Instead of white sand, it became bumpy and black rocks began to emerge. The rocks got bigger and bigger until they were mounds. And after even more walking, the sandy ground began to disappear altogether until the sandy shore was all but replaced with an entire wall of black twisted bubbly rock with a giant yawning opening rising up from the water's edge.

They stood on the outside of the cavern, staring into the opening in the black rock. "Is that a flicker of light in there?" Ivan finally asked, pointing deep within the cave. Tilly and Brody both scrunched their eyes and peered deep inside of the cave.

"Oh wow!" Brody said. "There's a light in there. Let's go in!

"I don't know if that's a good idea," Tilly said. "We're already so lost. At least we can see out here."

"We can't get lost. There's only one way in and one way out," Brody answered. "If we come to a fork, we'll go straight or we'll turn around."

"But we still could get lost. This place is strange," Tilly countered.

"I kinda agree with Brody," Ivan said. "If it's a cave, we might find a place to rest or at least some shelter. If we stay on a straight path, we can't really get lost. Might be worth a short try."

And so, after arguing back and forth, they finally decided to explore the cave and check out the light. Brody took the lead. Tilly laid her hands on Brody's shoulders, and Ivan placed his hands on Tilly's, and they slowly trudged deeper and deeper through the inky black rocky cave. The farther they went, the more the cave smelled like mold and old fish; and a few times, the path must have curved because they couldn't see the light at all. Every time that happened, they just kept shuffling along until it flickered again in the distance.

Now, if truth be told, you really should know that Brody was not happy about being in that cave at all; his knees felt rather weak and trembly, and little bits of sweat were running down his face. But since he had been the one who insisted on exploring the cave in the first place, he kept going and going and hoping to eventually reach the tiny light even though he actually wanted nothing more than to turn around and run back into the sunshine.

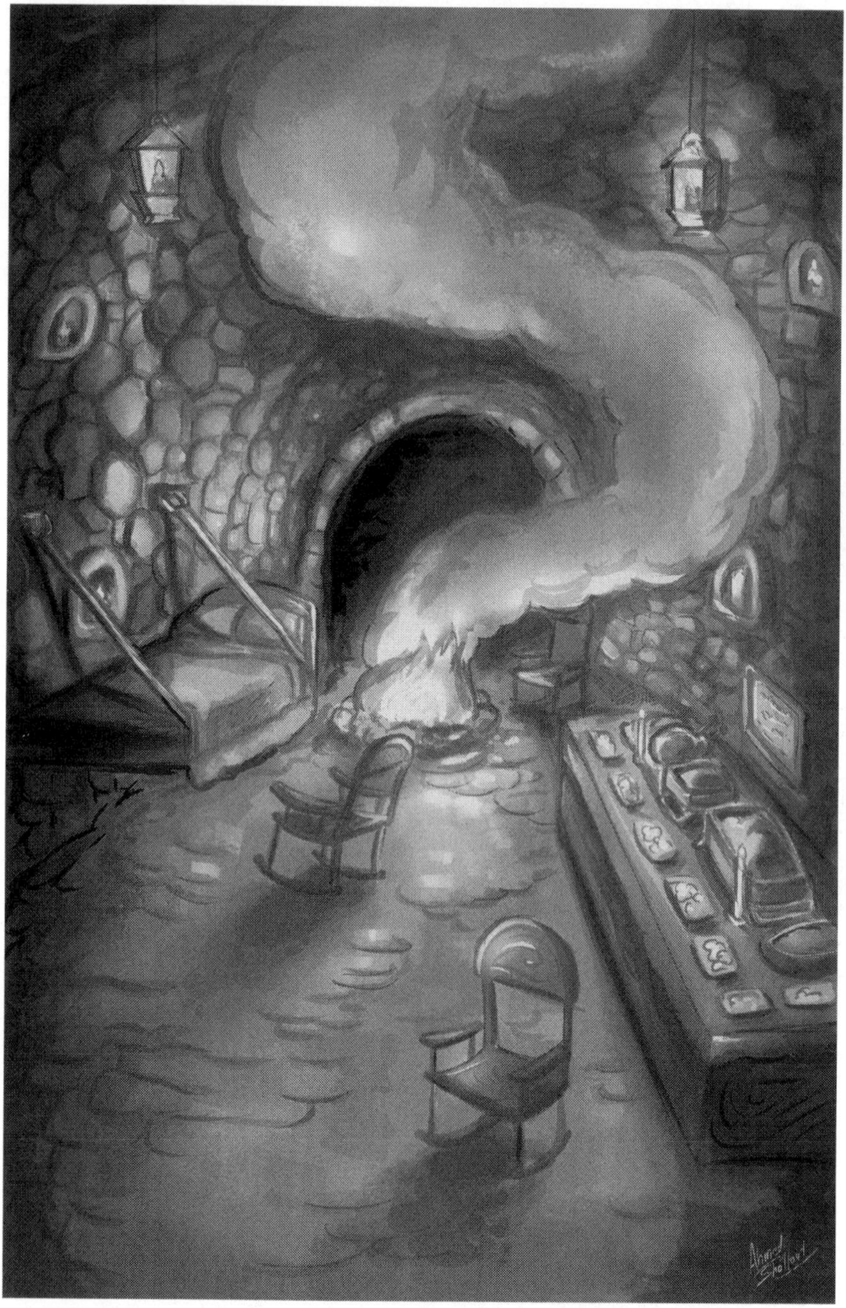

Chapter 22

Tilly, Brody, and Ivan: Craggy Walls Always Lead Somewhere

Brody ran his fingers along the craggy rocks as he stumbled forward. Except for their own shuffling feet and occasional words, Tilly, Brody, and Ivan were enveloped in silence and in thick black darkness. After a while, they heard a faint dripping. Brody ran his fingers along the walls, and a cool wet trickle glided across his fingers. He cupped his hands, letting a few drops accumulate, and then touched it to his tongue. "I thought so!" he shouted. "It's water!"

They cupped their hands, filling them with cold sweet water; and once their thirst was quenched, they moved forward, faltering and shuffling and even stumbling at times but still moving toward the light. And finally, when they had almost decided to give up and just go back, they rounded a giant bend in the path; and light flooded out from the entrance of a huge open cavern.

"Look at that!" Ivan yelled as they cautiously stepped through the archway and into the rocky room.

Flames flickered from lanterns hanging in recessed cubbyholes hewn into the stone walls and dangling from the curved dome at the top of the cavern. A blazing fire glowed and flashed from an open fire pit in the center of the room, and smoke circled up through an opening in the dome of the cave. Stacked beds covered with thick creamy-white fleece coverings hung on the side of the wall.

But the sight and smell that really made their eyes blink and their noses wiggle was an enormous wooden table with silver platters overflowing with all sorts of different foods. There were huge slices of roasted apples and baked pears and buttered fluffy biscuits and enormous pieces of chocolate cake and cherry pie and cookies with macadamia nuts and flakes of coconut in them. Aromas mingled, wafting through the air. Tall silvery white candles in silver candlesticks flickered in the middle of the table.

"OOHHH!" Ivan yelled as they raced toward the table ready to grab food.

But suddenly Tilly shouted, "Wait, wait, you dummies, how do we know this stuff isn't poison? It's kind of too good to be true, don't you think? In all the stories, if something's too good to be true, it can't be trusted."

Brody's hand was hovering over a large pan of baked apple slices with a toasted crust on top and a thick red sauce smothering the entire thing. Ivan was holding a macadamia and coconut flake cookie. He stopped just as the cookie touched his mouth.

Both boys stood very still, looking at the food and then at Tilly and then back at the food. A little dribble formed on the edge of Brody's mouth, and he licked his lips. Ivan drew in a breath and gulped. His tongue flicked inside his mouth. He stood there with the cookie an inch from his mouth, slowly pulling it away.

"But this looks like normal food, just lots and lots of it," Ivan muttered. "Hey," he added, "look at that sign."

Tilly scooted closer, the boys eyeing her, watching for her reaction as she read the sign aloud:

Follow your path with wonder and joy:
Savor the food, delight in the drink, bask in the warmth,
Relax in the rest, immerse in the illusion
But beware: Greed destroys with its cold grasp.
Gratitude in exchange for wonders,
Treasures spill first from within; then trickle out—
And not the other way around.

They all read the sign over and over.

Finally, Ivan broke the stillness. "Whoever put that sign on the wall is friendly, right?" he asked.

"Yes," agreed Tilly.

"Okay, tell you what, I'll try a tiny nibble. A nibble can't kill me and that way we'll know a little more."

Ivan didn't wait for anyone to agree. He licked the edge of the cookie and sighed, waited for a second, and then bit through a nut and a huge fluffy flake of coconut. With a full mouth, he "ummed" and "ahhhed" and took another bite and nodded. "Oooh, this is the best ever! Oh, man!"

Suddenly, out of nowhere, he fell to the floor, curling up into a ball, grabbing his belly, coughing and moaning. Tilly screamed, "Ivaann, oh no, oh, Ivannnnn!" She dropped to her knees to grab him.

Ivan's eyes popped open. "Got ya!" he roared, almost doubling over again from laughter as he got up. "Teach you to make fun of my sleepy leg!"

And at that, they burst out laughing and began devouring the most sumptuous food ever. And when their tummies were so stretched and taut they could not force even one more tiny bite of pie in their mouths, they shuffled over to the fire pit and tried to talk about clues and making plans and what they should do to get home and what happened to the others. And they even mentioned how scared they were and how they needed to stick together, but since Gramma didn't panic when Addie and Claire went missing, there must be a way to get home.

But after a while, no matter how scared or confused or even hopeful they felt, their eyes kept slipping closed, and their heads kept nodding down and then jerking back up; so they finally decided that it might be better to think after a teeny-weeny nap.

So they slipped over to the thick cushy beds that hung from the side of the cavern wall. After curling up and pulling the soft fleecy covers over their shoulders, they immediately drifted off into a deep sleep—sleep so deep they didn't shift or stir until rustling movements and dark shadows fell across Ivan.

Chapter 23

Claire and Addison:
The Problem with Hunger

Victoria sucked in a deep breath, rotating her shoulders and neck in a few circles, and sighed. Studying herself in the huge gold-framed mirror, she readjusted her clothes, carefully wiped the streaks of mascara from her cheeks, and fixed her makeup. She turned and smiled. Her perfect white teeth flashed; her eyes glinted and her dimples dinted.

"Now I did promise you, girls, sweet treats. It will only take me an itty-bitty moment or two. Sit, sit, be comfortable!" she said, indicating the white chairs. She glanced up at a clock as she strode through a stone archway. Her very shiny red high heels clicked on the shiny dark wood floor as she receded down the hall.

After the clicks had softened into little echoes, Claire whispered, "We really gotta get outta here!"

"No kidding!" Addison whispered back. "Let's go!" They turned around in a circle, and then they stopped and turned in another circle, and then they turned again.

"Oh my gosh!" Claire muttered. "Where's the door? It must be covered in a mirror, so how are we gonna find it?"

They scrambled around, desperately trying to find the entrance, searching for anything that would indicate a door—a latch, a knob, an indent, anything at all—but nothing. Nothing gave any indication of a door.

"What is it with doors today?" Claire whispered with a stomp of her foot. "First, we can't get back in at Gramma's, and now we can't get out of here!"

She started to kick the wall out of sheer frustration but abruptly stopped with her foot in midair, suddenly realizing that kicking glass mirrors might not be good at all, not at all.

And then, suddenly, tiny clicking sounds echoed from the hallway. They stopped and listened. *Click, click, click.* "She's coming back—hurry!" Addison whispered. They scurried to the sofa and sat sucking in deep breaths as Victoria, still chatting away, entered the room.

"Well, I did promise you a treat now, didn't I? Sweet treats for two, very sweet girls, and just the right amount to make you glad you came to visit! No one will ever say that Victoria does not keep her promise," Victoria said as she pranced over to the sofa, carrying an ornate silver tray with a round silver cover. She sat down on the white winged-back chair.

Addison and Claire smiled back; but if truth be told, their smiles were not very convincing. They glanced at each other and then turned back to Victoria, flashing their very best fake smiles.

Victoria sighed. "I told you my treats would be delightful and sweet and just your size," Victoria beamed as she trilled a little drumroll with her tongue and prepared to open the cover on the silver tray.

"I am so hungry!" Claire whispered in spite of herself.

"And here it is! Ready?"

Claire bent forward, her mouth watering.

"Taaaadaaaa!" Victoria lifted the silver cover.

Claire and Addison looked at each other and down at the silver tray.

"Carrot sticks?" Claire choked.

"Carrot sticks?" Addie repeated.

"I know, I know," Victoria said, her face flushing, "I cut them into just the right size for two delightful girls, and I know that these are particularly sweet. I just ate some myself this very morning. They are so good!"

Victoria cocked her head to one side and sighed, admiring the carrot sticks. She looked at the girls; her lips puckered into a pout. "Don't you girls like carrot sticks? You don't seem pleased."

Addison jumped in quickly, reaching forward grabbing one, and biting into it with feigned delight. "Sweet—yes, very sweet. Oh, we love carrot sticks, and these are certainly colorful and just the right size, just like you said."

Claire reached forward and took one, crunching into it; her shoulders kind of shivered, and her mouth developed a very small twitch (she really did not like carrots at all), but she ate the carrot. And it must be said that she crunched and smiled and was very polite indeed. And as soon as they were done with the carrot sticks, they both patted their bellies and went on and on about how wonderful the carrot sticks were and how they were very, very full.

Victoria regained her perfect smile and nodded as she ate one also, dabbing her mouth with a white napkin after each nibble.

Claire stood up. "Well, Ms. Victoria, we thank you so very much," she said. "It has certainly been wonderful, and your treats are especially sweet, but we really must be getting to Gramma's now. I just know she will be worried."

Victoria bent forward, her eyes squinting just a little around the edges. "Oh, not yet, my dearies. Remember we were going to coif you a little—you know, make you a little more presentable—for your dear lovely gramma." She smiled as her very red lips stretched across her very white teeth. Her eyes flashed. Her dimples dinted. "Ooohh," she said, "and since you love my treats so much, you simply must try the elixir. We will have so much fun looking into the mirrors. I don't mean to complain, and I do love my own company, but it does get a little lonely here in my mirror paradise. People come and go, and the ones that stay always seem to choose their favorite mirror too quickly, and, well, you know, things happen.

"But," Victoria continued, "as I sat here, looking at your cute little faces, I said to myself, *Why, Victoria, these girls are so full of youth and sweetness this might just be the exact right time to offer them a little swig of my elixir.* Well, not mine exactly. Mine would be too strong for you, but the young version—for your age. And if you want to stay around longer and choose a special mirror, we could have a fine time together!" She fluttered her hands back and forth, her shoulders shuttering with excitement.

She stopped for a second, gazing up at the ceiling, before continuing in a smooth, syrupy voice, "We do have to make decisions about what is important now, don't we? We need to grasp hold of our perfection when we are at that pinnacle. We need to hold tight and stand above the others. Why not choose to remain in such a wonderful place—at the pinnacle of beauty or love or whatever? What else matters except standing on the top rung of the ladder of perfection and/or beauty? We must keep our priorities straight!" Victoria finished her speech with a flourish as she watched herself in the mirror.

Claire's brow furrowed a little. "But that's not really true," she objected slowly. "Is climbing a ladder of perfection the most important thing? I mean, think about beauty, for example. There is always someone prettier, and there is always someone a little uglier—for everyone. It's like a circle, not a ladder."

"And," Addison added, "even that doesn't work because everybody looks way different once you really get to know them. Some people look prettier, and some look worse, and you kind of forget what they looked like at first. Don't you think?"

Claire nodded. Victoria looked rather horrified and puzzled. "What?" she questioned. "That can't be true—not at all. I'm an example of a person who maintains beauty at all costs. And look at me."

Addison turned to Victoria. "Yes, you are very pleasing to look at. And we thank you for the sweets and the conversation. It's been great, but we really need to go," she said.

Victoria's lips kind of twitched. "But you did promise you'd stay and take a small swig of elixir. I'll go get it now, and after a swig, I'm just sure you'll appreciate the mirrors even more, and you can pick your own favorite. Now, wait here. I'll be right back!" And clicking very rapidly, she went back in the direction of wherever she had come from with the carrot sticks.

Chapter 24

Claire and Addison: Hidden Doors and Elixirs

"We gotta go, NOW!" Claire exclaimed.

"I've got an idea!" Addison almost shouted before she caught herself and slapped her hand over her mouth, lowering her voice. She leaned forward, practically whispering, "When we came in here, we were smack dab in line with the middle of the room. I remember looking straight up into the center of the balcony right there and seeing that hourglass on the balcony. You wait here. I'll run up those steps, stand behind the hourglass, and point in a straight line. Maybe we can figure out where the door is."

"Great idea!" Claire agreed.

Addison ran up the steps, found the center, and pointed. Claire lined herself up and then turned to find the door. She quickly patted—moving her hands up and down, searching, groping, moving frantically all around—but she couldn't feel or see anything. No indentation, no latch, no knob, and certainly no handle.

Finally, she turned; and looking up at Addison, she said, "You must not be pointing right. Let's change places. I'll point."

"I am pointing right," Addison grumbled, scowling at Claire. "Come up here and see how I'm lined up, and then we'll trade places. I'll show you."

Claire stomped to the top of the steps, shaking her head. When she reached Addison, Claire looked over the railing, trying to find the center so they could figure out where the door might be; but there were too many mirrors reflecting everything. She held her arm out, finger pointing. "Addie, I think it might be right there, run down and—"

Suddenly the clicking again. "What'll we do? What'll we do?" whispered Addison frantically. "We gotta get outta here!"

"I found the girl's elixir. I found it. I fouunnd it!" Victoria prattled as she hurried into the room. "We can't give you the women's dosage. That would be too strong. I found just the right one for—" She stopped chattering midsentence as she entered the room. She stood there, glancing around, holding two little silver vials. Claire and Addison stood frozen at the top of the stairs.

Victoria finally looked up, noticing Claire and Addison standing on the balcony. "Why, what are you girls doing up there?" Her expression changed just a little.

"Oh, we just wanted to see the view. Such a lovely house you have, Ms. Victoria," Addison replied quickly.

Claire nodded. "Yes, very lovely," Claire agreed.

"Yes, it really is, isn't it?" Victoria stopped and looked around for a second, admiring her home. Her image reverberated up and down and around and above and below. "I love my home, and the mirrors are such a lovely accessory. Now, the clocks. I think the clocks are a little much, but—" Suddenly, she shuddered, turning to face the girls again.

"But I forget myself. Girls, girls, why don't you come down here now? You really should not be up there. There is a crabby old man who lives up there, and we don't want to disturb him now, do we? Come on now. If you come down right now, I will help you to choose a mirror of your own, and then we'll just pop the cork on this little vial, and you can drink the delicious elixir, and we'll just have a wonderful time. And I just know you'll want to stay here with me forever. Now, come here. Cooome heerrre." She shook the vials back and forth a little.

"Oh, no, thank you," said Claire, "It's very kind of you, but we don't want to wear out our welcome. We appreciate your offer, but we wouldn't want to deprive you of any of your elixirs, and we have plenty of mirrors at home."

"Well, none like these," Victoria said. "Come pick a mirror and have a tiny swig of elixir and then decide. You'll never know what you're missing if you don't give it a try."

Victoria started toward the steps. "Come on, girls, come on. Let's not play silly games." Holding the vials out, she walked across the room and stood at the bottom of the steps. "Come on, come on down here. You simply must trust me. There's a crazy man who lives up there who keeps these clocks going, and you don't want to listen to his tales, trust me. He can be so, well, confusing." She slipped up one step.

"Come, come, girls. The girl's version tastes so good. I brought the cherry flavor for one and the grape flavor for the other. Your choice. Now come, come." Victoria shook the little vial from side to side. She climbed up one more step, then another, and another.

Claire and Addison scooted closer to each other, and when their shoulders touched, they grabbed hands and stepped backward. Victoria climbed another step, still smiling; her eyes developed a strange glint.

Addison and Claire stepped back again. Victoria stepped up again. And just as Victoria lifted her leg to step onto the landing, in that very second, and quite suddenly, all the clocks—every single clock on every single wall—struck at the very same time. Again hundreds of clocks whizzed and bleeped and coo-cooed and chimed in perfect unison. Claire and Addison clapped their hands over their ears with a shriek.

Victoria stood frozen for a millionth of a second, looking around in horror. She turned, rushing down the steps, two at a time. "This can't be happening," she wailed. "It's much too soon," she screeched dashing toward her mirror. "Why so soon? It just can't be time! Did I waste time somewhere? Those horrible clocks. Oh no, no, no."

She stood in front of her mirror, twisting and turning and looking at everything, back and forth and up and down. "It's going to be okay," she finally said, gulping in deep breaths. "Oh, thank goodness! It simply could not be time for the clocks to toll. Not yet. Must be a glitch or something."

But just then, as she turned, she must have noticed something wrong with her bum. Claire always said that she thought there might have been a small bump on the one side or maybe an indent. The girls were never quite sure. But whatever it was, Victoria started screaming, "My elixir, my elixir, I need it now. I need it now. Hurrry, hurrryyyyy, my elixir!"

And the door opened, and the little bald man in the brown apron slipped out again and looked over the steps at Victoria. He fished in his pocket to draw out the vial. But just as he pulled the vial out, the clocks suddenly stopped their whizzing and bleeping and coo-cooing and chiming; and an eerie silence descended over the room.

With a mixture of horror, devastation, and confusion, Victoria stared into her gold-framed mirror and took a deep breath as she stood in silence. Suddenly a little snap shattered the silence as a tiny crack spread across the mirror. Victoria turned just a bit, glancing up at the little bald man who still stood with the vial in his upraised hand. "But this is my mirror," she wailed. "I love this mirror. It can't break. How did the clocks toll again so quickly?"

And suddenly there was a little pop and a crackle, and Victoria turned back to her mirror. She laid her body against the mirror, holding it, embracing it as the mirror wiggled as if it were made of tiny cubes of Jell-O, and then it jiggled back and forth. Victoria held tight and screamed as the mirror shattered, exploding her reflection into a thousand bits and pieces and parts like an elaborate jigsaw puzzle of Victoria pieces.

And even as it shattered, Victoria held on tightly, wailing, "I can't let you go. The clocks cannot have their way," as she grabbed both sides of the frame, pressing herself against the shattered glass. And there was a flicker and a shimmer as the fragments suddenly started wiggling again. The mirror vibrated and jiggled, and Victoria refused to let go. She began vibrating and jiggling in unison with it.

And after a bit, Victoria began to shimmer one second, and she became shadowy and somewhat ghostlike the next—almost as if you could almost see through her. Still, she held on tightly until she shimmered so much that it was hard to tell where Victoria ended and the mirrored image of Victoria began. And gradually, the shattered glass and Victoria seemed to become kind of gooey and gummy like sticky glue; and finally, there was a kind of slurping sound and then a type of crispy, crunchy sound and the fragments began to fuse, and Victoria fused into them. And then, there was total silence—just total silence. Claire and Addison stood motionless with their hands over their mouths, staring.

The mirror was smooth and solid, but it wasn't really a mirror anymore. It was more like a portrait of Victoria—a flat shiny glass Victoria inside a golden fleur-de-lis frame. And her very red lips were stretched into a smile over her very white teeth. And her dimples dinted. And her blue eyes sparkled. She didn't even seem to realize that she was inside the mirror or that she was stuck in one place and within a specific moment in time. It was more like she was looking at her own reflection, and she was very pleased.

"Oh dear. My, oh my," sighed the little bald Clockmaker with the brown leather apron, "and I had such hopes for that one. She seemed so resilient for so long," he muttered as he clicked his tongue against his teeth. He absentmindedly glanced at Claire and Addison. "Well, here we go again."

Clinging to the railing and muttering, he padded down one step at a time. "So I suppose you girls are here for some elixir?" he asked as he shuffled past Addison and Claire.

Chapter 25

Claire and Addison:
The Hall of Mirrors: Relentless Clocks

Reaching the bottom of the steps, the Clockmaker shuffled over to the mirror containing the trapped Victoria. With a grunt and a groan and a knee that popped, he lifted the mirror, carried it to another part of the room, and pressed a button on the wall with his elbow; a mirrored door slid open, and he walked through.

The girls heard pounding. Scrambling to the balustrade, they tried to peek through the wood railings, but they couldn't see into the room the pounding was coming from. Silently, slowly, they crept down the steps, tiptoeing to the open door. Craning their heads around the edge, they peeked in.

But in that very instant, as they peeked around the door and into that room, they forgot all about the tiptoeing and sneaking. Instead, their toes curled into tight little knots, the edges of their lips curled down, and they started flittering about with their hands in the air, saying things like "oooh" and "aaahhh" and "grrooosss."

Because in the very moment they looked in the room, the Clockmaker had just finished pounding a nail into the wall and he was lifting the mirror with the trapped Victoria and hanging it on the nail. Claire and Addison watched in horror as the Clockmaker stood back, cocked his head to the side, inspected the mirror, and then reached over, straightening it just to make sure that it was set perfectly straight on the wall. Turning his head slowly, he looked at the girls. Shrugging his shoulders, he muttered something about elixir getting out of control.

But neither Claire nor Addison paid him any mind at all; instead, they just kept curling their toes and fluttering their hands and blabbering things like "ahhh" and "ooohh."

For you see, it wasn't just a mirror with Victoria hanging in that room. Actually, it wasn't a room at all; instead, it was more like a very, very long hallway that stretched on and on and on. And the entire hallway, from beginning to end, was covered on both sides in mirrors. But not just any ole regular mirrors. Oh no, they were not regular at all; instead, they were the eeriest mirrors ever because every single one of them contained a trapped person. And all the trapped people in every mirror was different, and the mirrors just kept going on and on and on.

There were lots of rather young well-coifed women and men like Victoria, but there were also men in football uniforms, women in yoga pants, and people in business suits. There were even some holding fishing poles, and a few even looked like they were feeling rather ill. There were women standing with sorrowful eyes and outstretched arms and men with clenched fists and strange glares. Some had tears, some had smiles, some chewed on fingernails, and some simply looked up while others stared down. There were the young, the old, and the in-between. And they all hung in mirrors on the walls up and down that long, long hallway.

And after a long while, Claire and Addison stopped curling and fluttering and simply stood still, covering their mouths, staring into the grotesque room. "You can't do that!" Claire finally yelled. "Let them go! You evil man, you let them go!"

The Clockmaker smiled and shook his head with quiet resolve. "Oh dear girl," he said, "I only hang them here until the effects of the elixir overdose wears off and they are ready to move on. They all made the same mistake of thinking that one little image of themselves was more important than any of the others, and they refused to let go and move to the next mirror. Some stayed with one mirror out of love, some out of vanity, some out of sorrow, some out of glory. But for one reason or another, they would not move past one particular image of themselves when they should have.

"I warned each of them that the clocks stop for no one, that the elixir is simply a tonic to quiet the tolls and chimes for a quick second before moving on—for one last look—one last chance to learn a part of the song if necessary. "But," he continued as he pointed down the hallway, "they all ignored the warnings, and in the efforts to ignore the clocks, they got addicted to the elixir, and it just doesn't work that way."

He leaned forward, lowering his voice. "After a while," he continued, "the tolling just gets louder and louder until it shatters the mirror. That's what happened to Victoria. When the clocks tolled, she kept sipping elixir instead of moving on to the next mirror. Time waits for no one. Changes keep changing. I warned them. I really did. He paused and continued mumbling and murmuring—more to himself than to the girls.

"It's really so sad. What a waste, a sad waste of precious time clinging to only one. Each mirror has its own beauty, its own sweetness, its own alluring notes to add to the journey's song." He turned to go back up the stairs, pivoted around, and sighed.

"And I suppose you girls are here for some elixir of your own?" he asked.

"NO, NO, NO!" they both yelled in unison and a little too loudly. "We don't want the elixir. We just want out of this place. We can't find the way out."

"Really?" he said. "Then what? How? Why are you here?"

"We just came to eat some food and find directions back to Gramma's, but apparently, all you have around here is carrot sticks and no directions," Claire snapped.

"And a lot of very weird mirrors and clocks," Addison added.

The Clockmaker looked at them. "Gramma's? What do you mean?"

And with that simple question, Claire told the entire story of that afternoon starting with the treehouse and the slide and meeting Victoria and the carrot sticks and, finally, their failed attempts at escape.

After Claire had finished, Addison added, "If you just show us how to get out of here, we promise to go away and we promise to never tell anyone about this place."

"We promise," Claire said, holding her right hand in the air as though she was taking a pledge in court.

"Oh dear, oh dear," muttered the Clockmaker, rubbing his bristly chin. "Oh my, oh my! A treehouse, you say? I don't know anything about a treehouse. But now that you mention it, I do remember reading an old story about strange visitors from long, long ago. Kind of a weird story. Nobody really knows what happened on the other end. But there was a book about it. It had pictures and everything."

He rubbed his whiskers for a few seconds and then walked over to a grandfather clock that stood between two mirrors in one corner, its pendulum swinging back and forth, back and forth. He sifted through a set of books on a bottom shelf. "Here is it! I thought it'd be stacked on the shelf with the grandfather-clocks stuff," he said, picking up a smallish yellowed book. "Yes, yes, give me a second to think about this." He adjusted his glasses and flipped through crinkly yellowed pages, concentrating and reading.

When he finally looked up, he had a twinkle in his eye and a huge smile on his lips. "I just might have found a little solution," he said, tapping his finger on a picture in the book. "We just might be able to do this. We shall see. We shall see," he said as he continued flipping through the pages.

Chapter 26

Levi, Eleanor, and Esmé: Enjoy the Journey

Levi, Eleanor, and Esmé backed away as Grizzles laughed and rattled and coughed. As he bent forward in a fit of wheezing, they turned and fled across the field, stopping only when their breath was gone and they were gasping for air.

Esmé sucked in deep breaths, her eyes reddening as tears rolled down her cheeks. "I want Mama or Daddy or Gramma," she sniffled.

Levi took her, rubbing it gently while looking above Esmé's head at Eleanor. "I know, I know," he soothed. "Don't worry, Ezzy. We'll get back to Gramma's real soon." He plopped down on the grass and patted his arm. Esmé sat down beside Levi, leaning against him, snuggling into his shoulder.

"Eleanor, I'm going to say something strange," Levi said after a while, "and I want you to hear me out before you say anything. Deal?"

"Deal," Eleanor said.

"Lots of strange things happened today—things there's just no answer for—and I'm wondering if it's possible that, well, just maybe Gramma's ramblings might have been about actual stuff. We thought she was just saying stuff 'cause she's, well, Gramma, but maybe it was real. Remember the map book? It showed all these roads and paths all leading from the treehouse. What if each colored door led to strange places or something?"

Levi continued, "Remember how Gramma acted when we couldn't find Claire and Addison? She put out lanterns. Remember how that old man, Grizzles, said something about lanterns turning on and that lady, Lola, said he was right? What if the lanterns are signals of some sort?"

Eleanor leaned back on her elbows and looked up at the sky. "Actually, Levi, you might be right. You know, I do remember her saying—"

"Saying what?" Levi asked as Eleanor stopped abruptly in the middle of her sentence. Then he noticed her gaze and turned to see Lola striding toward them, her black hair flowing and her blue gown lifting and swirling as the breeze caught it. "Oh boy," Levi said, "listen, listen," he whispered, "act nice. This might be a chance to get a few answers. Be careful! She was sorta nice. Maybe she'll help us."

All three stood up, straightening their shoulders and plastering smiles across their faces, preparing to greet Lola; but then, they noticed Grizzles was also lumbering across the field, slowly hobbling and wobbling, but coming just the same. They groaned simultaneously.

"Be nice. Try to get information," Levi cautioned. "We can always make a run for it if we need to. If I give the signal, we run. Got it?" Eleanor and Esmé nodded.

Lola strode straight toward them. She was smiling and carrying a satchel across her shoulder. "Children, children," she said when she got close enough, "me and my Grizzles didn't actually mean to scare you. Well, at least I didn't mean to scare you. And Grizzles, well, he always exaggerates the number of kids he has eaten. It's not really all that many in the bigger scheme of things, and it was a long time ago—but whatever. The thing is, well, it's just that we would help, but we can't tell you exactly how to get home."

She slipped the leather satchel off her shoulder. Stepping closer, she stared directly into Eleanor's eyes and then into Levi's. "When you slipped through that door, you began a journey, a journey all your own. Didn't your grandmother warn you about such things?"

Levi looked down at the ground guiltily. "Well, yes, she tried to, but we didn't believe her. If only—"

Lola raised her right eyebrow. "If only, if only—such sad little words, powerful little sad words. Well, that's beside the point now. What you need to know is that it is possible for you to get home. Your grandmother did tell you that, didn't she?"

Levi stared across the field, thinking. "Yes, yes, well, kind of, but we . . . weren't—" Levi stopped as Grizzles staggered onto the scene, bumping into Lola, almost knocking her over.

"That's enough, Lola. You're going to make 'em soft." He looked at her. "Are you really going to give 'em that satchel?"

Lola smiled, shrugging her shoulders. She nodded. "Grizzles, you be nice now." She bent forward and lowered her voice. "These are the Treehouse Children. You saw the lanterns flicker. There's not much in the satchel, just a little to get 'em going. A little recompense. You do remember, don't you?" Grizzles rolled his eyes and grumbled something.

After gasping and wheezing and catching his breath, Grizzles stumbled forward, staring directly into Levi's face. "Well, boy, if that's the way it is, it seems your time has come." He raised his eyebrows and sniffed with his bulbous nose. "You chose this journey when you walked out that bronze door. It's time for you to go unless you want me to start nibbling on you, and you do look very tasty, and I am very hungry, and I don't like being disturbed.

"I cannot tell you what to do or where to go, but—and I only say this because I am in a very, very good mood today and because Lola seems to favor you three for some strange reason—choose carefully, boy. Choose carefully.

"There's lots of paths out there, boy, lots of paths. Lots of potholes, lots of briar bushes. Lots of roses but lots of thorns." He stopped and pointed directly at Levi with his gnarled, wrinkly finger. "Beware the forks in the road. Those forks can be treacherous things. Oh, and the dead ends. Stay away from dead ends. You can tell dead ends by the smell of rotten skunk cabbage and eggs and well—"

He stopped and sniffed the air and kind of growled and howled at the same time before he continued. "If you can't tell them by that smell, then pay heed to the eerie feeling inside. And don't be beguiled by old crones, dashing lads, or even beautiful maidens with their tales of elixirs and shortcuts and such. And especially, remember this: no, no, no shortcuts or lazy paths. Shortcuts are lazy tricks on these journeys and lead to dead ends, and if you take a shortcut to a dead end, you have to start over. Such a waste—a total waste. Just do it right."

And he threw his head back and growled again, raising his hoary old head and rolling it around, cracking his neck and snarling just a little. Then he turned to leave. Levi moved forward quickly, hoping Grizzles would give just a little more information.

"Please wait, please. We thank you for the advice, but please, before you go, could you just point us in the direction that leads to—get us started—and then we'll do just what you said?" Levi glanced over at Eleanor and shrugged. "We came to find my sister Claire and our cousin Addison. They went out the silver door. Is there a road leading from here to there to a path they might be on? I lost the map book, and we don't even know which direction to even start from."

The old man twisted around and cocked his head to the side, regarding Levi with a slight smile on his face. Suddenly he threw his head back and laughed and laughed and laughed.

"You tried to bring the map book with you? Here? Did you really say that you tried to bring the map book here?" Grizzles held his arms out, pointing his fingers in different directions as he twisted back and forth. "Lola, did you hear that? Oh, you, silly, silly child. Now, that's just funny—such a funny boy, you are!" Then Grizzles waved his hand dismissively; and turning, he began hobbling back toward his cabin, chuckling as he went.

Eleanor rushed after Grizzles, grabbing his arm. "Wait, wait," she pleaded. He stopped abruptly, shook her hand off his arm, and turned slightly, holding his gaze directly on her. She moved in front of him, staring straight back into his grotesque eyes. A shudder wiggled down her spine, but she did not flinch.

"What do YOU want?" he snapped. Eleanor took a deep breath. "Please, please," she begged him, "just give us a clue. Which way do we go? Which direction—which path leads us home?"

"Oh," the old man said, "is that all you want? You want to know which path will lead you home? Well, if that's all you wanted, why didn't you say so in the first place? Why, you, silly child! That's all? Why, that's easy."

He leaned in toward Eleanor, his rancid breath filling the air between them, his upper lip snarling as his scraggly yellowed teeth snapped. "You see, my little dear, that's the easy part because all the paths eventually lead home. But then, getting home has never been the problem. Getting home in one piece—now that's the problem." And with that, his whole body trembled into fits of laughter, which turned into fits of wheezing and then into fits of coughing until he finally doubled over and spat greenish-yellow blobs of phlegm onto the ground.

After he caught his breath and wiped the back of his hand across his mouth, he pointed his finger at Eleanor and continued, "But I will tell you this: each path has some good and each path has its bad some more than others, and it's up to you to choose. Just don't forget what I told you and no shortcuts. They only make it worse."

Then the old man turned and began hobbling away again. Lola smiled at the three of them. "Grizzles is right," she said softly. "Grizzles is always right." She sighed, watching him hobble away. Suddenly, she brightened. "I've got to go now," she said. "Good luck, children. I do hope you enjoy your journey. Oh, and the satchel is for you. But I really must go now. Things to do, things to do." She turned to follow Grizzles but stopped after just a few steps and turned around. Tapping her forehead with her forefinger as though she had forgotten something, she beckoned for Levi, Eleanor, and Esmé to come closer.

"I almost forgot to tell you," she whispered, bending forward. "Find the Oracle. Oracles are so good at journeys. So good—so very good."

"What's an Oracle?" Esmé asked, looking up at Lola.

Lola frowned. Clicking her tongue while shaking her head, she looked at Levi. "Didn't anyone ever read ancient stories to this child or teach her about important things?"

She patted Esmé on the head. "You are such a darling. So cute and so sweet. Oracles, my little dear," she said, "are everything." She stopped and glanced at the sky. "Actually," she continued, "they are everything, and they are nothing. They are everywhere and nowhere. But sometimes they are really hard to find. Just follow the signs—always follow the signs." And she scurried after Grizzles, who was hobbling as quickly as he could back to the ramshackle cabin.

Chapter 27

Levi, Eleanor, and Esmé: All Kinds of Signs

Levi, Eleanor, and Esmé stood watching Lola catch up to Grizzles, loop her arm through the crook of his elbow, kiss his cheek, and meander across the field with him, smiling and chatting. Eleanor watched for a while; and quite suddenly, she swallowed hard and kicked the ground. She took off running behind Grizzles and Lola, yelling, "Wait! Wait! Wait! You can't just leave us here! Give us a clue. Give us anything!"

But the contented pair just kept chatting as they rambled away without even a single glance back. Eleanor caught up to them. Grabbing the back of Lola's dress, she begged, "Please, please, help us." But Lola simply grabbed hold of her own dress, pulled it out of Eleanor's hand, and kept walking as if she heard nothing—as if she felt nothing.

Eleanor stood with her arms dangling at her side in complete confusion watching them. Finally, she plopped down onto the ground, rubbing her forehead with her fingers. Bottled-up tears of frustration rolled down her face. "Oh my gosh, oh my gosh, oh my gosh! I can't believe those horrible people or whatever they are!" She hit the ground with her fist.

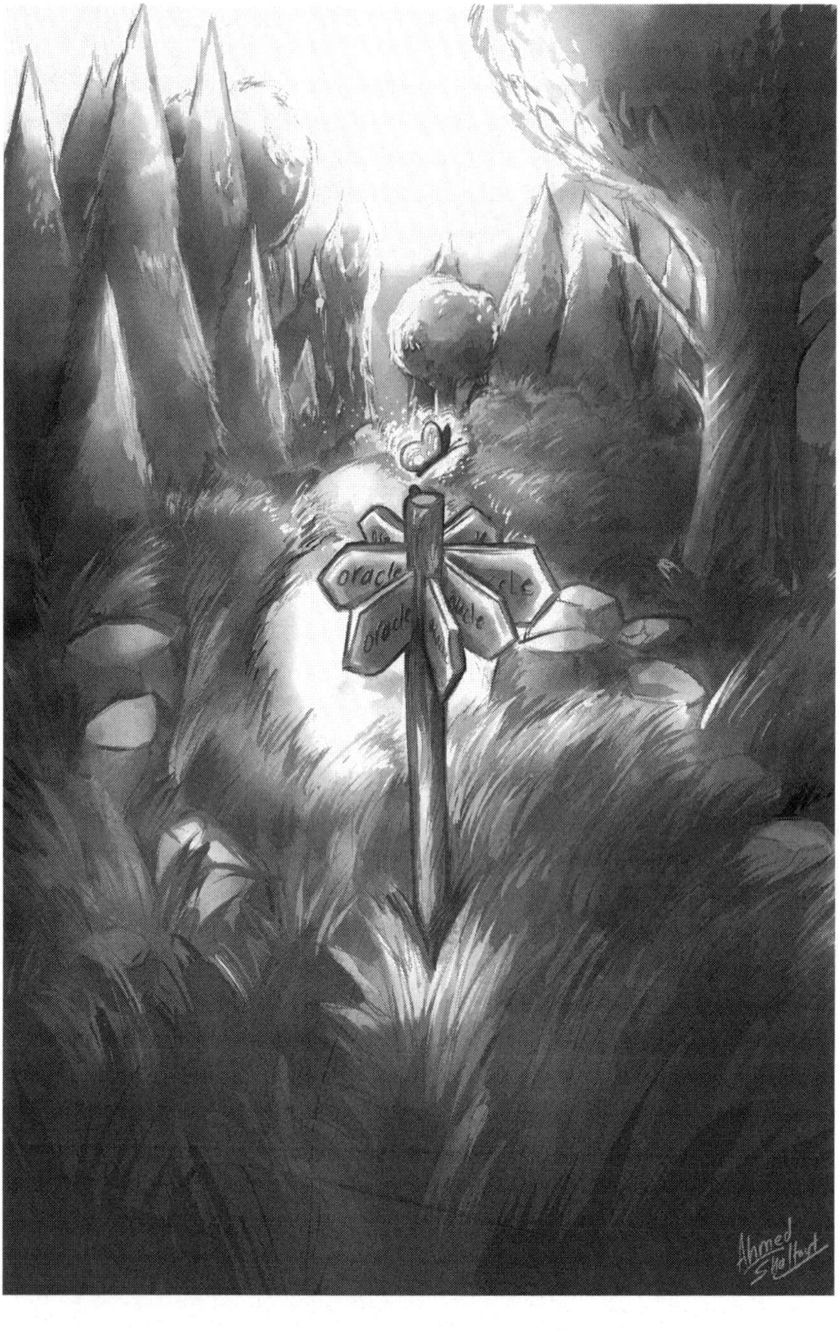
oracle
oracle
oracle

Levi grabbed Esmé's hand, and they hurried to Eleanor. Standing above her, Levi patted Eleanor's shoulder as they watched Grizzles and Lola stroll toward the cabin. "Ellie, please stop crying," Levi said. "Forget them. We don't need them. We'll find our own way back. Think about it, Eleanor. When Claire and Addison went missing, Gramma was upset, but she wasn't over the edge. She must have known they'd be back."

Eleanor's sobs slowed; she sniffed a few times and looked up at Levi. "Maybe you're right," Eleanor conceded, wiping her tears with the back of her hand. "Well, if that's true, we will find our way back whether that horrible old man and mean lady help us or not!" she yelled while pointing at Grizzles and Lola.

Eleanor stood up, brushing the grass off her pants. She watched Lola step onto the dilapidated porch and slip inside the cabin. Grizzles lingered on the outside for a moment longer. Slowly, he twisted around, staring across the field directly at Eleanor, his mouth fixed in a disgusting grimace. Eleanor kept staring right back at him, snarling and hoping he could feel her contempt.

Grizzles turned to shuffle across the porch, but he stopped at the threshold. He reached up, grabbing something out of the air. He raised his cupped hand to his shoulder, and then turning back around, he glared straight into Eleanor's eyes once more as the corners of his lips curled up just a little.

His hand flicked. She saw it. She was sure: a little movement, a flinch of his fingers—something. Craning her head forward, squinting her eyes, she saw something; yes, something flitted, something floated, something drifted above Grizzles's head before flickering up and away. She kept her eyes on it; a flash of excitement burst in her stomach. She saw Grizzles sneer, jerk his head to the side, and then after turning, he hobbled through the doorway.

Eleanor watched the something flutter and float, and suddenly she darted off across the field. "Levi, Esmé!" she yelled as she took off zigzagging across the field. Levi grabbed Esmé with one hand the satchel with the other as he hurried past it, sprinting to catch up.

"What's going on?" he shouted.

"Follow me!" Eleanor yelled while looping back and forth across the field. And then, quite suddenly and without warning, she abruptly stopped and stood silently watching something. Levi came panting up behind her. "What are you—" he started to ask.

But Eleanor waved the back of her hand at him, shushing him. "Keep your eyes on that butterfly!" she whispered. "I know you're going to think that I'm crazy, but when Grizzles twisted around, he stared at me. Then he let go of that butterfly, and I just had a gut feeling or something. I know it sounds really, really dumb, but I think he was sending a clue or something. Let's just watch and see. Stuff like this could be what Gramma meant with her gibberish."

Levi sighed, rolling his eyes, shaking his head; but he stood still, watching for Eleanor's sake.

The butterfly flittered and fluttered around and above them until it suddenly fluttered across the field, landing on the top of an old wooden signpost standing among the tall grasses. It sat there, fluttering its wings before suddenly rising and disappearing into the evergreens beyond.

And even though losing track of the butterfly was quite disappointing, still, it must be said, that they were so surprised to see the signpost standing in the midst of tall golden grasses in the middle of the field. They forgot to be upset.

"Is that one of those old signposts?" Levi shouted. "Why didn't we see that before?"

They rushed across the field, running and laughing and hoping and shouting. And they kept laughing and hoping and shouting until they were close enough to read arrows. And then they went silent, and then they looked back and forth at one another. Eleanor and Levi slowly walked around the signpost again and again until they just stopped under the sign post and began looking around in every direction. "I don't get it." Eleanor sighed with her fingertips over her mouth.

"The arrows are pretty," said Esmé. "They're the same colors as the doors at Gramma's treehouse."

"Yes, that is true, Esmé. That is true," said Levi, absentmindedly patting Esmé's head.

"Is that how you spell *oracle*?" Esmé asked.

"Yes, Esmé," Levi muttered. "That is exactly how you spell *oracle*."

"Are the arrows pointing to where the Oracle lives?" Esmé asked.

"Yes, the arrows must be pointing to where the Oracle is," answered Levi.

"So why is Oracle written on every single arrow?" Esmé asked.

"That, Esmé"—sighed Levi—"is the problem."

Chapter 28

Levi, Eleanor, and Esmé: Eight Arrows

The satchel lay open at the foot of the signpost; its tarnished latches unhinged, its used contents spilled onto the ground. To their surprise, the satchel had been stuffed with sandwiches, water, and even treats; and now, the crinkled wrappers, leftover bits of food, and empty water bottles lay scattered on the ground amid the cobbles and the stones and the tall grass.

Esmé was napping using Levi's wadded-up shirt as a pillow. Eleanor sat on the grass, cross-legged, elbows on knees, with her chin in her palms staring back and forth between the signpost, the mountain, the waterfall, and the cobblestone path stretching across the field. Levi was pacing, looking up and down and all around.

"Okay," Eleanor finally said, standing up and walking over to the signpost, "let's start at the very beginning one more time. We have a signpost. On the signpost, we have eight arrows, and every arrow points in a different direction. Every arrow is painted a different color, but each has *Oracle* carved into the wood. So what does this mean?"

"Well," Levi suggested, "since every arrow has exactly the same colors as the doors at Gramma's treehouse, there's gotta be an important connection—a clue or something. So," he continued, "it could mean that each destination has its own Oracle."

"But then again," Eleanor broke in, "it could be that there is one Oracle and eight different ways to get to him. Maybe the different directions are simply different paths people can choose, like the bronze points to that mountain, and the silver points to that waterfall, the red points to the open field."

"Or," Levi countered, "there could be one Oracle, and the colored arrows point in the directions we go according to the door we went through. The silver corresponds to the door Claire and Addison went through, and the bronze path corresponds to the door we went through."

"But the red path leads right through that open field," Eleanor said. "It looks easier and faster, and this is not a time to explore mountains or waterfalls for the fun of it."

"I vote we follow the bronze arrow," Levi broke it. "That's the color we started with. I say we follow it, find the Oracle, we ask him how to find Claire and Addison. You are right. There are other scenarios that could work, but following the bronze arrow is the surest bet, and, if there is only one Oracle, we'll be on the path we started with."

"But, Levi, even if what you are saying is true, the bronze direction is not really an option, and neither is the silver one," Eleanor countered with a grimace.

"Why not?" asked Levi.

"Because look at what we'd have to go through, dummy!" Eleanor snapped. "If we go in the same direction the bronze arrow points, we have to climb up that mountain. And the silver arrow points over to that waterfall. We can't go either way."

"Why are you saying that, Ellie? You love mountain climbing. And even if it's harder, it will be worth it if it gets us back home. Besides, Grizzles said not to take shortcuts or lazy paths, and while he is a horrible creature, I'm sure he was trying to warn us that the easy way won't—" Suddenly, Levi stopped midsentence. "Ellie, what is wrong?"

"As if you don't know!" Eleanor whispered, her tone turning harsh and raspy. Suddenly the heated words that had been sitting on her tongue ever since Esmé had fallen asleep tumbled out.

"You let Esmé come! Now our choices are limited because of Esmé! That's what's wrong. We might have to take the stupid shortcuts that Grizzles warned against because of her."

"What are you saying?" Levi asked, surprised at Eleanor's vehemence.

"You know what I'm saying! You've spoiled her. She just wouldn't take no for an answer. And now we're going to suffer or be delayed because she wouldn't listen—and you know it!"

"What is your problem?" Levi snapped. "She is here. She is fine. She hasn't done anything to hurt you."

"Yes, but she's going to delay us in one way or another no matter which path we take!" Eleanor snapped back. "What if we need to go up into those mountains? What if the only way out is to swim in that river by the waterfall? Do you think we can take her there? No, we can't! So what do we do now?"

"Stop it, Ellie. You just stop it!" Levi whispered through gritted teeth. "At least she is pleasant to be with unlike some people I can think of right now." At this, he stared directly into Eleanor's eyes. "What's the point of your argument anyway? It can't change anything."

"She creates problems and delays for us," Eleanor retorted sharply, "and you should at least admit it."

"I'll admit nothing," Levi snarled. "She just might surprise you. She's a tough little thing," Levi said, glancing down at Esmé. "She's been trying hard to be good all day. Can't you see that?"

At that, Eleanor turned away, grumbling and muttering under her breath. "Oh, forget it," she snarled after a little bit. "We have more important things to figure out." At that, she plopped back down to the ground, crossed her legs, put her elbows on her knees and her chin in her palms, and sat silently staring back and forth between the signpost, the mountain looming in front of them, the waterfall and the cobblestone path stretching across the field. Levi returned to his pacing.

And even though she had remained silent and feigned sleep, Esmé had been awakened by the harshly whispered words. Tears slowly welled up behind her closed eyelids, sliding across her cheek and plopping onto the ground. She wished she had never run out that stupid old door; she wished she was back with Gramma in a warm, cozy bed. Most of all, she wished Eleanor would stop being mean.

Chapter 29

Levi, Eleanor, and Esmé: Decisions Made

They had finally decided. Esmé was awake; their scattered mess was cleaned up. They wrote their names in pebbles and rocks, along with an arrow pointing to the path they had decided at the base of the signpost—just in case Addison and Claire, by some strange, weird chance, happened upon this particular signpost in the middle of this particular field in this particular part of whatever place they were in.

And while it was true that the mountain trail seemed much more foreboding and difficult with its ascent through huge evergreens, winding trails, mountain cliffs, and protruding precipices than some of the other paths, still, it was the direction of the bronze arrow. And since Grizzles had specifically cautioned them to beware of shortcuts—and, for all they knew, those easier paths could be taking a shortcut—they had finally agreed to take the bronze path.

Levi picked up the satchel, strapped it on his back, grabbed Esmé's hand, and started walking. Eleanor paused, considering the mountain face with its sheer cliffs and slate gray precipices. Under normal circumstances, she would be strapping on the gear and guide ropes, analyzing the heights and obstacles and preparing for a climb; but this was different—no climbing gear, no harness, no ropes. They would follow the path through the trees, remaining close to the mountain stream flowing down it, staying close to the source of water. She drew in a deep breath and then scurried to catch up as they began their ascent up the mountain trail and into the huge evergreens.

Chapter 30

Tilly, Brody, Ivan: Getting Out Is Hard to Do

The baby nestled against Mama, sporadically sucking her thumb, drifting in and out of sleep.

"Best festival ever, but I am totally exhausted." Mama sighed as she trudged along the cobbled path leading home. When no one replied, she turned, glancing back. "What'd you think, Jeslue? Papa?"

"Best ever!" Jeslue replied. "It was so great! Did you see how tiny those little green thingies were? And the red worms—I never saw so many! It'd sure be great to have pets of my own."

Papa brought up the rear, shuffling along, carrying the books and the bags and the giant stuffed turtle. "We'll get you your own pet someday, Jeslue," Papa said. "Watching the races today reminded me of my pets and showing them at the festivals when I was young, and it was great."

"Oh, Papa, that would be the best thing ever, and I will be so good to my pet! And next year, I'll take it to the festival and see if I can win the prize for the best pet of all."

Papa chuckled. "Well, I'm not promising you anything just yet, Jeslue. We've had a long day, and I'm worn out! But we can talk about it later."

They rounded the bend; the lantern hanging above the door cast a soft golden glow across the stone path, welcoming them home. Once inside, Papa set the bags and books and the giant stuffed turtle on the floor and reached over to adjust the wick on the lanterns, but Mama quickly shook her head. "Don't turn the flames up quite yet," she whispered. "Wait till I lay baby in her bed, so she stays asleep."

The dim light from the dying embers of the fire pit illumined the room just enough, and Mama carefully navigated her way to the baby's bed hanging from the wall. Mama quietly bent over the edge of the bed, shifting the baby in her arms and moving ever so gently to keep the sleeping baby asleep.

As she pulled the fleecy covers back and bent over, her shadow fell over the bed. Ivan's eyes popped open. He looked straight into the startled eyes of a huge face. He screamed. Mama jerked back, dropped the baby, and screamed.

The baby fell onto Ivan. Their heads bumped together. The baby woke up, and she screamed. Tilly jolted awake, saw a very huge face bent over the bed screaming straight into Ivan's face and a very startled Ivan screaming back into the huge face, and Tilly started screaming. Brody sat straight up, knocked his head against the wall, yelled "ouch," looked about at all the chaos, and then he started screaming.

The mother grabbed the baby out of the bed; she stumbled backward, falling into the chair. The Father ran over to see what was happening.

"What in the world?" roared the Father.

"Who are you?" yelled Brody.

"Who am I?" thundered the Father.

"Yes, what are you?" yelled Ivan.

"What do you mean who am I? What are you?" screamed the Mother.

"Who am I?" asked Tilly, pointing to herself.

"Yes, who are you and what are you?" shrieked the mother.

"Who am I or who is she?" queried Brody pointing at himself and then at Tilly.

"Who or what are any of you, and how did you get in our baby's bed?" bellowed the father.

Tilly, Brody, and Ivan huddled back against the wall, squeezing together as tightly as they could possibly squeeze.

"I'm a, well, I'm, uhh, Ivan. And that's Brody, and that's Tilly, and we are umm, well, we're people?" Ivan squeaked.

"Did you say People?" asked Jeslue.

"Yes!" shouted Tilly, Brody, and Ivan in unison, hoping he understood.

"Ohhh! Mama! Did you hear that? Mama, it's a people!" shrieked Jeslue.

"And what are you?" inquired Tilly, squeezing even tighter against the wall.

"What do you mean what are we? It's obvious, isn't it?" screeched Mama.

"Enormous elves?" Tilly wavered.

"Ellvves? Elves?" roared the Father. "Do I look like I make toys for a living? And did you not see my long white beard?"

"Giant Gnomes," suggested Brody.

"Aahhh, no!" spat the mother. She turned indignantly, glaring at Brody. She looked around in horror at Papa. "Did he just call us giant gnomes? Ah, ah, no! No, why would you think we are gnomes? Do we look low class? I think not! And," she continued with a sniff and a roll of the eyes, "And giants? I, for one, am only a little over nine footless, and I have always been considered quite petite in my family." A sob caught in her throat. "Perhaps I am a tad fluffy, but, I did just have Baby, after all. And if you must know, we are Biglings." She sniffed again and glanced over to Papa for support. He smiled and nodded at her.

Brody turned red. "No, no, no, no," he said, "I did not mean to insult you. It's just that gnomes wear pointy red caps and baggy pants like yours. You kind of look like, well, except you're so much bigger than us, you see." He glanced at Tilly for support, but she just shrugged and looked at the ceiling.

Jeslue interrupted. "Papa, Mama, who cares what they think we are? Mama, it's three peoples! We found peoples! I always wanted a people. Can I keep them? Please!"

"No!" shouted his parents in unison.

"Come on, just one, pleeeease," begged Jeslue. "I promise to feed 'em and take 'em out when they need to go, and if I'm sure that if I give 'em a bath, they won't stink anymore."

Tilly, Brody, and Ivan looked at one another with puzzled expressions, sniffed the air, and then shrugged.

"You can't keep us!" Ivan said, rubbing the egg developing on his forehead from the baby's head hitting it.

"Why not?" asked Jeslue.

"Because we're people!" Brody yelled.

"But I always wanted a people. Please, Mom. Pleeease," Jeslue pleaded.

The mother wavered for a second, considering the possibilities. Jeslue noticed. Rushing to take advantage of her hesitation, he grabbed Tilly, picking her up, setting her on his knee, and scratching her belly while running his huge rough hands over her hair. "This one has such soft hair," he said. "I like this one. I like its soft yellow hair."

Tilly panicked. For a second, she sat motionless, her eyes huge, blinking at Brody and Ivan. When she started squirming and struggling to get away. Jeslue set her down.

"But this one is cute too," he said, picking up Ivan. "Its hair is short and curly around the ears. It is smaller than the other two—not much bigger than baby sister. Must have been the runt of the litter, but it's really cute just the same. I kind of like its spunk." Ivan crossed his arms over his chest, frowning.

"But then again, this one is adorable too," Jeslue continued, setting Ivan down and picking Brody up. "I like its blue eyes. Look at how big and blue the eyes are, Mama! This one is sooo cute. How can I tell if it's a boy or a girl?" Brody's eyes got very, very big; and his face turned very, very red.

Just then, lanterns flared up throughout the cavern until the entire home was lit up as if it were daytime. The Father looked at the lanterns and then at the three cousins and then at Mama who stared straight back at him. "And just where did you people say you came from?" the Father asked.

Tilly, Brody, and Ivan began talking all at once, speaking over one another with a jumbled mass of words.

"Oh, never mind," the Papa snapped. "I am too tired to talk about it for tonight. But we can't just send 'em out into the night either. It would be bad if something got 'em or captured 'em out there. I'll tell you what, Jeslue, let's put them in the old cart-cage that we used for trapping. They'll be fine for tonight. We can figure out what to do with them in the morning."

Jeslue sucked in a deep, deep breath. "Oh goody! Oh goody! Oh goody!" he repeated over and over under his breath. He ran to the workroom and found the old rusty key under the workbench. He unlocked the cart-cage, spread an old ragged blanket on the floor, and yelled, "Ready!"

Papa came trudging in, carrying the wiggling, fussing, fighting Tilly, Brody, and Ivan under his arms; he shoved them into the cart-cage, and Jeslue slammed the door before they could scramble out.

"This is like the best surprise ever!" Jeslue said as he danced a little jig and jumped up and down in the workroom; bottles and jars on shelves jiggled and clattered together as he jumped.

Suddenly, he stopped. "Oh, little fellows, I bet you're thirsty. Do peoples drink out of sippers or bowls?" he asked.

Tilly shrugged. "Probably sippers." She sighed.

"Are you kidding me? Why'd you answer him?" Brody demanded.

Tilly shrugged. "Well, I'm thirsty," she conceded. "And the baby's sippers might be a better size for us than their huge bowls."

Jeslue brought water in the sippers and a big bowl of peas. Opening the side hatch, he pushed everything through. "Here you go, little fellows. The peas seem like a good size for you to nibble on."

Tilly, Brody, and Ivan stood there with their faces pressed against the squared iron mesh of the cart-cage, talking over one another, trying to explain why he just had to let them go. Jeslue simply stood there, staring at them and smiling. "It's okay, little peoples," he kept saying. And then he went on and on, and he just kept telling them that they were going to be so happy because he would be the best peoples' owner ever in the whole world.

He danced a little jig and then jigged some more until Mama and Papa yelled that it was time for bed. And then, just so his parents would not think he was assuming too much or getting his hopes too high, Jeslue straightened himself and walked evenly back into the cavern room as though it were an everyday event to find three peoples sleeping in your home and to hope that you just might get to keep one.

Chapter 31

Tilly, Brody, and Ivan: The Mother Lode

"Don't encourage him," Brody snapped. "Don't look at him. Don't say a word. He thinks the only problem is this stupid cart-cage. He thinks that once he gets a 'people house' for us, we'll live happily ever after with him forever and ever while he rubs our heads and walks us 'in the sunshine.'"

Just then, Jeslue entered the workroom, sat on the rocky floor beside the cart-cage, and stretched his arm through the bars, trying to reach the elusive cousins who shrank against the opposite side of the cart-cage and turned to face the walls. He sighed moving to the opposite side and trying to reach through the metal squares of the cage from a different angle. But the cousins simply moved away a second time.

"Act all hyper or angry or something. Maybe that'll make him go away," Brody whispered. They growled and hissed and scrunched their faces and wrinkled their noses and stuck their tongues out.

Jeslue only laughed. "You are so cute." He chuckled while trying once more to pat their heads, this time reaching down through the bars at the top. The cousins stopped making faces, rolled their eyes, and moved again.

"This is ridiculous!" Brody growled.

Jeslue sighed. "I know you hate the cart-cage." he said, "I promise that if I get to keep you, I'll make sure you have an awesome place to stay. We'll run and play, and I'll take you for walks in the sunshine. I promise to slip you the good food from the table when Mama isn't watching, and even if I can't keep all three of you, I promise to make sure that the others get the best home in the whole wide world. I'll make sure you have oodles of playdates with one another," Jeslue beamed and sighed. Brody rolled his eyes.

Standing up and dusting his hands against his baggy green pants, Jeslue continued, "I'm hoping to build you the best pet house ever, but for now, I better get my chores done. That way Mama and Papa will have one more reason to let me keep you."

Walking to the far corner of the room, Jeslue bent over a huge mound of rocks. After picking through several and shaking them, he chose a few and began tapping around the outside of each one with a tiny clawed hammer. Finally, he picked a particularly huge stone and set it on the worktable.

With a purple marker, Jeslue drew crooked lines around the outside of the stone and began sawing and cutting with little jibs and jabs. Around and around, he tapped and turned and shook and jibbed and jabbed.

"What's he doing with that rock?" Ivan asked.

"Shhhh," whispered Brody. "Don't let him know we're watching. He'll think we are interested, and then he'll come over here and try to show us what he's doing, and then he'll try to pet us."

A soft pop and a crackle echoed through the cavern. Jeslue kept tapping and jibbing and jabbing round and round. Slowly, methodically he listened and tapped. Finally, he grabbed a tiny wedge; and after prying it into the rock, he wiggled the wedge back and forth. Another loud pop, one more tap, and the stone cracked. Jeslue grabbed both sides, wiggling both halves until they burst apart.

He held the rock halves up the sunlight that filtered in through a hole in the crown of the cavern. Sparkles of color glinted and glimmered, bounced, and flashed around the room; tiny rainbows danced around the walls. Slowly, Jeslue set the rock halves on the worktable and sat in silence with his hand clamped over his mouth. Suddenly he jumped up, bouncing and hopping and laughing.

"Ooooh my, oh my, oh my! This is so awesome. So awesome. So awesome!" he chanted, dancing a happy jig around the room. "What a find! What a find! I'll get to keep a people—a people! I'll get to keep a people!" He sang and jigged and waved his hands in the air. He held the crystals up to the sunlight again. And then he jigged some more.

He dashed to the cart-cage. "We're gonna be a family. I'll get to keep you!" he shouted, and he rushed through the archway. "Mama!" he yelled. "Mama, you've got to see this!"

Tilly, Brody, and Ivan grabbed the bars and stretched up on their tippy toes. Even from across the room, they could see the glittering, sparkling red, blue, green, and purple octagonal crystals rising out of the stone halves even as all the walls sparkled and danced with the colored reflections.

Tilly slid down to the floor and put her elbows on her knees and her head in her hands. "I've never seen anything like that." She gasped. "And even though it's absolutely amazing, it only means more trouble for us."

"Obviously, we have to get out of here now!" Ivan exclaimed. "With the way he's jumping around, that must be the mother lode of crystals or something. If his parents are anywhere near as pleased as he thinks they will be, he'll definitely get to keep us."

"Oh my, oh my," sighed Tilly. "What are we going to do now?"

Chapter 32

Tilly, Brody, and Ivan: Nice Little Peoples

Jeslue set the food down on the outside of the cart-cage, opened the hatch, and stuck a bowl of tiny cookies through the slot. "You like cookies, don't ya, little fellows? Look, I made tiny ones for you." He tried to touch the cousins, but they cowered on the far side of the cart-cage. "Come on, little fellows," he pleaded. "It's gonna be wonderful. You'll see. I'll build you a people house and get you out of this cart-cage. I can pay for all the building stuff with the crystal rock I opened this morning."

He rolled his shoulders, stretching, and then yawned. Ivan glanced at Tilly and Brody and then back at Jeslue; and very quickly, before Brody or Tilly even realized what he was doing, Ivan slipped across the cart-cage and stood close to Jeslue and smiled up at him.

"Oh my! Ooohhh." Jeslue exhaled, a quaver in his voice. "Look at you, little fellow. Oh, come here, come here. You are sooo cute. You're starting to like me. I knew if I just waited, you'd come around. Oh, little fellow, I love you so much already. We're gonna have such great times together. You wait and see."

Jeslue's eyes reddened around the edges as he reached through the bars to pet Ivan. Ivan rolled his eyes and sighed, but he bent his head forward so that Jeslue could pat his head and stroke his hair. "I get to keep all of you," he said. "I made enough this morning to build you a big fine home. I'm going to put little steps and everything in it and paint it really cool colors. I'm the luckiest kidlet ever!"

"Jeslue!" Mama hollered from another room. "Time to get ready for bed. Put the peoples up for tonight." Jeslue sighed and got up. He patted Ivan on the head. Leaning forward, Ivan squeezed his arms around Jeslue who sucked in a deep breath and gazed at Ivan. His voice was husky; it quavered just a little. "Ooh, little fellow, I just love you so much. I'll be back in the morning first thing. I promise! But I gotta go and keep Mama happy." Jeslue patted Ivan's head one more time, and then he turned and hurried out of the room.

"Are you crazy? What'd you do that for, Ivan?" Tilly challenged crossly.

"You a traitor or something? What was that about?" Brody demanded.

"Well, I guess I feel a little sorry for him," Ivan confessed. "He really doesn't mean us any harm. He just doesn't understand. Besides, we're leaving tonight, so what can it hurt if I left him pat my head?" Ivan said, smiling and holding up a huge rusty key, waving it under Tilly's nose.

Tilly and Brody stared at the key and then at Ivan.

"How'd you do that?" Tilly whispered.

Ivan tapped his finger on his head. "Brains, Dr. Watson. Now, admit it. I am brilliant!"

"Okay, Sherlock!" Tilly chuckled. "I'll admit to anything that'll get us outta here," she conceded, "but how did you—oooh, you grabbed the key out of his pocket while he was petting your head. Wow! So what's next?"

"Simple. We wait till they go to sleep," Ivan continued. "We leave through that archway. The family comes and goes from there, so let's try that passage first. We just have to wait till they're all asleep."

"It's a plan!" Tilly agreed. They stood against the bars listening to the rustling and clatter from the cavern's family room. And after quite a while of waiting, they sat down to wait some more. Waiting, straining to hear any creak or groan or mumble or squeak. They waited.

Mumblings and murmurings rose and fell. Jeslue chatting. Mama's jabbering. Dishes clanking. A baby's cry. Water running. A baby babbling. Mama fussing. Jeslue muttering. A chair creaking. Sweet, simple melody of nostalgic notes. More creaking.

The dim glow from the lantern flickered and faded in and out as a draft from the cavern roof caught the flame and danced with it. The cousins scooted closer to one another and grabbed hands, hoping and wishing for the sounds to stop before the light flickered away. More hushed listening. Rustling. Whispered words? Quiet? Silence? Waiting, waiting, waiting. Silence. And, finally, pure quiet. Total silence.

Finally, Ivan whispered, "Ready?"

"One more minute—just to be sure," Tilly replied, holding her finger over her lips. Another moment. And then, "Okay, let's go."

They slipped over to the cart-cage door. Ivan reached his arm through to the other side and pushed the key into the enormous padlock. An echoing click reverberated through the silent cavern room.

"Shuushuu!" Brody shushed. Ivan drew in a sharp breath and stopped. More listening. Silence. Ivan twisted the key in the lock. It stuck. He twisted again. A squeaky groan. Tilly put her hands over her face. "Make it quick," she whispered. "Just do it."

Ivan jiggled it in the lock. Jiggle. Push. Click. Pop. Ivan slipped the padlock off the cage latch. They stood still in pure silence for a few more seconds. Listening. They grabbed the bars of the cage door and pushed. Grinding, creaking, groaning. A rustling movement from somewhere.

"Shhushh!" Brody whispered. "Quiet, quiet, quiet!" They waited. Silence. Quiet.

"Try again. One, two, three, now!" They pushed. The cart-cage door groaned. A huge creak from somewhere. Huge eyes and craned necks. Silence. Deep breaths.

"Now or never!" Ivan whispered. And at that, they ran. They ran over the cobbled floor and through the archway. They ran down a long passageway and through another workroom. They ran past lit lanterns setting in niches carved into the walls, and then, they ran through more cavern rooms. They ran until they rounded a corner and into a room where Tilly stopped so suddenly that Brody bumped smack dab into her and knocked her over. But Tilly didn't even fuss; instead, she just stood back up and rotated in circles, gawking and gazing and ogling. And Brody did the same. And so did Ivan. And it was no wonder.

For you see, that particular room was not just any regular ole cavern room like the others they had rushed through—oh no, not at all. If it had just been any regular ole cavern room, they would have just kept running, and everything might have turned out quite differently.

Instead, when they ran around that corner and into that room, they entered the most sparkly, the glitteriest, the shiniest, the most crystally, diamondy, gemstoney, colorful, rainbowy, gorgeous, and somewhat gaudiest room that they could have ever even imagined in their whole lives even if they had closed their eyes super tight and tried really, really hard to imagine such a place. And even though they knew that they should keep right on running straight through that room, their eyes made their legs stop.

They stood still for a moment in total silence; and then, they rotated in circles with open mouths and huge eyes as lantern light flickered against the gigantic gemstones and geodes and minerals, creating a mosaic of sparkles and flashes of color. "Unbelievable," Ivan finally whispered as he rotated one more time.

Chapter 33

Claire and Addison: To Stay or to Go?

"This won't be easy," the Clockmaker said while tapping the book with his finger, "but I think I can get you out of here. Have you girls heard of something like a theory of relativity or string theory or zero-point gravity or things like that?" Both girls scrunched their noses and nodded very tiny nods.

"Kind of, a little," Addison said.

"Well, according to this," the Clockmaker continued while concentrating on a picture that looked like lightning bolts flashing out of Spirograph designs, "getting you home has something to do with dimensional shifts or blurred timelines or parallel universes or some kind of gobbledygook?"

He stood there silently gazing off into the air; his forehead wrinkled, and his lip puckered. He looked up, drumming his lips with his fingers. "I simply have to create a glitch in the fabric of our time, and you have to slip through before the glitch tears a permanent hole, hmmm." Muttering inaudible tidbits to himself, he continued to study the pictures. Suddenly, his face broke into a huge smile. "Ah, ooh, I got it! I think I got it!"

He slammed the book shut and looked over at the girls. "I gotta be honest," he said. "It might not work. I think we can do this, but it is possible that it might not work. And you need to know that you really can stay here if you want to. We can play games, and you can help me keep the clocks in order."

Claire and Addison glanced around at the clocks, and both hesitated for just a second as they looked straight at each other with very pale faces.

"Gramma did say we might get lost, but she also seemed to think lost kids eventually got hhhome," Addison stuttered. "I-I-I-I don't want to stay here if we could get home. I think w-we have to try to go back. What do you think, Claire?"

Claire looked around at the room, at the mirrors and the clocks. She straightened her shoulders and focused her gaze straight into Addison's eyes. "Yes," she said, "I do think we should try. It is our best hope." Then she turned facing the Clockmaker. "Thank you very much, sir," she said, "but we want to try to go home if you will help us." She drew in a very deep breath and glanced over at Addison, who nodded.

"Then it is settled," the Clockmaker said. Beaming and rubbing his hands together, he said "This should be a most excellent adventure. I've always wanted to try something different." He adjusted his glasses, grabbed a little pad of paper out of his pocket, and flipped to page ninety-seven in the book. "I need your birthdates," he said.

"March 20?" Addison answered with some hesitation and a glance at Claire.

"December 22?" Claire said slowly with a glance at Addison.

"Good, good," the Clockmaker muttered as he scribbled on the paper. "And would both of you say that you look about the same age as you were when you got here?"

Addison and Claire looked at each other and then at themselves.

"Yeeess?" they both said at the same time, nodding rather slowly.

"Good, good," muttered the Clockmaker, nodding his head while continuing to read.

"Well, girls," he continued, "if you are sure, then we need to do this—RIGHT NOW. Follow me!" He pivoted, hurried to the staircase, and rushed up the steps—at least as quickly as he could with all his creaking and groaning and huffing and puffing. Though their legs were quite wobbly and their faces quite pale, the girls trailed resolutely behind.

The Clockmaker scurried across the balcony, stopping beside the huge hourglass. He inhaled three deep breaths, bent over, grabbed hold of the bottom of the hourglass, and tipped it on its side. He waited, watching until every single grain of white crystal sand had settled and everything lay perfectly still; then, glancing around at the clocks on the walls, he reached into his pocket and pulled his antique bronze pocket watch out. After flipping it open and pulling the stem, he wound it and fiddled with it for just a bit. He clicked it closed and slipped it back in his pocket.

"Not a second to lose, not a second to lose! Come quickly, come quickly. Walk with me, girls. There are things I have to tell you, and we must hurry. Time waits for no one!"

Claire and Addison sped up, rushing along beside him, Claire on one side, Addison on the other. They hurried across the balcony and under stone archways and down elongated hallways with various colored doors on both sides.

"Listen. You must understand what I am telling you," the Clockmaker said. "I've got to explain what you will be doing and what you must know to do it correctly. Moving through these mirrors is usually the work of a lifetime. But you will not have a normal lifetime for this journey—not if you want to get back while you are still the age you are—give or take a year or two," he said as he waggled his hand up and down.

"It will feel somewhat normal while you are there, but you will actually be going through at frenzied speed. Don't worry about your own personal life spoiler. Once you get back to your home, you should forget most of what you see, except perhaps for occasional bouts of déjà vu.

"Next," he continued, "and this is important. The mirrors, the clocks, and the elixir all have a specific purpose," he explained as they rushed down one hallway after another—through a labyrinth of passageways full of mirrors and clocks and doors, which the Clockmaker unlocked and locked again in quick succession. His breathing became labored, and his knees creaked; he kept moving rapidly as he talked.

"First, the mirrors," he said. "The mirrors will go on and on. Some are very pleasant, and some are not. But here is the important part: no matter what you see or how it feels, every time the clock tolls, you must move to the next mirror. It sounds simple, but the mirrors have stories that become hypnotic. It will be easy to forget that you are only looking at reflections of reality—kind of like when you get lost in a daydream and start laughing or crying—only much, much more real than that.

"You must keep going. You must change mirrors with every toll of the clock. There will be no relief, no dillydallying, and no time to waste, no time for hesitation, and no time to slow down to absorb the good or linger over the sad. If this were done in the normal way, you could linger a little here and there with a dose of elixir and absorb the repercussions of the story, but we are doing something different here, and the rules are different. Understand?"

Claire and Addison nodded as they continued scurrying along beside the Clockmaker, trying to keep up and understand at the same time.

"Now, for the tolling of the clocks," he continued. "Each clock chimes and tolls in its own way. In the beginning, the tolls are generally sweet, even innocent sounding, but they change. Oftentimes, by the middle of the passage through the mirrors, the tolls become somewhat harsher and generally a little more somber sounding. It is often in the middle of the passage that some people panic and refuse to move on. They don't seem to realize that even the more somber tolls are part of the song and that each tolling has something essential to add.

"And then there is the other side of the coin. Unfortunately, there are people who cling to the sorrowful tolls and refuse to let go and move on. They want the sad things to be the story. They seem to cling to the harsh notes and repeat sad notes over and over like when you press your tongue against an aching tooth. Neither situation is good.

"But if you just keep going, you will find that the tolls change back and forth. Sometimes the sounds are sweeter, sometimes harsher, but they always change. Near the end, the tolls are often more lyrical again, even lovely in a winter snow sort of way as if they are full and rich and full of nostalgia at the same time. But when all is said and done—and this is the important part—all the notes create the song, a most amazing song. Each song is unique. It is the song of the journey, and it is that song that must sing when you come to the last mirror."

Finally, they stood at the very end of the longest hallway in front of a huge white door with a rounded top, a black bar across the middle, a copper doorknob, and a slit of a window in the middle of the rounded top. The Clockmaker flipped his pocket watch open again and looked at the time.

"Now listen," he said. "You will need to hurry. There are forces at work—forces at work. For you, the speed will be mesmerizing, and the events will be real, but you must not forget why you are there. You will have no second chances."

Then, he glanced over at a grandfather clock standing in the corner. "You must go quickly, but do you have one last question?"

"I have a question," Claire said quickly. "If it is just a matter of changing mirrors when the clocks toll, what happened to Victoria and the others? I don't want to end up as mirror hanging on the wall."

The Clockmaker smiled sadly. "I almost forgot to tell you," he said. "On the side of each mirror, there is a small white shelf, and on each shelf, there is a bottle of elixir. The elixir is a temporary silencer. For most travelers, there are images either so special or sometimes so sad that travelers get so caught up in the story that they forget to listen to the notes of the song. It is sad but true. Sad, but true." He looked down at the floor and shook his head.

The Clockmaker's face dropped; his voice softened. "And there are times when the clocks toll that a traveler suddenly realizes they forgot to pay attention and learn the song. For those, one itty-bitty drop of elixir under the tongue quiets the tolling so they can hear the notes before they move on. In the end, the clocks still toll, and all the mirrors must be faced. The song must be learned. You must move to the next mirror as the tolling ceases.

"Unfortunately, after one drop of the elixir, some forget its power and become deluded. Some think they can stop time, and sometimes they even end up swigging the elixir. They trick themselves into believing they can make a lifetime out of one mirror, one event, one particular age or way of looking, or even one sorrow that they want to relive over and over. But in the end, it is all an illusion. Time waits for no one, and change always changes, and all the mirrors must be faced. Eventually, the tolling—the warnings to move on—become excruciating and no amount of elixir can quiet them. You saw what happened with Victoria. If only she had understood that she didn't have to be young and pretty to be beautiful."

The Clockmaker looked down at the ground, and then he paused. Looking up, he added, "Time," he said, "is a gift for keeping experiences separate, not a trap for illusions of self.

"And speaking of illusions, I almost forgot something," the Clockmaker said. He reached into the pocket of his apron.

"Here's a little gift from me," he said, handing each girl a tiny silver engraved hand mirror. He bent forward as if he were telling them a secret. "If you get mesmerized by the mirrors of your journey, these will remind you of who you really are—only the truth in those mirrors," he said with a soft smile.

They both smiled back. "Thank you so much for everything," Claire and Addison both said over and over a, and they both reached over and gave the Clockmaker a tiny kiss on his cheek, Claire on one side and Addison on the other. He blushed and looked down at the floor while twisting the toe of his boot around in a circle.

"Are you ready?" he asked.

Claire and Addison reached out; grabbing each other's hands, they turned toward the door and nodded.

"When you get to the last mirror—and you will know it when you see it—don't be afraid," he said. "The image you see looking back at you might not be what you expect. The experiences of the mirrors leave their marks on the prettiest, the sweetest, the ugliest, the meanest. When you see the reflections in that last mirror, try to remember that pretty and beautiful are not always the same. And"—he smiled gently—"when you finally gaze into that last mirror, it is my hope that you see beautiful.

He stepped back. "One last thing, but it is so very important," he said.

"When you come to that last mirror, lift your voice and sing that song that only your heart will know. That song will open that last mirror and reveal the last door. Just turn the knob and walk out."

He flipped his pocket watch open, twisted the stem one more time, and clicked it shut. "There is no more time."

As he reached for the padlock on the door, Addison froze and said, "Wait, wait, wait, hold on! How do we get home after we get out the last door?"

"Oh, I don't know," the Clockmaker said, shrugging his shoulders and gently shaking his head. "No idea at all. Find the Oracle. I hear that he is really good at telling lost people how to get home."

Addison started to ask a question, but the Clockmaker had already opened the padlock and lifted the iron rod from across the door. He placed one hand on Claire's back, the other on Addison's; and he gave them each a little shove into the room.

"Go quickly," he said. "Time waits for no one. Claire, go left. Addison, go to the right. Remember what I have told you." He slammed the massive white door; reverberations echoed the room. He snapped the padlock and slid the iron rod into place.

Claire shrieked. Addison drew in a huge breath and cried, "Oh my gosh, oh my gosh, oh my gosh!" They stood side by side staring about the pure white room, a totally empty room except for two oval-shaped mirrors, one facing right and the other facing left.

Chapter 34

Claire and Addison: The Gift of Time

They crept forward, Claire to the left and Addison to the right.

Claire leaned into Addison. "Promise, keep going," she whispered.

Addison laid a trembling hand on Claire's shoulder. "I promise," she said. "I'll keep going." They grabbed each other's hands, moved forward, and turned to gaze into their first mirror at the same time.

And in that first mirror, they simply regarded themselves—freckle faced with tousled hair. Girls with rosy cheeks and puzzled expressions looked back at them; but almost immediately images floated across the mirror—images that quickly began blending and spinning, changing into bits and pieces and flashes of happenings. Quarrels with siblings and hugs from parents, friends laughing, teachers teaching, boys winking, baseball games, family trips to Canada, kayaking, rock climbing, and Gramma and the treehouse.

And suddenly a clock chimed a very soft sweet note, and both girls startled. They had become so mesmerized by the feelings and images that they felt somewhat lost in time. They shook themselves out of their trance; each took a deep breath, closed their eyes, put their hands on the first mirror, and pushed.

They found themselves standing alone in front of the second mirror.

Outside, the Clockmaker slid down and sat on the floor, covering his face with his hands. "Oh please, keep going girls. Just keep going." After a few seconds, he scurried to his little clock room, found a ladder, and after pushing it against the door and climbing as high as he could, he watched through a little slit at the very top of the door.

In those first mirrors, both girls shook themselves and moved quickly when the clocks tolled; but after a while, the tolling seemed to startle them more and it seemed to take a little longer to snap out of the illusion.

And as the clocks tolled, the Clockmaker sighed at some times and wrung his hands at others. He watched, and they both did keep going every time the clicks tolled. "They are remembering. They are moving!" he almost shouted, his hand over his mouth, his fists nervously tapping the ladder rails.

In one mirror, he saw Claire pause and look around and laugh so hard she ended by wiping tears from her eyes. In another mirror, she smiled, holding her head high and sashaying back and forth, twirling in circles; and when the tolling began, she startled, looking about and holding her hand over her mouth. She started to reach for the elixir, but she caught herself; and even though she hesitated, she drew herself up and bent forward, straining to hear the notes. Finally, she smiled, pushed the mirror, and kept going.

Once he saw Addison stop and gaze into a mirror; she just stood there, staring as her face lit up. Suddenly, she swirled and bowed and threw a kiss into the air; and when the clock tolled, she kissed her fingers and touched the mirror gently as she turned and kept going.

A few mirrors down, the Clockmaker watched Addison; she seemed to be holding and snuggling something very close. Tears streamed down her face; and when the clock tolled, she clutched at the edge of the mirror as her entire body seemed to crumble.

But with her fists clenched, and after drawing in deep, deep breaths, she took one very long last look into the mirror; closed her eyes listening to the notes of the song; and then pushed the mirror open and kept going.

And as they neared the middle of the hallway, even the Clockmaker covered his ears as the tolling of the clocks reverberated with harsh tones. He saw both girls shudder and hold their ears as they gazed into the mirrors, touching their own faces a little sadly; and he guessed the mirrors revealed the betrayal of their youthful expectations and that time was having its way.

In the next mirror, Claire paused, stepped really close to the mirror, grabbed the engraved silver hand mirror out of her pocket, and looked at herself in it. Suddenly she leaned back and laughed and laughed and smiled sweetly while softly shaking her head and chuckling. She turned and went out the mirror when the clock tolled.

Near the very end, when he almost lost sight of them altogether, there was a time that Addison covered her face with her hands and tried to push at the mirror before the clocks even tolled. When it would not budge, she tried to avert her gaze; but finally, she straightened her shoulders and stared straight into the mirror. Just as it was time for the clocks to toll again, a smile finally wreathed her face, and she set her shoulders and held her head held high as she pushed that mirror open.

As the Clockmaker had predicted, as they neared the end of their journey through the mirrors, the tolling of the clocks was again softer and somehow more lyrical in a sad sort of way; and though both girls smiled in a wistful sort of way, still, it must be said that they also smiled in a softer sort of way.

And when at last Addison stood in front of her final mirror, she bent forward, scrutinizing the eyes looking back at her. She sighed and touched the face and held her hands up in front of her, studying them. She moved even closer, reexamining the image. And it was at that moment that Addison understood; she realized the face she saw gazing back at her was not pretty at all; it had lost its prettiness, its freshness, and the softness of the color; instead, it was worn and wrinkled and tired. And yet, while the face was not pretty or fresh as it once had been, it was, indeed, beautiful and, in a strange sort of way, even lovelier than it had ever been. She sighed and smiled a very soft, sweet smile; and her eyes crinkled all around the edges.

She reached her fingers forward, gently touching the mirror; and then, after a moment or so, she took a deep breath. Straightening her shoulders, she stepped back. She lifted her voice, and she sang her song—a song with notes so rich and so full—a song of a story, a song of a journey. A song that contained all the pain and the wonder, the joy, and the sorrow imbued in the image looking back at her from that final mirror. It was a song that only she knew, a song that only she could sing. And as her last note faded into silence, she heard a click as the last mirror released and slowly slid open.

She walked through and stood there motionless for just a second. And then she heard it, another song—a song very different than her own but just as sweet and just as lovely. And another mirrored door clicked, and Claire walked out, and they stood for just looking at each other, somehow surprised to see that they were still freckle-faced girls with tousled hair.

They grabbed each other and hugged as tight as tight can be. And they turned to face the final huge white door with the rounded top. Addison grabbed hold of the crystal knob and turned as Claire gave a gentle push, and together they walked out and lifted their faces to the pure warm sunshine.

Chapter 35

Levi, Eleanor, and Esmé: The Ancient Tree

Grizzles was right. Lola had said that Grizzles was always right, and he was. Already, the paths had been long, and there had been lots of them. There had been lots of potholes and lots of briar bushes. Lots of roses but also lots of thorns. At one fork in the road, they had taken a shortcut, but it had come to an abrupt stop at a stinky dead end, and they had been forced to go back to the trailhead and start all over. They had even passed a rickety old shack cradled into the mountainside; an old crone had emerged, trailing behind them, peddling her wares, trying to lure them with elixirs and such.

The path had twisted and turned, curving up ever higher and higher, until it ended where they now stood on the flat ledge of a rocky platform. But if that was not bad enough, the platform butted up against a sheer smooth rock face jutting straight into the air on one side while it dropped straight off the mountain on the other side. There were no ledges, no gaps, no divots, or notches for climbing higher even if they had wanted to try. So now, after they had forged through unbelievable obstacles, they stood confused and silent on a precipice, high above the valley floor where the path had come to an abrupt end.

Their arms were scratched; their limbs scraped from squeezing across rocky ledges, and their legs were wobbly and rubbery from the unending climb. They were hungry, thirsty, exhausted, and if truth be told, they were at the end of their metaphorical ropes.

Esmé's eyes darted back and forth. She had tried to hold everything inside; but finally, the sobs had burst out, shaking her little body, forcing her to cough and sputter as she broke down in tears. Eleanor stood with her hand over her mouth, shaking her head and drawing in deep breaths. Levi stood silently with his hand on Esmé's shoulder. The only sound was the sniffling of a very tired and very hungry Esmé.

The shadows were just beginning to creep across the mountain as the evening air chilled in anticipation of the night. And they stood grappling with their dilemma and the reality of their situation.

Levi finally broke the silence. "See that tree over there?" he said, pointing to an enormous sprawling curly corkscrew willow rising out of the ground at the place where the path, the platform, and the vertical rock wall converged. "I'm going to climb that tree and look around from higher up. A different viewpoint might just change everything."

He bent down, meeting Esmé's eyes with his own. "Ezzy," he said, "I need you to stay here with Ellie. I need to look around. We don't want to go back and start all over again, right?"

Esmé sniffed, wiping her eyes with the back of her hand. She frowned, shaking her head. "No," she snuffled, glancing up at Eleanor. "I'm coming with you, Levi."

Eleanor and Levi glanced at each other. Both had noticed Esmé's reticence toward Eleanor all day; they both secretly hoped that she simply felt safer with Levi, but now, they were beginning to wonder if there was more to it. "We'll go together," Eleanor said, trying to lighten the mood. "All for one and one for all! Besides, I'm the tree climber of the group!"

The tree was surprisingly intimidating once they stood under it. A huge mass of enormous roots lay tangled at the base of the tree, twisting, crisscrossing, and braiding over and around one another like heaps of unbound knotted ropes. They climbed up and over and across the gnarled roots until they finally stood at the base of the trunk, staring up through the profusion of branches.

"It goes up forever and ever," Esmé whispered.

Eleanor looked up, smiling. "Yes, but I think this might be the most perfect climbing tree ever. Look at those branches! They are close enough and tangled enough and big enough to climb all the way to the top! Let's do this!"

They circled the bottom of the tree, struggling over more roots until they found the lowest-hanging branch. "Here's where we start," Levi said, kneeling. Eleanor stepped on his knee and onto his shoulder; and with a little hop, she grabbed a nub, pressed her foot into a notch, and hoisted herself up onto the lowest branch. She wedged herself into a fork of the lowest branch of the tree, and after twisting herself around, Eleanor hung upside down, extending her arms and reaching down. "Grab hold, Esmé!" Eleanor yelled. Esmé climbed on Levi's shoulders, and he pushed her up.

Eleanor reached, and Esmé stretched, and Levi pushed; and finally, Esmé was sitting on a branch in the fork of the tree. And lastly, Levi jumped, grabbed the trunk, and after wedging his foot into the nub, he pushed off and climbed up.

"The branches get closer now," Eleanor said. "Let's go!"

They climbed and scooted and stretched ever and higher and higher until their arms were weak and their legs were trembly and until they simply had to stop and rest. As they sat on a strong fat limb, Eleanor grabbed Esmé's chin and held it, looking straight into her eyes. "You can look straight ahead, or you can look up at the sky," she said. "But do not look down. Promise?"

"Why not?" Esmé asked.

"Can you PLEASE just listen for once?" Eleanor demanded. "Now promise!"

"Eleanor is right on this one." Levi smiled gently at Esmé and nodded. "Don't look down, okay?"

"Okay, I promise!" Esmé conceded, rolling her eyes. And this time she obeyed.

Well, she kind of obeyed. Actually, if truth be told, it is probably more honest to say that this time she obeyed for longer than usual. And even if she didn't quite keep her word the entire time, you really must understand that after a while it became quite boring to just sit there staring straight ahead while Levi and Eleanor kept jabbering about plans and directions and paths.

And so, during a particularly tiresome interval, while Eleanor and Levi droned on and on about the landscape below and the possibilities of different routes, Esmé sort of rolled her eyes down just enough to catch a quick glimpse of what was down there.

And even though she immediately rolled her eyes right back up and stared straight ahead again, well, perhaps it should simply be said that her mouth had dropped open, her eyes had gotten very wide, and she started clutching at the limb and gasping with short quick little breaths.

After a little bit, after she had stopped gasping and clutching at the limb, and after her eyes had returned to their normal size, she began to wonder if what she had seen was really as bad as she thought it was. And so, she decided that perhaps she should just take another glance down just to reassure herself that her imagination was, in fact, exaggerating. She took a deep breath and rolled her eyes down again. Only this time she kept them down for a couple seconds, and this time when she looked back up, she almost stopped breathing.

This time, it felt like the blood was draining from her face and sliding straight toward her feet and that her feet were becoming very heavy from all the blood draining down to them. As a matter of fact, she was quite sure that they were going to pull her right off that limb and that she would fall down, down, down. Then she would die, and she would never get home to Gramma, and everyone would be so sad because she had died from heavy blood filling her feet and pulling her off the tree. And then, they would all cry, and none of it would have happened if Eleanor had just been nice in the first place because if Eleanor had been nice, then she would have stayed on the ground and waited when Levi told her to. So, the whole reason she was going to die was because Eleanor was mean. And that made her start sucking in the air very quickly. And then that made her start breathing very loudly and begin to cry.

By that time, Eleanor heard heavy breathing and snivels. She turned around and looked at the crying, very rigid, very pale, and very red-eyed Esmé. Eleanor rolled her eyes, shaking her head. "I told you not to look down," she snapped. "Levi, I think you might need to—" but Eleanor never finished because Esmé began to whimper and even screech a little, and Levi began quickly scooting closer.

"Shhh. I'm here. I'm here," Levi soothed. "It'll be fine."

And just then, in the midst of all the snivels, the eye rolling, and the scooting about, the branch next to them began to wobble and sway. "What's going on with that branch?" Eleanor whispered.

"It's just the wind blowing through," Levi answered.

"But I don't feel a breeze," Eleanor said, her voice rising a notch. "I see the branch move, but I don't feel a breeze."

And just then another branch—actually, one that was right next to them—moved and shuffled and kind of lifted straight up slightly. Esmé screamed. Eleanor froze. Levi sucked in a deep short breath.

"Branches don't move like that. It's got to be our imagination," Levi said, but his face drained of its color. They all scooted very, very close to the trunk of the tree as branches began to arch and twist, slither and slide toward them.

"Oh dear, oh dear, I don't like this one bit," Eleanor said, "and no, it's not my imagination!"

And suddenly, one of the curly limbs lifted straight up, creeping toward them like slow-moving tentacles on an octopus reaching through the water. And out of nowhere a gentle sweet voice asked,

"Is something in my hair? Just what is in my hair?"

All three cousins grabbed one another's hands and looked around in circles.

"Who said that?" Eleanor shrieked.

More branches moved and shuffled, tenacling closer and closer toward them, shifting and wiggling like fingers preparing to scratch a lice-filled head.

"You birdies need to settle down. It is quite unlike you to be so disorderly," the voice continued. "You're mussing my hair. And I spent all summer getting it just so." Branches continued sliding slowly toward the three cousins.

"Who's talking?" Levi shouted, whipping his head back and forth and around.

"Are there voices in my head? Why are there voices in my head? When did the birdies learn to talk again? Quite a conundrum, quite a conundrum! The birdies are talking again. Why it's been so long since I heard blue birdies talking. But you birdies must settle down and stop mussing my hair." The branches continued to move toward Levi, Eleanor, and Esmé, curling around as if preparing to touch them.

"We're not birds! We're not birds!" Levi shouted. "Stop!"

The branches stopped suddenly.

"Who said that? Who said to stop? Birdies never shout like that. They are too polite. Who are you? What are you doing? Why are you mussing my hair? I spent all summer getting it just so," said the soft voice.

"We're not trying to muss your hair!" Eleanor shouted.

"Who is talking?" Levi shouted.

"Who is asking?" the gentle voice asked.

"Us—we're asking!" Levi yelled.

"What is an *us* and a *we're*, and why are you in my hair?"

"We're, umm, people, and we are trying to find a way home," Eleanor said with a shrug as she met Levi's eyes with her own.

"And just where is home?"

"Earth?" Levi suggested.

"Tell me more," the soft voice continued.

"From a coastal town in—" Eleanor started to say.

"That doesn't help. Details please, details please," interrupted the voice.

"From behind the bronze door of Gramma's treehouse," Esmé shouted.

"The bronze door—oh my, oh my! Oh, that I understand," the gentle voice said. "Well, well, well, and just how did you get into my hair?"

Levi and Eleanor looked at each other, and after shrugging their shoulders, they attempted to explain a journey that neither of them understood. Unfortunately, they only ended up jumbling over each other's words and interrupting each other and making no sense at all.

It was Esmé who suddenly started telling the story of how they ended up sitting in the branches and mussing her hair. She skipped from one event to the next, filling in details from her perspective, putting the day in order as she remembered it: Gramma, cousins, treehouse, Addison and Claire get lost, running with Levi out the bronze door, Mean Eleanor, waterfall, Grizzles and Lola, signpost with arrows, More Mean Eleanor, mountain trail, rocky plateau, climbing huge tree, don't look down, and Even More Mean Eleanor—just want to go back to Gramma's house but have to find a guy named Oracle—and it's all worse because of Big Mean Eleanor.

Eleanor rolled her eyes. Esmé made an ugly face at Eleanor. Levi told them both to be good.

There was silence for a minute, and then the voice softened as the limbs and branches stilled their motion. "Oh, now I understand," the voice murmured. "Now I understand."

"And if you don't mind, who are you?" Levi asked, looking about in all directions.

"Well, Creatures from behind the Bronze Door," the voice continued. "It is so sad that you even need to ask. There was a time when you would have known and understood, but now even the birdies are forgetting. I will try to help you understand. Even then, you will not know. It is sufficient to say that I am an ancient tree of an ancient species from ancient times. And while I cannot get you home, perhaps I can help you to understand the path that will lead you there."

Eleanor looked hopelessly at Levi. "What in the world is this place? When we get home, I'm never ever going to doubt Gramma again—never ever."

"Hmmm," continued the tree, "where to begin? Where to begin?" What is the most understanding way? Hmm," the voice hummed. "Oh, I know. The oldest! Stand up!"

Levi looked at Eleanor; both sets of eyes widened with fear. He sucked in a deep breath, grabbed hold of a limb, and stood up. Though his legs wobbled and his knees knocked, Levi looked straight forward. "I am the oldest," he said, but his voice caught as he said it.

"What do you want from us?" Levi continued, squaring his shoulders and lifting his chin.

"I want nothing from you, Oldest Creature. It is you who asked me for help from me. If you want to find your way to the Oracle, there are things you must see so that you will know what you need to know. You, the oldest, will need to rise higher, climb more, up, up more and more.

"The others may wait where they are until the oldest gets back, but you mustn't muss my hair. I spent all summer getting it just so. And if you muss my hair too much, I will be left with a bald spot, and we would not want that now, would we?" The leaves on the tree jiggled a little.

"I think the tree just giggled," Eleanor said with a chuckle. "She thinks she made a joke." And the thought of a tree making a joke made them all smile—at least a little.

Esmé looked up into the towering branches of the tree; she grabbed Levi's leg.

"Don't go, Levi. Please stay here," Esmé pleaded.

Levi touched Esmé's hair, bent over, and whispered into her ear, "Ezzy, I have to try. Understand? It might help us get home. Can you be a good girl and stay with Eleanor, please? Eleanor does love you, Ezzy. She really does."

Esmé nodded, tears welling up in her eyes once more.

Levi's eyes met Eleanor's. "I have to take a chance," he said.

"I know," Eleanor replied, "but if anything goes wrong, yell, whistle, throw something—whatever works. I'll be watching and listening and ready for whatever. I know how to climb, and I'll be there." She sat down on the limb, wrapping her arm around Esmé, who scooted closer, accepting the embrace.

"Trust me, Little Creatures from beyond the Bronze Door, I know what I know. And since you do not know, the oldest needs to see so that the oldest will know and teach the others. He will return. Now climb, Oldest Creature from beyond the Bronze Door, climb."

And with that, Levi took a deep breath and grabbed the nearest limb. "Okay, here I go," he said as he began to climb. The voice kept urging him to go higher and even higher. And so, he did, climbing up and up until his breathing was deep and labored and his legs wobbled from exertion. One time, he glanced down, and his stomach twisted with such fear that he kept his eyes ever upward after that. And he continued up and up until the thin limbs snapped little snaps when he pushed against them. Finally, Levi had gone as high as he could go.

"Good enough, Oldest Creature from beyond the Bronze Door, good enough. Now, you will see and understand, but to understand, you must trust. The birdies trust and understand, and they always find home. You must trust me, Oldest Creature, so you can understand." And Levi nodded and swallowed. "Okay."

A small branch moved toward Levi, slithering toward his feet, wrapping around them, and continuing upward, encasing his legs, encircling his limbs with twigs and leaves, gliding up and around his waist. He stood paralyzed, gulping against the rising panic, watching as the shimmering leaves enclosed his body. Slowly, the twigs tightened their grip; and the branch lifted him, slowly moving up and out and away from the trunk of the tree. Levi clenched his eyes so tight that his face crunched and wrinkled, and he bit down on his lip so hard that he tasted blood. And he tried to trust; he really did try.

And after the limb had stretched as far as it could go, the tree spoke. "Now, you must open your eyes," murmured the soft voice. "It is time to trust, Oldest Creature from beyond the Bronze Door. I will hold you tight."

Levi sucked in huge gulps of air, shuddered, and clutched the branches and leaves encircling his waist. He slowly opened his eyes only to see that he was suspended, high in the air with only a tree limb and leaves and twigs keeping him from plunging to the depths below. His body tightened into little knots, and he whimpered and grabbed at the leaves and twigs. He panicked and froze, and his arms flailed about, seeking something to hold on to.

And it was then that one little limb slid up to his face and a little leaf tickled his cheek. "It is just fine, Oldest Creature. It is just fine. Trust and understand."

And so, Levi shut his eyes once more—gasping in and out, in and out—until finally, after he had mustered every bit of courage from every atom of every cell of his entire being, he was able to breathe almost normally. He slowly opened his eyes again.

And he looked around, and he looked up and down and into the distance and across the land and the rivers and the trees and the mountains and the villages. And it was all so beautiful and so boundless and so pure, and the sky was so blue that after a while, he forgot to be afraid, and he trusted; and he became so absorbed in it all that he became a tiny piece of what it was.

As he looked and thought and scrutinized and as he tried to understand, little flashes of ideas flickered in and out until finally a couple of thoughts stayed long enough for him to catch them. And then, other little flashes followed and combined until all the thoughts converged like little pieces of a jigsaw puzzle snapping together.

And so, it was that from that place high above the ground and being held by the limbs of an ancient tree of an ancient species from ancient times that Levi began to trust, and he began to understand as ideas gathered and took shape. And finally, Levi smiled.

"Now, do you understand, Oldest Creature from beyond the Bronze Door? Do you understand?" wondered the ancient tree. "The Oracle is out there, and you will find him, but he is not what you expect or where you expect," the tree murmured. "But do you understand?"

And at least in a little, tiny way, Levi knew that he did.

Chapter 36

Tilly, Brody, and Ivan: Crystals and Creatures

Tilly, Brody, and Ivan could not make their legs to keep moving; the crystals and gemstones, geodes, and colors were absolutely hypnotic. "Look at this place!" Brody muttered, staring about the room. "How much is all this worth? Can this even be real?"

"This is—my gosh! It's unbelievable!" Tilly muttered. "I feel like we landed inside a huge geode with every crystal and every jewel and every mineral all growing together. There are amethysts and quartzes and rubies and emeralds and topazes and sapphires, and it's like an explosion of glitters and crystals."

Ivan stood utterly spellbound; but finally, with a shake of his head, he cleared the stupor. "We really do have to keep going," he whispered, but even then, his feet refused to obey, and he stood there motionless a bit longer.

"Yes, yes, we do," Tilly muttered. But still, she hesitated, lingering until Ivan gave her a little push.

All three walked backward as they left the room, unable to stop looking. Finally, Ivan grabbed Tilly's arm, and they scrambled under the curved archway. Brody lingered for just a bit longer until Ivan yelled for him to catch up.

Now, it is true that Brody really did turn around to follow; but it is also true that as he turned, he just happened to notice the most beautiful purplish-blue crystal rock ever. And for some reason, and just out of nowhere, a little something kind of flickered inside his brain; it really was a strange little flicker—actually, more like a thought. But even though it was just a tiny, little flicker—a very, tiny, little thought—it grew almost instantaneously.

And then that flicker—that tiny thought actually—just darted right down out of his brain and into his arm and right down into his fingers. And as he turned, his fingers just kind of shot out and grabbed that most beautiful purplish-blue crystal that he had ever seen. And when a second little thought tried to tell him that grabbing the crystal was not a good thing to do, a third little thought in his brain assured him that it was just fine. Actually, his brain said something like "This'll teach 'em" and "We deserve this crystal for all the mean stuff they put us through."

Now, you must also understand that when his hand grabbed that crystal, it broke off quite easily; and since his brain had already told his fingers that what he was doing was just fine, his fingers somehow decided that they might as well grab some more. You see (according to his brain), he could sell the crystals and make enough money for all of them to get home. Or he could sell the crystals after he got home and be very wealthy indeed. And furthermore (according to his brain), since there were so many crystals in the cavern, it would be a good lesson for those Giant Gnomes or Biglings or whatever they were to learn how to share. And so, before he made it out of that room, Brody had grabbed (some might say he stole) an entire handful of green, red, yellow, and purplish-blue crystals, which he quickly stuck into his back pockets as he scurried to catch up with Tilly and Ivan.

Now, unfortunately, Brody was so busy stuffing crystals into his pockets and catching up with the others that he did not notice the tiny heads peeking out from the holes left from the broken crystals. And he did not see little slithery things lunge forward, pop out, and follow him with their eyes. He did not notice when they ran down the walls and sniffed the air and followed him. If he had just known any of those things, he would not have broken those crystals from off the wall; but you see, he really, really, really didn't know any of those things. Neither did his brain. And so, he turned and ran under the curved archway with beautiful crystals in his pockets and dreams of riches in his head.

Chapter 37

Tilly, Brody, and Ivan: Twisted Ankles and Nasty Critters

Sporadically placed lanterns hanging in niches cast gloomy shadows and spooky images across the walls and the cobbled floor as Tilly, Brody, and Ivan hurried through cavern passageways, searching for a way out. And when the corridor curved around a bend, a faint draft of air swirled about their feet. "We must be getting closer!" Ivan yelled. "I think I felt a breeze. Hurry!"

Tilly rushed across the uneven cavern floor, dragging her hands along the jagged grotto walls so she could catch herself if she stumbled. Her hand slid across a wet slimy bump on the wall; she jumped, muffling a little scream.

"Ooooh, gross," she said, slowing to a stop, grimacing while flipping her hand about and then wiping it on her pants.

"What happened?" Brody asked, slowing to a stop beside her.

"Ugh, yuck, I touched something slimy. I know I'm just being jumpy, but it felt so gross!"

shzshzhz

Wait! Did you hear that?" Tilly asked, leaning forward with her hand cupping her ear.

"Hear what?" Brody asked.

"That sound. Listen!"

shzshz

"That—did you hear that?" Tilly whispered, jerking her head from side to side, squinting her eyes, peering through the shadows and gloom.

"What's it sound like?" Brody asked.

"A sizzle sound—like a snake or a hiss or something."

Brody leaned forward, listening. "I don't hear—"

shzshz

Brody looked around. "Oh, Tilly, you're just jumpy! It's just water trickling down the walls or the wind blowing through. Ivan already said he felt a breeze."

shzshzshzshzshz

Tilly jumped and tripped, rolling her ankle as she stumbled against the cavern wall. "Ooouucch, ouch, ouch!" she howled, hopping about on one foot.

Ivan, finally noticing that Tilly and Brody were lagging behind, hurried back. "What's going on?" he asked. "I think we're close. Hurry up, will ya?" It was then that he noticed Tilly's grimace. "Tilly, what's wrong?"

"Oh, nothing really," Tilly said. "I touched something gross and heard a strange noise. I jumped and rolled my ankle. Brody's helping me. But don't worry, I'm coming. I want out of this place as much as either of you."

She gingerly stepped down on her foot only to stumble instead. "Oouchhh, ouch, ouch!" she yelled. "I think I twisted my ankle! Ooooh, not now! We don't have time for this!"

Ivan looked about impatiently, puffing his cheeks in and out. "Oh boy, oh boy! Well, listen. Tilly, take a minute to check out that ankle. Brody, you stay here with Tilly. I'll go around that bend and see how much farther we need to go to get out of here. I'll be right back." Ivan turned and hurried around the bend.

Leaning against the wall and pulling her shoe off, Tilly began rubbing her ankle. "It's too dark to see anything. We just need to get outta here," she said, testing another step. "Ouch! Ouch! Ouch! Brody, I'm going to have to lean on you."

Brody offered his shoulder, and Tilly bent down to grab her shoe.

SHZSHZSHZSHZ

She jolted, her eyes darting back and forth in the dim light.

"Did you hear it that time, Brody?" she whispered, her hand over her mouth.

Brody nodded quietly. "Ya, I heard it, and that's not water, Tilly, and it's not the wind either. Let's get outta here! Slip that shoe on, put your arm around me, and let's go! Come on! Hurry!"

Tilly's fingers trembled as she pulled her shoe over her foot. "I'll tie it later," she whispered. She felt a little tingle on her back, a little itch. The reached to scratch it. It moved.

She shifted her shoulders, rolling the muscles of her back. Something slithered up her spine. "Brody," she whispered, "do you see something on my back? I think I felt something." Brody leaned forward, grabbed her collar, and started to peep down the back of her shirt just as she felt another quick slither, heard a *SHZSHZSHZ*, and felt a snap as a sting of fire surged through her spine and rushed into her head.

"Ahhhh!" she screamed, falling to the floor, cracking her head against the jagged rocks. Brody grabbed for her, but the rock edge sliced into her skin before he could catch her. It slashed her shoulder as she slipped down to the cavern floor.

"Tilly?" Brody shrieked as he bent over her, studying her face.

She lay there, blood spurting, eyes rolled back, and mouth open. Brody plopped down, grabbed her head, and laid it in his lap. He screamed for Ivan, "Ivan, Ivan, where are you? Ivan! Hurry!"

Tears gushed down Brody's cheeks as he rocked back and forth, cradling Tilly's head and pushing her blonde hair away from her face. "Ivan! Ivan!" Brody yelled over and over as he shook Tilly and tried to revive her. "Ivaaaan! Ivaaaan!"

And then he heard it—or saw it—he never remembered which was first. But a little orange head at the end of a long snakelike body with itty-bitty legs slithered at him and stood on its hind feet glaring at him. Eyes between boy and creature met.

SHZSHZSHZ

Brody backed up a little, holding tight to Tilly and dragging her across the rocky floor with him.

SHZSHZSHZ

Brody kicked his foot at the creature, but the creature snarled and continued staring straight into Brody's eyes.

SHZSHZSHZSHZ

Brody kicked again and again, scooting backward, Tilly's head in his lap, her limp body scraping across the rocky floor with each shuffle.

SHZSHZSHZ

Brody kicked. The creature darted from side to side; each kick missed. Brody jerked back one more time and felt the cave wall against his back. He slowly gently laid Tilly's head on the floor. He slowly, slowly, slowly lifted his leg to stand and kick better. The little creature grimaced and smiled, leaping forward and slipping into Brody's pant leg. Brody felt the slither. He shook his leg, screaming, "Ivvaann!"

SHZSHZSHZ

A snap and a burst of fire raced up his back and into his head, and he slid down, cracking his head as he hit the rocks on the passageway floor.

Ivan heard Brody's desperate screams. Rushing back, he rounded the bend just as Brody slid down and cracked his head. Ivan ran to them, kneeling over them and placing his ear over Tilly's heart and then over Brody's. He saw blood gushing from Tilly. "Oh my gosh, oh my gosh, oh my gosh!" he whispered over and over with his hands over his mouth. "What happened? What happened? What now? What now? What now."

He looked back and forth, up and down. He tried to move Tilly, but he knew he couldn't lift her limp body. He tried to move Brody, but Brody was heavier and bigger than Tilly. He turned in several circles, bent over and felt their hearts, touched their faces, stood up, sat down, looked back and forth, pursed his lips, and finally tasted salty tears that were sliding down his face.

"What now? What now? What now?" he cried out over and over. Finally, he looked down at Tilly and Brody and began running down the rocky corridor.

Chapter 38

Tilly, Brody, and Ivan: Ivan's Decision

A dim lantern flame cast a shadow across Jeslue's face. He stirred, turning over. A creaking, a rustling, something crawling in his bed; and suddenly he startled from sleep, bolted upright, and knocked something off the bed. He looked over the edge of his bed, reached down, and grabbed an Ivan from off the floor.

"What in the world?" Jeslue burst out. "How'd you get out of—"

"Jeslue! I-I-I need your hel-help! Now!"

"Please, please!" Ivan stammered between sobs and more than a few tears.

Jeslue held Ivan in the air; curiously considered the tears, the sobs, and the broken words; and then he drew Ivan to his chest, patting his back. "What's the matter, little fellow? What's wrong?"

Ivan sputtered and gasped, attempting to catch his breath. He wiggled around, pushing himself far enough away from the furry chest so he could look directly into Jeslue's face. Between his sniffles, he told the story as quickly as he could make the words tumble out.

"I stole the key to the cart-cage padlock, and we tried to escape."

"You what? How? Never mind, just go on."

"We only meant to find a way home. We were going through a corridor. Tilly hurt her ankle. I went to check for a way out. I heard Brody yelling. I ran back and found Brody and Tilly lying on the ground, and they won't wake up. They won't wake up, Jeslue. Please help us—PLEASE! I promise to stay here with you forever—if you just help Tilly and Brody. I promise to stay."

Jeslue frowned. "Wait, hold on. Let me make sure I have this. You stole my key and opened the padlock?"

"Yes."

"You were running away."

"Yes."

"Tilly hurt her ankle?"

"Yes."

"Brody was yelling for you?"

"Yes,"

"Where is Tilly? Where is Brody?"

"She's lllyying there with blood aaaall over her," Ivan stuttered and sobbed. "Brody is too."

Jeslue sucked in a deep breath. "You peoples are naughty little creatures," he said, shaking his head. "Come on, let's go."

"You'll help us?" Ivan's sobs calmed at little; he sniffed, wiping his nose with the sleeve of his shirt. "You'll help us? Thank you, thank you! Come on, I'll show you where they are!"

Jeslue stopped, searching Ivan's eyes. "I know where they are." He sighed. "We'll take care of Tilly and Brody first, and we'll talk about the rest later. Deal?" Ivan nodded and sniffled again.

They rushed to the workroom; Jeslue jerked drawers open, rummaging through them, slamming doors open and shut, pulling bottles and jars out, searching through the back of cabinets. "Here it is!" he finally shouted, grabbing a huge shiny green bottle. "Hold on!" Jeslue yelled, flipping Ivan onto his back. Jeslue took off running with Ivan bouncing around like a child getting a horsey ride.

Jeslue sprinted down a long passageway through a workroom; straight through the sparkling, glittering, amazing, crystal room;

past the dimly lit lanterns casting shadows and gloom; and, finally, beside Brody and Tilly who lay still and motionless on the cold stone floor. Jeslue bent down on one knee; Ivan slipped off his back.

Jeslue bent down, picking Tilly up. Her head flopped back and sideways. He sat down, laying her head in his lap. "Her jaws will be clenched and tight," Jeslue said. "Ivan, pry them open for me. I don't want to hurt her with my big hands."

Ivan pressed his fingers between Tilly's lips and teeth, forcing them open. With his teeth, Jeslue twisted the cap off the shiny green bottle and then spit the cork onto the floor. "Keep her mouth open," he said as he began pouring thick green syrup into Tilly's mouth. Suddenly Tilly sputtered and wheezed and sputtered again. Her eyelids began to wiggle and flutter; she sucked in deep breaths, opened her eyes, and sat straight up face-to-face with Jeslue and screamed, "Aahhhahh!"

"Shhh, shhh," Ivan shushed her. "It's okay. I'm here."

"Oh, my head." She gasped, grabbing both temples and pressing.

Jeslue laid Tilly down and picked Brody up. Ivan stuck his fingers between Brody's lips and teeth and pried Brody's mouth open; the thick green syrup stuff went in. Brody wheezed, sputtered, and fluttered; sucked in breaths; opened his eyes; and sat straight up, looking straight into Jeslue's face. "Aahahah!" he yelled. He grabbed both sides of his head, groaning.

"Peoples sure do scream a lot," Jeslue muttered.

Jeslue poured some of the thick green stuff on his hands and wiped it on the walls, and he rubbed a little more on Tilly's ankle. He propped Tilly and Brody up against the cave wall, watching and waiting. Finally, they both shuddered, stopped holding their heads, and returned to their normal color instead of the grayish-green color they had while lying on the floor. Then they all just sat there and looked around and at one another until Ivan finally broke the silence. "Well, what now?" He sighed. "I gave my word, and I always keep my word."

Chapter 39

Tilly, Brody, and Ivan: Truth, Greed, and Gain

Jeslue sat with his back against the cavern wall. Pulling his knees to his chest, he stared directly at each of the cousins. "Just which one of you stole the gems from the crystal room?" he asked, his voice colder than they had ever heard it.

Glancing back and forth, Tilly and Ivan both shrugged, shaking their heads. Brody, however, stared at the ground; his face grew very warm and turned a reddish color as he puffed his cheeks in and out, pursing his lips. When he finally lifted his head, he averted his gaze, looking at anything except the three sets of eyes scrutinizing him.

"Me," he finally confessed. "I did it. But . . . but . . . I didn't think it would matter much. I mean there are so many! Who would even notice? How could anyone even—"

He glanced around, hoping for support or at least understanding, but then he stopped and looked straight up and into Jeslue's eyes. "I was wrong, and I am sorry." He reached into his pockets, pulling the crystals out. "I really am sorry," he said.

Jeslue held out his hand, and Brody dropped the crystals into it.

"You know," Jeslue said, "slizzards guard the crystals. That wasn't very smart."

"You mean those horrible things that bit us? They're called slizzards? Well, how was I supposed to know about slizzards?" Brody countered defensively, holding his palms up and looking at Tilly and Ivan; but he stopped again. "I know, I know. I shouldn't have taken them anyway. But at the time I told myself that it didn't matter since you had tried to capture us and steal us and keep us in cages."

Jeslue looked confused; he shook his head. "But . . . but . . . but I wasn't capturing you," he said. "What do you mean? I was keeping you safe in the cart-cage until I could build your house. I didn't want any bad Biglings to catch you. I thought you were lost and scared. I thought you were just scared of me like the peoples in all the stories are always scared. Besides, you are real, so I wanted to take care of you," he said. His voice cracked, and his bottom lip quivered as he bent forward. "What do you mean steal you?"

Ivan cocked his head to the side. He shuffled closer to Jeslue.

"Stories? What stories do you mean, Jeslue?" Ivan asked.

"Well," Jeslue started slowly, "you know, the stories that our mamas and papas told us when we're little. The make-believe stories about peoples who show up out of nowhere and hide behind lanterns and peek into our caverns and sneak around and steal food and run off into the woods. Some of the kidlings get scared and think that peoples are hiding under their beds, and they want to sleep with their mamas and papas. But when they get scared, the oldsters just laugh and say that peoples aren't real—that peoples are make-believe—and that there's no such thing, that they are only stories made up long, long ago. But the stories with peoples were always my favorites."

Tilly, Brody, and Ivan all just stood there with their mouths open like they were getting ready to talk; but then they just closed their mouths and scratched their heads and looked back and forth at one another with furrowed brows.

"Jeslue," Ivan finally asked, shifting closer and looking straight up into Jeslue's face, "are you saying that when you were little, your parents told you that people are make-believe?"

Jeslue nodded.

"So you thought people were just storybook characters—like fairies or something like that?" Tilly asked.

Jeslue shook his head slowly. "No, not like fairies. Fairies are almost impossible to find, but you can find them sometimes," he said, tapping his lip and looking up, thinking. "No, not like fairies, more like—ooh, I know—more like puppies and kittens." Jeslue chuckled. "In our stories, peoples had these furry little things called puppies and kittens. They were so cute, and they follow the peoples around!"

"But puppies are real," Brody said very slowly.

"Puppies are real?" Jeslue asked, his mouth dropping open. "Are kittens real too?"

Tilly, Brody, and Ivan all nodded.

"Wait? Hold on!" Tilly broke in. "Did you say that fairies are real?"

"Well, of course, they are!" Jeslue laughed, but then he stopped when he noticed their confused expressions. "Did your mamas and papas tell you that fairies were make-believe?" he asked.

Tilly, Brody, and Ivan all nodded and glanced at one another.

"Maybe we should talk," Tilly said slowly, and the cousins sat down in a semicircle on the rocky cavern floor facing Jeslue.

It was Ivan who finally asked, "If you thought people were make-believe, why weren't you more surprised when you saw us?"

"Well," Jeslue began, "Mama told me a secret family story when I was very young. She said that long, long ago, her father's father had seen peoples walking in the woods, holding lanterns, but when he tried to pick them up, they got scared and ran away. But when he tried to tell his friends that he had seen some peoples, they all laughed at him and said he needed to wear a pair of silly shoelets. But Mama believed him, and she always said that peoples just might be true."

"What else did your Mama say, Jeslue?" Ivan finally asked.

"Well," Jeslue continued, "Mama said that if peoples were true, they might just be using the lanterns to find their way home, and when they steal food and hide under beds, it might be because they are scared and hungry and lost."

Jeslue looked at the cousins and sighed. "I always hoped that peoples might be real, and I dreamed that if ever I ever did see one, I would build it a house with crystals and I would put lanterns inside so the people wouldn't be scared or have to run away or steal food."

Jeslue's voice cracked. "But now I know that it's not like the stories at all. Peoples run away 'cause they don't like us." Jeslue's face kinda crumpled, and his bottom lip kinda quivered, and then one very big tear rolled down his nose and plopped to the ground. He turned his face so the cousins couldn't see any more tears roll down his cheeks, which they did.

"Oh, Jeslue, oh, we didn't understand," Ivan said, and he stood up and wrapped his arms as far around Jeslue as his arms could stretch, and he laid his head against Jeslue's furry chest. "It's not that we don't like you or want to be with you. It's that we went through a door at our Gramma's, and we stumbled into this place, and we really have to find a way home because our families will be looking for us. Don't be sad, Jeslue, please. You've been wonderful to us, and if we didn't have to go home, I'd love to stay with you in the house you build. We didn't understand, Jeslue."

And then Tilly wrapped her arms around Jeslue, and she stood up on tippy toe, and she kissed Jeslue's cheek over and over until Jeslue smiled and blushed and told her that that was really quite enough.

And then Brody wrapped his arms around Jeslue and buried his face into Jeslue's chest and said over and over that he was so sorry and that he would never ever steal again and that he hadn't understood at all.

And finally, they all began smiling and chuckling and talking, and they all sat down very close to one another on the rocky cavern floor, and they chatted for quite a bit of time and even more than that. And the cousins told Jeslue that Brody had a puppy named Otis who got so excited when he saw people that he snarled his teeth into a grin and wiggled his behind so hard that he almost knocked the people over. And Jeslue laughed and said he wished he could have a puppy because puppies sounded much more fun than fairies.

Then, Jeslue told the cousins how he had caught a fairy the summer before, but he had let it go because it just didn't seem right to keep it in the jar.

And finally, when each of them understood what they needed to understand, and after each of them felt contented and soft and warm inside, they knew it was time to leave. Jeslue stood up and dusted himself off. "I don't know how to get you home," he said, "but in the old stories, the Oracle always knows what to do."

"How do we find him?" Ivan asked.

"Well, in the picture books, there's a signpost that points to the Oracle, but there's also a picture of the Snow Village. The Snow Village is up in the mountain. Maybe you could start there. I don't know if an Oracle lives there. Those are old stories. But somebody in the village might know."

And he pulled his marker out of his pocket and drew a little map. "Follow this until you get out of the valley. After that, stop and ask for directions. But stay hidden until you are on the other side of the mountain," he said. "If anyone sees you—"

"Oh, we get that part," Tilly said, interrupting. "We will stay hidden."

Suddenly, Jeslue reached into his pocket again. "Oh wait, one more thing," he said, drawing crystals out of his pocket and handing them to Brody. "You might need to sell these to get home," he said, smiling. "If you don't need to sell them, you can divide them equally among yourselves when you do get home."

Brody nodded and looked at the crystals and then back up at Jeslue. "Thank you," he whispered.

"These are amazing," said Tilly. "We won't sell them unless there is no other way. We'll try to keep them forever. They will always remind us of you, Jeslue."

"Jeslue," Ivan suddenly said, "I'm going make you a promise—and I always try to keep my promises. Jeslue, if I ever find a way home, and if I am ever able to find a way back here, I promise I'm gonna bring you a puppy!"

"And I'll help him!" shouted Brody.

"Me too," Tilly agreed.

Jeslue threw his head back, and he laughed and laughed. Then he reached down, and picking Ivan up, he hugged him and hugged him even more. "You're such a cute little fellow," he said, still jiggling from laughing so hard and hoping so much.

And after Jeslue set Ivan down, he picked Brody up; and then he picked Tilly up, hugging them both and squeezing them just a little too tight if truth be told. "I suppose I should say good-bye. I've got to hurry back now and find those slizzards and put 'em back before my parents wake up," Jeslue said with a smile; but his voice quavered, and the cousins knew that he just didn't want to say good-bye. And so, after patting each on the head one more time, Jeslue waved good-bye with his very big hands and then turned, slipping into the shadows before the cousins could see the tears rolling down his cheeks.

And as Ivan stood watching Jeslue hurry away through the gloomy corridor, his chest heaved, and his eyes turned a little red around the edges. He looked at the floor so that Tilly and Brody could not see his face crumple. Brody stood, rubbing the crystals between his fingers and sniffing very loudly more than a few times, and Tilly stood with her fingers over her mouth and a huge lump in her throat.

And finally, when he knew his voice would not crack, Ivan reminded them that it was, indeed, time to go. They turned and pushed against the big round wooden door and walked out into the night. They drew in deep breaths of fresh air, gazed up at the millions and millions of twinkly stars, and stared in wonder at the lanterns hanging from every tree as far as they could see.

Chapter 40

Gramma: Bugs and Things

Gramma sat in her blue rocking chair nibbling on one peanut butter cookie after another, drumming her fingers on the arm of the rocking chair and chewing on various fingernails all at the same time. The creaking and groaning of the floorboards kept time with the ticking and tocking of the clocks as she rocked back and forth.

Her eyes flittered from one timepiece to another, finally stopping on the tall slim grandfather clock in the corner. She quit rocking and sat motionlessly, her head cocked to the side, listening to the ticking of the second hand. Pressing her fingers against the inside of her wrist, she checked her pulse and stared at the clock again. Suddenly, jumping out of the rocking chair, she hurried over to the silver shelf and bent forward, staring into the tiny silver hourglass and watching the crystal sand slowly drizzle through the middle.

She plopped down in her blue rocking chair, rocked some more, chewed some more, glanced at clocks some more, and drummed her fingers on the arm of the chair some more. After finishing another cookie and brushing the crumbs off her lap, she began muttering, *What to do? What to do? What to do? What to do?"*

She patted her fingers against her cheeks and lips and then flopped her head back against the top rung on the back of the rocker, staring at the ceiling, rocking slowly. Suddenly her eyes flew open, and she bolted straight upright. She leaned forward, studying the mosaic compass tiled into the floor.

Slapping her palm on her forehead, she shook her head, rolled her eyes, and smiled. She scurried to the wood cabinet (the one marked Emergency, Catastrophe, and/or Armageddon Supplies in white tape). She flung it open and began rummaging through the disorganized clutter.

At the back of the cabinet—behind the plastic bowls, the duct tape, the expired jars of unopened mayonnaise, five jars of self-stir peanut butter, and a few cans of green beans—she found the three-quart glass jars she was looking for. She found the flathead screwdriver in the miscellaneous drawer under that cabinet, buried under the extra napkins, the plastic silverware, and the wooden spoons.

She punched three holes into each jar lid with the screwdriver and rushed outside. Just a while later, the peacock door flew open, and she rushed back inside carrying the three jars; each one was filled with bunches of flickering lightning bugs, a couple of iridescent dragonflies, a few butterflies, and a tiny blue egg. *This oughta do it,* Gramma muttered to herself.

Reaching into her pocket, she drew out her brass key ring, sorted through the keys, selected the sparkly silver key, and scurried over to the silver door. Sucking in a few deep breaths and bracing herself for an onslaught of wind, she unlocked the door and pushed her way outside.

A minute or so later, the door reopened, and she came stumbling back in with the wind at her practically knocking her over. She grabbed the second jar of bugs and butterflies, selected the green key, pushed her way out, and with wildly tousled hair and erratic movements came tripping back across the threshold as the wind forced her inside.

And finally, she grabbed the third jar, slipped the third key in the lock, pushed her way out the bronze door, and then came floundering back in. She placed her back against the door and heaved and pushed against it until it closed.

She patted her hair in place, straightened her sweater, and after grabbing a chocolate chip cookie from the wicker picnic basket, plopped back down in the blue rocking chair. Glancing around at the clocks once more, she sighed deeply, smiled gently, and began rocking back and forth, back and forth to the time of the ticking and tocking of the clocks.

Chapter 41

Grizzles and Lola: Growls and Twirls

"Grizzles, dear, it's time," Lola said, stepping across the threshold.

Grizzles slouched in an old wooden chair bending over the table, flipping through the tattered pages of an old worn book. He rolled his shoulders, popping and cracking his neck. "I know, I know," he growled. "I saw the lanterns flare."

Lola slipped over to him; bending forward, she gently kissed the top of his head while kneading his stiff shoulders. He snarled a grizzly kind of snarl.

"Why, oh why, oh why? Why not just eat 'em and get it over with? My friends could have a feast."

"Oohhh, Griiizzles," Lola countered, "you know we have promises to keep! These are not edible children. You know that. They were trying to help the others, and that is very sweet, you know."

"Yes, but what caused the first ones to leave? We can't help the ones you have a shining for without helping the original ones who were very bad indeed. They should have stayed put," Grizzles grumbled, his raspy voice betraying his contempt. He scratched at the sides of his face with his long yellowed curling talons; little flakes of dirty skin and old whiskers floated in the air. He pushed his chair back, scraping the legs against the stone floor of the cabin, and looked up, staring directly at Lola.

"Oh, all right," he complained, "I suppose I can. But why, oh why, oh why didn't they stay put?" Slowly, his squinty eyes narrowed, almost disappearing into his wrinkled face. "Why, Lola, you are all lit up today," he gruffled. "You really are lovely when you are lit like that. Almost makes it worth it." Lola turned slightly red and looked down at the floor, but she smiled ever so sweetly just the same. "Oh, Grizzles, dear, you are so sweet."

He lumbered toward the door. "Well, come on, come on," he growled. "Let's get this over with."

"I'll be right behind you," Lola said, waving a dismissive hand at Grizzles. "You go ahead. I have a couple tiny little details to take care of before I go."

After hobbling and wobbling to the field, Grizzles stood gazing up at the hills, at the waterfall, and the mountains beyond. Creaking and popping and groaning, he slowly lowered himself down until he sat on the ground in the midst of the overgrown grasses. He hunched forward, rolling his head from side to side; his white curls tousled wildly as gusts of wind blew across the meadow.

He rolled his shoulders in circles and slowly began writhing and thrashing, growling and groaning as his ancient hideous face contorted and wrinkled. He bent forward, clawing at the dirt with his long yellowed talons. He raised his hideous head to the sky, sniffing with his huge bulbous nose, snapping his teeth together, and bearing them with snarling lips and puffing cheeks. Finally, he howled a long cruel guttural howl, and he bayed and heaved even more and more until the howl became one long piteous reverberation of echoes ricocheting from hill to mountain and back again like the unrelenting rumbling of thunder rebounding on and on and on and over and beyond.

And in the hills and in the mountains, wolves perked their ears and lifted their heads; and they joined in the howling and baying and growling as each picked up the echoes and added their own howls and growls to it, passing the message from one to another on and on and on. And the wolves trotted out from dens and caves and stood beside the rivers, and they sniffed at the air, and they began following the scent that only they understood.

And when Grizzles heard the growling echoes bouncing off the mountainsides, he heaved a great sigh; and lifting back up, he straightened himself into his own hunched form. He snarled and snapped and shuddered, and he hobbled and wobbled back to the cabin.

But when he reached the threshold, he did not go inside; instead, he turned, gazing back across the field, watching Lola move toward the signpost at the far corner of the opposite meadow. The wind caught her skirt, and the blue-and-purple silken layers flowed and swirled as she walked. She swung an old lantern in rhythm to her steps, and the flame flickered as she strode along.

Grizzles tilted his head, watching her movements. And he smiled gently. "Don't be gone too long, my dear," he muttered under his breath. "I will miss you." And Lola, somehow sensing his gaze, turned; and her eyes met his, and she smiled a very sweet, wistful smile. She touched her fingers to her lips and blew a kiss to Grizzles. He reached up, pretending to catch it. He snatched at the air with his gnarled hands and laid his hand on his cheek while patting his heart to let her know he understood. He blew a kiss back to her. And she pretended to catch his kiss and laid it against her heart. And then, smiling again, she turned and continued walking across the field, swinging the lantern at her side until she reached the signpost.

She stood there in silence for a minute or so, looking about. After hanging the lantern on a little hook under the bronze arrow, she stood watching the flame flicker and dance in the glass globe. She stepped onto the path. Gazing up at the darkening sky, she drew in a very, very deep breath and began to sing a very melancholy ancient song with deep mournful sounds, something like the tune of an old spiritual or perhaps a tune about somebody wanting to find their way home or maybe like an old refrain about walking a lonesome valley all by yourself.

And as she sang, the breeze grew more forceful, and the blue-and-purple silken layers swirled about her even more.

As her song ended, she raised onto the very tips of her toes. Stretching her arms high above her head and touching her fingertips together, she slowly and rhythmically began to sway and spiral within the wavering pulse of the wind.

As she twirled, the layers of her skirts began wrapping around her legs and then around her body. She sucked in more air, twirling and spinning around and around and around faster and faster until it was impossible to see where the silken layers ended and where Lola began. After a bit, and quite abruptly, little bits of blue and purple seemed to flick off the bottom of her silken layers of skirt and float up into the air. And then more and more layers flew off until bits of shining blues and purples were scattered and floating all about her.

But those bits did not filter to the ground. Instead, they swirled and bounced about in the air—little bits of blue and purple and iridescent specks suspended and whirling in the air as if Lola was the center of a cyclone in the midst of chaos. And the more bits that flew from her skirts, the faster she spun until Lola was a spinning streak with hundreds and hundreds of flickering, pulsing bits of light and color flickering about, like the embers of a bonfire sparking into the air.

There was a whirring and snap; and suddenly, just like that, where Lola had been, nothing was. And in the place where she had been, hundreds of flickering fireflies lit the sky, and whole bunches of iridescent dragonflies drifted here and there, flying around the signpost; and in the midst all of that flickering and drifting and darting, innumerable beautiful butterflies hovered, languidly flapping their purple wings.

From the threshold of the old ramshackle cabin, Grizzles watched as the fireflies and the purple and blue butterflies rose into the air and flew away, as tiny flickers and tiny lights sparkled and fluttered through the evening sky heading in the same directions that the silver, bronze and green arrows pointed.

Chapter 42

Claire and Addison: Another Journey

They stood in silence with their faces tilted up and their eyes closed, soaking in the beams of soft sunshine. And after a while—after the warmth had soaked in and after their jumbled feelings had calmed—they turned around, scrutinizing each other's faces just to make sure that they were still who they thought they should be. Once they were content that everything was back to normal, or at least as close to normal as could be expected after escaping all those mirrors and clocks, they turned to consider their setting.

"This is so confusing and weird. The Clockmaker told us to find the Oracle. Why didn't he just tell us how to get back the treehouse? What's going on?" Addison asked as she shaded her eyes, looking around in all directions.

"We should be able to find the water by going west. If we're close to the treehouse, everybody will be looking for us by now, and the water is one place they'd go. Let's keep the idea of finding an Oracle in mind just in case there's something that we don't understand," Claire said. She grew silent, but suddenly her face lit up. "Addie, even if things are strange, everything is going to be just fine. I don't know what happened, but things will eventually get back to normal."

Addison nodded. "Let me guess. You saw our families with us in the mirrors."

"Yes, I did! And that can only mean one thing: we will get home just fine," Claire said.

"Well, you're probably right," Addison replied. "But there might be other possibilities. I mean, what if the mirrors were only showing one version of our lives? What happens if we make changes now? What if the mirrors were showing the life we would have led if we had not gone down the slide? And if we already made changes by going down the slide, what happens then? I mean, will the mirrors change if we change? If we have choices, can life be predestined? Therefore—"

"Oh my gosh! Stop already!" Claire laughed. "Let's worry about the parallel universes or the butterfly effect or the string theory after we get home. Right now, let's just figure out which direction we should go in."

"You're right." Addison smiled. "And it is nice to know that the mirrors showed us being back home. Remember, the Clockmaker said we'll forget the stories except for a little déjà vu here and there. So I guess we'll never know anyway."

"It's so weird." Claire sighed. "Things are already getting fuzzy. It's like when you take a test at school, and you forget the questions as soon as the test is over."

"Well, first things first, any ideas for finding the coastal waters?" Addison asked.

Claire studied the field they were standing in. "I got nothing," she said, "except that cobblestone path over there seems to go in the direction of the setting sun, which should lead us west and back to the water."

"Yup, that's the only thing that makes sense at all," Addison agreed. "Let's go that way."

And once they had decided on a plan, they both felt somehow better and lighter. "It's you and me, kid," Claire said, pointing straight at Addison and then back to herself. "Let's follow the yellow brick road and see where it takes us!"

"You watch way too many movies." Addison chuckled, shaking her head.

And with that, Claire drew her elbow through Addison's; and together they walked across the grass, stepped onto the cobblestone path, and (even though they would never admit to such a thing) began giggling and skipping down the cobblestone path the same way they had when they were very, very young. Unfortunately, the cobblestone path just kept going and going; and when nothing seemed familiar, they began to feel rather deflated and a little worried.

"The sun is too high in the sky," Claire said after a while. "Wasn't it getting late when we went down the slide?"

Addison frowned and nodded. "Maybe we should just sit down for a bit and think about this. It's been a long day. It can't hurt to just rest and think for a minute."

And so, they sat down on the cobblestone path; and after a bit, they lay back on the grass and closed their eyes, letting the warm sun fall on their faces. They tried to think of anything that might give them a clue, but nothing made any sense.

It was about that time that Claire felt something tickling her nose and Addison felt something fluttering on her eyelid. When the tickling and fluttering didn't stop, both girls popped up to see what was going on. It was then that they realized they were surrounded by blue and purple butterflies fluttering and floating all about them and into the trees. "Ah, look at this!" Claire exclaimed. "A butterfly must have landed on my nose!" Claire giggled.

"Well, I had one kiss my eyelid." Addison laughed. "Come on, I wanna get a closer look. We just have to make sure to keep the cobblestone path in sight."

"I've never seen so many beautiful butterflies in one place." Claire agreed, "I would like to see if there are more in those trees."

And with that, both girls stood up, stepped off the cobblestone path, and began chasing butterflies.

Chapter 43

Claire and Addison: Butterflies, Dragonflies, and Wolves

They sat on a stump in the middle of a grassy field. There was nothing around them except grass—nothing at all—just grass and the stump. Claire sat with her head down, her elbows on her knees, her forehead pressed against her palms, shaking her head back and forth and occasionally kicking the ground. Addison kept gazing around in circles.

Throwing her hands in the air, Claire shot up and began pacing. "Why, oh why, did we leave the cobblestone path? Now, we're lost, and for what? To chase a couple of stupid butterflies?" She flicked the back of her hand at Addison. "You and your bright ideas!"

"Claire, you can blame me all you want for this little catastrophe," Addison snapped. "But, Claire, we didn't go far. We never left the field. This doesn't make any sense. We stepped off the cobblestone path, but we never left the field," Addison continued. And she just stood there chewing on the inside of her cheek, looking down at the ground, shaking her head.

Harsh words were sitting on Claire's tongue, fighting to burst out; but just as she opened her mouth to let them fly out, she glanced over and noticed Addison's downcast eyes. A tiny nagging voice reminded Claire that she was the original cause of their predicament, so instead of spewing the words that were fighting to get out, she just shook her head and gritted her teeth and kicked the ground a few more times until she stubbed her toe. Then she started hopping around on one foot and grumbling quite harshly even more.

But it was at that very moment, as Claire was hopping on one foot and Addison was standing with downcast eyes and a very confused expression, that another beautiful purple butterfly floated in between them and just kept gliding around and up and down.

And then a dragonfly with iridescent wings flitted around on the ground at their feet. Claire was so irritated and Addison was so frustrated that neither of them paid the butterfly or the dragonfly any attention at all. In fact, Claire even swatted at the butterfly; but instead of floating away, the purple butterfly landed on the stump where Claire had been sitting and the dragonfly hovered in the air, its wings shimmering in the sunlight.

After a while, another particularly large indigo butterfly floated in front of Addison's face. She grew silent, watching it flutter about. "You know, Claire," she said after a while with a hesitant smile, "Think about it. Since we are totally lost and since we don't know where we're going, any direction will get us there." She kind of chuckled at her own words, knowing that they didn't make much sense, but continued anyway, "And hey, maybe the butterfly is going there too. Since we don't know where we're going, why not follow the butterfly? At least it's pretty!"

Claire groaned. "Oh, Addie! Get real!"

"I am," Addison countered. "We are lost. Since we have no direction, one way is as good as another, so why not at least follow this very persistent butterfly? Maybe it will naturally drift toward water or something edible or something like that? Maybe not, but it's as good as anything we got right now."

And with that little bit of logic, Claire looked around and relented just a bit. "Okay, she said, "I suppose we could follow it while we're looking for other things. Oooh, all right, let's go." And at that, they were back to chasing a whole bunch of butterflies and a few shimmery dragonflies darting across the open field and into a grove of trees.

They laughed as they followed, but they kept watching for dirt trails or cobblestone paths or roads or people or houses or any sign of civilization. And so, it was. They both took in deep sighs of relief when they finally saw a dirt path intersecting the field.

"Addie, look! There's a path over there!" Claire shouted. As they hurried toward the path, they were almost disappointed when they glanced back around to see that the butterflies and the dragonflies were gone. They sprinted through the grasses; and even though the narrow dirt path was not nearly as nice as the cobblestone path had been, still, it was a path and paths always lead somewhere.

They hurried along the path, hoping to find something; but after a long while, they both gave up and realized that the dirt path didn't seem to go anywhere either. Both girls plopped down onto the ground. Claire pulled off her shoes and socks to examine the swollen toe she had given herself while kicking the ground, and Addison leaned back on her elbows.

"We've walked so far. What's going on?" Claire complained while rubbing on her sore foot. "There are no directions, no people, no anything."

Addison stood back up, bending from side to side, stretching her tired muscles. And that was when she heard it. "Claire, listen! Shhh, listen! Claire, do you hear that? Claire, I think I hear water. Do you hear it, like waves rolling up on the shore—maybe? Could we be close to the water? Shhh, listen."

Claire quickly slipped her shoe back on and jumped up. "Oh, Addie, you're right! I know that sound! It's far away, down that road, around that bend, but that's the sound of waves. Let's go!"

And they took off, sprinting and running and laughing, racing toward the bend in the road. "We're almost home!" Claire screamed, leaping into the air as the roar of water got louder and louder (even though it hurt Claire's bruised toe every time she landed). The soft, gentle spray of moisture filled the air as they ran around the bend.

But after rounding the curve in the road, Addison slowed to a stop and Claire (whose bruised foot caused her to run just a little slower) slowed to stop right behind her. And they both just stood there staring up and down and all around. For you see, they were not where they had hoped they were at all.

There were no ocean waters surging and crashing into misty bursts against the ocean cliffs and bluffs. No, no ocean waters at all. The soft and gentle spray was not from high tides and ocean waters battering the coastal cliffs—no, not this time. This time the mists burst forth from the plunging, pounding waters of a resplendent, pristine waterfall surging over the rock face and cascading down the sides of a magnificent towering mountain.

They both just stood there in silence, staring at the water flowing over the rocks. And even though it was a beautiful, mesmerizing sight, they couldn't even see the splendor because of all the tears filling their eyes and blurring their view. And they both just stood there without a word. They reached over and took each other's hands with big fat tears rolling down their cheeks. After a long while, they both wiped their eyes and turned away from the waterfall.

"Well," Addison said, drawing in a deep breath, "well, maybe we aren't any worse off than we were before—maybe, I guess. So, well, let's just get back on the path and get going again." She wiped her nose with the back of her hand. "I wonder what time it is. How long have we been gone anyway? I bet they're looking for us. Remember, Gramma said we could get lost. Oh, Claaairre, what has happened?"

"They've gotta be worried by now," said Claire. With sighs and groans, they turned to go back to where they had started;

but as they did, Claire seized Addison's arm, this time pointing to the far corner of the field. "Addison, look at that—over there," Claire asked cautiously. "Is that one of those old signposts with directions on it?"

"How did we miss that before?" Addison asked. "Oh wow! What if it has directions on it?" Addison shrieked. And again, they ran across the field, wishing and hoping and wishing and running until they reached the signpost. But this time when they reached their destination, they did not stand with tears in their eyes—no, not this time. Instead, they stood scratching their heads and walking in circles around the post over and over. "Well, we seem to have directions to the Oracle," Addison muttered slowly.

"But how can he be in eight different places and why," Claire whispered, "and why would this old lantern be hanging from the signpost?"

A dragonfly grabbed Addison's attention, and she watched it flicker through the air and land on the ground. "Wait a minute, Claire," Addison said. "Look at that over there, on the ground. It looks like there's another arrow in the dirt. Maybe it's another clue."

They hurried to look more closely at the arrow formed by rocks and pebbles on the ground. In the second they stood over it, both girls simultaneously gasped and slapped their hands over their mouths, looking up at each other and then down at the ground again. They both screamed and jumped about. And this time the tears rolling down their faces were happy ones.

Addison bent on one knee, touching the stones.

"Claire, is this possible?" Addison gasped.

Claire sat down on the ground reading the names Levi, Eleanor, and Esmé over and over. "Oh my gosh! Addie! What if they were here trying to find us? They must have been here! But where is here?"

And they both turned staring up in the direction the arrow pointed—at the trail ascending through huge evergreens and into the mountain with its cliffs and protruding precipices. "The arrow points in the same direction that the bronze arrow on the post points," Addison murmured.

"The bronze arrow!" Claire gasped. "Wasn't Levi looking at that map book from the shelf beside the bronze door?"

"Yes, he was!" Addison replied. "Talk about synchronicity or serendipity. Maybe the butterfly did lead us in the right direction! Wow, this is so cool!"

"Oh, Addie!" Claire replied with a grin, a roll of her eyes, and a shake of her head. "Maybe it's just plain ole regular coincidence or a really great stroke of luck." But, it must be said, that even while Claire rolled her eyes, inside she had a curious feeling that just maybe Addison might be onto something—maybe.

"Just the same, it's unbelievable!" Addison finished.

And so, Claire and Addison wrote their names in pebbles beside Levi's, Eleanor's, and Esmé's names. And they wrote the words *we were here* just in case Levi, Eleanor, or Esmé happened to come back to this particular place in this particular area of wherever they were.

They picked up the lantern from the signpost; but just as they were about to begin their trek up the mountain, Claire and Addison glanced at the darkening sky and realized it would be better to wait for the morning. The sun had spent its last rays for that day, and the moon was beginning its ascent. Thick clouds were rolling across the sky.

And if those were not enough to make them stop for the night, they heard growls coming from somewhere in the mountain. So instead of beginning the journey into the mountain, they decided to find a soft place to rest and wait until the light returned.

But just as they lay in a patch of soft moss under an ancient old cottonwood tree, they noticed a dilapidated cabin across the field. Tilting their heads from one side to the other, they both rubbed their eyes and stood up. "Is that an old cabin over there?" Claire asked, pointing across the field.

"I think so," Addison answered, nodding slowly.

"Why didn't we see it before?" Claire asked, looking back and forth between the cabin and Addison.

"I don't know," Addison answered with a shrug and a frown.

"Are those lanterns hanging from the porch?" Claire asked.

"I think so," Addison answered.

"What are we waiting for?" asked Claire.

"I'm not for sure," Addison answered. "Maybe our luck has changed! See, there is serendipity and signs and synchronicity!"

Laughing and hoping, they scurried to the cabin and jumped up on the porch. As Claire tapped on the door, it creaked open, and they peeked inside. Since it was empty, they slowly crept in. A piece of paper pinned to the side of the table read, "Go ahead and sleep and eat, leave the lantern on the post where you found it, and get out of here in the morning. I don't like children."

"I'm not staying here," Addison said, her eyes wide with fear. "I'd rather take my chances under that tree."

"You and me both," agreed Claire.

They turned, running out the door; but as they stepped onto the porch, they froze as a deep guttural growl rumbled across the bottom on the porch steps. Claire and Addison stood motionless except for their eyes, which were flickering back and forth and all around. And then, they saw it, an enormous gray wolf sitting on his haunches at the bottom of the steps, baring his fangs and growling deep guttural growls and snarling with his lips pulled back over his pointy teeth. He slowly rose and began pacing back and forth at the bottom of the porch steps, growling, snapping, glaring with cold yellow eyes straight into theirs; his tongue darted out from his mouth. He licked his lips, snarling and licking and snapping.

They unfroze, slowly backing into the cabin, slamming the door, and standing with their backs against it, shaking. Without a word, they pushed a heavy chair against the door.

"This is gonna be a long night," Claire whispered.

"Maybe if we sleep, the night will get over faster," Addison suggested. Both girls crept over and lay down on the bed;

neither said one word as they lay there staring straight up at the ceiling.

"So, Addison," Claire finally asked, breaking the silence, "how's that serendipity working for ya now?"

"Oh, shut up!" Addison snapped back, but she moved very close to Claire anyway.

And though they thought they would never sleep and their eyes would never close in that very strange place, the truth is that sleep slipped over them the second after Addison said "shut up." Their sleep was deep and sound, and they both awoke with a start as the first rays of sun filtered through the open window. They heard a deep howl and peeked out the window just in time to see the wolf hurdle off the porch and trot across the field.

"Let's grab some food and get outta here," Claire suggested. They jumped up, snatched food from off the table, grabbed the lantern, and scratched thank you on the bottom of the note with a nub of a pencil they found lying beside the paper. They ran across the field, put the lantern on the little hanger hanging from the post, and hurried to the path leading up into the mountain in the same direction as the bronze arrow pointed.

And just as they set their foot on the first step of the path, a huge beautiful purple-and-blue butterfly flickered past and floated off into the woods. Addison smiled. Claire noticed Addison smile and shook her head. And off they went following the path up into the mountain.

Chapter 44

Levi, Eleanor, and Esme: Eleanor Musses the Hair

Glimmers of fading sunlight filtered through the trees as light and shadow mingled and merged. The leaves quivered as the mild breeze strengthened into a gentle but persistent wind. The air chilled in anticipation of the night as the sun continued its slide into the horizon. Esmé sat clutching at the limb and whimpering like a lost, lonely puppy each time the wind blew across her.

Jumbled feelings fluctuating from anger to worry to concern and back again raced through Eleanor's mind. "When he gets back, I am going to let him have it. I cannot believe that he is taking so long. But wait—what if something is wrong? What if he got hurt? Oh my gosh! What if something happened to Levi? Oh, he is just fine. We would have known if he fell out of the tree, I think. What is taking him so long? Just wait till I get my hands on him! But what if something bad has happened? Where is he?" Eleanor craned her head one way and then the other, trying to look up through the branches, biting her fingernails, and patting Esmé's knee with each new whimper. And still, Levi had not returned.

After a long while, and after the jitteriness and worry and concern had filled Eleanor from the soles of her feet to the top of her head, she stood up, wiggling first one foot and then the other as she stretched her entire body.

She stood there a few moments resting against the trunk of the tree, biting her lip, and thinking. The shadows were creeping across everything. She glanced down at Esmé and rubbed her forehead.

Finally, she bent forward, looking straight in Esmé's face. In her calmest sugary sweet voice (used only for extra special occasions), she drew in a deep breath. "Sweetie," she said, "I really need to climb up just a little more and see if I can see Levi. It's starting to get dark, and I'm very, very worried. Can you handle that, sweetie? I will hurry so very fast and call to you all the time."

When Esmé whimpered a high-pitched whimper, Eleanor stopped pleading. But then, expectantly, and without saying a word, Esmé began scooting as close to the trunk of the tree as possible. And when she was as close as close could be, she grabbed the trunk and tried wrapping her arms around it; but the tree was far, far too big, and Esmé was far, far too small. All she did was scratch her arms and whimper some more.

So instead, she shuffled around, pressing her back against the trunk, and grabbed a large nub sticking up from the branch. And though she was quite pale and very trembly and very, very scared, she whispered, "Okay, go look for Levi. But don't go too far—promise?" And then Esmé closed her eyes as tight as anyone can close their eyes. She whimpered just a little every time the wind blew across her, and she could only breathe in short rapid little gasps, but she sat there all the same.

It all made for such a pitiful sight that Eleanor almost decided to stay, but the dark was closing, and she needed to make sure about Levi. "Okay, little Ezzy," she said, "I promise." And with that, Eleanor grabbed a limb above her head and began climbing up higher and higher.

After a while, the darkening gloom and the relentless wind created eerie flickers of light and shadows on the leaves and limbs, so Eleanor decided to move sideways along a thick branch to a more exposed place. She kept sidestepping toward the edge of a bough, continually calling down to Esmé. Finally, just where the limbs were getting weaker and floppier, Eleanor realized that she could not go any farther.

By twisting her body up and around and raising up on her toes and leaning out as far as possible, she was able to see around the leaves and up into the sky. "Esmé," she yelled, "I think I see Levi!" After shuffling over just a tidbit more and bending forward just a tad more, she yelled, "Esmé! Esmé! I see him! Oh my gosh! He is . . . Esmé, you won't belie—he's fine!"

Now, Eleanor was so amazed at seeing Levi far above and suspended out in the air with a long leafy branch holding him that she quite forgot—for just a tiny moment—her own precarious situation. Instead, she craned her head up and around, stretching onto her toes and bending forward even more.

And it is sad to say, but during that tiny bit of time when she was craning and stretching and bending, her foot slipped just as she was adjusting the angle with her hand. The limb snapped back, and when she snatched at the limb, it flopped down. She lost her balance, and suddenly Eleanor found herself holding on to a different limb altogether and leaning forward in a very strange position. She froze. Only her eyes moved, searching, probing. Thinking. Gasping. Frozen. Eleanor held on, sucking in shallow quick breaths.

"I told you not to muss my hair," came a gentle voice. "It is not good to muss my hair. Oh dear, oh dear, oh dear, you really ought not to muss my hair."

Now, Eleanor tried to push up, but the branch kept wobbling; and that, of course, made it even more difficult to push up. And the truth is that if you have ever been high in a tree, all straddled out like that and leaning way too far forward, then you certainly know that in just a little bit of time, your muscles get very tired and rather shaky, especially if you are already a little frightened. And Eleanor was more than a little frightened, what with her strange position looking downward and with a tree talking to her and Esmé yelling up to her.

And so (as you can probably imagine) it wasn't long until Eleanor's shaky foot slipped just a little, which caused her to jerk and lose her grip; and though she was able to grab the limb, she was in an even worse position than she had been in originally.

"Oh dear, you are mussing my hair. It took me all summer to get it just so. You really ought not muss my hair."

Eleanor looked down, breathing heavily and sucking in air and, if truth be told, thinking some naughty words about the talking tree. About that time, Esmé yelled up, "What's the matter, Ellie? Are you okay? I heard the tree telling you not to muss her hair."

"I'm just fine, Ezzy."

"No," said the soft, gentle voice, "I don't think you are. You mussed my hair. It's never good to muss my hair."

Eleanor trembled. The branches continued swaying as the breeze grew stronger, which made them sway even more.

"Eleanor, are you okay? Is Levi okay?"

"Yes! Yes! Yes! I'm fine. I'll be back in a minute. Levi's fine, Ezzy."

"Actually, you aren't, and no, you probably won't be—not in a minute at least. But, yes, Levi is fine. He did not muss my hair."

Eleanor tried to push up, but she had slipped even more; so, between the pressing and the wobbling and the slipping, Eleanor's hands were stretched wide on one limb, and her feet were stretched wide on another so that she was rather like a giant *X* sprawled across the branches looking downward. But then, quite suddenly, a blast of wind rustled through the tree, and the branches began swaying even more. Her hand slipped sideways off the limb, and when she grabbed, nothing was there.

Now, it really is very difficult to explain what happened next; but it is probably sufficient to say that when Eleanor's hand slipped, she lunged forward and lost her balance and she fell through a few branches. Then she kind of rebounded and fell through more branches. And Esmé screamed as Eleanor bounced by continuing her downward fall, landing on and tumbling through one limb after another. Each branch broke her fall just a little as she passed from one limb to another—down, down bouncing, hitting, dropping, screaming as limbs slowed her plunge and rebounded her to the next one until she bounced into a thick cushion of leaves on a thick leafy branch. She lay there looking up at the sky and wondering if she was really still alive.

But while she was still wondering if she was still alive, the stinging and hurting and the bleeding started, and she knew for sure that she was. She lay on the leaves for a few minutes; but when the wind blew through again, and the limbs swayed with the breeze, she shook herself and worked her way over to the trunk, one hand over the other, pulling her way along until she was in a safe place. She sat catching her breath and examining the cuts, the scrapes, the blood, and the places that would obviously be black and blue very soon.

And after just a tidbit of time, she yelled up to Esmé. But she could not see Esmé through the leaves and branches and shadows. Esmé could not hear Eleanor because of her own weeping and sobbing.

And far above and around on the far side, close to a sheer rock face, the branch was moving Levi back toward the trunk of the tree, slowly unwrapping him and guarding him as he climbed down, down, down. And after much climbing down, he finally found a panicking, crying, wailing Esmé sobbing and choking so hard that she could not explain where Eleanor was; all she could do was just point and sob and point some more.

"She is fine, little one," the gentle voice kept saying the entire time. "She is fine, but she is where she will be for now."

And Levi looked out into the darkening sky and up at the ascending full moon, and he knew they would climb down to

Eleanor if she really needed them, so Levi simply sat there with his arm around Esmé. "It's okay, Ezzy. We'll go down if she needs us."

"Promise?" asked Esmé.

"I promise," comforted Levi, looking straight into Esmé's eyes and smiling. But he looked the other way as his chest tightened, and he bit down on his lip and dropped his head forward as a terrible frown covered his face. And so, he did the best thing he could for that moment.

"Esmé," Levi said, "you have to help me. We are going to call down to Eleanor. You need to yell as loud as possible, okay?" Esmé nodded. And Levi and Esmé yelled and yelled and yelled; and far, far below, Eleanor heard their voices. Though she could not hear everything, she heard enough to understand, and she yelled up until she was hoarse that she was fine and she was in the crook of the tree, that coming down might only make things much worse.

"She is fine, Little One," the voice said again. "I will keep her."

And even though the wind was blowing very hard by this time, they heard enough to know that Eleanor was understood. And as the wind blew colder, she huddled against the fork of the tree because Eleanor was as brave about that type of thing as anybody could be. And about the time that she was beginning to feel very alone and somewhat scared, little lights began flickering all around her. Tiny lights flashing off and on. So many that Eleanor laughed in spite of herself. "So lightning bugs have come to visit." She sighed. They were so beautiful as they glimmered and flashed and flickered. And one even sat on her nose with its little tail blinking off and on, making little sparkles of light in the night—little bits of joy in the dark. And just a tad after that, a branch moved up and around, covering Eleanor with leaves so that she felt as cozy as is possible on such a night.

And far above, high in the tree, tiny little lights flickered around Esmé and Levi. Esmé stopped sniffling and watched, and she finally giggled. Levi chuckled as they hovered all about—tiny sparkles of light flickering off and on, off and on, tiny fireflies giving them just enough light to resettle themselves into a giant fork of the tree branches.

And as Levi snuggled into sleep in the tree, he pulled Esmé close. The trunk was on one side and a heavy branch on the other, and a leafy limb slipped over them. And though the wind was cold, it was still such a beautiful place that Levi forgot all about those silly ideas that usually hindered him from doing such things. And he began humming, and his humming turned into a song, and he sang a sweet old tune that he remembered his mama singing to him when he was very, very young. Esmé drifted into slumber.

Levi lay very quietly on the limb. He gazed down through the tree and smiled because he could see little flickers of light flashing far below. And Levi smiled gently. "Eleanor is fine, isn't she?" he whispered.

"Yes, she is," the tree murmured. "And soon she will understand." And that night Levi, Eleanor, and Esmé slipped into deep sweet sleep high up in the branches of an enchanted ancient tree.

Chapter 45

Levi, Eleanor, and Esmé: Even Wolves Have Their Place

They opened their eyes slowly as the sun filtered through the leaves. Esmé, still curling into Levi, woke first and lay silently looking up. Levi startled awake, popped up, looked around, and plopped back down, shaking his head and remembering. Eleanor far, far below woke stiffly, stretching her limbs, yawning, groaning and complaining. With a whole bunch of "oohs" and "aahs" and "ouches," she pushed herself up gradually one inch at a time, examining her cuts and bruises. While running her fingers through her long dark hair to straighten it, she noticed a big bump on the back of her head. She groaned again.

"Well, Creatures from beyond the Bronze Door," the gentle voice spoke, "this is a big day, a very big day indeed. You have places to go, things to do, people to see—so let's start by getting you three back together. But don't muss my hair. It's never good to muss my hair."

Eleanor rolled her eyes.

"First things first," the voice continued, "the ones up high must go down. I will send a little help, so Little One is happier. The one who mussed my hair needs to stay put."

Eleanor rolled her eyes again.

A small branch slithered toward Esmé, the twigs and leaves gently wrapping around her small body. At first, she gulped and sucked in air, and her eyes were as huge as huge can be; but Levi kept telling her that the same thing had happened to him. So before long, Levi and Esmé were climbing down, and Eleanor was looking up and smiling as they drew nearer. Esmé, wrapped in twigs and leaves, seemed to practically float down as Levi climbed beside her.

In practically no time at all, Levi and Esmé were sitting on a huge limb next to Eleanor, and there were sighs of relief and hugs all around and talk of lightning bugs and exclamations about how restful it actually is to sleep high in a tree and a talking tree at that! And it was quite a fine time until Esmé broke in with "I'm hungry."

And they suddenly remembered that they really did have places to go and things to do and people to see and food to find, so they turned their attention to the final climb down. And it went quite well and quite quickly until they made it back to the last branch where they had begun their climb in the first place. They sat down on that huge branch to catch their breath to get a plan for the last leap to the ground. (The distance between the lowest branch and the knotted, twisted tree roots looked different from up to down than it had looked from down to up.)

As they were sitting there thinking and contemplating on the best way to get Esmé down, the ground kind of rumbled, and they stopped chatting and glanced around. They heard a baying and howling and turned to look down, and that's when they saw them: a huge pack of wolves running straight toward the tree, yelping and growling and snarling with teeth bared and snapping.

The entire pack of wolves just trotted right up to the bottom of the tree and sniffed about and looked up at the cousins, staring into their eyes and howling as loud as only an entire pack of wolves can howl. After the wolves had finished howling and snapping and snarling quite a bit, they dug at the dirt between the roots and then sat back on their haunches with their raised heads and seemed to stare straight at Levi.

One particularly big wolf kept licking his chops, and though they couldn't be quite sure, he sorta looked like he was drooling every time he looked in Levi's eyes. And the wolves just kept digging in the dirt some more and turning in circles until then settled in and just sat there on their haunches, staring up and then staring around and then staring up again and snarling and growling with bared teeth here and there. And once in a while, they all took to howling and snapping at the same time which made for a particularly frightening ruckus.

"Well, this is not good," gulped Eleanor. "What now?"

"I have no idea," said Levi. "But the plan is to go up the mountain, not sit here in the tree."

"I'm hungry," sighed Esmé. Levi sighed and reached into the satchel and gave Esmé the last piece of biscuit. "That will have to hold you till we get down, so eat slow," he said.

"Don't muss my hair," said a soft, gentle voice. "It's never good to muss my hair."

And Eleanor rolled her eyes.

Chapter 46

Tilly, Brody, and Ivan: Escaping Through the Night

They stood on a stoop outside the cavern door in stunned silence.

It was still the midnight hours, and yet the light from the full luminous moon and from millions of twinkling stars and from all those flickering flames from all those lanterns in all those evergreen trees created a gentle, mystical quality. It was so still, so ethereal, so ghostly—as if they had been plopped down into the midst of one of those long ago and faraway tales, one of those ancient stories that somehow always end in happily ever after. And yet—and yet—it was imposing and impenetrable and so very strong and so very bold.

It was as though an entire mountain had been split in half and the middle section scooped out, leaving a deep wide gap between two sides of sheer rock that jetted straight into the air on both sides. An enormous broad cobblestone passageway meandered through the gap and continued winding ever upward until it ended at the jagged, snow-covered peaks of the mountain pass.

Giant doors faced each other across the broad cobblestone road; and each door opened to towering evergreens, vines, and tall grasses, which created a green forested barrier between the doors and the cobbled road. A lantern flame flickered from the bottom limb of the trees.

Jeslue had said that once they were outside the door, just follow the cobblestone road up into the mountain pass where they would be able to ask about the Snow Village or the Oracle without danger of being captured by biglings. But now as they stood there, they realized that the journey was going to be very long and very uphill.

And so, with a quick glance at the foreboding rock face on both sides and a long gaze at the mountain pass in the distance, they hurried off as quietly and quickly as possible. It was a noiseless night, eerie in its somberness; but they kept jogging until they were forced to stop and gulp in the air. They bent forward with their hands on their knees, sucking in the air until their breathing was normal and their legs less wobbly before quickly taking off again, sometimes jogging, sometimes walking quickly, but always climbing gradually upward toward the mountain pass.

They kept pushing forward until the first subtle shafts of sunlight wavered through the mountain clefts until the evergreens of a thick forest lined both sides of the cobblestone road instead of sheer rock. By that time, the morning fog shrouded the air with dreary cold mist. And finally, they slowed to a stop and sat on the edge of the passageway.

As the sun finally flooded the clefts between the peaks, the cousins heard the deep voices and laughter. They scanned the cobblestone road. Biglings were walking up the cobblestone road.

"They look like lumberjacks or something like that," Ivan suggested.

"They probably work in the forest," Tilly said. "Let's hide till we know."

They scurried into the forest to hide, hoping and planning to move back into the warmth of the sunshine as soon as the Biglings moved on. Unfortunately, that simply did not happen.

Chapter 47

Tilly, Brody, and Ivan: Into the Murky Darkness

The ancient trees and heavy vegetation shrouded the entire forest floor in murky darkness, and yet, the dark paths through the thick dense forest was the only way to stay hidden. What had begun in the very early morning as a quick dash into the forest to hide from lumberjacks had turned into hours of winding through a lush nightmare of shadowy gloom with creepy noises and strange whoops and whirrs and unanticipated slithery movements startling them at every turn.

As the sun ascended, a steady stream of Biglings flooded onto the cobblestone road, wandering up and down, leisurely meandering here and there, forcing the cousins to remain hidden in the dense forest. Jeslue had warned the cousins to hide until they got to the other side of the mountain or to the Snow Village; he said Biglings might try to capture them—not because Biglings were mean but because the cousins would be a novelty.

So the cousins crept through the forest, waiting for the right time to emerge. Instead, they heard continual sounds. Mothers shrieking in laughter and then fussing at toddlers, papas chatting about their exploits, and older youngsters pleading "Can

I please?" and "Oh, Mom!" babies crying, and moms shushing, and all of them going somewhere and nowhere on the road.

"Where are they all going?" Brody asked disdainfully. "Do they just wander up and down the road all day? Don't they have something to do?"

Two different times Brody had moved close to the edge of the forest, sticking his face through the foliage, trying to feel the sunlight or suck in a bit of the fresh breeze instead of the breathless dank air of the forest undergrowth. But both times, a youthful passerby had slowed, tilted their heads to the side, frowned, and turned back, pushing the vegetation open again while quizzically peering into the forest; and the cousins were forced to quickly slide into the undergrowth to hide.

Fortunately for the cousins, parents shouted for their kidlings to get away from the forest and to stop dawdling. So with final longing glances through the brush, the faces had disappeared; and the cousins had jumped up, brushing away the slimy bugs and gross stuff that lived in the vegetation before they hurried off in the darkness again.

After those close calls, the cousins kept to the darkness, sneaking along, staying as close to the road as they dared, but remaining in the hidden depths. And though it was gloomy and rather miserable, at least they were able to keep creeping along and making slow progress toward their mountain destination— that is, until a couple of hours later when they heard deep husky laughter and heavy boot tramping toward them through the forest gloom.

Silently grabbing one another's arms, the cousins scurried behind a huge old cedar, cowering in breathless silence in the thick undergrowth at its base. They could barely see shadows as they crouched in the shrouded gloom, waiting, watching, hoping the boots would just keep tramping past and continue on into the forest.

From their hiding places, the cousins bent forward listening to the husky, burly voices. Tilly leaned forward, cocking her head to the side, and holding her breath, listening. Brody grabbed Tilly, motioning for her to stay down. Ivan scrunched down on one knee, leaning forward, watching for clues that they would continue moving down the trail. But the Bigling trappers didn't keep moving on; instead, they slowed to a stop directly across from where the cousins were hiding. They grew quiet as they threw ropes and hooks and stuff off their shoulders and began walking around, examining trees and cutting marks in them.

Their talking resumed in halted serious tones. There was some swooshing and crackling as one of them threw a rope into the air; it hit something and bounced back, and one of the trappers yelled a few very harsh words that should not have been said at all. Finally, there was some pounding and a whopping and some laughing as they examined their work.

"Maybe we should check out that area on the other side of the trail. That tree over there might work," one of the trappers said. The trappers moved across the trail, stopping directly in front of the cousins who squished down as flat as possible onto the forest floor even though it was very creepy and very gross. (Ivan was always quite sure he felt something crawling under his belly, but he stayed very still and didn't move even one inch anyway.) The boots stopped so close that Brody could touch them. Tilly scrunched her eyes totally shut. *Please, please, please, please. Keep going, keep going, keep going,* she kept repeating over and over silently.

"What is that horrible smell?" one of the trappers asked. And at that, the other two started began laughing and telling stories about running into a certain animal that smelled like skunk cabbage and how their wives made them wash in juice to get the smell off. They drove a stake into the ground to mark their place and decided to come back and finish their work after lunch. They tramped away.

The cousins breathed again, but they also continued lying in the vegetation at the base of the ancient cedar until they were absolutely sure that they could not hear the tramp of boots or laughter or burly voices. And then, they slowly crept out from among the trees and scurried back onto the dismal forest path. "Just keep going until we get there," Ivan insisted. "This is just awful."

As silently as possible, they hurried along the path—that is, until Ivan felt something round and hard under his foot and heard a slight crackle. He stopped, bending forward to listen, but he could not see anything in the gloom of that trail. Tilly did not notice that he had bent over until she knocked into him, and then Brody knocked into Tilly, who fell into Ivan, who lost his balance, and fell face forward onto the ground. Something snapped and groaned and whooshed, and suddenly the three cousins who had been standing on the ground just the second before found themselves all tumbled together in one big heap swinging in a net from a very tall tree.

"You've got to be kidding me!" Ivan screamed in a whisper.

"What is it with traps in this place?" Brody whispered back. "Aaahhhh."

Tilly just lay there, breathing deeply, gritting teeth with her lips pressed together, staring at the tree branches above her and trying really hard to keep her words as they should be rather than as they wanted to be, but she growled anyway as she slapped Ivan's foot. "Get your foot out of my face, Ivan!" she yelled in a whisper.

"Well, get your head off my leg!" Ivan yelled back. "Wait, is that—"

"Get your bum outta my face," Brody finished.

And at that, all three of them rustled around, hitting and swatting at one another and trying very hard to untangle. But if truth be told, untangling when you're swinging from a net that is hanging from a very tall tree is a very difficult thing to do, and there was quite a bit of grumbling going on.

They eventually got themselves turned in a fairly decent position. At least everybody's head was at the top, and their feet were all at the bottom. As they lay there deciding what to do, in a strange sort of way, the swinging of the net hanging from the tree was rather soothing. It almost felt like being in a hammock (except they were trapped inside surrounded by ropes). After struggling and fussing and figuring, they eventually decided to just lay there for a bit and rest until they could think up a plan to get out of the mess.

Now, you must understand—you really must, or you will think they were quite careless (and they really weren't)—that it had been a very long night and a very long day and their eyes kept fluttering even while they were talking and planning. Without even knowing what had happened, they slipped into a sweet sleep and probably would have stayed asleep way too long except that suddenly there was a jolt as if they were falling. All three of them jerked straight up, smashing their faces into the net, shrieking and looking straight up into the face of Jeslue's papa who smiled at them and continued cutting at the ropes that held them in the tree. "I thought you'd be somewhere around here," he said.

But when he saw their expressions, he stopped cutting and looked at them. "Jeslue told me everything this morning," he said. "And Mama insisted that I bring you some food. You three are costing me time and money, but I think I can help get you on a better path. Now, if I let you go, you must promise not to run or make any noise at all. Promise?" he asked with a serious frown. They each nodded silently; he finished cutting the ropes and set them on the ground. He tousled the hair of each one. "Oh, you little ones, you are such cute things, but what a pain you are."

Brody interrupted, "How did you know we were here?" he asked.

"Oh, well, Jeslue gave me the first clues, and then there was some village gibberish about a couple of youngsters who swore they saw something strange in the forest, and then a couple of trappers were at the pub going on and on about strange smells in the forest. So with a little common sense and a lot of luck, I found you," he said. "I just didn't expect to find you swinging from a tree and sleeping," he added with a chuckle. "But we'll talk later. For now, we gotta go."

The day was getting late; the sun beginning to slide behind the mountains, and the broad cobblestone road was strangely quiet after the chaos of the day. Papa looked down the road and hurried the cousins into the back of the cart. "Lay down, cover up in the straw, and stay quiet until we stop," he said.

They jostled off—jerking and jolting, bouncing from side to side—but after a short while, the jostling turned into a more rhythmic back and forth sway. Finally, Papa pulled on the reins, brought the cart to a stop, and turned around. "You can sit up now," he said, handing them some sandwichy type of food, a sipper of water, and a bag of Jeslue's tiny cookies.

As soon as they finished eating, Papa sighed, looking over at a side road winding through an open field. "You might as well get some sleep, little ones," he said. "We have a long way to go." They lay back down, nestling together, curling into the straw, gazing up at the millions of stars in the sky and the hundreds of lightning bugs flickering around in the darkness.

After a while, Papa began singing rich, warm melodies from that land with his deep baritone voice. And it was warm and cozy and homey all at once, and they began drifting into sleep. They slept as the wagon jostled on through a forest, across one pass, and onto another mountain road where it circled up and around as wolves howled in the distance and lightning bugs flickered in the sky.

Chapter 48

Tilly, Brody, and Ivan: Hooks on the Mountain

Just as the sun's golden streaks flooded the valley below, the wagon slowed to a halt. Papa climbed off the wagon seat, groaning and stretching as he hobbled stiffly to the back of the wagon, rubbing his sore back. "We're here," he said, gently prodding Tilly, Brody, and Ivan. The cousins sat up, gazing about with sleepy eyes. "I can't take you any farther because of the terrain. So I need to show you where you are."

"We're high on a mountain somewhere?" Tilly asked softly, her voice cracking just a little with apprehension.

"Well, yes, you are," Papa continued. "But you don't need to be afraid. You only need to follow that trail," he said, pointing, "and you need to climb across that edge curving across the side of the mountain."

All three stared at the mountain and then at one another. Papa saw their expressions. "Others have taken that trail," he said, "and they hammered hooks into the mountain rock to use on the trek around the mountain."

He smiled gently at them and laid his hand on Ivan's shoulder. "You'll be fine. Just hold on to the hooks and don't look down. When you get to the other side, stay on the cobblestone path until you come to a flat plateau. A huge old ancient corkscrew willow—the old legends say it is enchanted—sets across from the plateau. The tree is massive. Its roots are twisted and sprawling, and legend has it that it is so tall and wide that whole families could be in it and never know one another even exists, but that's beside the point," he said with a smile.

"You need to circle around the bottom of the tree until you find an old decayed tree stump sticking out of the ground that was once connected to the tree. Climb inside. The old stories say the stump has a tunnel that leads directly to the Snow Village. It could be that the Oracle still lives there, but if not, it is a place to ask questions. Somebody will know something."

Tilly, Brody, and Ivan stood looking at the mountain and then at one another.

"And one more thing," Papa said. "Mama and Jeslue sent a couple of tokens just in case you need them."

Rustling around under the seat of the cart, he pulled out a leather case and handed it to Tilly. "This is actually one of Jeslue's old wallets," he said. "Mama sewed a strap on the outside and put some food on the inside. She said the food will keep you on your journey and the wallet will give you a reminder of us when you get home." He leaned forward and gave Tilly a wink. "It's very, very old, and there is supposed to be magic in it. I don't know about the magic," he said with a chuckle, "but the food should keep you going!"

Tilly draped the strap over her shoulder and then peeked inside. "Perfect!" she said, grinning. "Wow, thank you!"

"And for the runt of the litter," he said, turning to Ivan, "this is for you." He handed Ivan a lantern. "It's actually one of baby's old toys, so it's small enough for you to carry on your belt. It folds together, and you can stick it in your pocket. If you need a light in that tunnel, just squeeze it."

"Hey, thank you!" Ivan said. "If we have to go in tunnels, this will be perfect."

"And by the way," Papa said with a chuckle, "we know you're not a runt. It's just Jeslue's sweet name for you 'cause he's so proud of you." Ivan grinned and nodded, but his eyes got a little red around the edges.

"And finally," Papa continued, "Jeslue sent this for Big Blue Eyes. I guess that's you," he said, looking at Brody. Fishing around in his pocket, Papa drew out a tiny blue crystal. "Jeslue said to keep this as a reminder of him just in case you have to use all the others to get home. He said to remind you that greed destroys but gratitude creates." Papa handed the crystal to Brody.

"Oh, wow! I love this!" Brody said, holding the crystal up to the sunlight as prism rainbows wavered through the air.

Papa stood looking over the mountainside and the valley below. Finally, he turned and smiled at the three cousins. "It's time for me to go," Papa said. "But you three have given us more than you'll ever know." He picked them up one at a time, giving each a gentle squeeze and a pat on the head before he set them back down on the ground.

"Will you please give Jeslue a message from me?" Ivan whispered as Papa embraced him. "Please tell Jeslue that I will keep my promise if ever I can."

"What promise?" Papa asked as he set Ivan on the ground.

"I promised Jeslue that if we ever find our way home and if I can ever find my way back, I promise to bring him a puppy. You'll tell him, right?"

With a furrowed brow, Papa cocked his head to the side. "Puppies are real?" he asked. And Ivan nodded, smiling.

"Well, will the wonders of the world ever cease?" Papa muttered, scratching his head. "Hey, if that's true, then maybe that tree really is enchanted, and maybe that old wallet really is magical too," he said with a chuckle. "Maybe someday, I might take a journey myself and find out. Jeslue would love that." And he looked over at the mountain once more.

And so it was that after many, many thank-yous and after more tousled hair, and after sending love and more love back to

Jeslue and Mama, Papa climbed back into his old rickety cart. He waved once more and then jostled away as the cousins turned the opposite way.

They trekked through magnificent trees, across a bubbling creek, and beside a roaring waterfall that burst out from the mountain spilling water over the tumbled rocks. And finally reaching the narrow ledge winding across the side of the mountain, they stood examining the shelf of rock protruding out from the rock face.

Ivan took a deep breath, and reaching up, he grabbed the first metal hanger hammered into the rock and stepped onto the shelf. "Come on, we gotta get home, don't we?" he said as he slid his foot onto the small ledge.

And although the thought of scooching along the edge of a mountain on a narrow ledge made them more than a little queasy and more than a little panicky, Tilly and Brody grabbed the handles beaten into the stone by those who had come before, and they stepped onto the rock ledge. And all three slid across the shelf with their faces pressed against the rock and their feet sliding and sometimes slipping off the sides. They refused to look down, but they continued grabbing one handle after another until they stepped off the shelf and onto the solid stone of another cobblestone path. They hurried until they rounded a bend and stopped—just stopped and stared.

"That," Brody said, "has got to be the tree. You could get a hundred people in it at one time. But where is the plateau?"

"It's over there!" Ivan shouted, pointing. "We must be on the back side."

Brody and Ivan hurried over to start their search for the stump. But Tilly just stood there, staring at the tree, watching the sunlight play with the delicate leaves as they twirled and flickered in the gentle breeze. The boys were creeping across the gnarled, braided roots when Tilly stopped them.

"You know, guys," she said, "what if this tree is enchanted as the legends say? Maybe there's no such thing as magical trees, but just in case—let's climb the tree and sit on that branch and eat our lunch in it!"

"Why not?" agreed Brody. "I'm hungry anyway." So they climbed across the gnarled roots until they stood at the trunk of the tree. Brody kneeled down, and Tilly stepped on his knee and pushed off, pressing her foot into a knothole; and after pushing and shoving and helping and climbing, up and over, all three finally sat on a branch in the tree, grinning and eating and chatting.

And as they sat there, chatting away, one of the curly limbs lifted a little and began creeping toward them. "Is something in my hair? What is in my hair? It is not good to muss my hair. It took all summer to get it just so."

And Tilly, Brody, and Ivan all stopped grinning and eating as they caught one another's very big eyes and stared at the little curly limb tenacling toward them. "My gosh! This is an enchanted tree!" Tilly gasped, jumping up and dropping her food.

"Oh, Precious Ones." The gentle voice sighed. "Sit and eat, little birdies. Stay a while. The butterflies are coming. The wolves are howling. But do not muss my hair. It is never good to muss my hair. It took all summer to get it just so."

And though it seemed quite strange, the three cousins sat down and took another bite and slowly chewed their food and smiled at one another. Tilly giggled, and Brody and Ivan chuckled, and they all decided to stay for just a little bit more. After all, it just didn't seem right to climb down and leave so quickly after being invited to stay and sit and eat on the branches of an enchanted tree.

Chapter 49

Levi, Eleanor, and Esmé: Wolves and Cousins

The cousins sat in the tree watching the wolves lying among the gnarled, ropy roots of the tree and hoping the wolves would forget that they were sitting in the branches right above them. "SShhhh," Levi whispered. "They're rustling around. Don't remind them that their supper is sitting right above their heads. Maybe they'll forget about us and leave."

It seemed like forever; but finally, the wolves did rise, slowly extending their front paws, lifting their haunches in the air, stretching and yawning with wide open mouths revealing sharp, pointy teeth. And after licking their chops and staring up at the cousins in the tree one last time, they suddenly trotted off.

"Come on, hurry," Levi said. "Maybe they actually ran down the mountain, but we need to make sure those horrible wolves are really gone and not just camping out, waiting for us to get down before we get out of this tree."

"Even wolves have their place in the bigger scheme of things," the gentle voice said very softly.

"Did the tree say something?" Levi asked.

"It said something about wolves," Eleanor said as they began scooting across the tree limbs, "but I didn't understand what it said either." So they continued shuffling across the branches, holding on to some and slouching under others, stopping every so often to push limbs aside and look at the ground to see if any wolves remained around the roots of the tree. When they finally reached the far back side of the tree, they pushed the limbs aside one last time before descending from the tree, but they immediately stood back up and looked straight into one another's eyes. "What in the world?" Levi muttered.

They both stood there for another second until Eleanor bent forward again, pulling the branches aside to see below. "What? How? Can't be? Did they go—" Eleanor asked.

Levi glanced into Eleanor's very big eyes. He shrugged very slowly with his palms in the air. And then they both bent forward, pushed the curly leaves aside, and looked down one more time.

Suddenly Esmé saw what they were seeing; she burst out screaming, "Tilly! Brody! Ivan! Tilly! Brody! Ivan! We're here!" And when Tilly, Brody, and Ivan heard their names, they jolted, jumped up, startled, jerking their heads around in circles, wondering how the tree knew their names and why the tree was yelling at them.

"We're up here! Turn around! We're here!" Eleanor screamed. "Tilly, Ivan, Brody, Tilly, Ivan, Brody, Tilly, Ivan—oh my gosh! How in the world?" All six of them just stood there, staring through the limbs and branches at one another for half a second. But after blinking a few times, quite suddenly, all six of them began rushing toward one another as quickly as anyone can rush when hurrying across the branches of an enchanted ancient corkscrew willow.

And it is very true that when they finally reached one another, there were bunches and oodles of hugs and bunches and oodles of laughing and some shouting and talking over one another and lots of pandemonium. By the time the chaos ended, Eleanor was standing with one arm around her sister, Tilly and the other around her brother, Ivan. Levi had one arm on Brody's shoulder and the other on Esmé's, and everybody was grinning. "Don't worry, we'll find Claire and Addie," he assured the cousins.

The tree remained quiet as they raced toward one another and let her hair be mussed. But finally, as the sweet chaos calmed and as the cousins stood together smiling and chatting and explaining, the sweet, gentle voice whispered once again, "You really shouldn't muss my hair. It's never good to muss my hair. It took all summer to get it just so." And they all looked at one another and burst out laughing because it really is amazing to stand on the limb of a magical, enchanted tree.

Finally, Levi broke in, "I hate to be the messenger of bad news, but we need to start searching for a way home. There was a pack of wolves keeping us trapped in the tree, and when we came over here to make sure they were gone, we found you instead. Talk about a coincidence! What're the chances of that?"

"Even wolves have their place in the bigger scheme of things, Little Creatures," the gentle voice said. And this time, as the voice murmured, Eleanor stopped chatting with the others. She glanced at Tilly, Ivan, Brody, and even at Esmé. She touched the tree and scanned the forest path where the wolves had run. A strange expression crossed her face; she looked about, caught in her thoughts, while the others droned on about their experiences since leaving the treehouse.

"But do you understand, Little Creature from beyond the Bronze Door?"

Eleanor nodded in a very hesitant way. "I might," she whispered, "but if I do, I'm not sure I like it."

"Then you do understand, child. You do understand."

Levi stopped talking and nudged Eleanor. "Did you say something?" he asked.

"Oh, just thinking, just thinking," Eleanor said with a smile.

"Well then," continued Levi, looking around at them all, "let's get going. We can tell our stories while we're on our way. But we need to find some food. Esmé is hungry, and after that, we need to find an Oracle. The problem is that we don't have the slightest idea of where to find him."

"Well, I can solve your first problem," Tilly said, patting Jeslue's wallet. "We have food right here in this wallet turned satchel!"

"And I can help with the second problem," Brody said. "We know how to get to the Oracle."

"Or at least to a place where he might be," Ivan added.

"What? How?" Levi asked. A startled, confused expression crossed his face.

"Wait a minute. Let's get this straight. You know how to get to the Oracle?" Eleanor asked.

Tilly, Brody, and Ivan nodded and smiled.

"What? Where? How? Well, then let's go, I guess!" Levi grinned.

And so, they grabbed hold of the trunk and shimmied and climbed and pushed and held on and dropped and caught until everyone was down. Once the others were standing on the twisted roots at the base of the tree, Levi put his arms around the trunk and his foot in the knots and hopped, jumping down.

They began searching around the base of the tree, moving foliage aside, climbing over the thick twisting roots, and pushing aside the tall grasses. It was Esmé who found the large old stump decayed through in the middle with sharp points and dips around the jagged woody edges camouflaged among the ivy, foliage, and moss. "I think I found it!" she yelled. "Come here, everybody! Come here!" They found her standing proudly in front of the serrated stump at the base of the tree.

Eleanor picked her up and squeezed her tight. "Ezzy! You found it when none of us were having any luck," Eleanor said as they stood looking at the stump sticking up at an angle out of the ground. Levi circled the stump, touching it, looking inside the yawning hole. "This isn't actually a stump," he said. "It must have been a thick root that was sticking above the ground, and somebody hacked into it. It must be a root from the enchanted tree itself. Amazing."

But as they began discussing the complications of actually getting into a dirty old ivy-covered stump of a root, they were interrupted by voices from somewhere. Levi, Eleanor, Esmé, Tilly, Brody, and Ivan all stopped investigating the stump and glanced around. And then a deep husky voice came into focus.

"Just stop it. Obviously, the butterfly did not lead us to the right place! I don't know how I let you talk me into this stuff!"

"Well, you don't need to be so cantankerous," came the stubborn reply.

"Will you look around and notice where your bright idea about chasing butterflies got us?" insisted the husky voice. "Just admit you're wrong, for goodness' sake!"

"Well, maybe we should just reconsider certain other ideas," retorted the other voice. "I seem to remember someone daring me with a chicken dance, and it's pretty obvious that that wasn't the best of ideas now, was it? So get over it!"

"Don't you ever just forgive and forget?" yelled the husky voice.

With a huge grin on his face, Ivan pointed toward the plateau. "They're over there," he whispered, shaking his head and rolling his eyes.

They all listened for another second until they couldn't hold it in any longer. And suddenly six voices rang out, "Claire! Addie! Claire! Addie! We're over here!" For a second, Claire and Addison just stood there, kind of blinking with their heads tilted to the side.

Then came the screaming and yelling and shouting as all eight cousins leaped in the air and rushed toward one another. Esmé jumped right into Claire's arms. Brody grabbed Addison and hugged her and hugged her more; he even kissed her cheek, and Addison hugged him back and kissed his cheek. And each and every one of the eight cousins hugged and cried and shouted and talked over one another and hugged some more.

And when at last they were ready to start on their journey, they waited for a bit so Claire and Addison could climb into the tree and sit for a couple of minutes. After all, it would be a shame to be so close to an enchanted tree and not see how it felt to sit in it.

The tree murmured its sweet good-byes to each of them, and after they had all gazed up into the curling leaves one last time, they gathered around the stump. It was tilted to the side, and it curved up from the ground. The edges were jagged and uneven as though it had been carelessly chopped down and left to fall over and rot. "Are you sure about this?" Claire asked as she looked at the stump. Tilly, Brody, and Ivan shrugged and nodded hesitantly.

"It's what Papa told us to do," Brody explained. So Levi climbed over the edge and down into the dank, musty, and cobwebby innards of the stump of the tree. Ivan dropped his lantern down, and Levi shone it through the insides as far as possible. With a grimace and a shrug, he climbed back out and told the others that he did see a hole and a tunnel.

And everyone hesitantly agreed that even though it seemed very gross and very strange, they might as well give it a try—at least for a bit—since that is what Jeslue's papa told them to do and they didn't have any better ideas. So they circled the stump, looking inside and trying to decide how to proceed.

And just as they did, several majestic purple and blue butterflies fluttered over their heads and floated down into the ivy, lazily flapping their beautiful wings. And far, far below, down the mountainside trail, a pack of wolves stopped and turned; and after sniffing the air, they raised their heads and howled until their cry echoed across the mountainside. The cousins stopped for a second, listening. Addison glanced at the butterflies hovering around in the ivy; and Eleanor looked down the mountainside, listening to the howls of the wolves.

And then they turned; and one by one, they began climbing up and into the gnarled, wrinkled, and jagged stump of a root from the ancient enchanted corkscrew willow tree.

Chapter 50

Signs and Decisions

Now, if truth be told, the cousins were not happy at all about climbing down into the stump of that tree. Cobwebs stretched across the insides, and tiny bugs were crawling all over the edges. They kept brushing little bits of stringy spider web off their faces and out of their hair and off their arms. There were lots of grimaces and lots of "Oh, yucks" and even more "This is so gross."

But once Ivan shone his light through the passageways, it became obvious that others had traveled this way before. Air flowed through the underground tunnels, and it was much more open than they imagined it would be. It is true that stringy, mossy stuff dripped from the walls, and it did have a musty smell like old dirt; but they shrugged and hurried down the corridor anyway. They walked in the only direction they could go and used the time to tell the tales of their strange journeys since leaving the treehouse and finding themselves in this strange and oftentimes scary place. And they began talking about all that had happened.

Claire and Addison apologized for causing so much trouble, and they explained how they thought it was just a trick mirror; they hadn't expected to find themselves wherever they were.

The others nodded and agreed because they understood that no one could possibly expect what happened. And so, as they walked and talked, they told their stories about Victoria, and Grizzles and Lola, and Jeslue and Papa and Mama, and the enchanted tree and the wolves and the butterflies and even the lightning bugs. The one thing they had in common was they had all been told to find the Oracle. So they continued making plans and feeling quite hopeful that home and Gramma was a very short time away.

And before they even realized how much time had passed, the passageway ended abruptly. When Ivan shone his lantern about to see what had happened, they realized that the passageway did not end; instead, it had narrowed into a huge round tube that plunged down and twisted around, and they could not see where it went.

"It looks like a giant waterslide without the water. I hope it's not like the slide me and Addie went down," Claire said, turning rather green just from the thought of it. Nevertheless, since their only choice was to go down or go back, they all knew that their only real choice was to keep going.

So Eleanor sat down first (since she volunteered) and Ivan behind her (since he had the lantern) and then Tilly, Brody, Esmé, Addison, Claire, and, finally, Levi. They wrapped their legs around one another so that they formed a long line that seemed rather like an upside-down caterpillar or perhaps a bobsled. Levi shouted the command. They pushed forward with their hands while scooting forward on their behinds, and in just a bit, they were swooshing down and through a small round chute.

There was quite a bit of screaming and yelling as they swished and swirled up and down and around the bends. Until they dove down, swooped around a curve, and finally popped out of the chute landing in a jumbled mess on the ground. As soon as their heads cleared, they looked around and found yet another cobblestone path only a few yards from where they landed. They followed that cobblestone path through a wooded area, along the side of the mountain, and into a field where it ended abruptly by forking into two separate paths. One led to a huge iron door wedged into the rock on the side of the mountain. The other path led through a field of tall golden grasses.

They stood at the fork in the cobblestone path for a long time, trying to decide between the two choices. Now, you must understand that both paths had some good, but both paths also had some bad. It only made it worse that they were hungry, tired, and the air was starting to cool as the sun began sliding closer to the horizon. And so, they stood with their arms crossed tightly over their chests, trying to decide the best way.

"Maybe we should go ahead and knock on that huge door," Brody suggested.

"But look at that path through that grassy field," Addison insisted. "I know it's getting cold and we're all hungry, but the butterflies keep fluttering past and going into those grasses and over that ridge. I think we should follow that path."

"Those butterflies are simply a coincidence, Addie," Claire said with a shake of her head. "It's time to stop chasing butterflies and to just think logically. Esmé's teeth are chattering. She's cold and hungry, and so are the rest of us. We need to try the door."

"But what's to say there's not food and shelter just over that ridge? The wolves keep howling every time we get close to that door, and I think it's a warning or something," Addison countered.

"Shouldn't we at least try to find out if the Oracle is in there?" Ivan asked.

Eleanor stood, tapping her fingers against her thighs. "I've got it!" she said. "We try the door."

Addison groaned, dropping her head forward, shaking it.

"But," Eleanor continued, "just listen before you get upset, Addie. We also make a pact. We will not go inside unless we know for sure that the Oracle is in there. And if something seems really wrong, we leave immediately. We get both. We don't get trapped, but we give the door a chance. How does that sound?"

"We're not even sure we can get in," Levi said. "I don't see a handle on that door. Let's go take a closer look, and then we can decide."

Chapter 51

The Iron Door and the
The Ginger-Haired Man

They stood in a semicircle, studying the imposing iron door with a thick perfectly round iron knocker hanging in the center and a giant round keyhole positioned directly beneath the clangor, but there was no handle. The door towered above them, wedged into the side of the sheer rock face of the mountain.

"Well?" Levi finally asked, breaking the silence. "Take a vote?"

Tilly and Brody glanced at each other, nodded, and slowly raised their hands. Ivan hesitatingly raised his elbow and a couple of fingers—not very high, just a little. Esmé raised hers straight into the air (but her vote didn't really count because she was so little). Addison stood with her arms crossed and shaking her head while watching the butterflies float off into the distance. Claire and Eleanor looked at the door and then at Addison and, finally, raised their arms into the air uncertainly.

"Addie, you might be right, but we are so tired, and this looks as good as anything for now, okay? It can't hurt to try. We can leave if we need to," Eleanor pleaded, looking over at Addison. "We can knock and ask anyway."

"Okay, whatever," Addison snapped.

Levi nodded at Claire. She stepped onto the raised slate slab; and after taking a deep breath, she grabbed the thick iron clangor, lifted it, and let it drop against the massive iron door. The sound was deafening; echoes reverberated, bouncing off the sides of the surrounding cavern walls. As the echoes ceased, the cousins remained standing in silence, watching the door, waiting, wondering if their hesitant voting, their hopes, and their concerns about this place were, perhaps, all for naught.

"Try again," Eleanor suggested, "just one more time."

Picking up the clangor, Claire dropped it again. Esmé cried out, covering her ears. But just as she did, a perfectly square previously unnoticed peephole at the top of the door screeched open and a squinty eye under a bushy ginger eyebrow appeared in the opening, oscillating back and forth, scrutinizing them all. Suddenly the eye disappeared, and thin straight lips with a thick ginger mustache appeared instead. A deep baritone voice bellowed, "Who are you?" and "What do you want?" And they shouted back that they were lost humans and they were searching for the Oracle.

"The Oracle, you say?" probed the baritone voice. "Are you sure?"

"Yes, we're sure," they agreed with nods and assurances.

"Hold on." There was silence. The thin lips with the ginger mustache reappeared in the square hole. "There is a time tomorrow for an audience with the Oracle. Is that satisfactory?"

The cousins grinned and whooped and patted one another's backs as Levi gave the assent. "Yes, that is perfect," he said.

The lips disappeared, and fingers holding a key slipped through the square slot. "Use this key to unlock the door and then push it through the keyhole." He dropped the key to the ground; and Levi picked it up; inserted it, twisting it until they all heard the resounding click; and then pushed the key back through until there was another click and then with a swoosh as it was sucked back into the keyhole.

They heard jangling and clanging of chains and a grunting and groaning as the iron door screeched off the ground, lifting up into a slot in the rocks above it. "Hurry!" the voice demanded. "This door is heavy."

They slid under the door as the man behind the baritone voice, the thin lips, and the ginger mustache released the chains, letting the door smash into the floor with a crash and thud, sending reverberations and rumblings throughout the room.

The cousins stood awkwardly, glancing back and forth between the heavy iron door behind them and the man pacing back and forth in front of them. Thick wavy ginger hair fell around his shoulders and around his grim, haughty face. The edges of his thin lips curled down; his nose was wrinkled into a perpetual haughty sneer. Little ginger hairs hanging from his nostrils quivered with each breath. He was dressed in black from his fur hat to his long fur-lined cloak and his knee-high laced boots. And he was definitely not what they had hoped for.

And the room was not what they hoped for either; it was dismal in a very uncomfortable sort of way. A single flaming torch and a tiny flickering candle were the only lights, and a square wooden table with a straight-backed wood chair were the only pieces of furniture. But if the ginger-haired man was unexpectedly grim and if the tiny dark room was appallingly dismal, it was the stone cold of the room that was shockingly horrible. It was not just regular old wintertime cold; no, it was a bitterly, miserably freezer kind of cold.

As they stood shivering, the ginger-haired man paced back and forth in front of them, staring at each of them. The cousins tried to look back and smile politely, but they felt so uncomfortable under his scrutinizing eyes that they averted their own, choosing instead to look around the room and at one another.

Finally, his upper lip curled into a sneer as he shook his head slowly and rolled his eyes, clicking his tongue against his teeth. He strode over to the table and sat down, stroking his ginger hair with one hand and dipping his quill pen in a bottle of black ink and writing in a little register book with the other. "Well, as I said before, we do have an Oracle here. You can go to the Inn tonight and prepare for tomorrow's audience," he said quite curtly.

Levi glanced around at his cousins; each had their arms crossed against their chests. Each was shivering. Esmé's teeth were chattering."

"It's freezing in here!" Claire grumbled, squeezing her crossed arms even tighter against her chest. "Why is it so cold?"

"What did you expect? It's part of the price. If you wanted comfort, why would you search for the Oracle?" he snapped while muttering "Stupid newbies" under his breath and continuing to write in his book.

Slowly, he looked up from his writing, his bushy right eyebrow arched. "There is a price for the honor of an audience with the Oracle. Adjusting to the cold is just the first lesson of many about price and sacrifice and responsibility and that sort of thing," he said while flipping his hand nonchalantly in the air. "We must all accept sacrifice if we want to experience the way of the Oracle."

"And yet," Claire muttered sarcastically, "you seem to be bundled up quite warmly with your fur cloak and thick boots. Just a tad hypocritical, aren't we?"

The ginger-haired man's lips turned up a little at the corners but not in a nice way at all. He bent forward, his eyes taking on a glassy appearance. "I hope I did not hear what I thought I heard. I didn't hear a rude comment, did I?" Claire's eyes got very large, and she took a step backward; the cousins surrounded her. Levi jumped in quickly.

"I think it is best that we leave. Thank you. We'll find the Oracle on another road. This is, perhaps, not what we are searching for. But thank you," Levi said. Each of the cousins nodded. They quickly turned to leave.

The ginger-haired man frowned, shaking his head and chuckling (but not in a very nice way at all). "Hmmm," he said, cocking his head to the side, "perhaps I should ask a question just to make sure we understand each other. Is there actually a part of you—even a teeny-weeny, itty-bitty, tiny part of you— that thinks for one itty-bitty, teeny-weeny moment that I can or will reopen that iron door for you?" He tilted his head to the side, an eerie smile crossing his face as he stared at them.

"No, sir, we would never ask that, but I am quite sure we can lift it ourselves, thank you," Levi answered, and all eight cousins nodded and then turned to examine the door.

"Oh, I'm so sorry, but did I forget to tell you that door only opens when someone unlocks it from the outside, kinda like what you just did? It won't open unless the key is inserted in the keyhole, and I don't see a keyhole on the inside, do you?"

They jerked their heads around, gasping as they realized the door had no handle, no keyhole, no markings, nothing at all except a square peephole at the very top. "So let's both win. You pay the price, and I get paid. And for that payment, I make sure you get to the Oracle," the ginger-haired man said. "It can be mutually positive experience—a win-win situation so to speak. And it will ultimately be worth the price when the Oracle tells you how to find your way home, so suck it up and pay the price."

Rubbing his forehead with his thumb and forefinger, Levi turned to face the ginger-haired man. "Okay, just what is that price for something warm and directions to the Oracle?" Levi sighed.

"Well, just what have you got?" the ginger-haired man asked, staring at each of them, stroking his thick bushy beard. Brody glanced over at Tilly and Ivan; they nodded at him. He reached into his pocket, sliding his fingers over each crystal and grabbing a middle-sized one. He shuffled past the others until he stood in front of the ginger-haired man. Holding up a perfect green crystal, he said, "I'm sure this will pay for what we need."

The ginger-haired man snatched the crystal out of Brody's hand, holding it up to the tiny candle flame. The corners of his mouth turned up just as tiny glints flashed in his eyes. Nonchalantly, he turned toward the cousins. Clicking his tongue against his teeth, sighing deeply, and shaking his head, he continued, "Oh, I suppose I can accept this in payment but only because you look like you are in such need. I am, after all, such a compassionate soul—just like the Oracle teaches us to be."

He strode to the corner of the room and pulled a black curtain open. He sighed again, waving the back of his hand at them and pointing to a mass of coats, wool socks, and thin black booties jumbled in a corner. "It just so happens that we keep a few things over in that corner for newbies who want to traverse our fair city. Pick out what you need—one blanket or cloak for each, one pair of socks and boots—no more than that. And I assume you know that there is no return on your time, money, crystals, or anything else. And now, our deal is done."

He returned to the flickering candlelight, holding the crystal up to examine it again. Levi slipped up behind him. Swiping his hand through the air before the ginger-haired man realized he was there, Levi snatched the green crystal out of his hand. The ginger-haired man jerked around, glaring straight into Levi's face. "Give it back! NOW!"

Levi crossed his arms across his chest. Setting his shoulders, he stared directly into the man's face. "We need to know how to find the Oracle. Without that information, there is no deal." All seven cousins stepped forward, standing with Levi.

"You certainly are troublesome, demanding little things, aren't you?" the ginger-haired man said, shaking his head. "You get your stuff. I open that door. You follow the cobblestone path through the village. You come to a bunch of cabins and some stone steps built into the hillside. Climb the steps. Go past those cabins until you get to the last place before the plateau. It's called the Oracle's Inn. The nice lady there will make sure you get to the Citadel and have your audience with the Oracle. He lives at the Citadel. You'll know it when you see it.

"And now," he said emphatically, grabbing the crystal back out of Levi's hand with his voice rising with each word, "unless you want to travel that road in your skivvies, get your stuff and get out of here!" He wrinkled his nose, snorted up a wad of mucus, and spat on the floor. He grumbled and complained and then spat on the floor again, making ugly faces all the while.

The cousins quickly rummaged through the jumbled mess, finding cloaks, slipping on the heavy socks, and pulling snow boots over their shoes. The ginger-haired man opened a door before they even finished buttoning or tying the laces. As he stood pointing toward the road, they scurried out under his arm. He slammed the door behind them.

They looked around at the slammed door, shivering and buttoning their cloaks. "Well, I'm glad we're outta there. But how can it be snowing out here when it wasn't snowing just outside the door? How can that even happen?" Eleanor asked, bending forward to tie her laces.

"It should be impossible," added Claire, wrapping her cloak tightly and crossing her arms.

They all stood, looking in circles at the snow falling around them.

Esmé giggled, sticking out her tongue to catch the flakes. But as she looked up into the flurries, she shrieked. Grabbing Levi's arm, she pointed up.

"What's the matter, Ezzy?" Levi asked, following the direction of her pointed finger and patting her small shoulder. "Don't worry, it's all gonna be—oh my gosh!"

The others looked around as Levi went silent. Following Esmé's pointed finger and Levi's gaze, they looked through the flurries and into the sky.

"Oh my gosh! What is that?" shrieked Addison.

"That's not possible, is it?" Ivan mumbled. "How?"

"What is it?" Brody asked, "It looks clear like glass or—"

"Does it surround this whole place?" Ivan continued.

They all drew closer to one another and stood there, touching shoulders, staring into the blizzardy sky.

"It's like we're inside a giant snow globe," Eleanor muttered.

"Maybe we are," Tilly whispered, remembering the snow globe back on Gramma's shelf with the tiny village of snow and the castle on the hill inside. "Maybe we are."

Chapter 52

Domes and Snowstorms

They kept staring up at the dome, encircling them as if they were figurines inside a giant snow globe. Even the snow seemed to be falling from the inside of the globe instead of from the real sky on the outside. But since the snow was falling in blustery flurries, they knew they didn't have time to stand around and try to understand it. They needed to find the village. Maybe there was a reason this entire place was enclosed; maybe the Oracle could explain it when they had their audience with him the next day. So because it was the best thing to do at that moment, they started walking down the cobblestone road.

"What is it with this place and cobblestone roads? Always cobblestone roads," Claire complained.

They huddled in, shoulders drawn and hunched, wrapping their cloaks and hoods as tightly as they could around their bodies as the flurries turned wilder and harsher. They tried to encourage one another, chatting about possibilities; perhaps the dome was simply a protection against the elements or something they didn't understand in this world of strange things. Unfortunately, the expressions on their faces did not match the hope in their words; and after a short while, they grew silent. They just kept walking, furtively glancing up time and time again at the dome encasing them.

The snowstorm raged more harshly. After a while, a strange roundish lorry rolled past the cousins, forcing them to jump into the snow as it swept and brushed the road and continued rolling on. Claire ran after it—yelling, pleading for it to stop—but the strange round snowplow just kept going. And the snow continued to fall, and the wind continued to blow.

The cousins walked and trudged and plodded and walked some more until their legs ached and their heels blistered from the weird boots. They walked until the frozen, blizzardy day had turned into a frozen, blizzardy twilight.

They walked on and on until the cobblestone road led up a very high hill and stopped. And they finally stood in stunned silence looking down at a mountain hamlet situated against the mountainside. Their silence quickly turned into relief and excited shouts; and they hurried down the hill, racing toward the cabins, forgetting their weariness as they hoped and wished for a kind face and some warm food.

"We're almost there now," they kept encouraging one another. "Maybe someone will give us a place to stay tonight. If we can't find a room, we'll find those stone steps. How bad can it be? We'll have an audience with the Oracle tomorrow and go home!"

And that's what they kept saying, and that's what they kept hoping and wishing for as they finally passed under the entrance gate and hurried through the winding streets of the snow-covered hamlet. But sometimes hopes and wishes just don't appear to come true, and unfortunately, this was one of those times.

Chapter 53

Candlelight and Snow

Snow had drifted against houses and lampposts, into the crevices of the diamond-shaped panes of the gothic windows with their flickering candles and hurricane lamps, casting an amber glow onto the winding streets.

At first, they hoped for an invitation into the candlelit warmth. Eleanor even tried knocking on a couple cabin doors, but only silence met her entreaties. And so, huddling together, they trudged through the village, still hoping and searching for a friendly face or a welcome sign; instead, they caught glimpses of eyes peeking out from behind the candlelit windows and hastily drawn curtains.

Esmé kept slowly trudging along behind the others, but when a tiny whimper finally escaped her throat, Levi picked her up and carried her. "Cuddle in," he said. "We're almost to the stone steps now, little Ezzy." But as they continued on and on, Esmé slipped into sleep; and after a while, when his arms burned from weariness, Levi reluctantly passed her over to Eleanor.

Eleanor silently took Esmé into her arms. After glancing down into the sleeping face, Eleanor smiled gently, bent forward, and lightly kissed Esmé's forehead. She reshuffled Esmé a bit to resettle the weight and continued trudging along behind the others. Esmé sighed in her sleep and nestled closer, burying her face into Eleanor's shoulder. And the cousins continued silently plodding along, hoping for a kind face or an open door. There was none.

After what seemed like forever and ever, the blizzard had, at last, subsided and the powdery snow lay thick and sparkling over the landscape. Still, the search continued until the cousins rounded a bend and slowed to a stop in the middle of a quiet, desolate street. Standing side by side with heads tilted back, they gazed around and upward.

A full moon had risen in the cobalt sky, casting a bluish glow over the icy, snow-swept mountainside, illuminating the entire hamlet. Icicles dangled from the steep high-pitched roofs of cottages nestling here and there, jumbled together at odd angles wherever the mountainside allowed. Jagged, ice-covered stone steps, cut into the mountainside, curved up and around the icicle-laden cottages until finally reaching a summit: a high flat plateau. And it was on that plateau, high overhead and overshadowing the village, that a Citadel, a snow-covered stone fortress, overwhelming with its massive and imposing presence, rose up out of the mountain as though etched and carved from the rock itself.

They stood exhaling puffs of frosty mist, entranced by the ethereal beauty of their snow-laden destination and shocked by the terrible price they must pay to get there. Finally, they realized the price for warmth and comfort for the night so they would have an audience with the Oracle tomorrow was a midnight climb up jagged icy stone steps tonight. It was foreboding and frigid; it was ethereal and sublime.

"We can do this," Eleanor whispered. She slipped over and laid one arm on Ivan's shoulder and the other on Tilly's. Addison silently reached down, grabbing Brody's hand, and he let her do it. Claire moved over to stand beside Levi, who had taken Esmé back into his own arms. He smiled a grim smile; and then he turned, planting his foot on the first jagged, icy stone step as each of the cousins formed a silent line behind him, breathing in the cold, frosty air and preparing to follow.

Chapter 54

The Oracle's Inn

And so, they did what they had to do because sometimes the only thing you can do on journeys is to just keep going. So that's what they did. They climbed icy, jagged stone steps under the full moon of the midnight sky. And once in a while, one of them would stop to catch their breath or rest their weary legs. And for just a second, they would look around, noticing the absolute beauty of the place with the full moon creating twinkles on the snow and illuminating the frozen icicles that dangled from the high-pitched roofs.

Sometimes they would stop and notice but not often. Mainly they just kept climbing, and their legs kept burning. Mainly they slipped on ice and had to pick one another up, and mainly Esmé cried, and they got bruised, and mainly it was dark, and they were scared, and it was hard and cruel, and mainly the miserable climb seemed to go on forever and ever.

But then, just before reaching the final plateau, the steps twisted around a bend and passed directly in front of a brightly lit log cabin tucked into a grove of towering snow-covered evergreens. The evergreens were sparkling in the moonlight as if they had been smothered in marshmallow crème and sprinkled with iridescent blue glitter. And it looked like home.

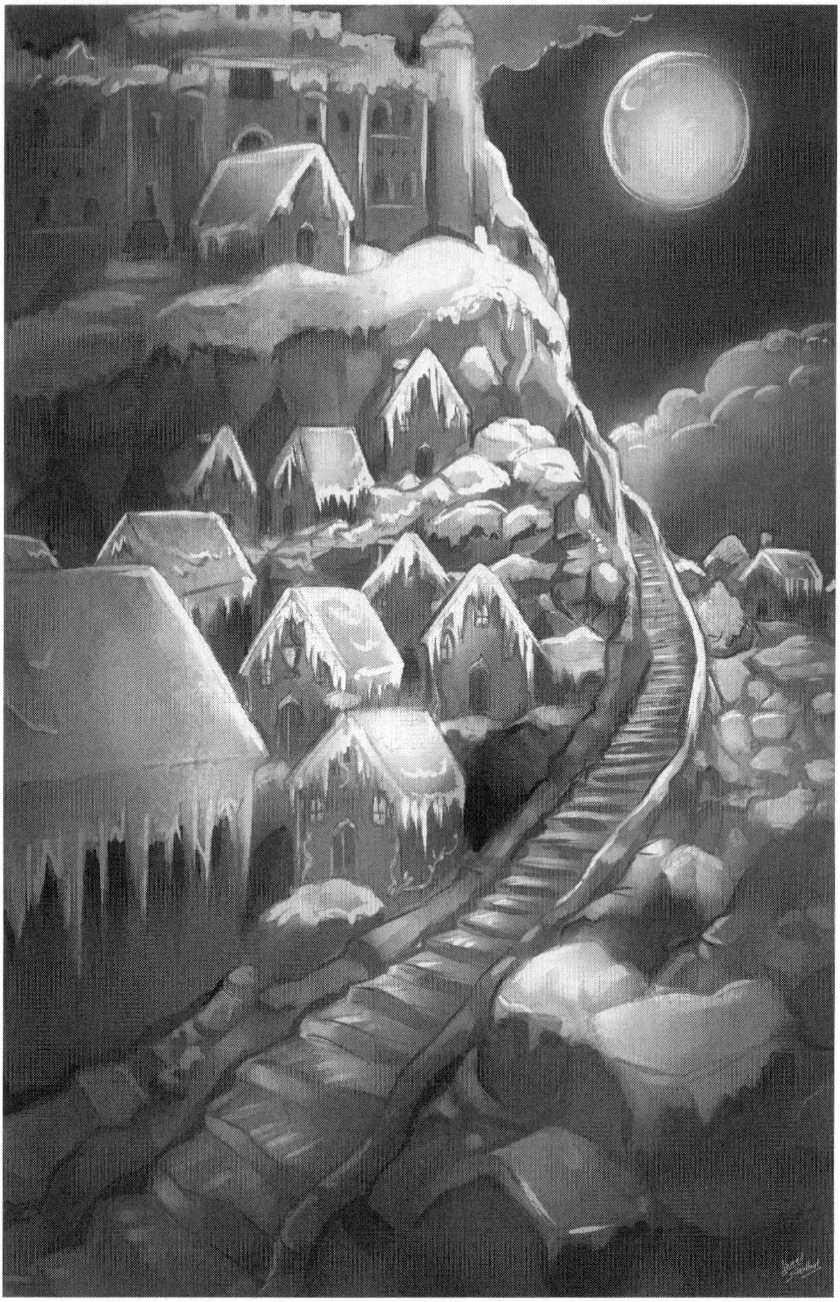

A wooden sign in the front yard screeched and groaned as the wind bantered it about on the chains holding it to a wooden post. "This is it! The Oracle's Inn!" Ivan shouted, reading the sign and slapping his hands across his legs to restore the circulation in his frozen fingers.

"Well, what are we waiting for? Come on!" Claire yelled as she hurried across the yard and up the steps. She raised her fist to knock on the door; but before she touched anything, the door popped open, and a cheerful, wrinkly face with long white braids popped out.

"You are here. Oh dear. Oh dear. Oh dear, you are finally here!" the little round lady with the long white braids exclaimed, bustling out onto the deck, grabbing each of them, and planting a kiss smack dab right in the middle of each forehead and even adding a little pinch to Esmé's cheek. "Come in, come in, come in!" she cried, hustling them in one at a time, patting each one on the back as they crossed the threshold. "Just look at you. My, oh my!" she said, bustling around the cousins.

"Let's get you kiddies out of those clothes and get some warm porridge in your tummies and set you in front of the hearth fire and get you all warm and cozy. Now, let's see. First things first," the Inn Keeper declared. Grabbing a measuring tape out of her apron pocket, she began measuring each of them from the top of their shoulders to their bottom of their feet.

Suddenly, she turned around and hustled away as the cousins all just kinda stood there, looking at one another with awkward grins and hesitant shrugs. And just as quick as that, she hurried back in, carrying an armload of fuzzy footie pajamas. "Here ya are. Here ya go," she said, handing pajamas to each one.

"Now, there are, in fact," she continued, "ten small bathing rooms in our little Inn, so I have drawn a warm tub of water for each of you. Take a quick soak. When you hear the bell tinkle, that will be your sign that the porridge is ready. Put the jammies on and come back out."

She waved her hand at them, shooing them off to the bathing rooms. "Hurry now," she said, "and wash your dirty hair while you're at it. There's shampoo on the shelf. Oh, and roll your dirty clothes in a ball and bring 'em out with you. I'll wash 'em, and you'll be fresh in the morning."

And so, with more awkward grins and hesitant shrugs, they did as they were told. The water was warm and lovely with honeysuckle-scented steam floating out as each cousin slid in and lay back. They soaked and smiled and sighed, even Esmé. When the bell tinkled, they slipped on the fuzzy footie pajamas and came back out into the main room.

Now, if truth be told, Levi felt rather silly in those fuzzy footie pajamas. His legs were quite slim and long, and the jammies were a rather soft purplish color, and he did look rather funny, but he was so warm and comfortable that a part of him just didn't care one bit even when Brody and Ivan burst out laughing. By that time, they were all so warm and cozy and smelling so good that nothing really mattered anyway except the jolly feeling they had while they were laughing; and so, Levi just rolled his eyes, smiling and wiggling his toes in the air. They all laughed even more.

The rich aroma of porridge drifted through the room, and the Innkeeper skedaddled them over to a long wooden table. Just as they were slipping their spoons into the steaming bowls of porridge, she scurried out and back in, carrying three wicker baskets of freshly baked bread. A red-and-white checkered cloth laid over the top kept the bread all warm and toasty (it was crispy on the outside and soft on the inside). She scurried back out and scurried back in with little bowls of soft yellow butter for each one—and honey too.

And then she plopped down at the end of the table and laughed a deep hearty laugh, waving the back of her hand at them. "Eat, children, eat!" And she laughed some more. They ate and ate and ate, and they didn't say a word except to mumble "Thank you" and "This is so wonderful" and "Oh, this the best food ever" many, many times. And when they were done, and when their tummies were so tight that they could not eat even another spoonful of steaming porridge or even another tiny bite of fresh warm bread or even a small lick of butter and honey, the Innkeeper laughed some more and told them to go sit by the fire. And she simply would not even hear of any of them helping to clear the table.

The fire snapped and flickered with red-and-orange flames. After they were as warm as warm can be and as cozy as cozy can be, and when they were yawning and their eyes were dropping, the Innkeeper opened the door to a large side room with ten beds in it and told them to crawl into bed and rest.

The pillows were fluffy, and the quilts were made of soft down feathers. And almost as soon as they laid their heads on the fluffy white pillows and pulled the fluffy covers over their shoulders, they fell into the deepest of deep sleep so quickly, in fact, that when the Innkeeper cracked the door just a couple of minutes later, all she saw was eight sleeping cousins nestled under thick down quilts with gentle snoring coming from two of them.

She smiled, quietly closing the door, and set about clearing the last dishes, singing a little tune as she wiped the table. She looked down and noticed the piles of rolled-up clothes in the basket. *Oh dear,* she thought, *I almost forgot those wet clothes.* And at that, she began sorting the clothes and checking pockets just to make sure there wasn't anything in those pockets that was not supposed to be washed.

"Oh, what's this?" she said, as she grabbed the crystals out of Brody's pockets. "My, oh my!" she gasped. "Just where have these kiddies been?" As she was holding each crystal up to the light, she saw something in the corner of her eye, and she startled. With a tiny shriek and a jump, she looked around. Brody stood behind her. "Did something wake you?" she asked pleasantly.

"Yes," Brody said, "I forgot to empty my pockets, and you said that you were going to wash our clothes."

The Innkeeper looked at the crystals in her hand and then at Brody. "Oh, are these yours?" she asked, holding out the crystals.

"Yes, yes, they are," he said.

"Well, they are lovely," she said.

Brody nodded with a hesitant smile. He held out his hand, and she dropped them into his palm.

"Where did you get them?"

"A Bigling gave them to me as a reminder about gratitude and greed," Brody said, looking at the ground.

"Oh, I see." The Innkeeper chuckled. "It is true that greed does very bad things. That's an interesting way to remind you. Well, off to bed with you," she continued as she returned to the laundry, checking and sorting the clothes.

As she pulled the small silver engraved mirror out of Addison's pocket, she smiled as she glanced into the mirror, patting some hair into place, but then stopped and leaned forward. After staring into the mirror for a second, her right eyebrow arched up, and she chewed on her thumbnail.

Glancing into the mirror one more time, she laid it on a shelf and continued sorting the wash, checking the pockets. She flicked Ivan's lantern on and off a few times and then set it on the shelf beside the mirror and continued sorting.

And when she was done, she sat down in her rocking chair. *An interesting situation, to say the least,* she muttered. *And perhaps this is the time. Only time will tell. Only time will tell.* And she rocked back and forth in her chair.

Chapter 55

Gifts

The Innkeeper bustled into the room. "Rise and shine, sleepyheads. Today is your audience with the Oracle. It's time to rise and shine. I've got the food on," she said with a smile. She set the mirrors and Ivan's lantern down on the dresser. "Be sure to pick up your treasures," she added. "I'll set them here." She watched as Ivan picked up his lantern and as Claire and Addison picked up the mirrors. "And here's your clothes," she continued as she walked between the beds, handing out their fresh, clean clothes.

As she passed Tilly's bed, she noticed Jeslue's wallet lying on the pillow. "Where'd you get this precious little satchel, honey?" she asked.

"Oh, it's actually a gift from a Bigling. It was his wallet, but for now, it's our food satchel," Tilly said with a smile as she rolled her shoulders, slipping out of bed, stretching her arms, and wiggling her fingers.

The Innkeeper noticed the satchel that lay on the floor beside Eleanor's feet as she handed Eleanor her clothes. She sat on the edge of the bed, running her fingers over the soft leather, touching the buckles. "This is beautiful." She sighed.

Eleanor smiled, nodding. "A gift from a lovely but very strange lady who made me furious, but it's all ending fine, I guess."

"Was she wearing a blue swirly-type gown?" the Innkeeper asked.

"Actually, yes, she was. But how did you know?" Eleanor asked.

The Innkeeper just smiled and then walked over and stood by the window, looking outside. "Oh, just guessing, just guessing," the Innkeeper replied. Suddenly, she spun around, faced the cousins, clapped her hands a couple of times, and looked at each of them. "It's a very big day," she said with a hearty chuckle and big grin. "So off to your washing rooms and get yourselves ready to go! And as soon as you're done, come to the table! You can't very well have an audience with the Oracle on empty stomachs now, can you?" She hurried to the kitchen as the cousins hurried to the bathing rooms.

Chapter 56

Treasures

Eight clean, combed, and pleasant-smelling cousins hurried into the huge open room. The sizzle of crispy bacon, the hiss of eggs hitting the frying pan, and the smell of blueberry waffles steaming from the waffle iron wafted through the air. Eight steaming bowls of warm oatmeal with strawberries and real peach bits and little dabs of whipped cream were already sitting on the table next to the miniature pitchers of cream and the tiny bowls of soft creamy butter.

The Innkeeper scurried in with the blueberry waffles and poured real, organic maple syrup all over them, assuring everyone that since it was fresh maple syrup, it was quite healthy and it was just fine to have as much as they wanted. And after that, she brought frosty glasses of freshly squeezed orange juice and set them on the table.

She sat at the head of the table and chatted, laughing and asking questions about their gifts and the acquaintances they had met along the way. And they ate, and they ate, and they ate and ate. As they were finishing their food, the Innkeeper glanced up at a round-faced clock with ivy painted around the edges, and she exhaled loudly before suddenly standing up very straight and squaring her shoulders.

"It's time to move on now," she said. "You have places to go, things to do, and people to see, and my part, for now, is done." She grabbed their clean snow clothes from the corner. "Put these on," she said. "It's cold where you're going." As they were slipping them on, she walked over to the huge picture window; and she stood there staring at the towering evergreens, the glistening snow, and the engraved sign flapping back and forth in the wind from the wooden post in the front yard.

Finally, she took in a deep breath. "It is time to go," she said, moving to stand in front of the cousins, "but first, I have to tell you something. It's very important." The cousins stood with puzzled expressions watching her as she began tapping her lips with her steepled fingertips. She squared her shoulders again.

"You are almost there now," she said. "Just go on up the path that brought you here." The cousins glanced back and forth at one another, nodding and smiling.

"But here is what you must know," the Innkeeper continued. "The Oracle lives in a beautiful Citadel. And that Citadel is surrounded by a thick stone wall with a massive gatehouse in the middle. The Citadel has been there forever, but the stone wall was built recently.

"But—and this is the important part—" she said, wagging her finger in the air as she looked at them, "the wall that surrounds the Citadel has a huge gatehouse. It also has twelve arched portal gates built into it—six to the right and six to the left of the gatehouse. Usually, anyone who desires an audience with the Oracle is required to pass through one of the twelve portals. And there are merchants and vendors of every imaginable type and style who try to make a profit by selling keys through one of those twelve portal doors.

"Some of the merchants are honest, but others are not. Some merchants speak in whispers. Some shout. Some are shysters, some are sincere, some are fools, some are honestly trying to help, and some honestly believe they know the best way to approach the Oracle. Some are only trying to make money by persuading you to buy their passes. But whatever happens, do not trade your own treasures for their expensive keys because even though all the portals do eventually lead through the wall and into the presence of the Oracle, none are essential if you have this."

She looked at Levi. Digging down into her apron pocket, she brought out a key—a skeleton key with a round red jewel-encrusted top. "Here," she said, handing it to Levi. "Show this key to the Commander at the stone gatehouse. You'll recognize him by the ribbons and medals on his coat. He will instruct the guards to lift the gridded portcullis of the massive gatehouse, and the guards will allow you to pass. Do not give up your treasures or sell the gifts you have received during your journeys no matter what anyone says. The gifts should never be sold, and they can't be given away."

The cousins passed the key around so each could see it before returning it to Levi. He slipped it into his pocket and then hugged the Innkeeper. "Thank you, thank you," he whispered as he was hugging her. "You have no idea what you have done for us. We thank you."

Tilly and Ivan glanced at Brody and gave him a nod. He reached into his pocket, drawing out a crystal. "Thank you for everything," he said. "This crystal should cover our expenses, but your kindness has been priceless." And all eight cousins smiled and nodded.

"Ooohh," she said, looking down, her face turning a little pink, "no, no, no. I could never accept anything from you. I loved having you here. Now skedaddle. It's time for you to go. You have an audience with the Oracle. But promise me one little thing. Don't let go of your gifts. You'll need them on your journey home, okay?" They all nodded even though they were quite perplexed at her request. The Innkeeper walked to the door and opened it.

Each of the cousins stepped forward, hugging the Innkeeper one by one as they stepped over the threshold and into the snow once more. Addison was the last to pass over. "Thank you," Addison whispered, and then tilting her head to the side, she looked into the Innkeeper's eyes. "Before I go, there is something I need to ask since I might never see you again," she said.

The Innkeeper smiled and nodded. "Okay," she said.

"Why did you do all this for us? Why didn't you accept the crystal?"

For a second, the Innkeeper's eyes lost their sparkle. She glanced out at the cousins who were standing in the snow before looking back into Addison's eyes. "I guess it's because I know how hard a journey can be. I'm still trying to understand my own journey," she said, wistfully looking toward the plateau. "Those icy steps up the mountain are much longer than most expect when they begin searching. Without their gifts, they might never find their way home. I've seen it before, and I want to make sure that you find your way home."

Addison's brow furrowed. "Thank you," she said hesitantly as she turned to go out the door and join her cousins who were impatiently waiting for her on the trail. "I'll never forget your kindness. Thank you."

"Oh, one more little thing," the Innkeeper said, grabbing Addison's arm.

"Yes?" Addison asked.

"I don't know how to say this," the Innkeeper said, "but you don't have to reveal your gifts if down inside there is a voice that says not to. And remember that your tiny mirrors are precious. You should look into them once in a while. Trust me."

"I don't understand—"

The Innkeeper shook her head. "Oh, I'm just being a silly old woman."

"You are not!" Addison chuckled. "You are the most generous, loveliest person ever. Thank you for the comfort and the help. Thank you, again," Addison said one more time. She wrapped her arms around the Innkeeper, hugging her tightly, and then she walked across the threshold and into the snow and then hurried to catch up with the others.

The cousins were chatting and laughing and preparing to climb the last section of icy, jagged stone steps. But this time, their destination was just up and around a few bends and twists on the mountain ledge. And this time their hearts were quite merry with the anticipation of going home.

Chapter 57

The Citadel

Nothing, nothing at all, not the ancient tales of lore or the fables of old could have prepared the cousins for the imposing power or the exquisite beauty of the Citadel. It rose up out of the snow like an elaborate ice sculpture, with belfries and pinnacled towers climbing into the clouds and reaching higher than the peaks themselves.

There were arches and turrets and cupolas and parapets and round keeps with lanterns flickering in spade-shaped windows, and all of it as pristine and intricate as though carved from ice and decorated with snow.

The castle was hewn from the mountain itself, forged from the stone so that the posterior of the castle was fused into the rock face of the mountain. A high thick stone wall with ramparts and battlements like the strongholds of old curved around the castle, surrounding it like a giant horseshoe with the massive gatehouse setting the center and the two prongs fusing back into the mountain. The only way into the castle was through the massive gatehouse with its portcullis or through the twelve arched portals set into the stone wall, six to the right and six to the left of the gatehouse.

A broad raised walkway, an esplanade, ran straight from the stone steps to the gatehouse where it split continuing around the entire perimeter of the wall passing in front of the twelve gated arched portals and not ending until the prongs of the stone wall fused into the mountain on either side of the castle.

The cousins had hurried up those final stone stairs and through a small tunnel that curved up and around ending on the top of the plateau. They stood utterly shocked, gazing at the majestic Citadel forged into the mountain at one end of the plateau and at the chaos—shouting merchants, guards, bartering vendors, and moneychangers—they would have to avoid to get there.

"Just ignore them all no matter what they offer or try to sell. Ignore them," Eleanor said emphatically. "Just keep walking and stick together until we get to the gatehouse." With Esmé in the center, they shuffled along together, refusing to make eye contact with anybody or anything for fear of encouraging a vendor to approach them.

A man in black robes and a turban approached them from the side, opening a velvet box, offering an assortment of shiny keys and claiming that his portal (the one on the far right) was of ancient origins and the Oracle was a wise man who appreciated such things. They passed by without even a glance; but as they did, another man in a black suit grabbed Levi's arm, whispering in low tones, "I have the key to the only real portal. I'll let you in on a little secret—just between us. Many of these peddlers are just shysters. Their promises are empty. They sell worthless keys that won't open the portals at all. See that man over there begging for coins? He spent all his money on worthless keys. But look at my key. This key will open the portal over there, and I'll even go with you to make sure that it opens properly. It is the only one that leads straight to the Oracle. And as you pass through my portal, you will gain wisdom and knowledge—all things the Oracle will respond to and respect." Levi politely said, "No thank you," as he brushed the man's hand off his arm. And they kept going.

A little old lady with white curly hair sat in a chair on the side of the road, muttering that love was the only real key. Then she started crying because she said she didn't have any keys to offer anymore—that hers had been stolen.

The closer they got to the gatehouse, the more frantic and chaotic the atmosphere seemed as the merchants became even more persistent and sly and pushy.

A woman with a turquoise scarf wrapped around her head and with jewels dangling from her neck, her ears, and her arms grabbed Eleanor. Eleanor startled. Whipping around, she found herself staring straight into a set of black eyes. "Listen, lissssen," the woman said, "I see goood things for you iffff you pass through my portal. I see things that show me that you are special. I can tell you what you need to know so thaaattt the Oracle will recognize your specialness, and the Oracle will give you what you need. Cooome, come with meee."

"No, thank you," Eleanor said, jerking her arm away.

An old crone with a hunched back and a long nose walked straight up to Tilly, offering her a silver vial, promising that a swig of elixir from her vial would make her more attractive to the Oracle and that he would grant her wishes due to her beauty. "Look at me," she said, raising her nose into the air. "I am not beautiful, but the Oracle believes I am and he refuses nothing to me. Nothing. I offer my elixir and the key to my portal for a small price."

Claire and Addison grabbed Tilly, pushing her away from the old crone. "No, do not listen to her or anyone with elixir!" they both warned rather loudly and at the same time.

A young tall man strode quietly up and down the road with a placard over his shoulders. "What's that sign say?" Esmé asked as they passed. The young man heard her and hurried over, looking directly into Esmé's eyes. "Why I'd be happy to read it to you, little one," the man said with a syrupy voice. "And perhaps you can persuade your companions to consider my truth and pass through my portal of knowledge." Levi started to grab Esmé's hand, but she jerked it away. "I wanna hear what he says," she said. The young man smiled and began chanting in slow rhythmic tones.

> Thoughts and wishes; hopes and dreams,
> Creating with words, with visions and scenes.
> Crystals and cards, stars and rings
> What makes it all work; what fulfills our schemes?
> Buy keys from me, and soon you shall see
> That the Oracle will give you all that you need.

"Thank you," Levi said to the man as he grabbed Esmé's hand, pulling her away. "Don't do that again," he scolded her. Esmé pouted, her lips puckered, and a tear dribbled down her cheek, but Levi kept hold of her hand and he would not relent.

And on and on they went down the entire esplanade amid shouts for attention and promises of success as merchants scurried behind them, grabbing at them, pulling them aside, and blocking their paths, whistling, shouting above the chaos, vying for their attention. But the cousins kept moving—sometimes pushing, sometimes pulling one another through the crowds—until they finally reached the raised stone platform leading to the massive gatehouse with its gridded gate, the portcullis.

Chapter 58

Commanders and Keys

With a sigh of relief and a huge grin on his face, Levi glanced around at his cousins and his sisters, Claire and Esmé. They were excited and chatting, combing their fingers through their hair, and adjusting their clothes in preparation for their audience with the Oracle. With his heart pounding, Levi jammed his hand into his pocket, grabbed the Innkeeper's key, and beckoned for the excited group to follow as he stepped up onto the platform.

But the second his toe touched the stone rising, a penetrating blare of trumpets stopped him. Drill commands and shouts, double-time marching, and warning whistles echoed across the expanse as soldiers appeared from everywhere and nowhere, rapidly funneling onto the platform from both sides of the gatehouse, instantly forming a rigid impenetrable barrier between the cousins and the portcullis.

An erect dark-haired Commander, embellished with braids and medals and ribbons dripping from the chest and shoulders of his uniform, stepped forward. He pivoted to face the cousins and shouted a single command; rifles and bayonets flashed as soldiers rotated their weapons, dropped the butts to the ground, and stood motionless with their black-gloved hands grasping the shaft of their rifles.

"No entrance here! Proceeeed to the portals!" the Commander demanded, snapping one arm to the left and the other to the right. "Leave immediately!"

Levi instantly stopped, his eyes huge, as he drew in sharp little breaths. Without turning, he lifted his foot to step backward off the platform. Every eye—soldier, sibling, and cousin alike—watched the slow movements of his foot. Until he stopped. With his foot suspended in midair, he simply stopped. Lowering his foot back down on the platform, he shifted his shoulders and looked directly at the Commander.

A slight frown flickered across the Commander's forehead. Dropping his arms, the Commander clasped his hands behind his back, shifting his feet. His eyes met Levi's; his lips curled. Levi looked down at his own feet and then back up, straight into the Commander's eyes. Total silence. Nobody moved. Nobody took a breath. Slowly turning his head, Levi looked over his shoulder at the others. Levi's gentle smile was gone, replaced with something fierce Claire had never seen on her brother's face before.

Claire shuddered. "Levi? What are you doing?" Claire demanded, her harsh whisper filling the silent void.

"Stay here," Levi ordered. "I'm not going back. I can't. We can't."

Still gripping the key in his pocket, Levi took a decisive step forward. "Halt!" the Commander demanded, simultaneously raising his right arm high with an open palm. Instantly, the entire regiment dropped to one knee, aiming their rifles and bayonets directly at Levi. Levi froze. Esmé screamed. Claire grabbed Esmé and snapped her hand over Esmé's mouth. "Shhhh, quiet, Esmé, quiieett. Shhh, quiet now, quiiieeet," she whispered frantically.

Levi stood motionless except for his fist grasping the key, clenching and releasing, clenching and releasing. Slowly—very, very slowly—still staring directly into the eyes of the Commander, he spoke, "We have the key," he said. "We have the key."

The Captain's eyelids flickered; his brow furrowed. His eyes fastened directly onto Levi's, holding them there. Hesitantly, he lowered his arm just a bit; slowly, very slowly, he turned his palm sideways—just a little. He kept his eyes staring directly into Levi's. Levi sucked in a shallow breath, and very, very slowly he took the key out of his pocket. Very, very slowly he raised the key into the air. Something strange flashed across the Commander's face. He stood for a second staring at the key, and after a bit, he flicked two fingers in Levi's direction.

Holding the key out on his palm, Levi cautiously, slowly picked his foot up and inched it forward, up and down, up and down, one step at a time.

And when they stood almost toe to toe, the Commander reached out, taking the key into his own black gloved hand. He touched it, running his fingers along the smooth metal, and held the key up to the light, examining it. His face remained expressionless except for the slight quiver wavering across his bottom lip.

He regarded Levi. Glancing across the platform, he flicked two fingers at the rest of the cousins who stood on the edge, staring with white faces and bated breath. They hurried across the platform.

The Commander pivoted. Facing the portcullis, he proclaimed, "Honored guests for the Oracle. Make way!" With exact precision and flawless movements, the soldiers simultaneously rose and maneuvered around, forming two exact perfect columns. With a slight bow and a sweep of his hand to indicate their path, the Commander ushered the cousins through the aisle formed between the two columns of soldiers.

The click of the Commander's boots and the patter of the cousins' footsteps on the stone walkway echoed across the platform, filling the otherwise silent void. The cousins kept their eyes directed at the gate, hurrying past the stiff rows of soldiers until they finally stood in front of the grid bars of the portcullis.

"Honored guests for the Oracle!" the Captain shouted once more, and instantly eight guards in black fur hats and long red cloaks appeared on the opposite side of the barred gate, parading into place amid the blare of trumpets and rolling beat of drums.

The Captain, erect and still, watched each movement of the trumpeters and the drummers and the red-cloaked guards. At the last command, as the soldiers were stepping into their final position to face the portcullis, he shifted his feet and leaned sideways, ever so slightly toward Levi. "Where'd you get the key?" he whispered with hushed urgency. Levi, still captivated by the precision of the eight guards and somewhat confused by the question, frowned and wavered.

As Levi leaned to the side to answer the Commander, the movement of the guards ceased, and silence dropped once more. With a swift imperceptible shake of his head, the Commander shushed Levi while continuing to stare straight ahead. The Commander lifted the key into the air, and stepping forward, he inserted the key into the keyhole of the gate. He rotated the key. It clicked. He exhaled and stood for a second with eyelids closed.

Suddenly he turned, motioning for the cousins to move into place beside him. Guards on the opposite side of the gate grabbed a chain, hoisting the thick black iron grate higher and higher. The portcullis rose, screeching and grinding against the rock sides as the gate was lifted into place.

The Commander turned once more. He held the key in the air; and then, while a trumpet blared and the drums rolled, he handed it back to Levi. As the key touched Levi's hand, his eyes met the Commander's. "From the Innkeeper," Levi whispered through unmoving lips staring straight forward. The Commander's bottom lip twitched.

Eight guards marched under the gate opening. Each procured a place beside one of the cousins. A deep resounding bell tolled, echoing across the entire plateau. And as it did—and for just a second or two—the merchants and vendors and old ladies and young men, fortune tellers and preachers, the crying children, and bustling teens hushed their shouts and looked about with curious expressions for just a bit and then quickly resumed their yelling and shouting and manipulation as though they had not heard a thing.

One guard picked Esmé up, holding her on one arm. Each of the others looped their elbows through the elbows of one of the cousins. As though marching down the aisle during a marriage ceremony, the guards escorted the cousins under the barred iron gate, across a stone walkway, and through the frozen white courtyard. They stopped in front of the massive doorway leading into the castle—a thick black iron door with a huge gold handle and a jewel-encrusted red keyhole. The first guard gave a nod toward the door.

Levi stepped up to the door. He glanced back at the Commander who stood motionless, staring directly at the door from across the courtyard. Levi inserted the key into the jewel-encrusted red keyhole and twisted. It clicked. Eight cousins exhaled. A smile flickered across the Commander's lips. Levi looked at each of his cousins. Each nodded a quick encouragement, and Levi raised his hand to grab the golden handle; but before he even had a chance to touch it, the door silently swung open entirely on its own.

Chapter 59

Anybody Home?

The guards pivoted and marched back to the gatehouse, leaving the cousins standing there, slightly bewildered. After a bit, Brody shrugged and stepped onto the entrance landing. He stuck his head around the edge of the doorway. "Hello! Heellllooo. Anybody here?" he shouted. "Hellllooooo?" He turned back around, shrugging with his palms in the air.

"What are we wait'n for?" Claire finally demanded. "We're here. The guards dropped us off and left. The door's open. I'm cold. Let's go!" And so, after a few shrugs of hesitant mutual consent, the cousins slipped through the marble entrance and stood staring around at the massive empty room.

There was a huge winding staircase curving up from both sides of the room joining in the middle, creating a catwalk across the back of the room. And there was a gold chandelier dripping with teardrop crystals hanging from the high ceiling in the center of the room, and there were long gold velvet drapes with gold tassels covering the tall windows around the room. But other than that, the room was totally empty. Not a chair, not a picture, not a sofa or a cabinet. Just a big eccentric empty room.

"Helloooo," Brody called out, his voice bouncing off the walls. "Anybody here?" The echoes fell dead. The cousins waited for a while, hoping someone would show up and invite them in;

but no one came, and there was no place to sit in that empty room and nothing to do. So after a little while, Brody slipped to the far side of the room and peeked around the corner. "Nobody's here," he said. "Should we try another room?"

Hesitantly, slowly, they quietly moved deeper into the castle; mushy footsteps and soft clicks interrupted the silence as they shuffled across the marble floors.

"Maybe we shouldn't be roaming around this place," Eleanor said softly. "I feel like a crook or something." But they all just shrugged, agreed with her, but kept going. They passed under arched doorways and looked around corners, calling out here and there until they finally stood at the entrance to a long wide hallway with doors running along both sides.

"Hello? Anybody here?" Brody called out again.

A door behind them rumbled open, sliding into the wall, revealing yet another enormous room. However, this time, everything in the room was red.

"This is just weird," Ivan said.

"Now whaaaat?" Tilly stammered.

"Seems like another creepy invitation. Maybe Oracles have a sense of humor or something. Let's peek inside," Eleanor suggested, moving through the doorway. The others followed. But as soon as they were all inside, the door lurched shut behind them.

Esmé shrieked and began crying. Eleanor grabbed her up, patting Esme's back and whispering in her ear, "Don't worry, little Ezzy, don't worry. The Oracle lives here, and he's gonna help us get home, okay?"

Esmé nodded, puckering her lips, and laid her head on Eleanor's shoulder. Eleanor looked over at Levi, meeting his eyes with her own, and grimaced. Levi shrugged, sending back a confused smile while shaking his head. The cousins glanced backward at the door and then moved closer to one another as they stood gazing about at the very, very red and very, very creepy room.

Chapter 60

The Red Room

The room was red, the walls were red, and the stuffed velvet sofas were red. There were a few black leather armchairs—and it is true the carpets on the floor had meandering green ivy leaves woven into the red flower motif—but mainly, everything was red. Perfectly arranged leather-bound books filled tall narrow red bookcases; crystals and keys hung from red wrought iron hooks. Kaleidoscopes and perfectly synchronized gold clocks set on skinny red shelves.

And then, there were the red candles in the red candleholders. Hundreds of candles with melting wax dripping and sliding into little blobs on the sides while tiny flames danced about, creating flickering shadows across the walls and books and curios, and across all the faces—all the faces of all the life-sized portraits hanging on every part of every wall that was not already covered with books or keys or kaleidoscopes or wooden shelves.

Portraits were hanging from the doorway, leading into the red room, all the way around the red room, and continuing all the way up the winding white marble staircase that rose from the center of the room, snaking its way up higher and higher until it ended at the pinnacle high above.

They stood with heads tilted back, amid the melting, dripping candles at the base of the spiraling stairs, glancing past all the portraits lining the walls all the way up and around. After a bit, they lowered their faces. With mumbled words and curious expressions, they began cautiously meandering about the room, touching the red velvet cushiony sofas, running their fingers across the crystals, and occasionally peering into one of the kaleidoscopes. But they kept to the center of the room and away from the walls with all the strange portraits with candlelight flickering across all those faces.

Because you see, though the red walls and red furnishings and red candles and all the keys and books and clocks and such bewildered them, it was the portraits that totally intimidated them. It was all the portraits and all those faces with all those eyes that seemed to follow them no matter where they stood or what angle they stood in that made them feel as though all the people in all the portraits were watching them, observing everything they touched.

"Maybe this is what we get for wandering around in this place without an invite," Eleanor whispered. "Do you think this is a message or something?"

But after a bit, when nothing happened, and nobody came to check on them, curiosity and boredom took over; and gradually, one by one, the cousins began slipping a little closer to the walls. And before you know it, they were examining the portraits, scrutinizing the faces, noticing slight differences, considering similarities, and quietly pointing out oddities as if they were in an art museum.

A different person stood in each portrait; but each of them—male or female, old or young—was dressed in red flowing robes and red skullcaps. There were stone-cold, wrinkled faces, and there were youthful happy faces. Some sneered, some appeared weary or even broken, others seemed vibrant and pleasant, but each held something, offering treasures on outstretched hands and open palms. They held crystals or tiny clocks or amulets or rings or keys or closed books with titles in fancy calligraphy or open books with fingers pointing to specific passages. There were scrolls and shiny rocks and candles and lanterns. One very ancient smiling woman even held a glowing piece of light almost as though she was offering a bit of a star.

As the cousins wandered around the room, scrutinizing the portraits, Addison stood by herself, in front of the winding staircase, looking around, and silently watching the other. After a while, Claire noticed and walked over. Shaking her head softly and rolling her eyes, Claire started talking before she even reached Addison.

"No, Addie, I do not think this has anything to do with Victoria's house," she said. "I think these are all pictures of old wise Oracles. Maybe all these Oracles knew something special, and this is a place where all that knowledge is saved. Maybe the portraits show their power or their discoveries. So don't let your mind go to weird places, okay?"

Addison shrugged. "Ya, but how do we know? I mean—"

"Well, think about it, Addie, and use your head instead of your imagination. This place was hard to get to. Nobody made it easy for us. It's more like we had to pay the price for getting to the Oracle. On the other hand, Victoria practically forced us into that situation. And," Claire continued, sweeping her hand around the room, "as creepy as they are, all these people seem to be offering something. They aren't trapped in mirrors."

Addison shrugged. "Okay, maybe you're right. But I've felt weird about this place from the moment we knocked on the door on the side of the mountain. The butterflies flew away, and the wolves keep howling."

"That's called nature, Addie. That's what animals do. Just leave this alone, okay?" Claire retorted. "This is how we get home, and Oracles must be strange. That's why they're Oracles, and we're not. I agree that this is all very weird, but if it gets us home—" Claire shrugged, but then her face lit up. "And I'll tell ya what," she said, "if this doesn't work, I'll be the first one chasing butterflies with you."

Addison smiled. "Oh, all right," she muttered, plopping down on the bottom step, putting her elbows on her knees, her chin on her palms as she continued watching the others.

But after a bit, curiosity won; and slowly, hesitantly Addison got up and began wandering up the steps, gazing into the eyes of the people in the portraits and puzzling over the objects they offered. She got lost in time as she bent forward, scrutinizing expressions, peering into eyes, noting markings on clothing and the objects they held as the quiet chatter from the others drifted up the stairs and turned into background static. And everything was curious, but everything was fine.

Until suddenly, Addison gasped, slapping her hand over her mouth, bending forward to examine the portrait or an old lady with wide startled-looking eyes and a tight-lipped mouth. The lady held two objects in her extended hands: a tiny silver engraved mirror on the one hand and a tiny lantern on the other hand. Addison moved closer to the portrait, studying the engravings of the mirror.

She reached into her front pocket, drawing her own mirror out. Touching the silver engraving around the edges, she examined the mirror in the portrait again. And that is when she noticed a tiny leather pouch, a miniature of Tilly's wallet hanging around the lady's neck. The pouch was almost hidden in the folds of her red robe.

Addison stood on the step, biting the inside of her cheek and thinking. She slipped her mirror back into her pocket. Her eye caught on another picture. She moved up a few steps to look closer, and there stood a lovely lady with long black wavy hair and beautiful dark eyes. And she was holding two butterflies: a blue one and a purple one.

Addison stood there amid the dripping candles. She stepped back down, and bending forward, she gazed at the silver mirror once more. Suddenly, forgetting everything else, she yelled. "Claire, Eleanor!" she yelled. "Claire, Eleanor, come now!"

Eleanor and Claire ran toward the spiral staircase. Actually, all the cousins rushed to the staircase; but just as Claire and Eleanor jumped onto the first step, they stopped, instantly freezing in place, staring straight past Addison and up the steps. Addison frowned and slowly turned. She clapped her hand over her mouth, staring up the spiral stairway.

Because there he stood, on a step, high above them, all watching and smiling. Thick black ringlets tumbled out from the small red cap encircling his head. Everything else about him was full and rich and noble from the cardinal-red velvet robes wrapping his tall handsome frame to the wide golden sash encircling his waist and the amulets and gold chains and crystals hanging around his neck. Deep crinkles bounded his eyes and mouth, as though his face had never known a time without a smile crumpling it. And there could be no mistake at all but that this was, indeed and at last, the Oracle.

Like a wax figure coming to life, he suddenly animated and began gracefully flowing down the spiral staircase toward them. "Children, children, I heard you were coming," he said with outstretched hands. "Oh my, oh my, you are here at last. Finally, and at last. There have been signals and murmurings from all over to expect children from beyond. And now you are here. You are finally here."

He steepled his fingertips, tapping them against his lips, and then gently shook his head back and forth as he flowed past Addison and then continued on until he reached the bottom step. "Ohhh, and here is the little one. What a little sweetheart." He bent forward, gazing directly into Esmé's eyes with his own startling clear blue ones. She glanced around at Levi, who encouraged her with a wink and a nod, as the Oracle picked Esmé up, wrapping his arms around her, enfolding her tiny body within his own velvet red robe.

He looked around at each of them; his eyes met each one. "I know why you are here," he said, "and yes, of course, I can get you home. But there is timing involved, so I only ask one little thing. I ask that you join me for a meal before you leave so I can hear about your adventures and share in the wonder of your journey. The meal is being prepared as we speak. May I ask your indulgence and company for an hour before I send you home?" he asked with a smile of the richest, loveliest, and gentlest kind. And all the cousins could do at that moment was to smile back and nod.

"Then, let us proceed to the alcove," the Oracle said with a slight bow and a flourish of his hand. And with that, he turned and walked to the far end of the red room, under an archway, and into the most quaint and cozy alcove ever. Windows reaching from floor to ceiling arched around the circular nook. A long polished oval wood table set in the center of the room with nine high-backed chairs around it. A cracking fire roared in a huge open fireplace.

Outside, soft fat snowflakes drifted past the windows while the snow-covered mountains rose majestic and proud in the background. Amid smiles, sighs of relief, excitement, and stunned silence, they all pulled out their high-backed chairs and sat down to have one last experience in this land of frozen beauty before finding their way back home.

CHAPTER 61

Dinner with the Oracle

The Oracle sat at the head of the long polished table, beaming with assurances and reassurances; they had done good—very good. This was it; they had really done it. They sat breathing deeply, wavering between giddy joy and profound relief, trying to soak in their new reality. They sat as honored guests of the Oracle, experiencing one more extraordinary event before entering the portal where a little magic mixed with some special power would propel them back to home, to Gramma, and to normal.

The Oracle jingled the tiny silver bell, setting beside his plate. The room came alive as waiters balancing trays of steaming soup on their shoulders flowed into the room from nowhere and everywhere, placing the first course in front of the cousins who suddenly remembered their manners, spread their red napkins on their laps, and waited to begin.

"Eat, eat!" the Oracle chuckled, waving the back of his hand at them as he picked up his own spoon and began slurping up the savory sage and cabbage soup from his red bowl.

And before long, everyone was as happy and cheerful as happy and cheerful can be. The Oracle was asking questions about their journeys, and they were all talking around and on top of one another as they told their stories, laughing about many of their ordeals through strange places.

And all the while, waiters with the red aprons whisked in and out, continually replacing empty dishes with full dishes. When the main entrée was finally set before them, the Oracle cut a piece of roast goose, sighing as he lifted it into his mouth. "Is anything better than roast goose?" he asked as he chewed for a second with his eyes closed. When he opened his eyes, he almost startled as he looked around the table and realized the eight cousins were watching him and each was smiling.

And they all laughed and reached down and picked up their knives and forks, anxious to taste their own roast goose. It felt rather like Christmas, if truth be told, with the fire crackling and the snow falling and the warm spirits and the laughter and the tales of adventures and the succulent roast goose.

They all chewed and smiled; and, after a while, the Oracle laid his fork down on his plate and sat back in his chair, looking at them with his kind face with the crinkles around the eyes. "Your stories are so amazing," he said. "But I would love to hear more about the treasures you gathered on your journey through these lands." He tinkled his bell, and servants scurried in again, clearing the table. "And I would love to see—"

But at that very second, a sudden ferocious howling and baying of wolves interrupted him, piercing the cold mountain air and sending chilling echoes between the snowy mountain peaks, reverberating throughout the alcove. All of them stopped and turned to gaze out the massive windows surrounding the nook. When the howls stopped, they all slowly turned back to the table.

"Oh, those wolves," the Oracle explained as he looked at all the pale faces and huge eyes around the table. "I've never quite gotten used to the wolves around here either," he continued as he smiled once more and the crinkles lit his face up again. Now, about those adventures you have been on, did you ever run into wolves? If so, you must tell me all about it."

And with that, Addison and Claire began telling of the wolves trapping them in the cabin. And then, Levi and Eleanor told about being stuck in the tree, and everyone laughed at their adventures because now that the danger was over, in a strange sort of way, their troubles seemed almost funny instead of scary.

As they told their stories, the Oracle was laughing so hard that his entire body shook. "So where was this cabin?" he asked between laughs. "Where was this fabulous tree?"

That led Ivan and Brody to talk about their adventures with Jeslue, and Tilly told about the cart ride and the wallet. The Oracle said he had never seen a wallet from that land, so Tilly passed it over to him; and touching it almost reverently, he examined it from all angles before laying it down on the table in front of him.

"My gift is a silver engraved mirror," Claire broke in. "Would you like to see it? Me and A—"

The Oracle's eyes flashed. "A mirror you say? Yes, show it to me!" he interrupted abruptly, holding his hand out. "I mean, please, I'd love to see it." And he smiled, and his face crinkled. "I've always love silver engravings and just always wanted to uhh—"

"Oh, of course," Claire said, standing up and taking the mirror from her pocket. As she reached across the table to hand it to the Oracle, a wolf howled so suddenly and so ferociously that Claire dropped the mirror onto the table. The Oracle looked down at the mirror and then up again at Claire. "Pay no attention to the wolves," he soothed. "They are up in the mountains and can't hurt us in here. Come look out the windows with me. I need to show you something that will help you understand," he said, pushing his chair back and standing up.

Everyone jumped up except Addison; she turned to look out the windows, but she remained sitting as the others gathered around the windows, pointing and talking. Absentmindedly, she picked up the mirror that Claire had dropped on the table. After running her fingers around the engravings, she held it up to look at her own face. As she straightened her hair, a flash of black crossed the mirror just as the Oracle and her cousins returned to the table. She turned her head. *What was that?* she wondered, laying the mirror down and looking around.

"See, all is well," the Oracle continued as he sat down. "Now, let's see that mirror." Addison picked up Claire's mirror, handing it across the table; but as it passed over Tilly's wallet, she noticed a reflection, an inscription or something reflected in it. She glanced down at the wallet and then up at the mirror again, catching the eyes of the Oracle as she did.

He quickly dropped his gaze as he grabbed the mirror and ran his fingers around the silver back of it, examining the intricate silver design. "These are amazing treasures, indeed," he said as he held it at various angles.

"The silver engravings are beautiful, but the mirror itself is perfect too," Claire suggested. "Turn it over and see what you think."

"No, I don't think so." He chuckled. "Not a reflection that I want to remind myself of." The cousins laughed at his self-deprecation and assured him that he was handsome indeed. And so, after running his fingers across the delicate engravings a few more times, he turned the mirror over and glanced at it. "Well, just as I thought," he said. "One very old Oracle."

And with that, the Oracle glanced out the windows at the deep darkness and then at the huge grandfather clock in the corner, and he sighed. He set his napkin on the table and stood up. "Well, it seems that time has slipped away too quickly," he said, "and unfortunately for me, I suppose it is time for your journey home to begin." The bottom of his red velvet robe swirled about his feet as he turned to leave. "Come on now. We must hurry."

Each of the cousins glanced at one another, pushed away from the table, grabbed their treasures, and hurried behind the Oracle as he began the ascent up the grand spiral staircase.

Chapter 62

Portraits and Mirrors

Addison held back, waiting for the others to climb the winding steps ahead of her. And then, cupping her hand around the silver engraved mirror, she slipped it from her pocket and held it inconspicuously at her side. She casually caught up to Tilly and turned the mirror just enough to catch the reflection of the wallet. *I knew it! I was right,* she thought. *There is definitely writing on it—inscriptions or instructions or something. But it only shows up in the mirror. But why? So many weird things around here.*

As she stood on the step, trying to decide what to do, the others went ahead of her. Brody jabbed her arm as he walked by. "Come on, Addie," he said, "we don't have time to dwaddle right now."

"I know," she said. "I'm coming. There's a picture over there that I wanna look at really quick on the way up."

Brody smiled, nodded, and hurried to catch up with Ivan.

Addison found the portrait of the lady with the mirror, examined it, and then stood on a step, chewing on the inside of her cheek. *Okay, this portrait is saying something. There was a shadow that crossed the mirror, the wolves have been howling, and I know there is something on Tilly's wallet. I need to tell them just in case something is wrong. But if I say anything and I'm* wrong, then that could cause problems. *How do I do this?* she thought as she stood there tapping her finger against her thigh.

I got it! she said a little too loudly. *Trick Claire into using her own mirror. And then, when she sees the inscriptions on the wallet, they will pay attention, and I can tell them about the rest of the strange things around here before we get up to the portal—hopefully.* She turned to hurry up the stairs and catch up with the others, pausing for just a bit as she passed the picture of the lady with the butterflies. She turned to dash up the steps at the same time that Claire was looking down at her from over the winding balustrade.

"Addison!" Claire yelled from a landing high above. "Will you hurry up? We don't have time for you to look at pictures. Come on!" Claire demanded. "We don't have to go all the way up to the top. The Oracle's portal is right here. Everyone is waiting for you! It's time to go home! Hurry!"

Addison scurried up the steps two at a time and stepped next to Claire. "Claire, I have something to tell you," she whispered in Claire's ear. But she was shushed. "Just a minute, Addie. I wanna hear what the Oracle's saying."

The Oracle had closed his eyes; he was muttering strange, unintelligible words while holding his hands in the air and wiggling his fingers. Suddenly, his eyes flashed open. "Once I open this door," he said, "there is no turning back." Put your lantern, crystals, and your mirror into your pockets. Fasten the satchel and wallet tightly over your shoulders. This can be a slightly bumpy ride, as they say. Everyone understand?"

They all nodded. Eleanor and Tilly checked the clasps and tightened the straps on their satchel and wallet.

"About the mirror," he continued, "that situation is extremely important. Mirrors must stay inside your pocket until you are home. Mirrors create false illusions in the portal, and those illusions could take you in wrong directions. It is more than essential that you do not use your mirror until you get out of the portal. Understand?" he asked.

"Yes." Claire nodded as she reached into her pocket, touching her mirror.

"You too, Addie," Claire whispered, and Addison nodded.

"Okay, then," he said, "the time has come." He looked into the eyes of each cousin, and his face crumpled into a benevolent, sweet smile. He raised his right arm high. Flashes, like bolts of lightning, sparked into the air as he opened his fingers.

"Let the games begin!" he shouted as he turned toward the door.

Addison took a deep breath, nervously stepping forward. "Wait, I have a—"

"What games?" a voice interrupted from the stairs.

They all snapped their heads around.

"I do so love games. Wait for me!" The Innkeeper laughed as she hurried up the last steps.

The entire group whooped a very loud whoop, turning to hug her. "Oh, stay where you are. I'm coming!" she called out. By the time she reached them, she was huffing and puffing and had to catch her breath amid all the shouting and hugging.

"Were you going to say something?" Levi asked Addison.

"I was, but it's okay now. The Innkeeper seems content, so I'm good," Addison whispered with a sigh of relief. Levi shrugged and turned back to listen.

"What are you doing here?" the Oracle asked the Innkeeper with a slight frown. "I have prepared, and it is time for the travelers to go home."

"Well, then I'm not a minute too late, am I?" laughed the Innkeeper. "You didn't think I could let these precious ones leave without a last hug, did you?"

The Oracle smiled at the Innkeeper. "How did you get here?" he asked.

"Oh, I just climbed those steps like everyone else," she replied with a chuckle as she patted the cousins on their backs.

"But how did you get through the gate?"

"Oh, I have my ways." She chuckled. "We can chat all about those silly incidentals after the children leave. Time is a-wasting, and I certainly don't want to slow you down. Time, time, time. Can't be late! But I just had to be here for this send-off," she beamed at the cousins.

"It is time to go," the Oracle said. "Say your good-byes. We need to enter the portal room now."

"Well, I'm here. Time's a-wasting. Let's go. This'll be wonderful. It's been so long since I've seen the portal," the Innkeeper beamed.

"But you don't really want to come into the portal with them," the Oracle objected. "There are so many distractions and time constraints once we enter the portal room. Wouldn't you prefer to say your good-byes out here?"

"Oh, goodness, no!" the Innkeeper exclaimed. "I certainly wouldn't climb all those silly stairs if I didn't want to see them off in the proper fashion." She smiled a huge smile. "But I promise I won't go into the actual portal with them. Wouldn't want to end up living in the treehouse now, would I?" She laughed again.

The cousins chuckled, and they all agreed that they especially wanted her to be with them as they entered the portal.

"Well," she said, bending forward and looking the Oracle straight in the eyes, "I didn't mean to mess up any timing. Now, where were you?" She stopped and looked around. "Oh yes, I remember now! Drumroll, please!" She laughed as the cousins created a drumroll with their tongues. "Ready?" she said. "Then, if I remember right, I think you were at, 'Let the games begin!'"

"Yes, and we must hurry now," the Oracle said soberly as he turned to face the door, taking a key out of his pocket. "You must pay close attention," the Oracle said as he held a key high in the air. "This is the key to the portal. Once we are inside, I will lock the door behind us, and the process will begin. Are you ready?"

They all nodded. The Oracle slipped the key into the lock; the massive white door slid open. One by one, the cousins passed in front of him; the Innkeeper swept by at the end. He closed the door and locked it. He led them through a short opening, under an archway, and into the most perfectly and totally white room that any of them could have ever imagined (even if, for some odd reason, any of them had actually tried to imagine a perfectly white room, which none of them ever had).

Everything was white. The walls were white marble; the windows were surrounded by carved white wood and covered with thick white velvet drapes. The floor was white marble with a thick shaggy white carpet in the center. There were several pictures hanging here and there on the walls, but they were all pictures of snow-laden mountains, and even the sky behind the mountains was more like a soupy white misty fog instead of blue. And those pictures were enclosed in thick white frames.

White taper candles set in white candlestick holders flickered throughout the room. A white marble spiraling staircase with white wrought iron railings curved up to a white ceiling high above. A massive white chandelier with strands of tiny crystal balls sinuously wrapping around the white metal arms hung from the exact center of the room and right above the white throne that set in the middle of a round white platform. A giant round white clock facing down from the pinnacle at the top of the white winding staircase lurched forward second by second.

The room was uniform and perfect. It was magnificent. It was cold and austere. It was overwhelming, and it was, indeed, very, very white. And very, very silent and very echoey.

Chapter 63

The Portal

They stood in the center of the room looking up at the strange white clock that faced down from the pinnacle at the top of the spiral staircase. When they turned to examine the white throne, they were shocked to see the Oracle sitting on it. He was staring at them, but he was changed. He was no longer the genial, pleasant man laughing and telling stories around a cozy table; instead, power emanated from his very being. His face was bright, and his eyes flashed as though he was looking into their very souls. He had transformed.

"Gather around," he commanded. "Timing is critical."

Stepping forward, the cousins assembled in a semicircle at the base of the platform. They averted their eyes; the Oracle's were too powerful or perhaps too direct. "Pay attention," he said. "What I have to say is especially important. The journey through the portal is exacting. Are you ready to begin?"

They all nodded uncertainly.

"There is a portal door over there," he said. "Look at it." They turned, and indeed, there was an arched door opposite the throne.

Each of them nodded and stood silent, waiting for him to continue.

"When the clock tolls at exactly eleven seconds and eleven minutes after eleven, you will pass through that portal. You will have eleven seconds to go as far as possible before the door slams shut. There will be no turning back or changing your minds after that portal door closes. Do you understand?"

They all nodded, glancing nervously back and forth to one another.

Suddenly, his face crinkled into a smile; and once more, he seemed almost like the Oracle they understood. Almost. "Don't look so worried," he said with a gracious smile. "I will make sure it all goes exactly as it should."

"At exactly eight minutes after eleven o'clock, it will be time to begin the final preparations. You will say your farewells and then form a line in front of the portal. Levi first. Esmé next to him. Then Claire, Addison, Brody, Tilly, Ivan, and, finally, Eleanor. Do you understand?"

They all nodded.

"When the clock tolls at precisely eleven minutes after eleven o'clock, Levi will take this key and insert it into the portal door. Do not open the door. Just insert the key and be ready. Do you understand, Levi?"

Levi nodded. The Oracle handed him the key.

"While Levi is doing that, all of you will grab one another's hands. Eleanor is to make sure that everyone is ready to go through the portal door one by one. Do you understand, Eleanor?"

Eleanor nodded.

"When the clock strikes eleven seconds after eleven minutes after eleven o'clock, I will give the final signal. Levi will open the portal door and grab Esmé's hand. You must all walk across the portal doorway in one chain. Does everyone understand?"

They all nodded.

"Once you enter, you must keep walking. When you eventually see the light on the other side, walk straight into the light. There will be a flash when you pass over the final barrier, walk through, and you will be close enough to home to find the way."

He looked at each of them. "Are your mirrors, lanterns, crystals, small things in your pockets, and the satchel and wallet strapped tightly over your shoulders?"

Every cousin nodded.

They all looked at the clock. The minute hand lurched forward. Eight minutes after eleven o'clock. The Oracle looked at them. "Well, my sweet visitors, it is time to get into place. Unfortunately, the Innkeeper will need to stand across the room so that there is no interference when the time comes. So give her your last hugs now."

They hugged the Innkeeper and the Oracle, and with wobbly knees, and shaky smiles, they walked over and stood in front of the portal door. Levi stood closest to the portal door, then Esmé, Claire, Addison, Brody, Tilly, Ivan, and Eleanor last. Each cousin sucked in deep breaths as they gazed around the room, trying to capture their last moments in that enchanted land. The minute hand lurched forward. Nine minutes after eleven.

"Well, this is almost it," Eleanor said. "I would like to say thank you so very much. You know we will never forget any of this or your kindness, don't you?" She smiled at the Oracle and then at the Innkeeper. The rest of the cousins nodded and added their thank-yous, love, and wishes. They looked up at the clock. The second hand lurched forward. Thirty-five seconds and nine minutes after eleven o'clock.

The Innkeeper stood across the room, patting her lips with her fingertips; her face scrunched into an ugly cry face as her eyes misted. "Wait!" she suddenly shouted. "We only have a little more than a minute. One last hug, please before you go." She began moving toward them. "And I have one small strange request while I hug you," she said quickly as she moved.

"An Oracle from long ago had a mirror just like Claire's and Addison's. She said it did magical things in this room. I'd love to glimpse in the mirror together with all of you. We will share an unforgettable memory. Addison, can I have your mirror for all of us to glance into?"

"No!" snapped the Oracle. "Mirrors create distortions and delays. They must keep them tucked away until they get home. It is essential on every level. It is also important that there is no interference at this point."

"Oh, you are right, of course," the Innkeeper said. Her face reddened as she looked about uncomfortably and moved back. "I am sorry. I so wanted to look into the mirror one last time so we could share the final memory," she said, looking straight into Addison's eyes.

The second hand lurched around the giant clock face facing down from the pinnacle at the top of the white winding staircase struck, sending vibrations through the silent room. They all looked up. Ten minutes after eleven o'clock. The Oracle stood on the platform of his throne, watching the clock, preparing to start the final countdown.

Addison glanced up at the clock. Ten seconds and ten minutes after eleven o'clock. She broke loose from the chain. "Well, one last hug anyway," she said as she wrapped her arms around the Innkeeper. "You can keep it," she whispered. Addison put her hand over her own heart and then touched the Innkeeper's heart. "Always," she said as she pulled back, slipping the mirror into the Innkeeper's apron pocket. She turned and rushed back into place. She slipped back into place, grabbing Claire's and Brody's hands again. The cousins glanced at the clock. Forty-five seconds and ten minutes after eleven.

The Innkeeper fingered the mirror. Her eyes met Addison's. Cupping her hand over the mirror, she slipped slightly closer to the cousins. While the Oracle watched the clock in the pinnacle, the Innkeeper continued slipping closer to the portal door.

The clock tolled and the sound reverberated throughout the room once more.

"Exactly eleven eleven!" the Oracle called out. "Levi, insert the key. But do not open the door." Levi pushed the key into the door; his hands were shaky, and the key was sticky—he had to wiggle it back and forth several times—but finally, the key slipped into the keyhole.

"Grab hands, everyone. Eleanor, make sure they are together!" shouted the Oracle. Eleanor bent forward and looked up with a nod and a slightly scared smile.

The Innkeeper watched the Oracle watching the clock. She slowly crept closer to the portal door, blowing kisses to the cousins as she moved in.

Tolls vibrated throughout the room.

"Eleven eleven and eleven seconds!" shouted the Oracle, "Levi, open the door. Your eleven seconds begins!"

Levi turned the key; it stuck just a little. "Aaahhh!" he hollered, jiggling it frantically. Suddenly, it clicked. The portal door swung open wide. "Go!" yelled the Oracle.

The Innkeeper lifted the mirror into the air, turning it, so it reflected the open portal. Levi turned, grabbing Esmé's hand.

"Go!" shouted the Oracle. "Go now!"

"Stop!" screamed the Innkeeper. "Stop!" she screamed. "Don't go!"

Levi's foot was on the threshold. Addison glanced at the Innkeeper and yanked back with all her might; the cousins stumbled, pulling Levi back.

"NOW!" shouted the Oracle. "Go. Go. Before the portal closes!" Levi faltered forward.

"No, no, no, no!" screamed the Innkeeper, still holding the mirror high. "No!"

The Oracle rushed forward, knocking the mirror from her hand. It crashed to the floor, shattering the glass.

"Run!" yelled the Oracle, "Go now!!"

The Oracle grabbed Esmé, pushing her through the portal door. Addison flung herself in front of Esmé. "No!" she screamed, pulling Esmé back.

The Innkeeper grabbed Eleanor, yanking her back. Still holding hands, the cousins lurched forward and then fell back again and again as the Oracle and Innkeeper fought for priority. They stumbled, and Claire fell, tipping Esmé over. Esmé screamed.

The portal door slammed shut.

Ten bewildered, horrified, scared, and/or relieved people turned, silently staring at the door.

"What just happened?" Ivan muttered. Seven cousins, one Oracle, and one Innkeeper looked directly at him. Then they all looked at the door, and for a few seconds at least, nobody said a word.

Chapter 64

Drapes and Darkness

The Innkeeper collapsed to her knees. "Oh my gosh!" she shrieked, her shoulders shuddering as she crumpled forward onto her elbows, her fingers wringing through her hair. "All this time, all those people, all those hopes, and dreams."

The Oracle slipped over to her, gently laying his hand on her shoulder. "You are mistaken," he said. "But I will help you. It will be just fine."

She slapped his hand off. "Don't touch me, you grotesque, filthy snake or whatever you are."

The Oracle looked at the cousins, his face grim and tired and full of concern. "As you can see, she needs rest. I will send for help. I am so sorry that you had to see this." He pursed his lips, shaking his head. "The nightmarish delusions from mirrors in this place—I tried to warn her." He smiled gently and bent forward. "And don't worry about your own situation. We'll send you home through the portal. Nothing is lost, only slightly delayed."

The Innkeeper jumped up, stretching her arms across the front of the cousins. "No, never again!" she screamed. "You won't ever do that again."

"But it is the only way for them to go home," the Oracle said. "Now, you must calm down. You are confusing them. I am going to call for help. You need a little help, my dear. There is a reason mirrors are not allowed in this place."

The Innkeeper turned and held out her hand. "Claire, give me your mirror!" she demanded.

"Mirrors only create distortions in here," the Oracle said, shaking his head. "You can see the possible outcome." He looked at the cousins, sighing with his palms raised as he glanced at the Innkeeper and then back at them.

"Please give me the mirror, Claire."

Claire hesitated, looking back and forth between the two.

"Claire, I think you should give her your mirror," Addison said softly. "I've seen some things," she said.

"And it will be wonderful to hear all those things," the Oracle broke in. "Do not use the mirror, Claire. I am going to pull that rope over there and summon help. So hold your wonderful stories until they come. Then, we will be able to hear all about the things you saw. Just trust me, dear."

"But I don't trust you," Addison said, a tremor catching in her throat. She stared directly into the Oracle's eyes. Her knees quivered. She squared her shoulders. "There's a portrait of a lady with a mirror like mine above the steps, and when the mirror passed over Tilly's wallet—"

"My child," the Oracle interrupted, "first things first." He turned to walk to the edge of the room as a long white rope hung from the ceiling. "Let me summon help, and then we can all sit down in the alcove with some hot chocolate and hear about your discoveries." He smiled at Addison as he turned.

"Give me the mirror now," the Innkeeper shrieked, "before he summons his guards!"

Claire looked at the Innkeeper, and then she looked at the Oracle who was hurrying across the room. She looked straight into Addison's eyes. Reaching into her pocket, she drew out the mirror. "This one's for you, Addie," she said as she slapped the mirror into the Innkeeper's open palm. "And I hope you're right."

"What have you done? Do not use mirrors in here!" the Oracle shrieked.

"Look!" the Innkeeper screamed, holding the mirror over the fleeing Oracle. "Look at the truth, children! Look at the truth!"

The Oracle cowered forward with his back toward them and his hands over his face.

"The black shadows on the mirror were him?" Addison gasped.

"Stop, you crazy woman!" the Oracle shouted as he grabbed for the white rope. Brody seized his arm, pushing the Oracle off balance so that he fell onto the floor. "Another one for Addie!" Brody said.

"Don't believe her!" the Oracle snarled. "It's a lie. I tell you—a lie. Don't believe her magic tricks. Mirrors lie in this place, and if the Innkeeper has her way, you will never get home. You must not believe the illusion!" he shrieked as he turned to hurry out the door. Instead, he stopped and stood there, calmly looking at them, and then moved toward his throne, a sly smile etched across his lips.

The Innkeeper closed her eyes. "Ivan," she said with a shudder, "Ivan, quickly, take your lantern out. Shine it on the windows." Frowning, Ivan reached into his pocket and drew out his lantern.

The Innkeeper hurried to the windows. "If I am right—if I am right—if the rumors are true, we will know now. If not, you can banish me forever."

She grabbed the white velvet drapes covering the window and snapped them open with a wild jerk and continued jerking one set of drapes after another until all the windows were exposed.

The room darkened with each jerk of the drapes until everything was pitch black, except for the flickering of the candle flames and the light of the chandelier. It was ghoulish and dark as the room was buried in shadows. Even the chandelier disappeared in the darkness; the flickering flames seemed suspended in the air. In the darkness, the Oracle slithered on his throne and sat watching them; it was too late to stop the Innkeeper. Esmé began whimpering and crying. "Why is it so dark, Levi?" Levi picked her up, and she crumpled into him.

"Come here, Ivan, please," the Innkeeper said. "Shine your light over these windows. I think we will know." Ivan held his light over the windows, and then he slowly reached out and touched them. "Those are not windows," he muttered. "Those are mirrors. The drapes were covering mirrors." He shone his light against the wall. "This room is not white. This room is pure blackness." Confused, Ivan rotated in a circle, turning with his light to peer through the darkness.

Suddenly, Eleanor gasped. "Ivan, shine your light onto the throne. My gosh, look at the throne." They all turned to look. And there he sat, gnarled, wrinkled, hunched, snarling, slobbering, and licking his fingers, muttering defiant dark words through sneering lips and glazed eyes.

The Innkeeper slapped her hand over her mouth, sobbing. "Close the drapes!" she cried. "Close the drapes!" The cousins yanked the drapes closed, and all was white and beautiful again; and the Oracle was handsome and noble looking with cardinal-red velvet robes wrapping his tall handsome frame, a wide golden sash around his waist, and amulets and gold chains and crystals hanging around his neck.

Chapter 65

The Oracle's Usurper

The Oracle sat on his throne, grinning nonchalantly, tapping his fingertips together. He appeared so handsome—it was almost impossible to imagine the twisted, hunched, wrinkled being that actually sat there.

The Innkeeper stood with her face buried in her hands, trembling as sobs racked her body. When she finally looked up, she appeared dazed and confused. "Where'd the seekers go? They never went home, did they?" Her voice faltered. "You sent them into that blackness, into that darkness with the bugs and vermin that I saw in Addison's mirror. But where did they go?"

The Oracle grimaced. The corners of his mouth turned down as he shrugged with his palms in the air. "I don't actually know," he said, bending forward. "The travelers go through the portal door, it slams shut, and—*whoosh*—they're gone. Nobody ever comes back to tell the tale." He drew in a deep breath, sighing and smiling. "They are wandering around in there. I assume they pop out somewhere."

The Innkeeper's eyes flittered around the room, unfocused, searching._Finally, her gaze landed back on the Oracle. "But how?" she sobbed. "I was in that portal before. It was beautiful. And you, you were kind and wise and— what happened? What happened to you?" She focused her gaze on the Oracle's eyes and suddenly inhaled sharply. "On no! You're not the Oracle!" She gasped.

"Well, of course not, silly woman! It took you long enough to realize that little piece of information." He stared at her with a bright smile. "Come now, let's play a game. Don't you recognize me? Look closely. Look past the red robes and the altered hair and face. Consider the eyes. Recognize me?"

The Innkeeper stared straight into his eyes. "But you look like—no, I don't recognize—" She unexpectedly slapped her hand over her mouth. "Oh my gosh! It can't be! Are you the Oracle's apprentice from long, long ago? But you—"

"That's it, that's it!" the fake Oracle broke in. "Yes, long ago I was an Oracle's apprentice!" He chuckled, nodding his head.

Then his voice lowered as he glared at the Innkeeper. "But don't you ever call me an apprentice again! I hate that name! An apprentice, plahh! I need a better name," he muttered, drumming his fingers. Suddenly his face flushed with excitement. "I know! I know! You can call me the Usurper. Yes, the Usurper! Has a certain powerful ring to it, don't you think?"

The Innkeeper shook her head. "It doesn't matter what we call you!" the Innkeeper shrieked. "Where is the Oracle? What did you do with him?"

"That clown? Oh, I banished him long ago—way before the wall and the merchants and way, way before the dome." The Usurper glanced around. "He didn't even see it coming till it was too late. And then, even better, you villagers were so easily fooled by outside appearances, so you never noticed the difference between the real and the fake," he continued while wagging his finger. "Whoops! Got ya! But you can't say we didn't have fun now, can you?"

"But I don't under—why did you do this? Why?" cried the Innkeeper.

The Usurper shrugged, smirking as though it was the stupidest question he had ever heard. "Why? Why?" He paused, looking up at the clock. "Well, I suppose I did it because I could.

And, oh wait," he added, "and because I had an epiphany!" He crossed his arms over his chest as he inhaled and smiled.

"And it was such a wonderful epiphany too," he added. "It confirmed what I had known all along—that it was time for the Oracle to go, grow old, and give someone else a chance to play with time and portals.

"Besides, it was all his own fault," the Usurper said, shaking his head.

"He kept repeating the same old things about the price for being an Oracle. He insisted that the mirrors and the clocks be perfectly synchronized so the portal could be pure or something like that. He knew how much I hated looking in mirrors and setting clocks, but he insisted on old ways of timekeeping."

The Usurper bent forward as if appealing to the Innkeeper and the cousins for support. "That Oracle actually told me if I wanted to continue with my apprenticeship, I would need to look into the mirrors and understand the reasons behind my desire."

The Usurper paused, placing his hand over his heart, pursing his lips. "But the worst thing was when he suggested that greed for power and control might be holding me back from being an Oracle. He actually suggested that greed was keeping me stuck in one mirror. Then he said that before I could master time, I had to master myself. What does that even mean?

"Well, I'll tell you what," the Usurper continued. "Soon after the Oracle insulted me, I had my epiphany—a real epiphany! An unexpected flash! And just like that, I realized the truth. I realized that I didn't care one bit about being an Oracle. What I really wanted was the power and the control and the throne that comes with being the Oracle. There's a big difference, you see.

"And then, a little voice inside my head told me that I could have what I really wanted without years of frustration if I just took a little shortcut. And after all," he finished, "what's really wrong with an occasional shortcut?"

The Usurper sat up straight, tilted his chin up, and smiled. "And so, long story short, after a lot of ignoring mirrors, a little deceitful clock setting, a few questions, some sabotage, a few short cuts—oh, you don't need the grizzly details—but after some calculated risks, I sat on the throne. And here I am, and there you are, and you are just now realizing my little ruse. Funny how these things work. Twists and turns in fate. Whoa, right?"

"But," the Innkeeper's voice quavered, "that doesn't explain the blackness in the portal. It was white and pure light. Even if you stole the throne, how did the portal become gruesome and black?"

"Well, I suppose I'll have to let you in on another little secret," the Usurper continued with a roll of his eyes. "Unfortunately, there was one tiny, little flaw in my plan. I didn't have quite enough power and knowledge to use the portal when my little switcheroo took place.

"So anyway, I did the only thing I could do. I sent seekers into the portal and let them take their chances. Travelers went away and never came back, my secret's safe, and everybody's happy. In hindsight, I realize that the portal does need perfect timing, or it seems to get corrupted as time goes on, but, well, that's part of the price of experimenting with power, don't you think?"

The cousins had been standing around the Innkeeper, listening with horrified expressions to the confessions and secrets of the Usurper. Levi finally laid his hand on the Innkeeper's shoulder. "Let's go," he said. "We know enough to end his evil reign. Let's show the guards what happens when the drapes are opened." The Innkeeper nodded, but the Usurper began laughing.

"Don't even try," the Usurper snickered. "You don't really think you can simply walk out on me after I spilled all my valuable secrets, do you?"

"Your power is worthless now!" yelled Brody.

"No, my power is not worthless, little boy. You have no idea how much power I do have. One tiny example might be that you can't go out any doors unless I let you go out the door. I already took care of that little matter with a few tiny thoughts while you were opening drapes," he sneered.

"You see," he continued, "I've always had an alternate plan. I knew there might be a time when my ruse would be discovered and I might have to leave quickly. So I continued developing my powers, and I began creating a new portal. I have even chosen a very special place to go—a sweet little paradise where it's warm and sunny and mirrors only reveal the outside flaws instead of the inside desires. I actually needed just a bit more time to complete my plans."

He stopped talking and looked at them. He sighed deeply. "And yet, just now my plans changed very suddenly. While all of you were opening drapes and looking in mirrors, I realized I don't have time to finish my portal. I need to leave a little sooner than expected."

He paused, staring straight at the Innkeeper. "And wouldn't you know it, on the very day that my little deception is discovered—on that very day, mind you—a map to another place altogether, but nevertheless, a place where mirrors only reflect what's on the outside practically fell into my lap. And who needs an unfinished portal when they have a map?" He shrugged with his palms up. "An exceptionally nice little coincidence, don't you think?"

He turned his head slowly and gazed straight at Tilly. "Give me the wallet, sweetie."

Addison snapped her head around. "Oh my gosh!" she screamed. "It's a map. Tilly's wallet has a map."

"What?" Tilly asked, staring at Addison.

"Tilly, there are inscriptions on your wallet. They show up in the mirror's reflection! You have the map to get us home."

"You are the clever one, aren't you?" the Usurper said, staring at Addison as he gracefully moved toward Tilly with his hand outstretched.

"Let me have the wallet, child. I promise to drop you off at your treehouse and never bother you again. Of course, you could also stay here, and I will give you the keys to the castle, to use an old cliché. And then again, if you don't want either of those two options, you can take your chances with the black portal. I can't promise you'll like where you end up, but it could be quite the adventure, don't you think? Take your pick, child. Take your pick."

"No!" Tilly screamed, shaking her head. "I won't give it to you."

"Stay away from her!" Levi yelled, jumping in front of Tilly. Brody, Ivan, and Eleanor stood beside Tilly. Addison and Claire wrapped their arms around Tilly, shielding her. Esmé tried to hit the Usurper.

Waving his hand in the air, the Usurper exhaled a long deep breath, twisted his finger around in a circle, and pointed. Frigid wind blasted against the cousins, forcing them backward, crashing them into the wall. The Oracle gazed at the cousins. "Quiet," he demanded. "Your chaos is distracting. Stay there. I just want to talk to sweet little Tilly." He stood in front of Tilly, gawking into her face.

Tilly stood frozen in place, her breath in short quick gasps, her feet refusing to move.

The cousins jumped up, immediately preparing to rush back to help Tilly. "Wait! Stop!" the Innkeeper whispered frantically. She held her hand up to stop them from moving forward. "I need Tilly to listen to me. Trust me, he has powers you can't match. Act scared so that he thinks that he's won, so I have time to give a message to Tilly." The cousins nodded and cowered against the wall.

The Usurper saw them. Shaking his head and sneering, he gazed at Tilly. "Didn't take much to make those cowards stand down." He chuckled. Bending forward and twisting his face up, he moved forward so that his face was right next to Tilly's, his rank breath and stench filling her nostrils. Using his fingers to jab her, he circled her, jabbing and breathing into her face. "Give me the wallet, Tilly. It's the only way for all of you to go home unless you want to just take a little trip through the black portal."

"Tilly, listen," the Inn Keeper pleaded. "Listen!" Tilly turned around, staring into the Innkeeper's eyes. "Shut up, Innkeeper! Shut up!" He grabbed Tilly's face, forcing her to look into his own face.

The Innkeeper spoke rapidly. "Don't give him the wallet. He's lying. He will leave you here. He can't force you to give it up or take your map from you unless you hand it over willingly. It's your treasure."

"Shut up, shut up, shut up!" the Usurper shrieked at the Innkeeper. "Haven't you done enough damage for one day?" He waved his hand through the air; and a bolt of lightning shot from his hand, flashing through the air, striking the Innkeeper. She screamed and fell, writhing around on the ground. The cousins started to run to her, but she waved them away, pointing to Tilly.

"What the Innkeeper said may be true," the Usurper sneered. "But let's reconsider." He walked around Tilly several times, jabbing at her. Her eyes followed his movements as far as possible as the Usurper moved around and around. The Usurper began pacing back and forth instead. Each time his back was turned, Tilly looked around at her cousins who kept sending reassuring signals. Tilly nodded that she understood, but her face was white. She stood with trembling legs, clenching the wallet behind her back.

The Usurper suddenly turned, beckoning to the cousins. "Oh, come on over here. I see what you are doing," he said to the cousins. "Yes, come and give Tilly some help. She needs some help. She is trembling, and she should not have to hold on to the wallet by herself. Come, help her." The cousins passed confused glances among one another and hurried to Tilly.

The Innkeeper watched, frowning, thinking. Suddenly, she screamed. "Tilly! Tilly! Don't hand the wallet over to anyone. He can take it from them. It's only safe with you. Your gifts are what you gain for your journey. They can't be transferred."

"Will you shut up?" the Usurper screeched at the Innkeeper. Once more, he waved his hand through the air. A bolt of lightning shot from his hand, flashing through the air, striking her. Once more, she screamed and fell, writhing around on the ground; and again she motioned frantically for the cousins to stay with Tilly.

The Usurper sat down, drumming his fingers on the arms of the white throne. "She is only making it harder on you," he said, a sinister smile creeping across his lips. "I will get that wallet. I need that map. I have more power than the Innkeeper, and I definitely have more strength than a mere child. I was giving you a chance to give it to me the easy way, but now we'll have to try something a little more difficult. Oh! What to do? What to do?"

Suddenly, he shot up. "I've got it," he said. "I know what to do!" He looked around, his eyes flashing with excitement. "We all love games, don't we? Well then," he continued, "I've got an idea. Let's play a game. And here's the rules. The game ends when you give me the wallet. Yes, that's fair and easy. You give me the wallet, and I promise to stop playing the game. Ready? Let the games begin! I go first!"

He reached up as if grabbing something out of the air. He threw whatever he had grabbed toward the cousins. They instantly felt little bits of cold, and they looked up curiously. Gentle flakes of snow floated around them, glancing against their confused faces, touching their upturned fingers. Tilly stood for a few seconds, raising her face as the drifting flakes began swirling around her. She felt the kiss of a snowflake on her nose, and for a second, she almost smiled.

But the Usurper knew that the kiss of snow was too gentle, that she would never relinquish her gift simply because he had the power of sweet illusion. And he took another deep breath, and he blew again, and the snow turned into flurries. The Usurper chuckled as he sat on his throne, excited that he finally had his chance to play with the power he had striven for: the power to create illusions, the power to deceive, the power to control.

He sneered imagining Tilly kneeling before him, handing her gift to him so the game would end. He watched her and realized that she was not in enough awe of his power to create; she was only confused. If his power to create did not influence her, what about his power to control? He studied her. He wondered what would cause her to relinquish her gift. Cold? Fear? Isolation? Could she endure his power if she felt isolated and alone?

So he uttered malicious words, sucking in air and exhaling sharply, breathing his words into reality. He inhaled and exhaled again and again, forcing his breath out with violence, waiting for Tilly to buckle to her knees and hand her gift to him. He waved his arms about, triggering the winds to blast around and against her. He twirled his hands, and suddenly Tilly stood in the center of a whirlwind of snow.

Though the cousins frantically fought to get to Tilly, the wind repelled every attempt; they could not pass through the furious cyclone encasing her. The spinning wind encircled Tilly, the harsh snow bombarding her, pelting against her. And so, with each breath, the Usurper's storm raged harsher and harder. Tilly continued to rise again and again, fighting against the fierce blasts, but she was toppled again and again. The storm was too fierce.

But finally, Tilly fought through the force, and she rose in silence. With her face upturned and her arms outstretched, she stared straight into the Usurper's eyes. *Go ahead and do your best,* she thought. *I will feel it all. And you will not overcome me.* The Usurper's face distorted. His expression was one of pure evil; his stomach lurched with hatred that a mere child would attempt to withstand his power. And so, he knew the time had come to blow her over once and for all, and his breath became a raging gale.

The snow changed into ice biting into her skin, and the wind pelted the crystals against her. And she stood silent and firm with her rosy lips softened into a still, defiant smile, and she closed her eyes. She had felt it all from the gentle kiss of the floating flakes to the stinging wind and the bite of the ice jabbing at her skin. And as the Usurper continued breathing against her, she thought how each part was simply another layer of the other parts, and she would feel it all in its completeness, but she would not let go of her gift or let his evil overcome her. And in her silence, the Usurper finally became exhausted, and he gradually gave up, and his breath slowed into a breeze, and only a few flakes caressed Tilly's face as they floated down once again. And she opened her eyes.

She stared straight at the Usurper who was staring straight at her. "You cannot have my gift!" she cried with tears spilling down her face. "And we will go home, and you will not come with us." And her cousins surrounded her, holding her tight, and she smiled through the tears as she crumpled into Eleanor's arms and Ivan wrapped his arms around them.

With his power spent, the Usurper curled up, cradling himself against the back of his throne, moaning and whining about the unfairness of it all. And the Innkeeper rushed up the steps to the pinnacle where she grabbed the rope and pulled, sounding the alarm to the bell tower.

From the highest point on the Citadel, the watcher pulled another rope again and again. The bells tolled over and over and over, and soldiers awoke to commands and rushed across the snow-swept expanse to the Citadel. The people in the village woke and pulled their curtains back, peeking out, wondering why bells were tolling.

And the Commander rushed with his troops into the castle, through the hallways, into the red room, up the marble steps, past the portraits, and into the white room. He glanced around the room, immediately taking inventory of the situation, the cousins, the Innkeeper, and the groveling wizard. He smiled, and his eyes met the Innkeeper's.

"You were supposed to sound the alarm at the beginning, not when it's all over. Now it's all done, and I'll have to hear the entire story secondhand."

"Trust me," the Innkeeper said, "It happened too quickly." And then she smiled at the Commander. "But they did just fine. They did even more than just fine."

And in the mountains, the wolves bayed long deep howls that echoed across the valleys and then turned to trot back into their forest dens.

Chapter 66

I Told You So

By the time the sun flickered through the mountain clefts, the world inside the dome had changed forever. The Oracle's apprentice, the Usurper, had been exiled along with the merchants and false prophets, the evil vendors, the malevolent magicians, and even the ginger-haired man who had opened the thick iron door.

Bells tolling from the highest bell towers in all the pinnacles of the Citadel had awakened sleepy people. Rubbing their eyes and stretching, they had peeked out through curtained windows and cracked doorways as soldiers hurried throughout the hamlet, proclaiming the news that the Usurper was gone.

Gates were opened and the portal dismantled. Most people seemed confused at the change and commotion. Some people rejoiced, and some cried, some were sad, and some were happy, and some were afraid. Most were somewhat bewildered, but almost all felt little bubbles of joy as they realized the tiny fears and doubts they had tried so hard to ignore had been justified. And fear began tiptoeing away like disappearing shadows.

And by the time the sun had climbed above the mountain peaks, the cousins stood in front of the imposing iron door with the thick perfectly round iron clangor wedged into the sheer rock face of the mountain, the same door that the ginger-haired man had opened for them not so very long before.

The Commander and the Innkeeper stood with them. The Commander held Claire's mirror over the wallet, studying the map instructions. "You are close now," he said, pointing to a trail on the opposite side of the cobblestone path. "Just follow that path through those tall grasses and then over that ridge and follow the path until you come to the river."

"Wait, wait, wait," Addison broke in, holding her hand up. "Let me get this straight. Did you just say we should follow that trail over there—the one through the tall grasses that lead over that ridge, the one over there?"

The Commander nodded. "Yes, that's the one," he said.

"Oh, really?" Addison said, glancing around. Eleanor smiled, gazing at the ground, shuffling rocks around with the toes of her shoes. Levi started whistling and inspecting the iron door. Brody and Ivan began discussing the weather and looking at the sky.

"Don't you dare say it!" Claire broke in quickly with a chuckle.

"Oh no, I get to say this!" Addison said. She looked Claire straight in the eyes. "I told you so. I really, really did tell you so!" And this time, all the cousins laughed. Eleanor bowed; and with a flourish of her hand, she admitted, "Addison, you were right!" And they all laughed a little more.

The Innkeeper sighed and sat down on the stoop in front of the iron door, breathing in the fresh forest air. "This little journey into our world wasn't what you expected, but I'm sure glad you came. What if you hadn't come?"

And they all stopped and glanced at one another for just a second. "Yes, what if," Levi muttered.

"I've been thinking about that," Addison said.

"You've been thinking about that?" Levi asked, looking quite puzzled.

"Yes, I have," Addison continued, "and I think the end result might still be the same, but the way it happens might vary."

"What are you talking about, Addie?" Brody asked.

"Look at it this way," Addison continued. "It was obviously time for the Usurper to be found out. If we hadn't come, perhaps somebody else would have stumbled on this place or something like that. They would have done it differently because different people would have created different circumstances, but something would have happened to get rid of the Usurper because it was his time to go.

"And, on the other hand, if we had followed the butterflies in the first place, we might be home already, but we made a choice to go into the village, so we temporarily changed our path. We took a detour, a loop around. But since we stuck together and remained true to our original goal, we still end right back here. Maybe we changed our timeline, but if we did, then maybe we gained something that we will eventually need in the new timeline that we created when we looped off the original path. So I guess all's well that ends well."

The cousins just kind of looked at Addison and then at one another.

Brody scrunched his nose. "Gee, Addie, where do you get this stuff?"

Addison shrugged and chuckled. "I said I was thinking about it. I don't know. It's a guess." The entire group simply smiled and shook their heads.

Claire touched the Innkeeper's arm. "What about you? What will you do now?" she asked.

"Oh, we'll stay for a while," the Innkeeper said, glancing over at the Commander who was glancing back at her. "There is a lot of work to do. The people are going to need us when they realize how we were all deceived for so long. We have to search for truth again." She looked at each of the cousins.

"You know, we stumbled on this place the same way you did, searching for answers. And in the beginning, it was wonderful; travelers and seekers flowed in and out of the village, asking directions about their journeys, seeking wisdom from the Oracle, or searching for a way home. And it was all so good and fresh and free.

"But one day, something subtly changed. Now we know why. We didn't understand then. The Usurper, who we believed was the Oracle, asked for small donations. He assured us that travelers would be more fulfilled if they learned to pay the price for their journey. It seemed somewhat strange, but we accepted it. After all, we thought he was the true Oracle who understood the mysteries. And the price was so small at first.

"But soon after that, he commissioned the stone wall and installed the merchants to sell passes through the arches. Eventually, iron doors and the dome were built. Strangely, during that same time, the winters become colder and longer and deeper until finally the stone steps leading to the Citadel became frozen and icy and treacherous.

"We were told the dome was a protection against the harsh weather and blizzards. Secretly, we wondered if the dome was trapping us inside rather than protecting us from the outside, but when the Oracle came out to speak, we felt pride in our efforts to guide the few weary seekers who entered the village. Fewer and fewer came as the winters grew longer and harsher, but there were always a few seekers searching for a way home, and we proudly pointed the way to the Oracle."

"After a long while, rumors began floating through the hamlet, concerns about merchants and portals. Some people grumbled and whispered their concerns, but nobody wanted to admit to their doubts. But then, one day a young man stumbled into the village. He was ranting and shouting that the Oracle was a fake and the portal was a maze of tunnels and false paths, and people were lost inside. Some of the villagers jeered and mocked him, and the young man was immediately silenced by the Citadel guards."

The Innkeeper paused, glancing up at the Commander. He smiled at her, and she continued, "The Commander went and found the young man who had been silenced. He had been thrown in jail. And he talked to the young man. That evening, the Commander stopped at the Inn on his way back to the Citadel, and we chatted by the fire. One thing led to another. By the end of the evening, we had whispered our doubts and worries to each other. And we made a pact to watch for signs of deception and to send a signal if we discovered anything that might confirm the rumors. We wanted to believe that we were living a life of truth, but our doubts were troubling.

"Soon after that, you cousins came straggling into the Inn. And my heart broke as I saw the price you had paid to find your way home: a midnight climb up jagged stone stairs, hungry and cold and weary. But even then, I was confused until I began cleaning your pockets, and I saw the gifts that others had given freely to help you find your way home. And at that moment, I remembered something I had once known but that I had somehow forgotten.

"The cost of the passage home is not something a seeker pays for. The price of getting home is the journey itself. The experiences along the way are the cost and the reward of the journey. They are the same thing. The Oracle enticed the seekers into paying what they do not owe so that he could gain what was not his. And that is why he could not take the map from you unless you passed it to him or gave it away. Your gift is your own."

As the Innkeeper finished, her face crinkled into a smile even as tears rolled down her cheeks. The Commander laid his hand on her shoulder. "But now, we are going to clean this mess up and start again!" he said.

"Yes, we are," she agreed, and her face lit up almost like the first time they had seen her. Almost.

"Thank you for helping us," the Innkeeper said as she gave each cousin a big sloppy kiss smack dab in the middle of each forehead. "We will remember you forever and always."

And so, after hugs and smiles and more than a few tears on both sides, the cousins took their leave of the Innkeeper and the Commander. They walked across the road to the opposite side of the cobblestone pathway. After reaching the ridge, they all turned and waved a final good-bye before walking into the tall golden grasses and disappearing over the ridge.

And after the Innkeeper and the Commander waved back and blew kisses, they opened the iron door; and with a deep sigh, they stepped back inside the Snow Village to begin the process of tearing down the dome and starting all over again in their search for truth.

Chapter 67

Scraggly Silver Hair

The old man sat on a massive round stump under an ancient oak tree, observing the swollen river buckle and churn as it raced downstream. With his palms resting on the smooth rounded top of his timeworn walking stick, he leaned forward, looking around at everything and at nothing. Once in a while, he groaned his way up and meandered along the bank of the river, making note of the currents and eddies and the flow of the flooded edge.

Time and time again, he hobbled back and sat on the stump, the wind playing with his long scraggly silver hair and his bushy white beard. Every now and again, his head would droop forward, and his eyes would close. And then, after a second or two, his head would jerk up and his eyes startle open, reminding him once more that it was not yet time for sleep.

⌘

Eleanor stood high on a boulder, scouting the river. "There's just no way to get across right now—at least not here!" she shouted, shaking her head and trying to make her voice heard over the roar of the water. She finally climbed down off the rock and joined the others. "Even if we had our kayaks, we couldn't take a chance on these rapids right here. We need to follow the

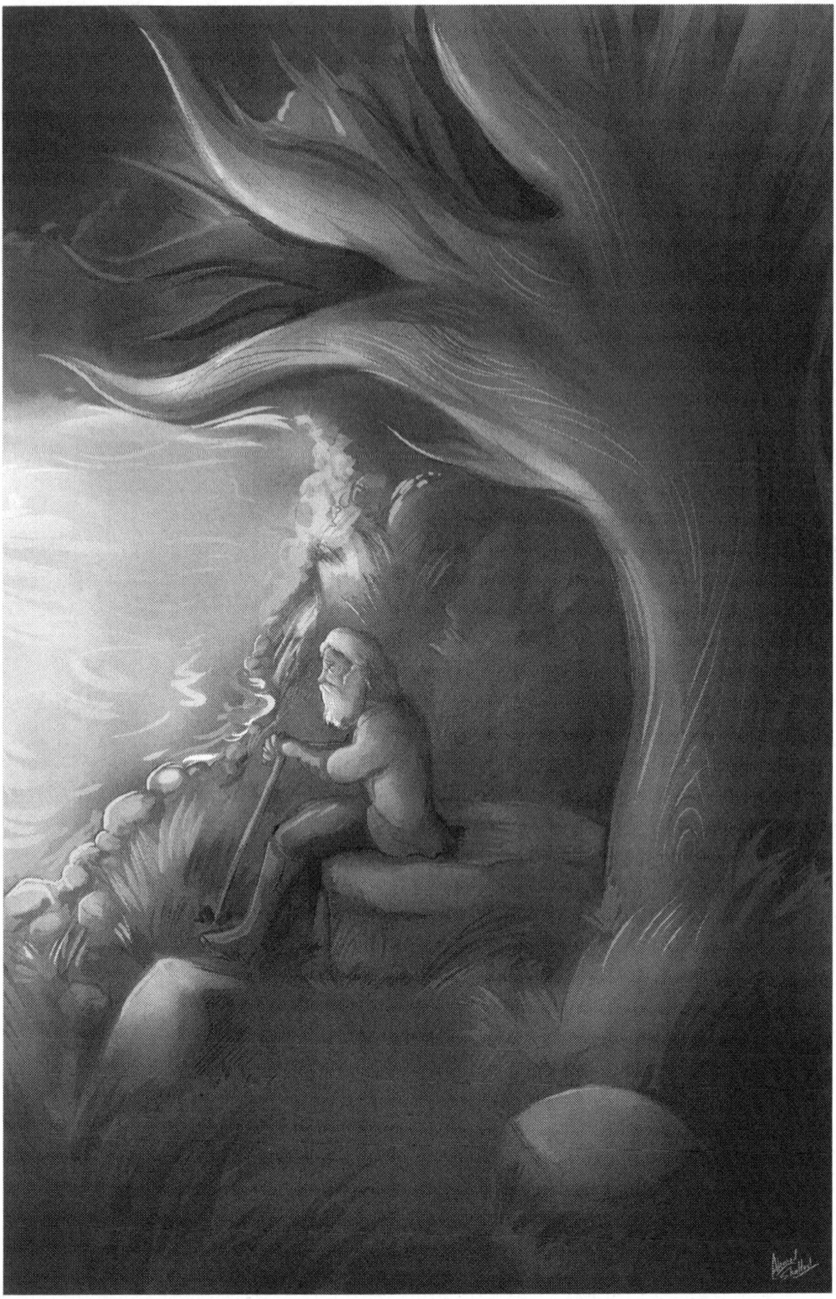

river downstream until we find a better place to cross. The map shows two good places to cross, but we'll just have to cross at the next one even if we have to hike back up on the other side."

And it was true. The water buckled and sprayed as it crashed against the tops of the heavy boulders sticking up from the midst of the river. Log jams pressed against the edges of the bank, tangled and twisted and stuck in the eddies. Massive logs floated swiftly downstream, some getting caught in the log jams, others arrogantly riding the waves by as if they were in a race to the bottom.

⁂

The old man sat very still. He saw them coming. He shuffled up the path toward them, exaggerating his limp and his need for the walking stick as eight slightly quarrelsome and rather frustrated and tired cousins hurried along the path beside the river.

"Would you young'uns help me? Could you help me, please?" the old man pleaded as he hobbled toward them.

"No, no, no, no, no," Eleanor muttered under her breath, "not another interruption—not now. I just want to get home, and we are so close," she continued gritting her teeth, pursing her lips, and groaning.

But Levi stopped anyway. "What do you need, sir?" he asked.

"Well, as luck would have it," the old man said, "I have been delayed. Delays, delays. I was delayed, and now I need help if you would be so kind."

"Of course," Brody said, glancing around at the others. "What do you need?"

"I would appreciate a fire and enough wood to keep the fire going during the night for warmth, and so the animals won't attack while I sleep."

Levi looked over at Eleanor, who was rolling her eyes and shaking her head but trying to smile because she really did feel sorry for the old man. "Of course, we can help you," Eleanor said.

And at that, they all hurried into the woods, found enough firewood to last during the night, stacked it up under the tree, and lit a fire to keep the old man warm and safe. Eleanor even ran to the river's edge and brought some water so he would be comfortable. Once he seemed comfortable, she reminded the others that they really needed to get going since they needed all the daylight they could get to find the best path and make it across the river.

But as they turned to leave, the old man grabbed Brody's shirt. "Couldn't you stay just a little bit and warm the heart of an old man with some of your youthful tales? How did you come to be here on this lonely path anyway?"

Brody glanced over at his cousins who were already moving toward the river's edge. "Just a minute," he said. He hurried over to the others. "Let's stay for just a minute. He seems kinda lonely. What can a few minutes really hurt in the bigger scheme of things?"

"Come on, Brody!" Eleanor fussed. "We got his fire going, and he has water and food. We gotta go." But as she looked around at the others, she felt a little guilty. "Ohh, all right," she moaned, "but just for a few minutes." They went back and sat around the fire even though they didn't really need a fire yet because the sun was so warm.

The old man smiled and seemed so pleased to have a little company. He asked how they happened to be on that particular path just then since it wasn't a regular route at all. One by one, they ended up telling just a little about their journeys—just enough to make the old man smile and nod. Now, if truth be told, they were more than a little anxious to be on their way, but he did seem so interested that after a bit they relaxed and chatted just a wee bit longer than they had originally planned.

After a while, the old man leaned forward on his walking stick and asked how they planned to get home. Tilly said they had a map. The old man nodded and stared into the fire; and after just a bit more, his eyes started blinking, and finally, his head fell forward onto his hands, which rested on the smooth top of the timeworn walking stick. Eleanor put her finger to her lips and pointed in the direction of the road. But just as they were slipping away, the old man's head jerked back up.

Claire reached over, gently touching his arm. "Sir," she said, "we would love to spend more time, but we do have to keep going. We have quite a while to go before the night falls."

And the old man looked at her and sighed. "I understand, child. If I am not mistaken," he finally continued, "and from the small amount you have told me, it seems that you have been on quite a long journey, and now you are very anxious to go home."

"Oh yes, we want very much to be home," Claire said softly.

"Well then, what is delaying you?" The old man glanced around at them. "Oh, you are being delayed because you are being kind to an old man who wants to ramble on and on?" His entire face crinkled into a grin, eyes and all.

Ivan smiled and nodded. And the old man smiled back.

"I understand," he said. "But I will tell you a secret," he said, rubbing his fingers and his thumb together. "No, not an idea actually." He sighed. "Now what is the best word—oh, a key. I will give you a key." He winked at Addison; and she titled her head to the side, confused by his choice of words, words that seemed strangely familiar.

Then he sat there gazing into the fire. The cousins stood impatiently shuffling around, ready to leave on the one hand and curious about what he had to say on the other.

"This is an important key," he finally continued. "Lock it away in your minds so you can pull it out when needed. Here it is. Helping your fellow travelers is not a delay on your path. It is part of your path—perhaps the best part. It's not a waste of time at all—not at all. It smooths the gears, shall we say. Actually," he continued, bending forward and looking directly at each of them in turn, "it's a wonderful way to spend your moment, and after all, all we ever have is a moment. We are just flashes, just sparkles you might say."

He chuckled as he flicked his fingers in the air. "Just flashes, just sparkles." And he grew very still and leaned forward, resting his chin on the smooth top of his walking stick, gazing out across the river. Suddenly, he jolted up as though he had awakened from a dream. "So if helping a fellow traveler is not the problem, what is really causing the delay in your journey?"

"Well, we have to cross the river," Brody said. "We can't just swim across."

"Yes, yes, I understand," the old man answered, rubbing his scruffy white beard. "It is true. It is true. It seems there are always rivers that need to be crossed on such journeys. So what is it that you want?"

"We want to cross the river," Ivan said with a shrug.

"Let me understand. So what you want is to cross the river?"

They all nodded.

"Well, it is true. It is quite true that knowing what you want is important. But it is also true—actually quite true—that wanting is easy. But, on the other hand, wanting does lead to pondering, and pondering leads to searching, and searching leads to experiencing, and experiencing leads to understanding, and understanding leads to finding keys, and finding keys leads to opening the doors, and opening doors always lead to home. So wanting is good, I suppose, but I would say intending is better. Intending for what you want is definitely better."

He stopped and rolled his eyes up and to the side. "I would say you should intend for what you want and then always say, 'Or something better.' That is good. That should work." He sighed and looked over at the river and then at each of them.

"And here you are," he continued. "And if I heard you correctly, even though you told your tales quite quickly because you are quite impatient to get going, you have been on a long journey and you have wanted and pondered and searched and experienced and understood and found keys. So why don't you use your keys to go home?"

"We didn't find any keys," Tilly said.

"Then you haven't been listening, child. As I listened to your tales, I heard enough to know that each of you found several keys along the way. Well, perhaps that one right there—what's her name?" he asked, pointing to Eleanor.

"Eleanor?" Levi answered.

"Yes," the old man continued, "Eleanor. Pretty name, it is. But, yes, perhaps Eleanor is still looking for one of hers. But it's coming. It's very close now. It's sitting on her fingertips, ready to be snatched up as soon as she knows for sure." He smiled and looked directly into Eleanor's eyes, but she just stood there looking rather bewildered.

"And I think that Levi has an important key to find. Perhaps. But the rest have enough. Yes, you all have enough for this trip." He stopped and stroked his beard, gazing off into the sky. Then he shook his head as if he remembered something.

"Now, let's try this again. Be specific," the Old Man continued. "What do you intend?"

"Well, we intend to cross the river," Ivan said with a shrug as he looked at his cousins.

"Oh, is that all? Well, why didn't you say so?" And at that, the old man groaned his way up. "Come on, come on," he said, hobbling toward the river bank. He stopped and pointed at an old wooden raft hidden among the rushes at the river's edge.

"You know," he said, "it was there all along. You just didn't see it because you were expecting other things. Sometimes nasty little delays that seem to be in the way are just what we need to find what we want." His eyes lit up. "But sometimes they're not." He chuckled. "Just leave the boat on the other side. People always cross rivers on these journeys. It seems some paths lead this way and other paths lead that way. Depends on the adventure, I suppose, but I will tell you this. Each path has some good, and each path has its bad, some more than others.

But in the end, it's all about the keys and the sparkles anyway." And he hobbled back to the fire.

Now, if truth be told, the cousins stood there slightly dumbfounded watching the old man hobble away. It was Eleanor who broke away.

"Thank you, sir," she said as she reached him. "Really, I appreciate what you've done. We all do." The old man smiled and looked straight into Eleanor's eyes. "You're real close to finding your key, little one," he said with a wink.

"Oh, and one more little clue since you are sweet enough to run over here and say thank you. The map's wrong," the Old Man said, bending forward. "The river changed course. Somebody must have diverged from their original path, looped around, and changed things—created a ripple and changed the map. These journeys are strange things sometimes. And so, you'll make better time if you drift about a mile and a half downstream before you cross. Then hike back up on the other side. Delays, delays, but sometimes delays are better than other things."

The Old Man sat down on the massive round stump under an ancient oak tree. Eleanor stood watching him with a puzzled face before she slowly turned and hurried back to the raft. In just a minute or two, eight cousins were pushing off from the shore and waving good-bye to an old man who was sitting by the fire, leaning forward, watching them with his chin resting on his hands on the rounded top of his timeworn walking stick.

CHAPTER 68

Rivers and Eddies

"The Old Man said the map's wrong and that we should float down before we try to cross," Eleanor said as she climbed on the back, guiding the raft while Levi watched from the front.

"There's only one problem with that." Claire chuckled. "He never saw the map. We told him about it, but he didn't see it. He's just an old man doing what old men do."

"That is true," Tilly agreed. "He didn't actually see the map."

Eleanor shrugged, nodding. "Well, the water looks really smooth for crossing right here anyway. I can't say for sure, but it looks like there's an eddy across there."

"Let's just follow the map," Ivan said as each cousin grabbed the makeshift paddles attached to the side of the raft and pushed off from the bank. And they all agreed.

And so, Levi and Eleanor navigated as the wooden raft slithered across the very wide and swollen river. The tranquil river lulled them all into a peaceful calm, and after a while, they laid their oars down and watched the clouds shape shift and the diamondy sparkles play on the surface of the water as they slid across the river.

And as they neared the middle of the river, they began watching for the eddy of the other side. Until quite suddenly and out of nowhere, Levi jolted everyone by yelling, "A huge hole straight ahead!"

Eleanor immediately saw it and hollered, "Right side back. Left side forward! Now! All forward!"

And instantly, and with every ounce of strength they had, the cousins dug their paddles into the water and paddled, trying to pull the raft to the right, straining to pull the boat one way while the current pulled the boat another.

A whirlwind of water grabbed the edge of the boat, lifting the boat to its side, rocking them violently from one side to the other, threatening to tip the boat and send them all into the swirling, seething hole.

Eleanor screamed, "Hold on!" as she and Levi dug in with their paddles, trying to keep the whirling, spinning mass of water from tipping them completely over. Esmé screamed, bouncing to the side as the boat tilted, sliding toward the water. Claire grabbed Esmé's arm, holding her with one hand as she held on to the edge of the boat with the other. Brody grabbed Esmé's other arm.

The water surged and buckled, whipped and sprayed. The cousins plunged and dove under the water only to be sucked down and spit back up to claw at the air and suck in gulps of air before tumbling into the seething mass again, twisting in violent circles, down and around and up and around again.

Rising up, sputtering, choking, gulping, gasping, then plunging, submerging, clawing at liquid for a way up, for light, for a taste of the air, grasping for anything solid. Until the whirlwind spit them out, the raft popped up out of the liquid hurricane and drifted on a patch of gentle water as though there had been no whirlwind at all.

They sputtered and spit, coughing and gasping for more air, and finally looked at one another as "I'm okay" and "We made it" and "I was terrified" and "Are you okay?" drifted back and forth among them all.

"Now what's wrong?" Ivan asked as he saw the relief in Eleanor's face change to frustration.

"There's no eddy here," Eleanor said. "We're gonna hafta go down farther and then hike back up. Everyone, look for a good place to land. We gotta keep going." It took a while, but they finally found a very nice eddy and landed the raft, pulling it onto the bank.

"We're down too far now." Levi sighed. "Looks like we have to hike back up to find the path we need to follow. I wonder how far off course we are now."

"Oh, about a mile," Eleanor said with a slight smile. And if truth be told, Eleanor kind of smiled the whole way as they were hiking back up and nobody really understood why especially since their journey had been delayed once again and they all knew how much Eleanor hated delays.

Chapter 69

The Hut across the Bridge

They were scratched and sore and rather miserable if truth be told. And if that was not enough, they were worn out, frustrated, and more than a little cranky by the time they reached the ridge.

They had spent hours wandering up this path, slapping at the grossly large mosquitoes, stumbling over briars and brambles. After a while, the motivation had lost its shine, and they were simply in nasty moods and generally fussing at one another.

"We just need to stop for the night and get some rest," sighed Levi. He had been prodding Esmé along; her little eyes had been threatening to shut and stay shut for a long time now. They had all pressed her forward, begging her to keep going for just a while more because they were all too tired and they didn't want to stop before reaching the summit where the map showed the trail ended.

The sun was slipping behind the mountain ridges, and the shadows flickered across the slate gray walls of the mountain as they reached that last rugged ridge. Levi glanced around at the scraggly crew and told them to rest for a few minutes. He would climb over the ledge and see if they should settle in for the night above the ridge or below it. They all looked around, somewhat relieved, and even Esmé's eyes popped open; she seemed to revive at the mere potential of rest.

Levi scrambled over the top, scraping his arms and legs even more on the near vertical wall until he finally maneuvered his way up and over. And then standing up and brushing himself off, he went silent.

"Hey," Claire called, "what's going on? Are you okay?"

Without explanation, Levi lay on his belly, stuck his arm down over the edge, and called down to the others, "Esmé, take my hand and come up, and then each of you, come on. I'll pull. Eleanor, you push."

And so, one by one, each topped the precipice; and just like Levi had done, they each went still as they stood in stunned silence gazing about at the profusion of color. Emerald and jade and lime green leaves melded together as ivy wrapped its way around the trunks of evergreens and dripped from the branches of huge oaks and delicate maples. Fiery reds and gentle yellows and vibrant blues and royal purples of wildflowers sprouted from the soft bluish-green moss that covered the ground and the gray rocks and even the trunks of the hoary old trees.

And just beyond the ledge, an old, very old, ancient swinging bridge made of creaking wood and held together with twisted gray rope swung between the ridge where they stood and a ledge on the other side. A waterfall spilled off the ledge, roaring down the mountainside, hitting the rocks, creating a haze of rainbows and mist in the air.

But they did not gasp only because of the colors and the beauty of the wildflowers and the ivy-wrapped trees—though that is what first met their eyes—or gasped because of the bridge and the waterfall, even though it was powerful and majestic. No, what made them stand in silence, shuffle closer to one another, and slap their hands over their mouths was a small stone hut with gray smoke curling from the chimney on the other side of the ancient swinging bridge on a ledge above the waterfall. The hut was set back against the mountain. Ancient trees surrounded it.

And without even talking, they walked through the ancient trees and across the creaky swinging wooden bridge held together with old ropes as the spray from the waterfall misted around them. The ground between the bridge and the hut was covered with moss and uneven with gnarled roots and lined with overgrown blackberry bushes with prickly thorns and scraping edges, but it did not matter as the cousins shuffled to a stop and the forest floor turned into a cobbled path leading to the front door.

"Well, let's not get our hopes up too much," Levi cautioned his cousins. "This may not be the Oracle's home, but whoever lives here just might let us sleep for the night or share some food or at least give us directions. And if this isn't the Oracle's home, then at least we are close. We have to be close. I'll knock and see if anyone's here. There's a fire in the chimney, so—"

"That's all well and good," Claire interrupted, "but the last places any of us entered hoping for some food ended with all of us in various types of captivity."

Levi looked at Claire and smiled with a shake of his head, and a lip skewed to the side. "You are right," he said. "But obviously we gotta try." And he paused, looking around.

"Eleanor," he continued, "why don't you take Esmé and watch from behind the bushes over there? Everyone, stay hidden. I will knock, and if everything seems good, I'll signal."

"I should go with you," Eleanor said.

"No," said Levi, "if something goes wrong, I need you to help get me out, remember? We're all in this together, but when it comes to going into places, it might be better to be cautious and watch."

Ivan stepped forward. "I'll go with you instead of Eleanor."

Brody stood up. "I'm going for this family. One of us from each family."

Levi smiled and nodded. "Sounds good. The rest of you, hide as much as possible and watch. If all goes well, we'll signal. If not, well, let's hope all goes well." The five girls scurried to find places among the foliage and scrubs as though playing a game of hide-and-seek.

Levi, Brody, and Ivan watched the others bend behind the bushes and peek out from around the ragged overgrowth, endeavoring to both hide and keep away from scratching thorns. Unfortunately, the two things could not happen at the same time, and there were several "ouches" and "shushes" emanating from the bushes. Once everyone seemed settled into their hiding places, Levi, Brody, and Ivan straightened their shoulders and began walking toward the hut.

Ivan tripped over a gnarled root; fell into Brody, who rolled his eyes; and pushed Ivan back up. They continued walking. Reaching the hut, they stopped, drew in deep breaths, and climbed until they stood on the steps in front of the thick rounded top wooden door.

Levi motioned for Ivan and Brody to stop; he held his head high and climbed the last step onto the landing. Stepping up to the door, he stood with his fist ready to knock; a slight quiver crossed his shoulders. He glanced down at Brody and Ivan and then back at the bushes. He took another deep breath, shut his eyes for just a second, and then raised his fist and knocked. No one answered. He knocked again. No answer. He pounded. No one answered.

He turned around and glanced back at the bushes and saw five heads peeking out, watching him. He shrugged, swallowed hard, put his hand on the doorknob, and turned it slowly. It clicked, and he pushed just a little. The door groaned and creaked, but he pushed a tiny bit more until there was enough of an opening to peek inside. He peeked around the edge of the door. He stood up, paused, and bent forward, peeking around the edge again. With a bewildered expression, he slowly turned and hesitantly beckoned to the others.

Brody and Ivan cautiously moved forward as the girls untangled themselves from their hiding places and hurried up the broken cobblestone path to the steps. One by one they peeked around the door, gasped or sighed, and silently slipped into the room. As each cousin entered, the others unconsciously moved aside as the new one scooted into place so that, in the end, all eight stood side by side, shoulder to shoulder.

"I think this just might be the Oracle's house," Levi said, staring at the wall straight in front of them and then turning in a circle, quickly scanning the rest of the room. "There's even eight colored doors just like the ones at Gramma's treehouse."

They all took a quick look around the room, nodded, and then turned back to gaze at the huge round bronzed clock with roman numerals for numbers. The clock was not only so massive that it took up the biggest part of the entire wall, but it was also an intricate conglomeration of gears within gears and even more gears making up the innards. And every space on that wall that was not covered by clock was crammed full of carved trees and tunnels and mountains and people and animals. Every carving was painted in rich colors so that an entire miniature world had been carved into the wall around a giant clock made of interlocking gears within gears.

Chapter 70

The Cuckoo Clock: Gears within Gears

"That is the most intricate, the most, the—" Eleanor started to say before she simply went silent for a bit.

"Look at all those gears. Too bad it's broke," Ivan mentioned. "Can you imagine how that wall would look if they were circling around one another?"

"There's a door in the bottom of the clock where the six should be. Is something behind there?" Addison muttered.

"Maybe a giant bird or something comes out and cuckoos or spins when the clock tolls," Eleanor added, chuckling. "But that'd be a little creepy."

"Ya, but anything's possible around this place," Claire muttered with a grimace. And at that, everyone just stood there, examining the wall in front of them.

Suddenly, Levi hurried to the wall, touching a thick blue line. "It's a map!" he almost shouted, "Look, there's the domed village. You can see the dome!" he yelled as he pointed to tiny elaborate details on the wall. "And there's the river we just went down. And here's the tree where we found one another! Oh, wow!" he continued as he ran his fingers across the miniature scenes of mountains and rivers and trees and cabins and tiny people and even tinier animals delicately carved into the wood of the wall. They all stepped up to the wall, touching the painted carvings.

But just then, and very suddenly and as they were all concentrated on the map on the wall, the wind rushed through the room, and the door behind them slammed shut. Esmé screamed, and the others jumped and startled and looked around with big eyes. And they groaned.

"Oh no, not again!" Claire yelled with a stomp of her foot. "Now we're trapped again. I knew it! I told you! It happens every time."

And just as Claire stomped her foot, the huge round bronze clock in the center of the wall began clicking and whirring. The gears lurched forward, rotating and grinding, slowly interweaving, snapping and clicking as the gears within gears began revolving like the innards of an old-time swiss pocket watch—only a very big old-time swiss pocket watch.

The long thin black second hand of the clock suddenly lurched forward spun around the face of the clock one time and stopped on the twelve. The door at the bottom of the clock, just where the six should be, popped open; and a life-sized nutcracker soldier with a tall red furry hat, gold-painted suspenders crisscrossing his dark-blue shirt, and black pants slid out of the open door. He slid around the tiny track so that he stood at front and center, his arm lurched up. The scroll he held in his hand unrolled. And they all just stood there, staring at it, until Claire hurried forward and read the message from the unfurled scroll.

> There are journeys, and there are times, and there are adventures, and there are dreams.
> Wheels within wheels, gears within gears, the test of time, the keys to wisdom.
> And each traveler has a mystery and each mystery a key. And each key has a time.
> Time has a purpose for all to understand. But it waits for no one.

And your one hour and eleven minutes and eleven seconds of time begins in this moment.

And just like that, the carved soldier slid back around and into the door of the clock, and the little door where the six should be closed behind him. The hands rotated on the clock. The time on the clock was set at twelve o'clock exactly. The second hand lurched forward one second at a time; and after it had rotated one time, the minute hand jerked forward, joining the progression. And it was as though time had just begun.

Chapter 71

Trapped Again

"Oh, boy," Brody said, "this can't be good." And again, they all just stood there with huge eyes staring at the closed door.

"Since that clock is set at twelve o'clock right now, an hour and eleven minutes will make it eleven minutes after one o'clock. The Usurper wanted us to go into the portal at eleven minutes after eleven o'clock. What's going on with the sequence of ones. Should we be worried?" muttered Addison.

"What if it's another trap?" Claire said as she turned around and rushed to the entrance door. But even after pounding on the door, and after pulling and pushing and kicking at each of the eight colored doors, and even after trying to open the door on the clock where the six should be, they only ended up proving what they had known all along: they were stuck once again.

"Okay, first of all, we followed the map to get here, so it's probably not a trap," Levi suggested. "Maybe the real Oracle will show up soon, but in the meantime, let's try to think this through." They groaned; but it did seem like the only thing that made any sense at all, so they all plopped down, sitting in a circle in the middle of the room to think about what to do next.

"Any ideas of where to start?" Eleanor began. "Let's think this through before we panic."

"Well," Addison said, "we have, for lack of a better word, a giant cuckoo clock that gave us a strange message."

"The doors are the same colors as the ones at Gramma's: red, green, indigo, purple, gold, bronze, silver, and orange. And they all have little shelves on them," Brody added, glancing around the room.

"And," Ivan added, "each shelf has a small lantern sitting on a shelf. Every place we've been has those same lanterns—different sizes but the same lantern."

Esmé sat cross-legged with her elbows on her knees and her chin resting on her palms, wanting nothing more than to lie down and sleep.

"Levi," Esmé said with a yawn.

"What, Ezzy?"

"Maybe there are clues in the signs and pictures on the walls," Esmé suggested.

And for the first time since they had entered that room, they shifted their attention away from the clock and the carved wall.

"She's right!" Claire shouted as the cousins hurried to investigate the walls in the hut.

Signs covered the walls except for the doors from top to bottom—juxtaposed and crammed together, a hodgepodge with no discernable pattern at all. There were scenes of mountains and pictures of lanterns and wolves placed next to sayings carved into the wood with fancy calligraphy. There were images of waterfalls and tiny mirrors. There were portraits of people in red robes and blue ropes and green shirts. There were scenes of children sitting around campfires and planets and moons.

There were pictures of things they had seen and places they remembered; there were images that meant nothing to them. And there were pictures that did mean something but only in flickers of thought. Flashes of ideas refused to come together but kept flicking through each of them, ideas like puzzle pieces needing to snap into the exact right place. And there were lots of things that reminded them of other things but nothing that seemed like something that could be a clue.

Until Tilly yelled, "Ivan, Brody, come here! You've got to see this!" All the cousins hurried to see what was so important. Tilly pointed to a small plaque next to the fireplace. "Remember that?" she asked, smiling as she glanced at Brody and Ivan.

"Oh my gosh! Will ya look at that?" Ivan said.

"It's a miniature of the sign at Jeslue's house!" Brody shouted.

"This is the saying that was hanging above the table. I've wanted to remember what it said, and here it is." Tilly glanced at the cousins standing in a semicircle and began reading:

> Follow your path with wonder and joy:
> Savor the food, delight in the drink, bask in the warmth,
> Relax in the rest, immerse in the illusion.
> But beware: Greed destroys with its cold grasp.
> Gratitude in exchange for wonders,
> Treasures spill first from within; then seep without
> And not the other way around.

As Tilly read, Brody unconsciously reached down into his pocket, grabbing the small blue crystal. As Tilly finished reading, he drew the crystal out of his pocket and held it up to the light.

"You know," Brody said, "I don't know about any clues, but I do know that saying is so true. When I got greedy and snatched those crystals, I made a mess of things. Those slizzards bit Tilly and she—" Brody swallowed hard, looking down at the floor, shaking his head. "It's just that—"

Tilly reached over, patting Brody's back and smiling at him. "It ended up just fine," she said.

"But," Brody continued, "it could have been so awful. Ivan had to take a chance and run for Jeslue. And all because I got greedy." Brody looked around at each of them as he continued,

"And look what happened to the Usurper. He got greedy for power, and he turned him into something hideous and cruel. He could have been an Oracle, but he lost it all because he was greedy for power instead of being grateful that he was an apprentice."

Brody stopped and looked at the miniature sign again. "But the other part is right too." His voice cracked, but his eyes softened. "Jeslue was generous and kind. Remember how grateful he was when he opened that big crystal and did that jig because he was so happy." Tilly and Ivan smiled. "He gave me this crystal to keep as a reminder."

Brody held his blue crystal out for all to see again and looked around at each of them. "Part of the problem with being greedy is that you don't appreciate what you got. I'm just glad that—"

But just then, and quite abruptly, the giant clock on the front wall whirred and clicked. And the huge clock began chiming and tolling with deep low melodic tones reverberating throughout the room over and over. The sound was overwhelmingly loud, and yet, it was crystal clear and mellow. When the chimes ceased, the little lantern sitting on the shelf of the green door flickered and lit up. A small square peephole set into the door under the lantern shelf creaked and cracked. The peephole slid out from the door. A little leprechaun figurine holding a pot of gold spun around and stopped. Something dropped to the ground with a cling and clang, bouncing as it hit the floor. The peephole slid back into the door.

"It's a green key!" Brody yelled as he bent down to pick it up.

"Oh my gosh! What just happened?" Claire muttered. "What just happened?"

Brody stood staring at the key lying on his palm. He looked up at the cousins who were watching him. "We got ourselves a key. Let's give this a try!" Brody shouted as he jigged a little jig. And they all gathered around the green door.

CHAPTER 72

Finding Keys

Brody grabbed the copper doorknob with his left hand and inserted the key with his right. He twisted the key, and when it clicked, he pulled the door open. "Oh my gosh! Oh my gosh! It worked! What now?" Brody cried.

Everybody scooted forward, looking out the door, and almost knocked Brody across the threshold. Addison reached across Brody and slammed the door shut.

Brody pulled his hand back just in time to keep his fingers from getting slammed in the door. His mouth dropped open. "What'd you do that for?" he shouted. "You almost caught my hand."

Glaring at Addison, Brody reached forward and turned the key again, but this time the door would not open. "And now the door won't open!" Everyone groaned and turned to stare at Addison. Brody glared and scowled at her.

"I didn't want you stumbling through the door," Addison said. "I-I-I'm sorry, bbbuutt something is very wrong. I-I-I don't know what it is, but something is wrong." And suddenly her face kind of crumpled. "I'm sorry, but—"

"Addie's right. It wasn't time to go out any door without thinking about it first," Levi said with a sigh even though he was disappointed too.

"But I wasn't going through the doorway yet," Brody objected. "And now the key won't open the door anymore. What if that really was our way out and we didn't take it? That's possible too."

"Addie's probably right, Brody." Claire shrugged. "I've always given Addie a hard time about her gut feelings and her notions about signs and synchronicity and serendipity and all those silly things. But she seems to have something there. It's helped us quite a few times on this journey. I gotta admit that chasing those silly butterflies ended up working for us."

"True," Eleanor added. "And those troublesome wolves seemed to stalk us just when we needed it. We ended up in the right place at the right time. I didn't like it while I was sitting in the tree waiting for them to leave, but I kind of think Addie was onto something with her ideas and intuitions." Eleanor chuckled as she reached over and laid her arm across Addison's shoulder. Addison smiled gratefully.

But just as she did, the clock stopped, and the chimes tolled, and the little lantern on the orange door flickered and lit up, the peephole slid out from the door, a wolf with a little butterfly on its shoulder spun out, and two orange keys dropped. And as they clanged to the floor, Claire ran over and picked them both up.

"I'm not exactly sure why this just happened," she said. "None of us went out the orange door, but this key fell out after me and Ellie were talking, so I'm keeping one of 'em." Claire chuckled and flipped one of the keys into the air, catching it and slipping it into her pocket as she handed the other one to Eleanor.

"Now we know!" Levi shouted. "Brody and Claire and Ellie got keys when they remembered something from the journey. That must be why Gramma said keys are hard to find! We'll wait for the Oracle to get here or decide later what to do with them. But for now, let's find keys in case we need them."

"Everyone, search!" Eleanor broke in. "Just don't use the keys until we get Addie's approval!" Everybody rolled their eyes and chuckled as they spread out, hurrying around the room again, searching the walls and the figurines and the signs and the pictures. But this time, they were looking for clues and keys.

And for a while, nobody seemed to find anything that helped until Ivan saw a picture of a snowstorm on a mountaintop. He called to Tilly, and she hurried over. "Tilly, I think this one is yours," he said, smiling gently at his sister. "It reminds me of the Usurper blowing that fierce blizzard at you, and you refused to give him the wallet or buckle even though he knocked you down over and over and over. I didn't know you had it in you like that. That blizzard was more than cruel and terrible. He raged against you."

Tilly blushed, wrapping her arm around her brother. "What else could I do?" she said with a shrug. "It's not like I had a choice. I couldn't let the Usurper have our map and never get home or go into the black portal. So I just did what I had to do, that's all."

She smiled and looked away, but Ivan knew that Tilly had done so much more than she would ever admit. He knew that she had stood up to fear and cruelty, and she had defeated them both by staring them right in the face and not backing down. Tilly gazed at the picture for a minute more. "The snow is soft and sweet, and the ice is hard and cruel, but it's all just a part of the other parts that make up the whole," she whispered.

"I guess you see what you're made of when you've got no choice but to stand or to fall. The bully and fear slithered away when you stood up to them," Ivan added.

And suddenly, the clock whirred; and the crystal-clear chimes tolled, sending reverberations through the room. The lantern on the purple door flickered and lit, the square peephole creaked open, and a tiny snow globe spun around, and two purple keys dropped to the floor. Tilly picked them up and held one close to her heart before slipping it into her pocket, and then she handed the other one to Ivan. "I don't know exactly what I said," Ivan said, "but I'll take it!"

It wasn't long after that until Addison looked across the room and saw Claire standing quietly in a corner with her fingers over her mouth and her faced scrunched as though she was close to tears. "What's the matter, Claire?" Addison asked as she hurried across the room. Claire pointed to a tiny picture high up on the wall.

Addison reached forward. "Oh my gosh!" She gasped, touching the picture of an elderly slightly hunched woman standing in front of a mirror with her head held high, singing.

"Oooh, Claire," Addison whispered, "you remember that too, Claire? You remember?" Addison stood for a second with her hand over her mouth.

"Most of the memories from those mirrors are gone just like the Clockmaker said would happen," Claire said. "But I remember that part. The Clockmaker told us that at the last mirror, we would sing a song that only our hearts would know."

Addison glanced over. "He said that *pretty* and *beautiful* are not always the same and that he hoped when we got to the last mirror, we would see beautiful. When I looked in that last mirror, I was not pretty anymore. I had wrinkles and stuff, Claire." Addison shrugged. "But in a strange way, I guess I understood. And then the song—it just came out of nowhere. I didn't even know where it came from, but it was the story from all the mirrors, the good and bad and the happy and the sad and it was—"

"It was so beautiful," Claire interrupted, touching Addison's arm.

Addison looked straight into Claire's eye.

"And your song was so beautiful and so poignant," Addison said. Claire and Addison stood with their arms around each other, remembering. "I just wish Victoria had understood that before she clung so tightly to that one mirror and got trapped," Claire said. "It's the combination that makes—"

And suddenly the clock began to whirr and make strange sounds. When the cousins turned to see what was happening, the lantern on the silver door flickered and lit, and the keyhole popped open. A small porcelain figurine of a family complete with grandparents, a mom and dad, and two kids and a baby rotating in circles spun out. It dropped two keys, and the peephole slid back in. Addison stepped forward and picked up the two silver keys. She stuck one in her pocket and laid the other on Claire's palm. They smiled at each other, and they understood.

Just a bit later, Levi and Ivan stood in front of a picture of a lantern. "Why just a picture of a lantern?" Levi asked.

But Ivan understood even though he didn't say a word until Levi had rushed off to search for other images. And Ivan reached over and softly touched the picture. He remembered Brody's scream. He remembered finding Tilly and Brody lying in blood on that stone cavern floor. He remembered feeling alone and desperate. And he remembered looking back and forth and trying to decide what to do when there weren't any good answers. *I didn't know what to do,* Ivan whispered to himself. *I didn't know how anything would end.*

And so, with flickering lanterns casting glimmers through the shadowy cavern passageway, he had run to Jeslue, making the only decision he could. He would make a deal with Jeslue. He would promise to stay if Jeslue would help Tilly and Brody. "Sometimes you just have to trust and hope and do the best thing you can do even if you don't know how it's going to end," Ivan whispered aloud. Ivan startled as he felt hands on his shoulders.

Tilly and Brody were standing behind him smiling, and as he smiled back, the clock whirred and the chimes tolled throughout the room. And when the cousins turned to see what was happening, the lantern on the red door flickered and lit; and the keyhole popped open; and a tiny soldier spun out from the peephole door, dropped a red key, and slid back in. "Hey, I was just thinking aloud about that night. I forgot about the keys," Ivan said. "But this is awesome!"

Levi was studying the intricate map carved into the wall around the clock when he got his key. Eleanor, Claire, and Addison stood beside him, scrutinizing the elaborate details for clues. "Look at this," Levi said, tracing the lines all over the map with his finger. "No matter which path we took, we would've ended up back on this main path. It might have taken a lot longer, and some of these routes are pretty sketchy looking while others appear easy, but they all end up converging eventually." Levi chuckled. "No wonder Grizzles said that getting home was not the problem, that getting home in one piece is the problem. I guess we all understand that one now." He looked at the girls and grinned.

"But," Levi continued, "I think that's what the enchanted tree was showing me. While I was viewing everything from up high, it's like all the paths branched off this way and that way, and then they all circled and looped around so that everything was a part of everything else. Like a tree. Even the leaves and limbs are attached to the trunk in a way. Look, how everything meets and intersects. Everything is part of the whole."

"Maybe that's why Lola couldn't tell us how to get home," Eleanor suggested. "Maybe some paths are hard, and some are easy, but everything depends on which path you choose."

"And maybe the butterflies are trying to get a person to follow the easier path with signs and synchronicity. But if you choose to ignore them, maybe it makes the journey harder even if you still end up going home," Addison added.

"Don't you dare say that again," Claire demanded. And this time, they all chuckled.

Again, the clock whirred and made strange sounds, and the chimes began tolling. And when the cousins turned to see what was happening, the lantern on the bronze door flickered and lit, and the peephole popped open, a compass spun out, a bronze key clanged to the floor, and the peephole slid back in. "Well, I think this one mine," Levi said with a smile.

About that time, the four oldest cousins turned to look at the big clock. Levi sighed, shaking his head; a frown crept across his face.

"I think we should all sit down together and decide what to do," Eleanor suggested. "We can hope the Oracle shows up soon, but in the meantime, it seems our Oracle is delayed and our time is almost over."

And as she said those words and glanced around the room to call the cousins together, she happened to notice Esmé who was still sitting in the middle of the room with her legs crossed, her elbows on her knees, and her head resting on her palms. Her eyes were threatening to close with sleepiness at any moment.

Eleanor's face softened. "You know," she said, "when we went out that bronze door, I was so upset because I thought Esmé was going to delay us or get in the way. But the Old Man was right. He said delays are part of your path. Esmé, wolves, an Old Man under a tree—they all seemed like delays and frustrations, but in the end, they all helped us get here." And Eleanor stepped over to Esmé, picked her up, and hugged her tight.

And the clock whirred, and the chimes began. And when the cousins turned to see what was happening, the lantern on the indigo door flickered and lit, and the peephole popped open, and a figurine of a girl holding a prickly ball on her outstretched hand spun out. An indigo key clanged to the floor, and the peephole slid back in.

"Is that mine?" Eleanor asked, looking around. Levi, Claire, and Addison grinned and nodded as Eleanor stepped over to pick up her key.

"But . . . but . . . I wasn't even thinking about another key," Eleanor said as she rushed over to pick up her indigo key. "Hey, Ezzy, look at this!" she said. Then Eleanor hugged Esmé again. And Esmé smiled a huge smile.

And there were other keys too so that by the end they all had two or three keys. Lanterns flickering from the shelves on the colored doors (except the gold one) created shadows and lights throughout the room. It was dark outside. They had been searching for clues for almost an hour. But they still did not know how to leave, and the Oracle still had not shown up. "Let's sit down and talk," Levi said, calling the cousins. "We have some decisions to make."

Chapter 73

The Purpose of Time

And so, Levi, Eleanor, Claire, Addison, Tilly, Brody, Ivan, and Esmé gathered and sat down in a circle in the middle of the room. They hadn't discovered what they needed to know, and time was running out, and the Oracle had not shown up.

"All of us have a key to a door. Maybe we should all go out separate doors," Claire suggested; but then immediately, she stopped, holding up her hand. "No, that's not good. We stick together." Everybody nodded.

"Yes, we do need to stick together," Ivan said. "We're not sure what's behind the doors and if we all ended up in separate places—"

Levi stood up and began pacing back and forth. "What is going on?" he said, his tone betraying his rising frustration. He stopped and scanned the room, trying to see if there was some obvious clue they were missing. He threw his hands in the air. "Where is the Oracle? We need to know what to do and which door to use. When that nutcracker came out from the clock door, the scroll said we had one hour and eleven minutes. If that was literal, we only have a little over eleven minutes left! Where is he? Where is the Oracle? We're running out of time! Where is the Oracle?" Levi yelled.

"Levi," Esmé said, pulling on his shirt.

"What!" he snapped.

But when he saw her eyes reddening around the edges, he took a breath, caught himself, and patted her shoulder. "I'm sorry. I'm just tired, Ezzy. What do you want?"

"Remember what Lola said?" Esmé asked.

Levi shook his head, a little impatiently if truth be told. But again, he caught himself. "Nooo, Ezzy, I don't remember. What did she say?"

"She said that Oracles are everywhere and nowhere. She said they are everything and nothing. But sometimes they are really hard to find, so you have to follow the signs."

"My gosh, how did you remember that, Ezzy? Wow!" Eleanor said, looking slightly astounded.

"That is good thinking, Ezzy," Levi said. "She did say that, didn't she?" He patted Esme's head, smiling at her. Then he stood there looking up at the ceiling, drawing in deep breaths, and thinking. "But how can an Oracle be everywhere and nowhere? How can anything be everything and nothing? What does that even mean?" He threw his arms in the air again. "And we've been looking for signs and keys and ideas, but how are they leading us to an Oracle that's everywhere and nowhere and everything and nothing all at once?" Levi ran his fingers through his hair and turned his back to the cousins. "And the signpost—it pointed in all directions. What was it saying?"

While Levi paced and pondered, the other cousins looked around and up and down, trying to unpuzzle the puzzle and solve the conundrum, but nothing made sense to any of them.

"Wait, wait, wait!" Levi suddenly shouted. "The enchanted tree said something like that too! What was it that she said? What did she say? Come on, what was it?" Levi muttered, pacing back and forth, occasionally tapping his forehead with his finger. He stopped and turned, gazing around the room silently, chewing on his thumbnail.

"I remember now," Levi said softly. "The enchanted tree said something like the Oracle is out there and that we'd find him, but he is not what we expect or where we expect to find him. She had just held me in the air so that I was looking down over all these intersecting paths. You could see people going all over the place like ants on anthills, scurrying here and there, and yet all the paths were more like branches of a tree crisscrossing and yet joined to the trunk, which is like the converging paths on the map on the wall with all the carving."

"So," Ivan suggested, "maybe the enchanted tree wanted you to understand that everything is part of everything else or something like that?"

At that moment, the clock struck the first hour. The crystal-clear chimes tolled, reverberating throughout the room. And just like that and quite suddenly, all the carved images surrounding the clock began revolving and spinning and moving up and down or around. Little people rotated around and through tunnels, and others climbed tiny mountains, and wolves' heads tilted back as though they were howling. And tiny, tiny butterflies seemed to flutter their wings up and down, and the tiniest little lightning bugs lit up here and there, and even a couple of itty-bitty blue birds sitting among the leaves of the carved enchanted tree warbled their songs.

All the cousins jumped up and stood with open mouths, staring at the beautiful, amazing chaos of movement and intricacy.

Claire snapped out of her stunned silence first. "I could watch that forever. There is so much going on, but we have less than 11 minutes to figure this out. Which door do we use? Is there one that puts it all together better than the other? We gotta concentrate on getting out of here."

"Which door would be most like the Oracle?" Eleanor asked cautiously.

"Which door? Which door?" Levi asked, looking around the room yet again.

Esme slipped over and touched Levi's arm. He looked down at her. "What, Ezzy? Hurry, we only have a few minutes."

"But, Levi," Esmé continued, "didn't Gramma say we had to go in the peacock door?"

"Oh my gosh, she's right!" Addison broke in. "Gramma said that over and over and over. So how'd we forget that? She made us promise, remember?"

"But there's no peacock door in here!" Ivan shouted, stomping his foot with frustration.

And again, Esmé reached up and yanked on Levi's shirt.

"What, Ezzy? What?"

"The clock door isn't peacock color, but it has peacock feathers around the edges like the one at Gramma's. I was looking at it while I was sitting on the floor."

Seven cousin's heads jerked around and stared at the door in the bottom of the clock where the six should be. They rushed to the clock door.

"Ivan, shine your lantern directly on the door!" Brody yelled. They all bent forward while Ivan shone his light directly on the wood.

"She's right! Look at this!" Tilly gasped. "There's tiny peacock feathers engraved around the edges." Tilly spit on her finger and began rubbing on the frame. She grabbed the bottom edge of her shirt and rubbed the wood some more. And the more Tilly rubbed away the dust and dirt and scruffy marks, the more the faded color came through. Though the color was washed out from wear and tear and age, it was, indeed, a dull peacock blue.

And suddenly the entire group was jumping and jigging and shouting and yelling things like "Oh my gosh!" and "Now what?" and "It's the peacock door! How did we miss that?"

"Maybe because we were expecting something else," Addison said softly.

Levi scooped Esmé up in his arms and kissed her smack dab in the middle of her forehead. Then he sat her down and looked at the door again.

"The color is so faded and cracked and it's got grime on it like it's been here forever," Levi said. "Is it older than the other doors or used more?" And then he glanced up at the clock and the minutes were still ticking away.

"Okay, guys," he said. "We have to figure this out. We still need a key to open the peacock door. What is it about the peacock door?" Levi stood there staring at the door and then glancing around. "Is there something that connects everything in the same way that the peacock door is the entrance to the other colored doors? Is there something that's a part of everything and nothing, and yet it's everywhere and nowhere, and it underscores everything else or connects everything?"

"This is ridiculous," Eleanor said. "You do realize you're starting to sound like Gramma, don't you?" The cousins all nodded and chuckled even though Eleanor really hadn't meant to be funny at all, and it really didn't seem like an appropriate time to laugh at all.

"Hurry! Think everybody! We're running out of time!" Claire shouted.

"Is there something that was the same that happened to all of us? Something we all have in common like the branches of a tree or intersecting paths that lead to one place?" Ivan asked.

"Hey, that's good, Ivan!" Brody said. "That sounds like a good place to start." The cousins all agreed. And Levi nodded, but his brow furrowed as he scanned the room again.

"Is there something that was a part of everything and everywhere?" Levi muttered as he paced. "Maybe we're searching for the wrong idea. Maybe the Oracle is a message or something?"

"We've only got a couple of minutes," Brody said, watching the second hand sweep around the clock. "Time is slipping away. We gotta hurry."

"There are always clocks in these places, reminding us of time," mentioned Tilly.

Levi looked at the clock and at all the intricate carvings of the map surrounding it. He stood tapping his lip, and suddenly he turned around and looked at each of his cousins one at the time. "Maybe that's it!" he shouted. "Maybe the one thing that all the experiences and paths and people have in common is time. Maybe it's something about time. Think! What have we heard about time while we've been here?"

"Well," Addison said, "the Clockmaker told us that time is a gift for keeping experiences separate."

"He kept saying, 'Time waits for no one,'" mentioned Claire with a shrug.

"And the Old Man by the river, remember what he said?" added Eleanor. "He said all we ever have is moments, just flashes, sparkles—something like that."

"That must be it!" Levi said. "So we found the peacock door, and maybe the key has something to do with time. How do those ideas fit with the Oracle that's everywhere and nowhere and everything and nothing?" Again, they all stood in silence, thinking, looking, feet tapping, chewing on fingernails or the insides of their cheeks.

Until Levi held his hand in the air. "I think I might have it," he said. He looked at the clock and the intricate carvings moving and sliding on the map around the clock. He glanced at the peacock door at the bottom of the clock where the six should be.

"I think," Levi said slowly, "that the Oracle has been here all along. I think that the Oracle is time, and the key is that time doesn't exist as we understand it. Time has a purpose. It's not for getting trapped in illusions about ourselves," Levi started speaking more rapidly and staring at the huge round clock and the wall around it.

"I think the purpose of time is to keep the paths separate so we can experience everything along the journey as moments. And when we experience everything as moments, we are able to understand and when we understand, we are able to discover the keys and the keys open the doors that eventually get us home. I think that's why the Old Man said all we ever have is moments. Levi paused and looked around with a smile. "Ya, I think that might be it!"

The others just kinda stood there looking at him with very strange expressions, glancing back and forth at one another.

"He really is beginning to sound like Gramma," Claire muttered. Everybody nodded.

But at that very instant, as Levi stood there smiling and as Claire was muttering, the gears within the gears began grinding to a halt and the second hand on the giant clock stopped. The ticking and the tocking went silent. They just stood there waiting for something to happen; but nothing did, just silence, just anticipation of something, but they didn't know what.

And suddenly the little lantern above the door on the clock where the six should be flickered and lit, and the door flipped open. The carved nutcracker soldier with the red suspenders slid out and stopped in the front; his arm lurched into the air, he dropped a key and slid back around and through the door, and the door slammed shut.

Levi quickly picked up the key. "It's peacock blue!" he shouted as his face almost scrunched into an ugly cry face and he almost sobbed. Almost. Instead, a single tear rolled down his cheek, and he quickly wiped it away.

And everyone jumped and shouted and then stood there staring at the door and then at one another. And suddenly the second hand on the clock continued to lurch forward again.

"I think we can go home now," Levi said, smiling. "We have our key, and we found the peacock door. I think it's time to take a chance. Addison, do you agree?"

Addison nodded. A huge grin lit her face.

"Everyone else agree?"

"Yes!" each one nodded and agreed.

"Ezzy, come here, sweetie," Levi said, beckoning to Esmé and laying the peacock blue key on her palm. "When I give you the signal, put this key in the lock and twist it. Our timing seems just about perfect. Everybody else, get in line!"

They all shuffled into place. Esmé stood closest to the door and then Claire, Addison, Brody, Tilly, Ivan, and Eleanor. Levi stood at the back watching the clock.

Esmé held the key, beaming at each of her cousins. When her glance landed on Eleanor, the two looked straight into each other's eyes and Eleanor winked at her. "Good job, sweetie," Eleanor whispered with a nod and a smile. "Good job."

The clock tolled again. They looked up. It was exactly eleven minutes after one o'clock.

"Okay, slip the key into the keyhole!" Levi shouted. Claire watched to make sure, but the key slid right in. And when the second hand lurched forward so that it was exactly eleven seconds after eleven minutes after one o'clock Levi shouted, "Now!"

Esmé turned the key, and the door clicked open. They all glanced around the room one last time as they grabbed hands, and one by one they walked across the doorway. And just before Levi grabbed Eleanor's hand, he stopped and took a very deep breath. "Thank you," he whispered. "It's been such an incredible journey! And when all is said and done, I guess I wouldn't change a thing." And then he took Eleanor's hand, stepped over the threshold, and pulled the door closed behind him.

And on the other side, in the treehouse, the cousins were yelling and smiling and bouncing around; and Gramma was laughing and clapping and hugging them all—and she even jigged a jig. Tears were flowing, and smiles were glowing, and hugs were tight and long. Gramma kept grabbing each face and kissing them smack dab on the forehead and on the cheeks over and over.

After clapping and jigging and laughing and kissing for quite a bit of time, Gramma stopped and put both hands over her mouth. "You didn't get lost," she cried as her whole body shook with sobs. "You didn't get lost. You remembered the peacock door." And she wiped her eyes.

But amid all the chaos and the bedlam and the happy, Brody suddenly held his hand in the air. "Sshhh, does anyone hear that? What is it?" he asked, glancing around. They all hushed to listen.

"Oh," Gramma said, "that's a couple of puppies fussing at the bottom of the steps. They showed up out of nowhere while ya'll were gone. Cutest little things ever, all golden and fluffy. You can bring 'em up if you want to."

Ivan startled. He stared at the peacock door and then at the green door. He glanced at Gramma.

Gramma's right eyebrow arched as her eyes met Ivan's. A slight smile flickered across her lips.

"Anyone hungry?" Gramma asked cheerfully as she began rummaging through the wicker picnic basket with the red checkered cloth. "Lots of chocolate chip cookies left, and I'm sure in the mood for some adventure stories." And at that, everybody began talking at once. Everyone, that is, except Tilly, Brody, and Ivan, who rushed down the rickety wooden steps to fetch those puppies.

*

And from somewhere behind a very ancient peacock door, a lock clicked, and the face of the huge round clock creaked open. An Old Man with a timeworn walking stick slipped out from behind the clock. He moseyed across the room, blowing the lantern's flames out one by one. He checked to make sure the doors were locked. He double-checked the green door.

He tottered across the room and out the door of the cabin, shutting the door behind him. A wolf sat beside the door. He stopped and stroked the wolf's head. A butterfly fluttered by and landed on his shoulder. "Time to go home," he whispered. "It's time to go home."

And the wolf trotted away into the forest, and the butterfly fluttered away over the waterfall. And the Old Man reached up, grabbed the lantern from the side of the entrance door, lit the flame, and shuffled down the cobblestone path and across the swinging wooden bridge with his ancient timeworn walking stick.

Made in the USA
San Bernardino, CA
06 October 2017